also by **David Handler**

Stewart Hoag & Lulu Mysteries

The Man Who Died Laughing (1988)
The Man Who Lived by Night (1989)
The Man Who Would Be F. Scott Fitzgerald (1990)
The Woman Who Fell from Grace (1991)
The Boy Who Never Grew Up (1992)
The Man Who Cancelled Himself (1995)
The Girl Who Ran Off with Daddy (1996)
The Man Who Loved Women to Death (1997)

Stewart Hoag & Lulu Short Stories

"The Man Who Couldn't Miss", *Ellery Queen Mystery Magazine* (2007)

Mitch Berger & Desiree Mitry Mysteries

The Cold Blue Blood (2001)
The Hot Pink Farmhouse (2002)
The Bright Silver Star (2003)
The Burnt Orange Sunrise (2004)
The Sweet Golden Parachute (2006)

other fiction

Kiddo (1987)
Boss (1988)

Stewart Hoag &
Lulu Mysteries

The Man Who Would Be F. Scott Fitzgerald

&

The Woman Who Fell From Grace

the third & fourth
Stewart Hoag & Lulu Mysteries
by
David Handler

Busted Flush Press
Houston 2007

The Man Who Would Be F. Scott Fitzgerald

Originally published by Bantam Books, 1990

&

The Woman Who Fell from Grace

Originally published by Doubleday, 1991

Published by Busted Flush Press

This edition copyright 2007
by David Handler

Introduction copyright 2007
by Dean James

Illustrations copyright 2007
by Colin Cotterill

3742 0287 3/08

Trade paperback ISBN: 978-0-9792709-1-8
First trade paperback printing, December 2007

Layout & Production Services: Greg Fleming, Jeff Smith &
John Ramirez

BUSTED FLUSH
PRESS

P.O. Box 540594
Houston, TX 77254-0594
www.bustedflushpress.com

Introduction
to the second
Busted Flush Press
Omnibus Edition

The lot of a ghostwriter can be a very trying one indeed. Witness the life of one Stewart Hoag, "Hoagy" to his friends. He was once the darling of the New York literary scene, thanks to a dazzling first novel. Then there was the romance with the beautiful, talented toast of Broadway, Merilee Nash. Hoagy and Merilee were the Big Apple's dream couple – until everything fell apart, that is. Hoagy couldn't come up with a second novel – we're talking writer's block with a vengeance. On top of that, things with Merilee went sour, and before he knew it, Hoagy was left with only Lulu the cat food-eating basset hound for company.

That's where the ghostwriting comes in. Washed up as the Next Big Thing in literary fiction, Hoagy turns his talents to ghosting "autobiographies" for celebrities of all kinds. Admittedly, his first two efforts were number one bestsellers (kindly see *The Man Who Died Laughing* and *The Man Who Lived by Night* for more details). At least he's now making good money, if not exactly earning the literary respect he desires.

Then there's the fact that, every time he takes on one of these celebrity ghostwriting gigs, someone ends up very dead. Hoagy and Lulu find themselves sniffing out clues and, ultimately, coming up with the solutions to some rather intriguing murders. Hoagy proves to be as good a detective as he is a ghostwriter, and Lulu – well, Lulu is inimitably Lulu, one of the most delightful canines in detective fiction.

Each of Hoagy's ventures in ghostwriting takes him into a different milieu, and the lucky reader gets a guided tour behind the scenes, with plenty of titillating hints and not-so-hidden skeletons in the closet. Just imagine *People* magazine or *Entertainment Tonight*, but on a much more sophisticated and intelligent level. Add this to Hoagy's wryly witty narrative voice, and you have a sinfully delicious and wickedly funny read ahead of you.

Hoagy's third appearance, *The Man Who Would Be F. Scott Fitzgerald*, earned the author an Edgar Award for Best Paperback Original from the Mystery Writers of America in 1992. Hoagy is hired to help another literary wunderkind, Cameron Noyes, finish his long-overdue second novel. The upper-class, extremely photogenic Cam is finding life one big party after another, and he simply hasn't got the time to write. Hoagy agrees to help Cam with his new book, a tell-all detailing Cam's rise to fame that threatens to expose some very painful scandals in the publishing world. When the bodies start piling up a little too quickly, Hoagy and Lulu find themselves playing detective yet again.

In *The Woman Who Fell from Grace*, the fourth novel in the series, Hoagy is again drawn in to the literary world, but this time he's working with a dead author, Alma Glaze. Back in 1940 she penned *Oh, Shenandoah*, a Revolutionary War epic, and though it wasn't exactly a literary triumph, it was a huge commercial success. One of the best-selling novels of all time, it spawned a Hollywood blockbuster that became one of the greatest movies of all time as well. Alma Glaze herself didn't live to see the phenomenon that her work became, but now her celebrity daughter is planning to pen a sequel. That's where Hoagy comes in, because he will be the one who actually writes the book. Before long, however, people start turning up dead, and inevitably Hoagy and Lulu turn to detection.

Astute readers of these two novels will quickly figure out the targets of David Handler's mordantly witty prose. In the guise of these two books he offers us inspired satires of the inanity and insanity that are endemic to publishing. You'll laugh your way through the books as Handler zings one target after another, and at the same time you'll wonder how anything every gets published at all – anything of lasting value, that is.

The minute you finish these two gems, you'll start looking for the rest of Handler's work. He's that good, and his body of work stands as proof that intelligence, wit, and sophistication will always find an audience.

Dean James
Houston, Texas
January 2007

The Man Who Would Be F. Scott Fitzgerald

the third
Stewart Hoag & Lulu Mystery

For my friend Lee Siegel
down at the plant

I want to laugh but nothing is funny. I want to cry but nothing is sad. I want to be loved but I want to be alone. The gun is cold in my hand as I pull the trigger. The pillow explodes before me, showering me with feathers. I laugh.

– *from* BANG, *the novel*
  by Cameron Sheffield Noyes

No – Gatsby turned out all right at the end; it was what preyed on Gatsby, what foul dust floated in the wake of his dreams that temporarily closed out my interest in the abortive sorrows and short-winded elations of men.

– *from* THE GREAT GATSBY,
  by F. Scott Fitzgerald

CHAPTER
ONE

Aside from the name it was the usual Soho art gallery in the usual converted cast-iron warehouse down on Spring Street and West Broadway. The door was made out of steel, and I had to buzz to get in and wait out there on the sidewalk in the rain while the surveillance camera mounted over the door checked me over to see if I was their sort of person. I'm not, but I fooled them.

Inside, the wood floor was polished, the pipes exposed, the lighting recessed. A tape of some Philip Glass nonmusic was softly nonplaying. A languid clerk wearing a tight black dress and heavy black-framed Buddy Holly glasses sat at the reception desk just inside, her nose deep into a copy of *Vanity Fair*, which is the *People* magazine of pseudointellectuals and social climbers. Me she ignored.

Like I said, it was the usual Soho art gallery – aside from the name, which was Rat's Nest.

I took off my trench coat and Borsalino and stood there politely dripping until she finally glanced up at me, then down at Lulu, my basset hound, who was wearing the hooded yellow rain slicker I'd had made for her when she got bronchitis one year. She always wears it on rainy days now. I don't want her getting breathing problems again. She snores when she has them. I know this because she likes to sleep on my head.

"I'm looking for Charleston Chu," I said.

"In there," the clerk said, one lazy hand indicating the main gallery through the doorway.

We started in.

"Sir?"

We stopped. "Yes?"

"No animals are allowed in Rat's Nest."

Lulu snuffled at me, deeply offended. I told her to let me handle it. Then I turned to the clerk and said, "We're going to pretend we didn't hear that." And we went in.

There wasn't much in there, and what was in there wasn't much. Some graffiti art left over from a couple of seasons before. A lumpy piece of statuary the size of a grand piano that looked to be from the postmodernist, neo-nonexistent school. A large white canvas that had a life-sized mannequin of a metallic-blue woman suspended from it by hooks. The prices were posted on small, discreet business cards. The lumpy statue was going for $15,000, which would have been an excellent investment if they also threw in a new Mitsubishi Galant.

Someone in the gallery sneezed. I looked down at Lulu. Lulu was looking up at me. That ruled out the only two so-called warm bodies in the room.

I approached the painted mannequin.

It was called *Blue Monday*. It had no price on it.

Its nose was running.

Lulu barked. She has a mighty big bark for someone with no legs. Also pretty definite taste in art.

"Shit!" cried the mannequin. "He won't bite me, will he?"

"He is a she," I replied. "And she won't go after anything larger than a baby squirrel unless challenged, in which case she'll hide under the nearest bed. May I wipe your nose for you?"

"Please. Damned tree-pollen allergy. Spoils the whole statement."

"Oh, I wouldn't go that far."

I dabbed at her blue nose with my linen handkerchief. It was a tiny snub nose, and some of the paint on it came off on the handkerchief. Her almond-shaped eyes were brown. The rest of her was quite blue. Her hair, which she wore close-cropped like a boy. Her leotard and tights. Her hands and feet, which were shackled to the canvas in a position that wasn't exactly Christ-like but wasn't that different either. She had a slim, firm body, the body of a gymnast or a dancer, which she wasn't. She was Charleston Chu, the Chinese conceptual artist who was, at age twenty-four, the new darling of New York's art scene.

"How many hours a day do you spend up there?" I asked.

"Six."

"It must get a bit uncomfortable after a while."

"I wish for it to. If I'm uncomfortable, I make you uncomfortable."

She had a girl's voice, with a trace of an accent, but she was no naive waif. This was a savvy self-promoter and entrepreneur who had climbed to the top of a rough business very fast, and on her own terms. She was her own dealer – Rat's Nest merely rented her gallery space.

"People like to sit back and judge art," she went on. "I won't allow you to. I judge you right back. Force you to have an intimate relationship with me."

"I'm willing if you are," I said gamely. "Just promise me one thing

– years from now, when you talk about this, and you will, be kind."

She narrowed her eyes at me. "Do you have some kind of problem, asshole?" she demanded coldly. She was in character now. Then again, maybe she wasn't.

"That," I replied, "may take us longer than six hours to get into. Tell me, how come there's no price tag on you?"

"I'm not for sale."

"We're all for sale. I know I am."

"What's your price?"

"A third of the action, generally. If I can find my celebrity. I had a lunch date with Cameron Noyes, and he stood me up. I was told you two . . ."

". . . Hang out together?"

"You said it. I didn't."

She smiled. Because of the blue on her face her teeth seemed unusually white, her gums a vivid pink. She had nice dimples. "We live together. Cam should be home working."

"I rang the bell. Also phoned. No answer."

"Then he must be lost in thought, or shitfaced, or out banging someone," she said mildly.

"And that's okay with you?"

"Cam Noyes is a genius," she replied. "His life is his work. To impose my will upon one is to corrupt the other. I have no right to do that. No one does. Besides, you know how writers are."

I tugged at my ear. "Yes, I suppose I do."

"Oh, I get it now – you're Stewart Hoag."

"Make it Hoagy."

"As in Carmichael?"

"As in the cheese steak."

"I'm a vegetarian," she said.

"I suppose someone has to be."

She giggled. It was an unexpectedly bubbly, delicious giggle. It reminded me of Merilee's. Almost. "Everyone calls me Charlie," she said, wiggling a shackled hand at me.

I reached up and shook the hand, and came away with more blue. "Pleased to meet you, Charlie. That's Lulu."

"She's a cutie."

Lulu turned her back on us with a disapproving grunt and faced the lumpy statue.

"I say something wrong?" asked Charlie.

"No. She's just had this thing about other women ever since my divorce. She always thinks they're coming on to me."

"Are they?"

"I seriously doubt it."

"Can't you tell?"

"A guy is always the last to know."

Her eyes gave me the once-over. I had just changed to my spring wardrobe. I wore the navy-blue blazer of soft flannel I'd had made for me in London at Strickland's, with a starched white Turnbull and Asser broadcloth shirt, plum-colored silk bow tie, vanilla gabardine trousers, and calfskin braces. On my feet were the Maxwell's brown-and-white spectator balmorals with wing tips. None of it did me any harm.

"Cam is very much looking forward to meeting you," Charlie said. "You're one of his idols."

"He has others?"

"He has few. I meant, he's excited about your new arrangement."

"There won't be any arrangement if he doesn't keep his appointments."

"Oh." She frowned, concerned. "Look, it's nothing personal, Hoagy. He's just very into chaos."

"Aren't we all."

"We were out late last night. He's probably just taking a nap. Tell you what, there's a house key in my purse at the front desk. Take it. Let yourself in."

"Kind of trusting, aren't you?"

"Am I?"

"Everything I told you could be a lie. I could be anybody. I could be trouble."

"No chance. Your eyes . . ."

"What about them?"

"They give you away."

So I rang Cam Noyes's bell again. This time I had Charlie's key in my pocket and my hat off. The rain had moved on up the coast toward New England, and it was sunny and fresh out. The green of spring across the street in the park was new and bright. Cam Noyes owned one of the Greek revival town houses that face right onto Gramercy Park, and that are about as prized these days as Yankee starters who can last seven innings. Only those who are both very rich and very lucky ever get to live facing the private park. Even they aren't allowed to bring their dogs in there with them. I'd have something to say about that if I were one of them, but I'm not. I've used up my money. Also my luck.

His house was white and sported an iron veranda with lacy ornamentation. He still didn't answer the doorbell. I glanced back at the curb. Parked there, as it had been earlier that day, was a gleaming, fully restored hot-pink 1958 Oldsmobile Super 88 convertible. The original Loveboat, the one that Olds boasted carried no less than forty-four pounds of chrome plating on it. It had to be the longest, gaudiest, most vulgar car ever made. It had to belong to Cam Noyes.

I rang one more time, and when no one answered. I used Charlie's key.

The decor wasn't what you'd call typical. Actually, it wasn't what most people would call decor. The walls, ceiling, and ornate molding of the ground-floor parlor had been stripped down to the bare, pitted plaster and left that way. Some tall plastic potted palms had been scattered about. In the center of the room a half dozen fifties, shell-backed metal lawn chairs in assorted pastels were grouped around an old Packard Bell black-and-white TV set. Over the marble fireplace hung a particularly awful Julian Schnabel original. It looked as if he'd dipped a dead gerbil in a can of yellow paint and hurled it against a wet canvas. The oak floor was unpolished and bare except for a twenty-foot length of Astroturf stretching toward the kitchen. Golf balls dotted it. At one end there was a putting cup with an electronic return. A putter leaned against the wall.

I called out his name. There was no answer. There was no sound at all.

Most of the kitchen was a raw, gaping wound. There was a refrigerator with some liquor bottles on it, and a utility sink, but everything else – stove, cupboards, counters – had been ripped out. The walls had been stripped down to bare, crumbling brick, the floor to the rough wood subflooring. Lulu found an open trapdoor with steep stairs down to the basement. A light was on down there, illuminating stacks of fresh lumber and Sheetrock, boxes of tile, buckets of joining compound, a new sink, copper pipe.

I called down there. No answer.

French doors led out back to the walled garden. A twelve-foot square of damp earth just outside had been cleared, leveled, and marked out with stakes and string lines. Under a wet blue tarp were piled sixty-pound bags of cement mix and pallets of bluestone. All the makings of a patio. For now the garden didn't offer much, except for a lot of dead leaves with one pink plastic flamingo standing guard over them. This Lulu carefully checked out with her large black nose before strutting back to me, snuffling victoriously.

The second-floor parlor had a higher ceiling and grander molding than the one downstairs, and tall leaded-glass windows overlooking the park. Also paint splatters everywhere. Charlie's studio. Worktables were heaped with paints, brushes, spray cans, contact cements. Huge blank canvases were stacked against one wall. Cartons were piled everywhere – cartons filled with gaily colored Fiesta ware, with empty Coke bottles, with old magazines and postcards and snapshot albums. On an easel in the middle of the studio sat a canvas to which she'd glued broken shards of the Fiesta ware as well as part of a Uneeda biscuit box. Welcome to the age of borrowing. The Museum of Modern Art and the Whitney had lined up to buy just such works of borrowed art by Charlie Chu. I'll still take Edward Hopper. He didn't borrow from anyone.

A dozen or so eight-by-ten, black-and-white photographs had been taped directly onto one of the walls. I walked over to them, broken bits of china and glass crunching under my feet. They were photos of literary wunderkind Cameron Noyes and his many hot young friends, snapped in restaurants, in clubs, at parties in expensive-looking lofts. Photos of him with Emilio Estevez and Keifer Sutherland, with Michael J. Fox, with Adam Horovitz of the Beastie Boys and Molly Ringwald and Suzanne Vega and Johnny Depp. There were no pictures of him with Charlie. She was the photographer. I found her darkroom in the bathroom off the studio.

A wide doorway opened into what had been the dining room. There was a dumbwaiter down to the kitchen below, and wiring for a chandelier in the center of the ceiling. Charlie made her heavier artistic statements in there. Hunks of iron, lengths of pipe, were heaped in a corner next to an acetylene welding torch and welder's mask. She had a heavy-duty circular table saw, a lathe, a workbench stocked with hand tools. Rough picture frames hung by the dozen from spikes in the wall. Did her own framing right here, too. Handy girl.

I called out Cam's name. There was no answer.

The third floor was somewhat more conventional. There was fresh white paint on the walls of the short hallway. A guest bedroom in back, simply furnished. The front room was where Cameron Noyes wrote. It was an austere room, and he wasn't in it. An uncommonly lovely writing table was set before the windows. It was made of cherry in the Shaker style and rubbed until it glowed as only cherry can. On it was a yellow legal-sized pad, blank, a pencil, an oil lamp, and a genuine fifteen-inch bowie knife of the 1850s with a wrought-steel blade and brass handle and hilt. The Arkansas Toothpick – glistening and razor sharp.

There was nothing else in the room – no books, no papers, no phone, no other furnishings.

I kept climbing.

The top floor was all master bedroom. A ceiling fan circled slowly overhead and made the curtains, which were of a gauzy material, billow. A brass bed was planted in the middle of the huge room like an island, and on that brass bed lay Cameron Noyes, naked on top of the covers. His mouth was open, his eyes closed. His head had lolled to one side in such a way that the blood from his nose had streamed down his face and onto the pillow, and dried there.

I looked down at Lulu. Lulu was looking up at me.

I sighed and crossed the room to the bed. He was breathing, slowly but evenly. There was a vial of white powder on the nightstand, next to a pocket mirror, razor blade, and length of drinking straw. Also a bottle of tequila, some wedges of lime, and two glasses – all the makings for a fine matinee horror show. I moistened a finger, dipped it into the vial, and rubbed the powder over my gums. It was coke, all right. I knew about the tingle. Also about the nosebleed. The inside of his nose was ruined from stuffing coke up it. A lot of coke.

I looked down at him. He may not have been the handsomest man I'd ever seen, but he was close. So handsome he was almost pretty. He had wavy blond hair, a high forehead, prominent cheekbones, and a delicate, rosy mouth. His complexion was fair and free of blemishes. The nose, aside from the blood caked on it, was perfect. So was the chin. His eyes were set wide apart. I wondered what color they were. I guessed blue. It was the face of a sensitive boy. It didn't go with the rest of him. He was a big man with huge, sloping shoulders and powerful arms. His chest was deep, his waist was narrow, his stomach flat and ridged with muscle. The words *Born to Lose* were tattooed on his left bicep. The hands were monstrous and work roughened. The legs belonged on a modest-sized plow horse. It was the body of a laborer or an outside linebacker, or the young Brando. It was a body that didn't fit with the face.

I looked down at him and wondered. Cameron Noyes had it all.

He was young, handsome, brilliant, rich, and famous. And he was trashing it. Why? This I would have to find out.

I heard something rolling on the bare wooden floor. Lulu had made a small discovery under the bed and was nosing it toward me. It was a woman's lipstick. Red. I picked it up and put it on the nightstand next to the tequila.

Then I went downstairs to the kitchen. The refrigerator was empty except for a half-eaten sausage-and-mushroom pizza from John's, the coal-fired pizzeria on Bleeker. I went to work on a slice. I'd missed lunch, and there's no greater delicacy than cold pizza, except for licorice ice cream, and there wasn't any of that in the freezer. Just a bottle of Polish vodka and four trays of ice cubes. These I dumped in an empty joining-compound bucket from the cellar. I filled the bucket with cold water from the sink, swooshed it around, and carried it back upstairs. When I got to the bed, I hefted it, took careful aim, and dumped half of its contents on the naked, fully exposed groin of Cameron Noyes. He instantly let out a lion's roar of shock and pain and sat right up, his eyes – they *were* blue – bulging from his head. I gave him the other half of the bucket in the face. Then I wiped my hands and sat down and asked myself what the hell I was doing there.

CHAPTER
TWO

You could take your pick with Cameron Sheffield Noyes.

You could call him the brightest, most gifted boy wonder to shine on American fiction since F. Scott Fitzgerald lit up the Jazz Age. Or you could call him an obnoxious, big-mouthed, young shithead. The only thing you couldn't do was ignore him.

Not since his sophomore year at Columbia, when this strapping young part-time male model and full-time blue blood had submitted the manuscript for a slim first-person novel to Tanner Marsh, who teaches creative writing there. Marsh also edits the *New Age Fiction Quarterly*, and happens to be the single most influential literary critic in New York. Marsh read the little manuscript, which told the story of a shy, privileged, young Ivy Leaguer who suffers a nervous breakdown while studying for finals and runs off to an Atlantic City hotel-casino with the middle-aged cashier at the diner where he regularly breakfasts. There, besotted by drugs, alcohol, and sex, he blows both of their brains out. The novel was called *Bang*. Marsh was so knocked out by it he showed it to Skitsy Held, editor in chief of the small, prestigious Murray Hill Press. She shared his enthusiasm. *Bang* was published one month before Cameron Noyes's twentieth birthday. A spectacular front-page review in the *New York Times Book Review* catapulted it, and its author, to instant celebrity. "It is as if young Scott Fitzgerald has come back to write *The Lost Weekend* while under the influence of cocaine and José Cuervo tequila," raved the *Times'* reviewer, who was none other than Tanner Marsh. "Indeed, Cameron Sheffield Noyes writes so wincingly well he must be considered the most brilliant new literary find since Stewart Hoag. One can only hope he will fare better."

Critics. One thing they never seem to understand is that everyone, no matter how gifted, can roll out of bed one morning and have just a really rotten decade.

I read the damned thing, of course. How could I not? I read all 128 pages of it, and I thought it was absolutely brilliant. Oh, I wanted to hate it. Desperately. But I couldn't. *Bang* captured the itchy ennui of the young as so few novels ever had. Cameron Noyes had a gift – for peering into the depths of his own soul and for coming back with pure gold. And he had the rarest gift of all. He had his own voice.

Lulu stayed out of my way for a whole week after I read it. I was not in a good mood.

Lonely, alienated teenagers who before might have turned to Plath or Salinger for comfort found Noyes much more to their liking. *Bang* understood them. It was dirty. It was *theirs*. It took off and stayed near the top of the bestseller lists for thirty-six weeks, the name of Noyes crowding out more familiar ones such as Michener and King. The paperback reprint went for close to a million. The movie version, which starred Charlie Sheen and Cher, made over $100 million, though fans of the book not to mention the movie's first director – were put off by the studio-dictated happy ending, in which the hero has only *dreamt* the violent climax and awakens from it sobered and determined to get his degree.

Cameron Noyes wasn't the only hot young novelist in town. It seemed as if a pack of baby authors had been let loose on the literary world with their hip, sassy tales of the young, the restless, the stoned. There was Jay McInerney, author of *Bright Lights, Big City*, Bret Easton Ellis with *Less Than Zero*, Tama Janowitz with *Slaves of New York*. They were a kind of universe unto themselves, an undertalented, overpaid, over-publicized universe at that. But Cameron Noyes was not like the others. He actually knew how to write, for one thing. And he knew how to grab like no one else. He appeared in ads for an airline, a credit card, a brand of jeans, a diet cola, and the Atlantic City casino where *Bang* was filmed. *Saturday Night Live* made him a guest host. MTV sent him to Fort Lauderdale to cover spring break as its guest correspondent. *Rolling Stone* put him on its cover. So did *People*, which called him the sexiest man alive. He was seldom lonely. Not a week went by without his appearing in the gossip columns and the supermarket tabloids, squiring one famous film or rock 'n' roll beauty after another to Broadway premieres, charity bashes, celebrated murder trials. He had been with Charlie Chu, his current live-in love, for two months now. It was, they both told Barbara Waiters on network TV, a "once-in-a-lifetime thing."

He made good copy. Indeed, Cameron Noyes seemed to revel in his own enfant-terrible outrageousness more than any young celebrity since John Lennon. "It's true, I brought the remote-control generation to literature," he told *Esquire*. "And they will keep on reading great books just as long as I keep writing them." When he wasn't blasting literary sacred cows of the past ("Hemingway and Fitzgerald are officially sanctioned culture – the boredom comes built in with the product") and present ("Saul Bellow's been dead since 1961. Isn't it time someone told him?"), he was acting out his own style of commentary. He became so outraged, for instance, when real estate developer Donald Trump's book hit number one on the bestseller list that he bought up every copy in every store on Fifth Avenue – several hundred in all – carted them into Central Park and made a bonfire out of them. For that he spent a night in jail. And while that little demonstration might have displayed a certain spirited cheekiness – not to mention good taste – a number of his lately had not. He ran over a pesky paparazzo with his car one night and nearly crippled him. He punched Norman Mailer at a black-tie benefit for the New York Public Library and broke two teeth. Currently, he held the unofficial record for turning over the most tables at Elaine's while in the heat of a drunken argument: three.

He was a powder keg, a troubled young genius blessed with James Dean's looks and John McEnroe's personality. He was the perfect literary celebrity for his time, so perfect that if he hadn't come along, someone would have invented him.

In a way, someone had. The mastermind behind the meteoric rise and phenomenal marketing of Cameron Noyes was twenty-four-year-old Boyd Samuels, who had been his college roommate and was now the most notorious literary agent in the business. Boyd Samuels had made a name for himself in publishing almost as fast as his star client had – for trying to steal big-name talent from other agents, for being unprincipled, for being a liar, and most important, for being such a damned success at it. Take Cameron Noyes's much anticipated second novel. He wasn't writing it for Skitsy Held. Samuels had simply blown his nose on his client's signed contract with her, snatched Noyes away, and delivered him to a bigger, richer house willing to pay him a reported advance of a million dollars. Just exactly how Samuels had managed to pull this off – and why Skitsy Held, no cream puff, had let him – had been the subject of much speculation around town. Just as Noyes's second novel was. Word was it was on the late side. Word was his new publisher was getting edgy. Hard to blame them. A million is a lot of money for a serious novel. Especially one by an author who had only just turned twenty-three.

It was Boyd Samuels who got me mixed up with Cameron Noyes. He called me one day and invited me up for a chat. I went. I had nothing better to do.

The Boyd Samuels Agency had a suite of offices on the top floor of the Flatiron Building, the gloriously ornate skyscraper built in 1902 at the elongated triangle where Broadway meets Fifth and Twenty-third. It was about 1957 in Boyd Samuels's outer office, and it wasn't so much an outer office as it was a diner – cute and kitschy as hell, too, right down to the shiny chrome counter and swivel stools, the pink and charcoal linoleum on the floor, the neon clock and the vintage jukebox, which was playing Eddie Cochran. It seemed as if everywhere I went that season I bumped into the fifties. I suppose young people are always nostalgic for a decade they didn't have to live through.

Phones were ringing, people were bopping in and out of different office doors, snapping their fingers to the juke. None of them looked over twenty-five. Lulu and I waited at the front door until one of them, a tall, gangly, splay-footed kid with a Beaver Cleaver burrhead crew cut, hurried over to us from behind the counter. He wore a Hard Rock Cafe T-shirt, jeans, and the look of someone who was used to getting whipped. His shoulders were hunched in the anticipation of blows, his eyes set in a permanent wince.

"Stewart Hoag, isn't it?" he asked timidly, fastening his eyes to a spot on the wall about a foot over my head.

I said it was.

"I'm Todd Lesser, Boyd's assistant. H-He's on his way."

"From . . . ?"

"Home," he replied, explaining quickly, "he's running a bit late this morning. He'll be here in just a few minutes. Really. Care to wait in his office?"

"Nice decor," I commented as we crossed to a corridor of offices. "If business is ever slow, you can sell burgers."

"Business," Todd said modestly, "is never slow."

Boyd Samuels was into ugly. Ugly, kidney-shaped desk of salmon-colored plastic. Ugly art-moderne love seat of chrome and leopard skin. Ugly specimen cacti growing uninvitingly in pots in front of the window overlooking Madison Square Park. These Lulu ambled right for, sniffing delicately at them so as not to honk her large black nose on a prickle.

Todd eyed her warily. "Uh . . . she's not going to . . ."

"Just getting the lay of the land," I assured him.

One wall of the office was floor-to-ceiling shelves displaying the many best-selling books by his many best-selling clients. Framed magazine covers and best-seller lists and rave reviews crowded the walls. Standing in one corner was a life-sized, full-color cardboard display cutout of Delilah Moscowitz, the statuesque, scrumptious, and sizzingly hot young sex therapist who was blowing Dr. Ruth out of the water, so to speak. Delilah's looks, frisky wit, and bold irreverence toward such touchy subjects as fellatio, bondage, and her own rather uninhibited sex life had made her a sensation. She had a top syndicated newspaper column, a radio call-in show, a regular slot on *Good Morning America*, and now, thanks to Boyd Samuels, a surefire bestseller, *Tell Delilah*. "Good sex is all in the head," read the promo copy on her cardboard cutout. "Take home the lady who gives the best head in the business."

"Nice subtle approach," I observed.

"Our newest star," said Todd, beaming. "Her book has already hit the B. Dalton chain list. She'll be appearing on *Donahue* and *Oprah* both, and Donna Karan and Norma Kamali are still fighting over her."

"For . . . ?"

"They want her to wear their clothes on her national publicity tour. She looks fabulous in whatever she wears. The camera loves her."

"Yes, she does give a whole new meaning to the word *bookish*," I said, admiring her cutout. "I see Skitsy Held is her publisher. Interesting, considering what happened with Cameron Noyes."

Todd frowned and shook his head. "No, not at all. B-Boyd always tries to make things work out even. Coffee?"

"Please. Black."

He shambled out. I sat down on the love seat, which was as uncomfortable as it looked, and gazed over at the shelves crammed with all of the hot books by all of the hot authors. I listened to the phones ring – publishers calling with feelers, with firm offers, with promises of gold and village virgins. And I sighed inwardly. Once, the raves and magazine covers and phone calls were for me. Once, I'd swum in these swirling waters myself. And drowned in them.

Maybe you remember me. Then again, maybe you don't. It has been a while since I burst onto the scene as the tall, dashing author of that fabulously successful first novel, *Our Family Enterprise*. Since the Times called me "the first major new literary voice of the eighties." Since I married Merilee Nash, Joe Papp's newest and loveliest leading lady, and became half of New York's cutest couple. Since I had it all, and crashed. Dried up. No juices of any kind. No second novel. No Merilee. She got the eight rooms overlooking Central Park, the red 1958 Jaguar XK 150, the Tony for the Mamet play, the Oscar for the Woody Allen movie. Also a second husband, that brilliant young playwright, Zack something. She got it all. I ended up with Lulu, my drafty old fifth-floor walk-up on West Ninety-third Street, and a second, somewhat less dignified career – ghostwriter of celebrity memoirs.

I'm not terrible at it. Two No. 1 best-sellers, in fact. My background as an author of fiction certainly helps. So does the fact I myself used to be a celebrity. I know how to handle them. A lot of the lunch-pail ghosts don't. On the down side, being a pen for hire can be hazardous to my health. A ghost is there to dig up a celebrity's secrets, past and present, and there's usually someone around who wants to keep them safely buried.

Danger is not my middle name.

My juices did finally return. Not like before they'll never be like before. But I did actually finish the second novel, *Such Sweet Sorrow*, the bittersweet story of the stormy marriage between a famous author and famous actress. Somewhat autobiographical. I felt certain it would put me back on the map. A choice paperback sale. Movie deal. Great part for Merilee Nash. Tailor-made for her, in fact.

Deep down inside, I also hoped it would help me win her back – she and Zack had split for good over his drinking and carrying on. But things didn't quite work out that way. For starters, *Such Sweet Sorrow* was not exactly a critical success. "The most embarrassing act of public self-flagellation since Richard Nixon's Checkers speech," wrote the *New York Times Book Review*. "The plot sickens." That was actually the kindest review I got. Written, incidentally, by Tanner Marsh, who, in case you haven't figured it out yet, is not one of my eight or nine million favorite people. But I can't blame the book's utter critical and commercial failure on Tanner. No one liked it. Particularly you-know-who. She called me in tears after she finished reading it to say she felt like she'd been stripped naked in the middle of Broadway, beaten to a pulp and left in the gutter, bleeding, for bums to urinate on. Her words, not mine. She also said she never wanted to speak to me again. And she hadn't.

That spring found her starring with Jeremy Irons in Broadway's hottest ticket, Mike Nichols's revival of *The Petrified Forest*. Sean Penn was bringing the house down as Duke Mantee. And Merilee was considered a shoo-in for another Tony nomination for her portrayal of Gabby Maple, the Arizona truck-stop waitress who reads François Villon and dreams of running off to France.

Me, I was facing the gloomy realization that my season in the sun had passed. I was closing in on forty and didn't have much to show for it – two small rooms, $657 in the bank, some yellowing clippings, a huge ego, and a basset hound who eats Nine Lives canned mackerel for cats and very, very strange dogs. I had no future. I was looking for one when Boyd Samuels called.

His assistant returned with a steaming *Bang* coffee mug. I thanked him. He lingered, examined the carpet. He was painfully shy. Not a positive quality in an agent, unless it can be harnessed into naked ambition.

"For what it's worth," he finally got out, "I thought *Such Sweet Sorrow* was an even better novel than *Our Family Enterprise*. I really loved it."

"That makes you and my mother – and her I'm not so sure about."

"What I mean," he added, reddening, "is I think the critics were wrong to punch you out."

"Could be. But don't forget they weren't necessarily right when they lavished praise on me before. They simply misunderstood me to my advantage." I sipped my coffee. "Todd, isn't it?"

"Why, yes," he replied, startled. He was not used to people remembering his name.

"Thank you, Todd."

"Sure thing," he said brightly.

"Been working for Boyd long?"

"Ever since he started out. We were friends in college. Well, sort of friends. What I mean is . . ."

Before he could finish explaining, Hurricane Boyd hit. The man seemed to explode into the room. He was a human exclamation mark. "Whoa, sorry about the delay, amigo!" he exclaimed as he hurled his bulging briefcase on his desk, whipped off his Ray-Bans, and stuck out his hand. "Glad to meet ya! Indeed!"

I shook it, half expecting to get an electrical shock.

Boyd Samuels was burly and bearded and over six feet tall in his ostrich-skin cowboy boots. He had thick black hair and he wore it shoulder length and didn't bother to comb it. He wore a denim shirt with the sleeves rolled up over his thick, hairy forearms, a bola-string tie of turquoise and hammered silver, and pleated khaki trousers.

"Coffee, Toddy!" he ordered as a greeting to his assistant.

"Right away, Boyd," Todd said, hurrying off.

Lulu stirred on the sofa next to me. Boyd fell to his knees and patted her. "Hey, pretty baby, what's happening?" She yawned in response. He made a face, turned back to me. "Jeez, her breath smells kind of . . ."

"She has funny eating habits."

"What's she eat – old jock straps?"

"We're going to pretend we didn't hear that."

Todd came back with the coffee. Boyd took it, dropped into his desk chair, and gave him the name of an editor he wanted on the phone at once. Todd nodded, retreated.

There was a bottle of Old Overholt rye whiskey in his desk drawer. Boyd poured a generous slug of it into his coffee, then offered me the bottle. I was starting to reach for it when a soft, low growl came from the sofa next to me. My protector. She was concerned that I was slipping back into my bad habits I had before when things went sour. I glowered at her. She glowered right back at me, baring her teeth like Lassie trying to protect Timmy from a hissing rattler. I was definitely losing the upper hand.

Boyd put the bottle away, struck a kitchen match against the sole of his boot, and lit an unfiltered Camel with it. Then he sat back with his boots up on the desk, smoking, sipping his laced coffee. The whole routine was pretty down-home shit-kicker; especially for an optometrist's son from Cherry Hill, New Jersey. Only the eyes spoiled it. The eyes taking me in from across that desk were shrewd and alert and as piercing as twin laser beams. The man didn't blink.

Not until his phone buzzed. Then he reached for the cordless headset on the desk and put it on. It had a mouthpiece and earphones and an antenna sticking out of it. It looked like a prop left over from an old episode of *Star Trek*, the one where somebody stole Spock's brain. Boyd jumped to his feet and paced around the office as he talked, coffee in one hand, cigarette in the other.

"Yo, amigo, you sound like shit in a microwave! Gotta start living clean like me! How's the little baby? . . . That's beautiful, man. Beautiful." Boyd shifted from chummy to grave. "So, listen, I have a firm offer on the table – buck and a quarter up front." (Translation: another publisher had offered one of Boyd's clients an advance of $125,000 for their next book.) He shifted to confidential now – the man worked through the gears as fast and furious as Emerson Fittipaldi. "None of this would be happening if it was up to me. You and me, we're like family. I want you to have it. And if you'll just match their figure by the end of today, you'll get it, okay? . . . Sure, sure think it over." He said good-bye, yanked off the headset, and flung it carelessly onto the desk. Then he sat back down, chuckling to himself. "Between you and me, the cheap bastard's been all alone in the bidding since seventy-five thou. But what he doesn't know won't piss him off, right?"

"I thought that sort of thing wasn't done," I said.

"It wasn't – yesterday. But that was when publishing was about books. It's about bucks now, and anyone who says it isn't is doing a yank on your frank." He picked up a football from his credenza and gripped it by the seams. "I know, I know. A lot of editors think I'm a douchebag, and guess what – I like it that way. It means I'm doing my job. What's important to me is that my clients are happy. And believe me, they are."

He tossed me the football. It had been autographed by a drug-dependent pro quarterback whose memoir Samuels had peddled for six hundred thousand. Happy indeed.

He took me in with his nonblinking lasers. "What would you say if I told you I've convinced Cam Noyes's publisher to accept a work of nonfiction for his second book instead of a novel. Exact same money."

"I'd say," I replied, "you're almost as good an agent as you think you are."

"It's going to be a kind of portrait of his time," he went on. "His life, his friends, his scene. Charlie Chu is doing original portraits and illustrations for it. An explosive collaboration, really. Like a labor of love for the two of them. Actually, there's no existing term to describe what it is."

"I can think of one – home movie."

Boyd's nostrils quivered, but he kept right on coming. "We're talking about the top writer and top artist of this generation. There's no doubt that it'll be major." He seemed utterly sure of this. And he was. Like all topflight salesmen, he was his own best customer.

"What's happened to his second novel?" I asked.

"Too soon. Cam has to wait for his ideas to percolate – especially because everybody expects so much of him. In the meantime, he needs product out there. And some help – pulling it together. He needs a good editor is what he needs, only there are maybe three in the whole fucking town and his isn't one of 'em. You interested in helping him out?"

"That's not my specialty. There are plenty of competent free-lance editors out there if you – "

"You're not gonna make this easy for me, are you, amigo?"

"That's not my specialty either."

He sighed, started to nibble irritably on the cuticle of his left thumb. Abruptly, he stopped himself. "Look, Cam Noyes is a cottage industry now. He has promotional commitments, personal appearance tours, speaking engagements – twenty grand a pop on the college campus tour. His time has become too valuable for him to spend it alone in a room generating material. Literary stars of his magnitude, they're stepping back from the day-to-day writing. Subcontracting it. At least the smart ones are. They're becoming like the great Renaissance artists. Those guys had a whole staff of studio artists grinding the shit out for 'em. Then they'd sign their name on it. Same thing."

"I still don't see anything here for me."

"What, you need to hear the words?"

"It would help."

"Okay. I want to hire you to ghost Cam's . . ."

"Labor of love?"

"I can't offer you any kind of coauthorship of course. But if you – "

"Not interested," I said, getting to my feet. I started for the door.

"Whoa, hold on, man! If it's the money – "

"It's not. You're talking about a book I wouldn't read. No one will. It'll sell seventy copies. The rest will be recycled into low-cost housing material."

"So make it a book people *will* read." It was a challenge.

"How?"

"If I knew, I wouldn't need you, would I?"

I hesitated. He had a point there. Besides, $657 doesn't go far these days when you have two mouths to feed. "First, I want you to tell me the part you're not telling me."

He lit a Camel and narrowed his lasers at me. "You don't beat around the bush, do you?"

"You want beating around the bush, get George Will."

He let out a short, harsh laugh. "What I'm not telling you . . . Okay, you got it."

I sat.

"I've known Cam Noyes since we were kids," he began. "I don't think of him as a client. I think of him as a brother."

"You forget, I already know how you treat family," I pointed out, indicating the headset on his desk.

"I'm trying to tell you I love this guy, okay?"

"And?"

"And . . . he's in danger of wearing out his welcome in this town. He's brought a lot of that on himself with his mouth. Genius or no genius, people are ready to bury him – no shit. And he doesn't care one bit. All he wants to do is party and chase puss. I keep telling him if he doesn't deliver some kind of class manuscript and deliver it on time, the party's gonna be over. But he won't listen to me."

"What makes you think he'd listen to me?"

"You've been there. You know the pitfalls."

"I didn't exactly step around them."

"But you understand what he's going through. He'll respond to you. You're what he needs right now. I sure ain't." He scratched his beard ruefully. "Will you talk to him?"

I shook my head. "No, thanks. I'm not in the market for a kid brother. Especially one who makes more money than I do."

"Just talk to him," Boyd pleaded. "You're gonna love the guy. I'm sure of it. Want to know why I'm so sure?"

"Not particularly."

He sat back in his chair, hands behind his head, and smiled expansively at me. "Cam Noyes is going to remind you of your favorite person in the whole world."

"And who might that be?"

"You."

CHAPTER
THREE

When he got done groaning and sputtering Cam Noyes asked me what the fuck was going on.

"What's going on," I told him, "is we had a lunch date three hours ago and you stood me up. I don't like to be stood up."

"I noticed. Sorry, I fell asleep."

"I noticed."

He sniffled and reached for a Marlboro on the nightstand. He seemed unconcerned by his nakedness. Also by the fact that he was sitting in ice water. He lit the cigarette with a silver Tiffany's lighter, pulled deeply on it, and let the smoke slowly out of his blood-caked nostrils. There was a mannered quality to the way he did it, as if he had practiced it in front of a mirror a few thousand times. When he put the lighter down, he noticed the lipstick Lulu had found. He picked it up and stared at it a moment, gripping it tight enough for his knuckles to whiten. Then he hurled it against the wall. It bounced off, rolled across the floor, and right back under the bed where it came from. Then he yawned, ran his hands through his hair, and smiled at me. It was a smile of straight white teeth, gleaming blue eyes, and long blond lashes, an unexpectedly warm and trusting smile with a hint of bashfulness underneath. It was a million-dollar smile.

"Cam Noyes, Mr. Hoag," he said.

"Make it Hoagy." I shook his big callused hand.

"As in Carmichael?"

"As in the cheese steak."

"Are you from Philadelphia?"

"I am not."

"Father was," he said.

"I suppose someone has to be."

Lulu put her two front paws up on the bed and barked.

"The name is Lulu," I explained.

"Of course it is," he said pleasantly.

He hoisted her up with one arm. She made a complete circuit around the bed, snuffling happily, flopped down next to him, and immediately began to sneeze like crazy, her big floppy ears pinwheeling around almost fast enough to lift her off the bed.

He watched her curiously. "Why is she doing that?"

"She happens to be allergic to a certain perfume."

Calvin Klein's Obsession, to be exact. The bedcovers reeked of it. She had not, I recalled, sneezed when she met Charlie.

He patted her. "I had a dog when I was a boy," he said, his voice tinged now with a kind of remote, aristocratic sadness. "A cocker spaniel named Johnny. I loved Johnny more than anything. He died when I was away at camp one summer. Mother was so distressed that I'd not been able to say a proper good-bye that she saved him for me. When I got home, she took me straight to the cellar and opened the freezer door and said, 'Here's Johnny!' And there he was, shoved in there with the Hummel skinless franks and Minute Maid frozen orange juice, teeth bared, his paws all stiff . . ." He shuddered at the memory, then looked down and realized he was petting the wet blanket. Lulu was long gone – under the bed. Not her kind of story.

"Get dressed," I said. "We'll put some food and coffee into you. Talk business."

He sniffed at his armpits. "Perhaps I ought to shower."

"Don't let me stop you."

He came downstairs a few minutes later wearing a stylishly dowdy white planter's suit, striped tie, pink oxford button-down shirt, and paint-spattered Top-Siders with no socks. His wet hair was slicked straight back. He looked scrubbed and healthy and ready for anything. He was still young enough to not show the effects of the life he was leading. It had been a long time since I was that young.

At the foot of the stairs he stopped to light a cigarette from his lighter. Again I noticed how self-conscious his gestures seemed. He posed there for me, one hand in his pants pocket, looking as if he were straight out of one of those Ralph Lauren ads, the ones where the members of an ultracivilized master-race family are lounging about their baronial country manse with their hunting dogs and their croquet mallets. There was a good reason for this – he had actually been a Lauren model before he took up writing.

"Forgot to give your key back," I said, tossing it to him. "Charlie's key, I mean."

He caught it and looked at it. "You met Charlie?"

"I did. She seems – "

"Brilliant? She is." He sighed. "She's also in love with me, the poor thing."

"Why do you say that?"

"I'm no good for her. Or for anyone. I can't love them back. You were married to Merilee Nash, weren't you?"

I nodded.

"What was it like?"

"Being married or being married to Merilee Nash?"

"Being married."

I tugged at my ear. "When it's going well, it's not the worst thing there is. When it isn't . . . it is."

"She seems like the perfect woman."

"Only because she is."

"How do you know when you're ready for it? Marriage, I mean."

"You're never ready. You just kind of feel it sneaking up on you, like the punch line to a bad joke. Not a terrible house, by the way."

"Thanks. Still no kitchen or terrace, as you can see. Charlie can't seem to get the damned contractor back for more than thirty minutes at a time, and at that only when we're not here to put our foot down. The man's uncanny. Friend of hers at *Architectural Digest* wants to do a spread when it's all done. He says it's a breakthrough in Found Minimalism."

"Play a lot of golf?" I asked, indicating the putting green. "Or is that the 'found' part?"

He went over to the putter and fingered it fondly. "One of my first loves, actually. As a boy I dreamt of being a pro. Do you play the game?"

"Some. Javelin was always more my style."

"What's your handicap?"

"An exceedingly low bullshit threshold. Yours?"

He grinned. "I don't know how to say no."

"That's not so hard. I'll teach you."

It was still sunny outside. The air was fragrant from the blossoms on the trees across the street in the park, where a black nanny was pushing a baby in a pram down one of the spotless gravel paths. An elderly couple sat on a bench together reading. They waved to the nanny as she passed. She waved back.

"Not a terrible neighborhood either," I observed.

"And steeped in a tradition of literary greatness," he agreed enthusiastically. "Henry James lived here in Gramercy Park. So did Stephen Crane, Herman Melville, Nathaniel West, S. J. Perelman . . . and now me."

Lulu stopped in her tracks and began to cough. Violently.

"What's she allergic to now?" Cam asked, frowning down at her.

"I'm afraid she got it from me."

"Got what?"

"The low bullshit threshold."

He froze, taken aback. Then he laughed and held up his hands in a gesture of surrender. "Boyd always says that if you keep telling people you're great, they'll eventually believe you. I take it you think that's bush."

"I think the work speaks for itself."

"As do I, coach." · He flashed that disarming smile at me. "But it never hurts to turn up the volume a little, does it?"

We hopped into his bright-pink Loveboat. It had a white interior and plenty more chrome all over the dash. Also enough room inside to seat six with space for a skating rink left over. He lowered the top as soon as he started her up. I put down my window. Lulu planted her back paws firmly in my groin and stuck her large black nose out.

"Unassuming little set of wheels," I observed.

"Yeah, I try to keep a low profile."

He pulled away from the curb without bothering to look and almost got nailed by an onrushing cabbie, who slammed on his brakes and gave us a sample of his horn and his upraised middle finger. Cam seemed quite oblivious of him – he ignored all of the other cars on the road, as well as things like lanes, street signs, and traffic lights. He just rolled along in the giant Olds as if the road were his and his alone.

"You spoke with Boyd about the book?" he asked.

"I did," I replied as he calmly drifted through a red light at Park, cut off three oncoming cars, and made a left onto it. "He wasn't entirely specific about what your concept is."

"Haven't got one."

"That might explain it."

He pulled up a whopping two blocks away on Park and Nineteenth in front of the Cafe Iguana and killed the engine and started to get out.

"Going to leave it right here?" I asked. The car wasn't exactly double-parked – it was more like in the middle of the street.

"Too big to take inside with us," he answered simply as he headed in.

Cafe Iguana was a big, multilevel Yushie hangout colored in peach and turquoise. Its trademark was a sixteen-foot crystal iguana suspended in the air over the bar, where Rob Lowe stood by himself drinking a beer and trying to look grown-up and deep. Seeing him there reminded me just how much I missed Steve McQueen. It was nearly six o'clock so the place was practically teeming with the Young Urban Shitheads – the power-suited male variety displaying plenty of teeth and swagger, the females showing a lot of treadmill-enhanced leg and stony gazes. A few artists and models and record producers were sprinkled around for flavor. There were tables, but no one was eating yet.

Cam made straight for the bar where he exchanged low-fives and a few lusty whoops with Lowe before finding us a couple of empty stools at the end. The bartender was ready for him with two shot glasses of tequila and a wedge of lime. The man wasn't unknown here. He took a bite out of the lime and threw one of the shots down his throat. Then a bite. Then the second shot.

Then the bartender turned to me for my order, his eyes flickering slightly when he heard the soft, low growl coming from under the bar.

"Make it a bellini," I said.

He frowned, shook his head. "Don't know it."

"Three parts champagne, one part fresh peach juice. It was invented at Harry's Bar in Venice in the forties."

He nodded. "Sounds perversely good, ace, but where am I gonna get fresh peach juice?"

I dug into my trench coat. "Where do you think?" I replied, rolling two ripe peaches onto the counter. "And don't call me ace."

Cam grinned at me approvingly as the bartender retreated to make my drink. "I'm beginning to like you, coach. You have style."

"Slow down. I'm complex."

"Tell me, is Harry's Bar still there?"

"Was the last time I looked."

"That's funny," he said. "I was just out there for the Oscar parties, and we ate down at the beach one night, place called Chinois. Stupendous eats. But I don't remember seeing any Harry's."

"Italy," I said tugging at my ear. "It's in Venice, Italy. Not Venice, California."

He nodded. "That explains it. Never been to Italy. Or anywhere in Europe. Would I like it?"

"There's nothing not to like."

The bartender came back with my bellini in a tall champagne flute and with two more shots of tequila for Cam. I took a sip. It was excellent – the champagne cold and dry and enlivened by the sweetness of the peach juice.

Cam drained another shot of tequila with a bite of lime. "Listen, when I said there was no concept for my book, I didn't mean I haven't given it a great deal of thought. I have. I just don't believe there should be one. Know what I mean?"

Before I could answer, an uncommonly leggy and lovely young blonde approached him from behind, ran her fingers through his hair, and leaned into him. "You didn't call me," she said. Then she kept on going down the bar, hips swiveling.

He gazed after her wistfully until she looked back at him over her shoulder and wiggled her fingers at him. He wiggled his back, groaning softly. "She models see-through lingerie for the catalogs. Not very high up on the food chain intellectually, but she happens to like it up the ass."

I sipped my drink. "I don't."

"Don't what?"

"Get what you mean."

"Oh, right." He lit a cigarette, dragged deeply on it. "I mean, I'm not interested in doing something that has quote-unquote form. I want this book's energy to be the energy of unvarnished chaos." He was warming up now – his voice was getting louder, his eyes brighter. Certainly the tequila wasn't hurting. "I want to surprise the reader. Ask them questions nobody's ever asked them before, like, say, do blind people *see* in their dreams? I want to have them turn the page and run smack into, say, the photographs Charlie has taken of dead bodies she's found on the streets of Manhattan." He laughed, tremendously pleased by his own brilliance. He had that special brand of cockiness that comes from never having known failure. Nobody had ever said no to Cam Noyes. Nobody had ever told him to shut up. He drained his tequila. "What do you think, coach? Don't you think it sounds stupendous?"

I glanced over at him. He was waiting for an answer. I gave him one. "I think," I replied, "that it sounds like one of the two or three biggest loads of bullshit I've heard in a very long time."

I never saw the punch coming. It caught me square on the jaw. The next thing I knew I was sitting on the floor watching that damned iguana swirl around somewhere up near the ceiling. Fireworks were going off, and somebody was ringing the bells up at St. Patrick's. And then the bartender was waving ammonia under my nose and Lulu was licking my hand. A bunch of Yushies were standing over me, murmuring. Personal-injury lawyers smelling a lawsuit, no doubt.

Cam Noyes knelt before me, his brow creased with concern. "Christ, I'm sorry." He sounded contrite.

"Kind of a short fuse you have there."

"I know," he acknowledged readily. "I've never been good at taking criticism. Ask anyone."

"That's okay. I believe you."

"Besides, you're not exactly gentle."

"You want gentle, get Sally Jessy Raphael." I sat up, rubbing my jaw.

"Care to punch me back?" he offered, quite seriously. "I deserve it."

"Not my style. But thanks."

He hoisted me up onto my feet. I was a bit wobbly, but okay. The Yushies dispersed. I got back up onto my stool. Cam started to climb back onto his. Just as his butt was about to land, I yanked it from under him. He hit the floor with a thud and a loud, surprised "Oof."

"Damn, that felt good," I exclaimed, grinning down at him.

"Is *this* your style?" he demanded crossly, glowering up at me.

"Generally."

"We even now?"

"As far as I'm concerned we are."

I helped him up. We shook hands. We ordered another round of drinks. He drained one of his shots after they came, gazed into his empty glass, and oh-so-casually remarked, "You've had it, haven't you? Writer's block?"

My stomach muscles tightened involuntarily. They always do when I think about the void. And the fear. I glanced over at him and swallowed. I nodded.

"How do you know when you have it?" he asked, his eyes still on his empty glass.

"You know," I said softly.

He looked up at me. The twinkle was gone from his eyes. There was only a hollowness, a hurt there now. He took a deep breath, let it out slowly. "Just can't seem to start anything. Doesn't matter what it is. The novel. A short story. Even a letter. I keep thinking – hold on, don't forget who you are. Don't forget you have to be brilliant, outrageous, natural, hip . . . You have to be *Cam Noyes*." He ran his hands through his wavy blond hair. "They've set this impossibly high standard for me, you know? And they'll only be happy if I exceed it. I'm not allowed to fail. They won't let me. So I end up sitting there. And sitting there. And . . . I don't know. I feel like I'm . . ."

"Exposing yourself in public?"

"Well, yeah. Kind of."

"That's what writing is."

"I suppose it is." He shook his head. "Christ, how did you survive this?"

"I didn't. I wrecked myself and my marriage. Drove all of my friends away – except for the real ones, the ones who were there before."

"I don't have many friends like that."

"No one does."

"And then what? How did you get over it?"

"I stopped caring."

"About your work?"

"About what everybody in town was going to think of it," I replied. "Half of them don't even know what the hell they're talking about anyway. You can't write for Tanner Marsh, only for yourself, the way you did before you became the famous Cameron Sheffield Noyes. Just concentrate on the work. Forget about everything else."

He lit another cigarette. "I can't."

"I didn't say it was easy."

"This book . . . what would you do?"

"If it were up to me?"

He sniffled. "Yes."

"I think the idea of you and Charlie combining forces is dynamite. As for the content . . . I'd try to get beneath your whole gifted and tragic rebel-genius image."

"Now you're trying to provoke me again," he said coldly.

"I'm not. What makes you Cam Noyes? That's what I'd like to know – who you are. How and why you became a writer. How you made it. What it took. What it has done to you – including give you writer's block. The average reader still thinks publishing is a word of tweedy, genteel people who sit around waiting to discover great books, and that authors are shy recluses whose sole aim in life is to write those books. Your story can be the story of publishing as it really is today. Unvarnished."

He scratched his chin thoughtfully, consciously. Portrait of the artist as a young brooder. "In other words, you want dirt."

"Not necessarily," I replied, sipping my drink. "Why, what kind of dirt?"

"Did you know Tanner Marsh and Skitsy Held were once married?"

"I seem to recall it."

"When they got divorced, *he* sued *her* for alimony, and won, on the grounds she couldn't have made it in publishing without him. He gave her her start, steered a lot of important young writers her way."

"That's common knowledge."

He lowered his voice conspiratorially. "Is it common knowledge they're thieves, both of them?"

I leaned forward. "Oh?"

"That is what you call someone who pockets money that doesn't belong to them, isn't it?" He waited, somewhat shyly, for my response.

"It is," I told him.

"Believe me, there's deliciously sleazy stuff to tell about the way those two do business. Stuff they'd positively kill to keep quiet."

"And you're prepared to tell it?"

He nodded eagerly. "It's perfect! It's ballsy. Subversive. High profile. It's *Cam Noyes.* God, I love it! Let's do it!"

"Slow down. Boyd may not be quite so enthusiastic."

"He could care less what people think of him," Cam scoffed.

"So he said."

"As long as it makes a splash and big bucks he'll be happy. And it will. I just know it will."

"Your editor may want to – "

"All he cares about is what month I turn it in. *We* turn it in. Will you do it with me, coach? Can we do it? Please?"

Christ, he *sounded* like a kid brother – one who was begging me to take him bowling with me. "You've made up your mind just like that?" I asked.

"Just like that."

"You're a snap – I should have asked you for all of your money."

He grinned. "Then I *do* know how to say no. Is it a deal?"

I said it was. Couldn't help myself. See, the truth is I'd always wanted a kid brother.

An involuntary shudder passed through me when we shook on it. A tingle of deep, dark dread, of snakes slithering through the undergrowth. Whatever it was, Cam clearly hadn't felt it. He was whooping and pounding the bar and buying everyone in the place a round, just a big, agreeable golden retriever puppy of a kid. I half expected him to lick my face.

We drank to our success when our drinks came.

"I do have one favor to ask of you," I said.

His face darkened. "If it's about the coke . . ."

"Not at all. It's your life."

"Glad you see it that way," he said, relaxing. "What then?"

"I'd like an associate of mine named Vic Early to stay in your guest room for a while. I find he comes in very handy."

"Sure. No problem. What is he, a typist?"

"Not exactly. You'll find him easy to get along with. Just don't get him mad."

"Why, what happens?"

"You don't want to know."

I pulled in at Tony's on my way home. It's a neighborhood place on Seventy-ninth off Amsterdam that hasn't changed its menu or its decor in twenty-five years. They make their own sausages. I had mine with ravioli and a bottle of Chianti. As always, there was a little fried calamari on the side for Lulu.

While I ate, I made notes of my initial conversation with Cameron Noyes. Most of them ended in question marks, such as how much did he really have on Skitsy Held and Tanner Marsh? How would they take to his writing about it? What on earth was I getting myself into?

Merilee's Woody Allen movie came on the TV over the bar while I was putting away my cannoli and espresso. Lulu scampered in there to watch it. She never misses one of her mommy's movies. The barman let her sit up on the top of the bar so she could see better. I stayed in the dining room. I knew all of the lines – by heart.

We walked home to Ninety-third Street on Broadway. Upper Broadway was in the intensive care unit now. A solid corridor of new, thirty-story, modern Frigidaire apartment houses was taking form. My old neighborhood merchants were losing their leases daily. In their place were coming the trendy boutiques selling distressed denim jackets and twelve-dollar chocolate chip cookies, the sidewalk cafes serving limp, watery arugula salads and mesquite-grilled snapper as moist and flavorful as chalk. In their place were coming more and more Yushies, who scurried around the neighborhood after dark like cockroaches, that new kind from Florida that the sprays won't stop.

I was losing my neighborhood. When you lose your neighborhood in New York, you lose your family, and there's no replacing it.

There was nothing in my mailbox except for another notice from the Racquet Club reminding me I'd forgotten to pay my dues.

I counted the stairs up to the fifth floor. I'd become convinced over the past few weeks that someone had added another flight when I wasn't looking. They hadn't.

My apartment was stuffy and smelled of the dried mackerel remains in Lulu's bowl. As unappetizing as her principal fare is fresh out of the can, it's even worse when it's been sitting in a warm room for twenty-four hours. I threw open the windows, scooped it into the trash, and opened a new can for her. There were no messages on my phone machine.

I undressed and brushed my teeth slowly and carefully, using the new circular motion my dentist said just might save my gums provided I also flossed. My jaw was too sore for that. I'd floss tomorrow. I've been telling myself I'd floss tomorrow every night for the past seventeen years. My problem is I always find something better to do than standing in front of the bathroom mirror poking a piece of wet string around in my mouth.

I went to bed with a collection of Truman Capote's early short stories, which I work my way through every couple of years to remind myself what good writing is.

I had just turned out my light – and Lulu had just assumed her favorite position with a satisfied grunt – when I heard it. A dull thud on the roof above me in the darkness. Then another. And another. Footsteps . . . Lulu growled. I shushed her. The steps quickened, headed toward the big skylight over my kitchen. At the skylight they stopped. Hesitated . . . checking it out. . . . The glass was reinforced with steel mesh, but all it would take was a pair of wire cutters and a swift boot and I'd have a visitor. I swallowed, glanced at the phone on the nightstand, thought about calling the police. But that meant moving, and I couldn't seem to. . . . The footsteps retreated now. Over toward the steel roof door. That was held shut from the inside by a hook and eye. A crowbar would pop it open easily.

He had a crowbar.

It opened with a sharp crack. Now I heard the footsteps on the stairs from the roof, descending quickly . . . in the corridor outside my door. Lulu growled again. This time I put a hand over her muzzle. The steps came to a stop at my door. Silence. A rustling sound . . . something being slid under the door. . . . The footsteps retreated now. Down the steps. Rapidly. One flight. Another. And then, far below, the street door slammed shut. Gone.

I let go of Lulu and my breath. Then I turned on my light and went to the door. It was a blank white envelope, folded shut. Inside was a three-by-five card that had a warning on it: *Write this book and you'll be very sorry. Get the picture?*

The warning was written in those LetraSet press-on letters they sell at artist supply stores. There was something else in the envelope – the ripped-up pieces of a magazine cover. I dumped them onto my bed and put them together like a jigsaw puzzle. They formed the cover of a *People* magazine from six years before. The cover story was on "The Lady Who Has It All." The face on the cover belonged to Merilee Nash.

I sat down on the bed and cursed. Yeah, I got the picture, all right. I got it just fine. Whoever it was certainly knew how to get my attention. And how to get taken seriously.

I glanced at grandfather's Rolex. It was after midnight. She'd be home from the theater now. Still wound up. I reached for the phone, stopped myself. Then I reached for it again.

It rang three times before she said hello. My heart started pounding immediately. It always does when I hear that feathery, proper, teenaged-girl's voice that belongs to her and no one else.

"Hello, Merilee," I finally got out.

Click.

I sighed, dialed again. She let it ring forever before she answered this time.

"Don't hang up, Merilee. Please. This is serious."

"Oh, no, it's Sweetness!" she cried. "What happened? Was it heartworm? A runaway sanitation truck? Oh, God, don't drag this out, Hoagy. *Please.* I can't stand it."

"Nothing like that. Lulu's fine. Obnoxious, but fine."

Merilee heaved a sigh of relief. "Merciful heavens, Mr. Hoagy. Don't ever do that to me again."

Lulu whimpered from the floor next to me. She always knows when her mommy's on the other end of the phone. Don't ask me how.

"Listen, Merilee. I seem to be in the middle of something . . ."

"Not again, Hoagy," she said wearily. "When are you going to stop this applesauce?"

"I didn't start it, believe me," I replied. "I've missed your quaint little expressions."

"Who is it this time?" she asked, sidestepping my attempt at familiarity.

"Cameron Noyes."

She gasped girlishly. "God, he's so gorgeous."

"Extremely well-hung, too."

"*Reeeeally?* How do you . . . No, don't tell me."

"You surprise me, Merilee. I wouldn't think he was your type. Kind of bratty."

"Meaning he's a pain?"

I massaged my jaw. "Meaning a lot of him is pose. I get the feeling it's almost as if he's performing a role."

"He's young," she said. "People that age are still in the process of inventing themselves. You're just not used to being around them anymore."

"Actually, his agent said he'd remind me of me."

"He *is* the new you," she said. "Gifted and handsome and full of doo-dah and vinegar."

"Ah, the me of my salad days."

"These are still our salad days, darling."

"If they are, the lettuce is wilting."

"Resent him a little?"

"Trying not to," I replied.

"And?"

"And failing," I confessed. "Charlie Chu seems like quite a girl."

"She's not a girl. She's a woman."

"Whatever she is, she's well aware he cheats on her, and seems to accept it."

"A lot of us do. We're afraid if we squawk, we'll get dumped." She was silent a second. "At least that's one thing you never did to me."

"Why, Merilee, that's the first nice thing you've said to me in – "

"I happen to be a very nice person. I'm not nearly as mean and petty and awful as you seem to think I am – in print."

"Look, we've been over that a hundred times. And that's not why I called."

"I've been speaking to Sean about us."

"Oh?"

"He's a very intelligent man," she added. "And I think he's gotten a bum rap from the press."

"Why should he be different from anyone else?"

"He said you had to do what you did, because you're an artist, and that you must write about your experiences or you won't grow from them."

"Merilee, that's precisely what I told you myself."

"I know, I know. I guess I just needed to . . . So you're in the middle of something?"

"I am. There's no reason for you to be alarmed, but they may . . . well, try to get at me through you."

"You mean you think a loon might go after me." She stated it matter-of-factly.

"I'm afraid it's possible."

"Not to worry," she said bravely. "I'm used to them. Come with the territory, I'm afraid."

"Still, I think you should be careful."

"I promised myself a long time ago I won't let them spook me. If I do, I'll become one of them myself."

"Promise me you'll be careful," I insisted.

"I'll be careful."

"Promise me and *mean* it."

"I'll be fine, Hoagy. I have a great big fierce doorman."

"Call me if you need me. It's probably nothing, but call, okay?"

"I shall. And thank you for the warning. It was very civilized of you."

We were both silent for a moment now.

"Do you ever miss us, Hoagy?" she asked, her voice softer.

I swallowed. "Only most of the time. You?"

"I miss us right now. When I've just crawled home from the theater, from all of the lights and the applause, all the energy, to this dark, still apartment. It's so quiet here. Hoagy?"

"Yes, Merilee?"

"You broke my heart, Hoagy."

CHAPTER
FOUR

(Tape #1 with Cameron Noyes recorded May 6 at the Blue Mill restaurant on Commerce St. off Hudson. Arrives punctually. Seems eager, clear-eyed. Wears blue-and-white seersucker suit.)

Noyes: The decor here is bizarre, coach. Don't they know what decade this is?

Hoag: This happens to be one of my favorite restaurants.

Noyes: Is that why you made me promise not to tell any of my friends about it?

Hoag: Precisely.

Noyes: Food's not bad. I take it you get off on simple.

Hoag: It doesn't get any better than simple.

Noyes: Think so?

Hoag: You know that cherry writing table you have in your study? Its beauty is in its simplicity. But it's a deceptive simplicity. Thousands of hours of work went into it – by a craftsman who knew what he was doing and didn't take any shortcuts.

Noyes: (silence) I made that table.

Hoag: You made it?

Noyes: You sound surprised.

Hoag: No, I'm impressed. You're very gifted with wood. You know, I wondered about your hands. They aren't a writer's hands.

Noyes: Maybe I'm more of a furniture maker than I am a writer. It's the only time I feel totally at peace.

Hoag: So that's your shop next to Charlie's studio?

Noyes: Yes. I make her frames for her. Am I? Better at that?

Hoag: I don't have to tell you you're brilliant. You know that. (pause) But I think you're at a crossroads now. You can come back down to earth, work hard, get even better. Or you can fizzle out. Become one of those people who are simply famous for being famous, like George Plimpton or Dick Cavett.

Noyes: All I did was put some words down on paper. I have no idea why people responded the way they did. I . . . I have no idea how to repeat it. And I sure as hell don't understand where it came from.

Hoag: That's why we're here – to find out where it came from. By the way, who knows about us?

Noyes: Everyone in town, I imagine. Boyd believes in getting the word out. I told him last night about our new idea, and he loves it. I knew he would. Why do you ask?

Hoag: Just curious. Tell me about growing up. Were you an only child?

Noyes: Yes. I grew up in a typical family – no one loved anyone. I was born and raised in Farmington, Connecticut, one of those quaint, historic New England villages the tourists from Fresno go so apeshit over. I come from *Mayflower* stock on mother's side, the Knotts. There are Knotts buried all over the state. Her great-grandfather, Samuel Knott, was a chief justice of the state of Connecticut. He helped slaves get away during the Civil War, when Farmington was a junction of the underground railroad. Her grandfather and father were clergymen. The family manse passed down through several generations. Mother grew up in it, as did I. It's a white, center-chimney colonial smack-dab in the middle of the historic district on High Street. The little plaque out front says it was built in 1790. Fireplaces and family heirlooms in every room. Like growing up in a museum, really. . . . Mother was a beautiful woman.

Hoag: She's dead?

Noyes: They're both dead. My parents died within a week of each other when I was fourteen. . . . She was a tall, fine-boned blonde. An only child. Jane Abbott. Knott was her maiden name. She studied at Miss Porter's School, of course, being that it was right around the corner. And a family tradition.

Hoag: So did Merilee.

Noyes: Did she? Mother could have become an actress herself. She was that beautiful. But she was much too devoted to her own special brand of pretense. The Mayflower Society. The Daughters of the American Revolution. The local historical society. Horse and flower shows. She lived in a permanent state of artificial grace. She insisted upon proper speech and dress. Proper manners at the dinner table at all times. If I pushed my food too close to the edge of my plate, she'd sweetly say, "Danger zone, Cammy. Danger zone." I never saw mother perspire. And I never could imagine her taking a shit. Still, I shouldn't be unkind. Mother believed in me. Loved me. Father never did. He always treated me like a stray someone had brought into the house. I often did outrageous things just to get his attention. I remember once, when I was perhaps five, he promised to buy me a penknife. I've always been fond of knives. He forgot. So to remind him I got a nail and ran it over the length of his Mercedes. He had to repaint the entire car.

Hoag: Did you get the penknife?

Noyes: No, but I got his attention. *(laughs)* He was of beef-baron stock. His great-great-grandfather built one of the big Chicago slaughterhouses in the mid-1800s. A multimillionaire who used to go on those expeditions out onto the plains to hunt buffalo. That bowie knife I have on my writing table belonged to him. Father's grandfather married into the Main Line and settled in Philadelphia. Father was named for him – Sawyer Noyes. He and mother met when she was at Wellesley and he at Yale. He was quarterback of the football team, a handsome, fearless campus hero. Father was the sort of man for whom college was the pinnacle of his life. Everything afterward was a gradual process of slipping away into ordinariness and disappointment. Once in a great while he and I would toss a football around in the yard. One time he caught the ball and stared at it, and continued to stare at it, and then he just laid it down softly on the grass and walked inside. He was an unhappy man. Had some family money left in a trust, but not much. He used his looks and mother's connections to sell real estate. Played a lot of golf at the country club. Drank, of course. So did his older brother, Jack . . . Smilin' Jack Noyes was father's idol. Had been a race car driver and flyer in his youth. By the time I came along he was little more than a sot and a bore – twice divorced and without a proper job. Hung out a lot at the Essex Yacht Club. Uncle Jack always had yachts of one kind or another. But he was nice to me, since he had no children of his own. Once, when the two of us were out on the Sound, he told me that it was vital for a man to have a place of his own – a hideaway where he could think and be himself and that when he died he intended to leave me his. It was a tiny fishing shack on Crescent Moon Pond in Old Lyme. Very remote. Had to row across the pond to reach it. He said no one else in the family knew of it, and that I wasn't to tell father, that it was our secret. *(pause)* I still have the damned place. It's little more than a tree house, really, and falling down at that. Town won't let me rebuild, because it's on state forest land. But I've kept it. And like Uncle Jack, I've told hardly anyone about it.

Hoag: So he's dead, too?

Noyes: Yes. *(pause)* Yes, he's dead, too.

Hoag: Something?

Noyes: (long silence) No, nothing.

Hoag: What sort of boy were you?

Noyes: Restless. Dissatisfied. I was a head-banger. Instead of sucking my thumb I'd bang the back of my head against my crib, sort of like a woodpecker in reverse.

Hoag: How old were you when you stopped?

Noyes: Who stopped? *(laughs)* I wasn't allowed the usual pacifier, television. Mother wouldn't have one in the house. It had, after all, been invented after the nineteenth century. So I spent a lot of time out in father's workshop in the carriage barn. That's where I learned how to work with wood. Also how to smoke cigarettes and wank off. Smilin' Jack was right – every man needs his hideaway. I went to the town elementary and middle schools. I had as many friends as I wanted. I was large for my age, and could do sports well. I spent six weeks every summer at a boys' camp in the Adirondacks, learning about canoeing and shooting and taking cold showers at dawn. The rest of the summer I'd play golf at the country club, sail, cherry-bomb the neighbors' mailboxes. The usual mischief. Mine was an idyllic New England boyhood, really. Safe. Sheltered. Secure. And I felt utterly suffocated by it. It was so narrow and confining. Everyone knew everyone, and everyone was well-bred and rich and white. All of them were hiding from the real word, hiding behind their fucking antiques and good manners and garden parties. You know what I mean, don't you?

Hoag: Quite well. I grew up in a town much like that. And fled as soon as I was old enough to.

Noyes: I know you did. I was thirteen when I read your book. *Our Family Enterprise* really influenced me. Made me feel like I wasn't crazy for hating the place. Gave me the courage to cut totally loose from it the way you had. Of course, it didn't hurt that it all kind of blew up in my face, too.

Hoag: How so?

Noyes: (silence) I suppose I'll have to deal with this, won't I?

Hoag: Deal with what? *(silence)* Come on, Cameron. Don't hold back on me.

Noyes: Mother . . . Mother was killed in a private plane crash in the White Mountains when I was fourteen. She and one other person, the pilot. My uncle Jack. They'd run off together, Mother and Smilin' Jack. She was a cheat, you see. She'd been banging Uncle Jack for years.

Hoag: Had your father known?

Noyes: Apparently not. The letter she'd left behind for him destroyed him. He brought all of her things down from the bedroom, laid them out in the dining room, and sat down at the table with a deck of cards. Sat there and played game after game of solitaire, surrounded by her things. Sat there for days. Didn't sleep or eat or speak. I'd ask him a question and he wouldn't even hear me. A week after the funeral I came down for breakfast and he was gone. I . . . I found him in the cellar. He'd hanged himself. I just stood there staring at him. Couldn't decide whether to cut him down first or to call the police. I stood there for a long time. Finally I cut him down. He was much heavier than I thought he'd be.

Hoag: Did he leave a note?

Noyes: Yes. It said, "Don't take this the wrong way, son." Christ, I still haven't figured out what he meant by that – what was the *right* way to take it? *(pause)* It wasn't easy, losing both of them that way. I'd lived so much for their approval. Or disapproval. Now that they weren't around I found myself in total wonder at what the point of anything was. Especially with father's suicide – to be told by your own parent that life is not worth living . . . I suppose the main thing it did, besides leave me totally alone, was make me realize there is no such thing as security or trust or happiness in this world. There's only chaos. And myth. I guess I've spent the rest of my life trying to tell people that, whether they want to be told or not.

Hoag: That's an excellent insight into your work. Keep it up. You had no other relatives?

Noyes: None. No aunts or uncles. No living grandparents. The local family lawyer was appointed executor of the estate, as well as my legal guardian.

Hoag: His name?

Noyes: Why?

Hoag: Just being thorough.

Noyes: Seymour. Peter Seymour. When the dust settled, it turned out father was in terrible debt. I had to sell off the Knott manse and all of the antiques in it to pay off his creditors. I was left with a small trust – just enough to pay for my education – and Uncle Jack's shack. Otherwise I was a penniless orphan the day when I was shoved out into the cold, cruel world at age fourteen.

(end tape)

(Tape #2 with Cameron Noyes recorded May 7 at the Blue Mill. Wears same suit as day before with torn black T-shirt, no shoes or socks. Is bleary-eyed, but punctual.)

Noyes: I ran into a friend at Live Bait last night who thought he'd seen you on a squash court at the Racquet Club yesterday, though he couldn't swear to it – he said you looked a lot older than your book-jacket photo.

Hoag: Tell him, whoever he is, that he's an asshole.

Noyes: It was you.

Hoag: Getting killed by a senior vice president of Kidder Peabody.

Noyes: I don't get it, coach. Why are you still hanging out at that gentleman's dinosaur pit? I thought you hated those people, like I do.

Hoag: I told you I was complex.

Noyes: But how can you write the way you do and still . . . I don't understand you.

Hoag: You don't have to. I'm the one who has to understand you. I meant to ask you yesterday, do you have any old photographs of your family? Pictures of you as a child? Charlie will want to sort through them for illustration purposes.

Noyes: Not a one. I threw everything out a long time ago.

Hoag: So tell me about the cold, cruel world.

Noyes: The lawyer, Seymour, decided that a boarding school made the most sense, so he sent me off to the Deerfield Academy. Deerfield became my home for the next four years, and the people there my family. Deerfield is where I came of age, though I don't give the school much credit for that. I hated the place on sight. It's in a small village in the middle of the cornfields in western Massachusetts. Deerfield Village is like Farmington, only more so. More quaint. More into itself and its past. The whole place is a living fucking colonial museum.

Hoag: I take it you don't go in for preservation.

Noyes: I go in for destruction. On the surface, the academy was a decent enough place. Lovely campus. Superior library and laboratories and athletic facilities, second-largest planetarium in all of New England . . . But it was, for all intents and purposes, a minimum-security prison. Instead of cells we were assigned dorm rooms. Instead of prison blues we wore blue blazers and ties. We were told where to go, what to do, when to eat. Curfew was at ten.

No drinking. No cars. No girls. Two proctors per corridor to keep an eye on you, and a corridor master to be your buddy. Mine was a prized dickhead named Darcy Collingwood, a middle-aged bachelor who taught algebra and wore Hush Puppies and ate Wheaties with diet raspberry soda on it. He smiled a lot. I didn't. I was used to coming and going as I pleased. Plus they really laid on that whole Eastern-elite prep-school mindset – the old-boy tradition of hearty good comradeship and spirited athletic competition. Sports do make the boy into a man. They also tire him out so he won't think about how horny he is and how there's nobody around to fuck except for the other boys. Deerfield just went coed this past year – actually joined the twentieth century. But when I was there, the nearest wool was three miles away at Stoneleigh-Burnham, and only then for purposes of organized activities like dances. It was a prison. I wanted no part of it. I would have fled, too, if it hadn't been for Boyd. As freshmen we were placed across the hall from each other in Plunkett, the oldest and ricketiest of the dormitories. I'd never met anyone like Boyd. He seemed conventional enough on the surface. Suburban middle-class background. But even then he was a visionary scam artist. Within weeks his room had become a working laboratory in the art of free enterprise. He bought and sold tests and term papers. Recruited smart kids to take the SATs for other kids at a fee, with an incentive program based on how far over 1400 they scored. When he turned sixteen, Boyd brought his car up from home and paid a local farmer to let him keep it in his barn. After curfew, he'd slip out his window, pedal his bike to the farm, drive over to Greenfield, and stock up on booze, using a forged driver's license. Then he'd bring it back and peddle it to the boys. Sold them forged driver's licenses at fifty dollars a pop, too, so they'd be able to buy it themselves on weekend leaves. He had a whole setup in his room – camera, printer, laminating machine. Probably stole all the equipment from the school. He was very resourceful.

Hoag: You sound rather proud.

Noyes: I am. Boyd and I have always shared the same vision of this world, which is that everyone in it lies, cheats, and steals to get what they want. Every single one of us. I accept that. What I don't accept is people who won't admit this about themselves. They, to me, are the liars. All that really matters to anyone is not getting caught, and Boyd never did, though one time the shit did hit the fan in a big way. A kid he sold a license to went a little *off* one night. Stole a car from the village, got a bottle, got wasted, slammed the car into a busload of kids near Springfield. Killed two of them, as well as himself. A major scandal on campus. State police said if they ever found out who sold the kid that forged license, they'd nail his ass but good. So Boyd got out of that line and into grass, hash, coke, ludes. He was the campus pharmacist our junior and senior years. Used his weekend leaves to buy quantities in Boston and Hartford. Once he even smuggled a bunch of hash back from the Bahamas when he was on vacation there over Christmas with his parents. He must have made five hundred dollars a week dealing, and he never got caught. Too smart for them. . . . I was fascinated by Boyd from the beginning. In awe of him, really. It was Boyd who got me through Deerfield, both in terms of slipping me test papers and in terms of my head. We spent a lot of hours together getting wasted and talking about life. Boyd wanted to become a rock promoter. He sort of ran things over at WDAJ, the campus radio station, until he used the word *Fuck* on the air and the dean of students wouldn't let him near the place again.

Hoag: And you? What did you want?

Noyes: I didn't know. I hadn't found myself yet. And I was different from the others. I had no future laid out for me – Ivy League education, seat on the Exchange, sturdy, well-bred wife who spoke in hushed, demure tones. Part of me was like Boyd – a rebel. Part of me desperately wanted to be accepted. The easiest way to become accepted was in sports. From the day I arrived at Deerfield I was the academy's best athlete. I was made quarterback of the varsity football team when I was still a sophomore. Everyone wanted to be my friend. I was a gung ho prince among men.

Hoag: Any resemblance to Sawyer Noyes would be strictly coincidental, of course.

Noyes: You don't miss much.

Hoag: I try not to.

Noyes: Believe me, that resemblance was short-lived. Died in the second half of the Choate game. That's when I finally got a good look at myself. We were trailing 7-0 at halftime. Not one of my better halfs. They were a big, physical team. On me before I had a chance to throw. Coach really let me have it in the locker room. Told me I was *spitting the bit*. Told me I wasn't playing like a *Deerfield* man. Made me feel like if I didn't win that game, I'd be a complete failure as a human being. And I *believed* that. I went out there wanting to win more than anything in the world. I was in the huddle calling the first play of the second half, all pumped up, when it hit me – here I was taking the same exact path as Father. Picking right up where he left off the night he threw that rope over the cellar support beam and hanged himself. That wasn't what I wanted. That was what I *hated*. I decided then and there to do something about it – I started completing passes, all right, only I completed them to the wrong men. Coach yanked me when I'd run the score up to 28-0. Screamed at me. Threw me off the team. Boyd hugged me after the game. Told me we were blood brothers. Everyone else treated me like someone with a serious psychological problem. I had, after all, repudiated everything that the school held sacred. Collingwood, my corridor master, sat me down and said to me, very sternly, "You are not a lone wolf, Noyes. You are a unit of society." He recommended counseling. And left me alone after that. Everyone did, except for Boyd.

Hoag: Is this when you started gravitating toward writing?

Noyes: Not really. The only writing I remember doing was in a sophomore English class. The teacher asked us to do an autobiographical essay. So I told my story – unvarnished. The dickhead gave it back to me with a poor grade and a note across the top: "Life just isn't this bad, Cameron."

Hoag: And reading habits? Who were you into?

Noyes: Jim Carroll, Kerouac . . . Mmm . . . you. I skipped almost all of the required reading. Did very little on my own. Still don't read much. I'm very poorly read. I've never read a word of Hemingway, for instance.

Hoag: (pause) Fitzgerald?

Noyes: Fitzgerald? No. I don't think I've read anything of his either. *(silence)* Why are you looking at me like that?

Hoag: I'm just a little shocked.

Noyes: I told you – I'm not well-read.

Hoag: I know. But you're always mouthing off in interviews about the great writers, putting them down.

Noyes: Oh, that. Boyd feeds me those quotes so I'll get attention. Just a lot of publicity. You know how that goes. Actually, I think I'm better off being so ignorant. It means I haven't been influenced by anyone who came before me. My style is *mine*.

Hoag: Tell me about your summers. Where did you go? What did you do?

Noyes: Deerfield fixed me up with a job as a lifeguard at a summer camp in the Berkshires. I think the dean had a piece of the camp. Wasn't terrible, just dull. The only hard part was when the parents came up to pick up their kids. All of them had homes to go to. I had nowhere to go, except back to Deerfield.

Hoag: Did you ever go back to Farmington?

Noyes: No. Never.

Hoag: What about girls?

Noyes: What about them?

Hoag: Tall, blond lifeguards tend to fare pretty well on moonlit summer nights. I wondered if there was one shy doe in particular.

Noyes: Nobody worth talking about.

Hoag: I'd like to be the judge of that, if you don't mind.

Noyes: I *do* mind. I told you, there was nobody worth–

Hoag: Look, Cameron. If I ask you a question I ask it for a reason. That's my job. Your job is to answer me. That's how it works. Understand?

Noyes: Okay, okay. *(silence)* When I was seventeen, there was this counselor named Kirsten. She was a Dana Hall girl from Brookline. Blond. Slender. Very into horses . . .

Hoag: And . . . ?

Noyes: Why are you so sure there's an and? *(pause)* And she and I . . . she was my first, okay? I was hers, too. On a blanket by the lake with the Clash playing on my boom box. She loved me, and I – I loved her back.

Hoag: I thought you didn't go in for that.

Noyes: That was the only time. Never again. Ever.

Hoag: I see.

Noyes: We were going to go to Bennington together. Get married when we were seniors. It was for real, coach. We were in love. I really felt like I belonged to somebody. And she belonged to me . . . And then it blew up in my face – just like everything else had in my life.

Hoag: What happened?

Noyes: Her mother happened. She forbid Kirsten to see me after the summer was over. She thought I was genetically unsound – no money, no living relatives, suicide in the family. I wasn't good enough for her fucking daughter. And Kirsten . . . she did what she was told. I couldn't believe it – after all we'd meant to each other. She blew me off. Just like that. *(silence)* I never saw her again.

Hoag: Any idea what happened to her?

Noyes: None. Probably became a rich perfect bitch. Married a rich perfect bastard.

Hoag: And what happened to you?

Noyes: Boyd was planning to go to Columbia. He was very into New York. The whole idea of New York seemed, somehow, very appealing to me, too. After that thing with Kirsten, I wanted desperately to get away from those quaint historic villages with those quaint placards out front of those quaint houses. I wanted to go someplace ugly and sweaty and *real*. I wanted to meet people who had ideas and dreams and passions. I wanted to disappear. Does that make any sense?

Hoag: New York is like the Foreign Legion. People flee here for a lot of different reasons.

Noyes: What was yours?

Hoag: Mine? There was a job waiting for me in the family business. I didn't want it. I wanted to sip martinis at the Algonquin with Benchley and Parker.

Noyes: Did you?

Hoag: No, they were good and dead by the time I got here. Martinis were damned fine though. So you and Boyd both got into Columbia?

Noyes: Yes. We paid a couple of the Deerfield computer nerds to take the SATs for us. Mine did so well I actually got in on an academic scholarship. *(laughs)* I like to think that Mother would have been proud of her Cammy.

(end tape)

CHAPTER
FIVE

Pub parties used to be small, dreary affairs. Three or four dozen writers, editors, and agents herded into someone's smoky, book-lined living room on West End. Wine and cheese on the dining table. Lots and lots of boring, pretentious conversation. They were never my idea of fun. Merilee used to say the only good thing about them was the chance to see so many men in the same room at the same time who looked exactly like frogs.

Pub parties are still dreary affairs, but they're no longer small. To celebrate the publication of *Tell Delilah*, Skitsy Held had rented a triple-decker cruise yacht, the *Gotham Princess*, for the entire evening. It was waiting there at Pier 63 festooned with *Tell Delilah* banners when Cam and I left his Olds in the parking lot at Twenty-third and Twelfth and made our way up the long, narrow ramp.

Two hundred glittering celebrity guests were on deck enjoying the free champagne, the late-day sun on the Hudson, and the complimentary *Tell Delilah* balloons, T-shirts, hankies, and panties. It was the usual crowd of smiling, chattering celebrities who turn out at Broadway openings and museum benefits and other such photo opportunities, people who had nothing in common with each other except that they were all celebrities, and no reason for being there except that the photographers were. Lensmen from the *Daily News* and *Post, Women's Wear Daily*, and the supermarket tabloids were busily snapping shots of Sugar Ray Leonard, of Paulina Porizkova, the Polish model with the $6 million Estée Lauder contract, of John John Kennedy and Maria Shriver and Arnold Schwarzenegger, of Ashford and Simpson, Jackie Mason, Bianca Jagger, Bill Blass, and Curtis Sliwa, founder of the Guardian Angels. Phil Esposito, the former hockey great, was there. So was City Council president Andy Stein and Ron Darling of the Mets and a former child star who had just written a scandalous book accusing Darryl Zanuck of waving his dick at her when she was nine years old. All of these people and more were there to celebrate Delilah Moscowitz's new book.

We lingered at the rail for a moment, Lulu sniffing hungrily at the air wafting up from the kitchens down below. Cam swaying slightly. He'd put away a great deal of José Cuervo that afternoon, and also taken a major toot in the Loveboat on the way over. He still wore his rumpled seersucker suit and torn black T-shirt, and no shoes or socks. I had on a glen-plaid suit of Irish linen and a straw trilby. I looked better than he did, but you'll have to take my word for it.

Skitsy Held hurried over to us almost immediately, her high heels clacking on the deck. She was a brusque, gristly little woman in her early forties with shoulder-length black hair, heavy black brows, nervous brown eyes, and the unlikeliest pair of breasts in all of publishing, if not the Empire State. They positively strained against her lavender knit dress, jutting so outrageously far forward that it was a miracle the woman didn't topple over. Those who worked for her swore that Skitsy's oversized mammeries would slowly deflate through the course of the year and that every winter she would disappear alone for a holiday – returning two weeks later tanned, rested, and uplifted.

"Well, well, you made it, young Master Noyes." She spoke in rushed, officious bursts and didn't move her mouth when she did. "Not that I ever doubted you, of course."

"Hey, sure," Cam said good-naturedly, bending forward so she could give him a maternal peck on the cheek. "Wouldn't miss it."

She gestured to a crew member. A moment later the ship lurched and began to pull away from the pier. She'd been waiting for us. She turned to me now and extended a small, bony claw. Her nails were painted red, as was her rather wide mouth. "And I know this gentleman."

"Using the term loosely," I said, taking her hand.

"We met at the Anne Beattie party, remember?" Her eyes darted over to Cameron, then back to me.

"As if I could forget," I said, trying to keep my own eyes .off her breasts, and failing.

"There seems to be a bar," observed Cam, glancing across the deck.

"Yes, go have fun, dear," she said. "And *please* say hello to Delilah. She's *so* insecure."

We watched him shoulder his way through the crowd, a big disheveled blond kid at a party of sleek grown-ups.

"He can be a very bad boy," said Skitsy, shivering slightly from the breeze that had picked up as we began to chug up the Hudson. "Be firm with him. He needs that. You see, he's always felt this need to act out his view of the world."

"Which is . . . ?"

"That all people, himself included, are trash."

A white-jacketed waiter passed by with a tray of champagne. She took a glass. We both did.

"I'd like to talk to you about him for the book," I said, sipping mine. "Get your side of his story."

She raised an eyebrow, on guard now. "The rumor I hear is it's some kind of publishing exposé."

"Not really. Just his story, honesty told."

"Still, I'd be careful," she warned.

"I'm almost always careful."

"Publishing is a very small, very social business."

"Tell me something I don't already know."

She eyed me over her champagne glass. "Friends look out for each other. Lend a hand. They don't screw each other. Not without paying the consequences. Am I making myself clear?"

I tugged at my ear. "Yes. You have something to hide."

Skitsy's eyes flashed at me hotly. "I was wrong about you. You're no gentleman."

"I tried to warn you."

"So I'm in it?" she demanded. "I'm in this book?"

"Of course. You discovered him. He was your biggest star."

"He's *still* my biggest star!" she snapped angrily. "And he always will be!"

With that, Skitsky Held turned on her heel and stormed off. Well, it certainly wasn't hard to locate her little hot-button. Actually, given that Cam had so ungratefully left her for another house, it was a wonder she still spoke to him at all. Loyalty means a lot in publishing. It's rarely practiced anymore, but it's still one of the two grand delusions book people cling to. The other is that they're smarter than movie people.

Had she been the one who slid that threat under my door? True, those footsteps on my roof had sounded as if they belonged to Andre the Giant, but the sound had been magnified by the darkness and my imagination. It could have been a woman up there with that crowbar. It could have been Skitsy.

Boyd Samuels was out there in the middle of the crowded deck, his greetings hearty, his laughter forced. He had on a white linen jacket and had tied a red bandanna over his head, Hell's Angel style. I saw no sign of Delilah. I did see Boyd's burr-headed assistant, Todd Lesser, who was standing by himself at the rail, nursing a beer and ignoring the views. He wasn't watching the sun drop over the Jersey Palisades, or the lights of the Manhattan skyline beginning to twinkle in the dusk. He had eyes only for the woman photographer who was across the deck from him snapping shots of the guests. She was a trim woman, light on her feet and graceful in an oversized men's white oxford button-down shirt, faded jeans, and black penny loafers. Todd was gazing at her the way a guy looks at the one and only woman he wants, and whom he knows he can never have.

I headed over to her with Lulu and said, "Blue Monday, isn't it?"

Charlie Chu lowered her Nikon and exclaimed, "You guys made it." Her dimples were even nicer flesh-toned, especially since that flesh was the color of honey and the texture of silk. Her black hair was glossy and parted neatly on one side. She wore horn-rimmed glasses that kept sliding down her nose in a way I knew I could easily find adorable. Her mouth was like a rosebud. There was no lipstick on it. She wore no makeup or jewelry of any kind. She needed none. There was an alive, eager beauty to her, a freshness you seldom find in New York women.

"How's the tree pollen?" I asked.

"Better, thanks," she replied. "Hi, cutie," she said brightly to Lulu, who glowered up at her disapprovingly. Charlie frowned. "She still doesn't like me."

"She's peeved because there's no clam dip."

"There's shad roe downstairs on the buffet tables." Lulu promptly waddled off in that direction.

"I waited at the house for you guys to pick me up," Charlie said gaily. "No show. Todd was nice enough to bring me."

"How chivalrous of him."

He was still over by the railing, conversing now with Boyd. Actually, Boyd was talking and Todd was nodding.

"Yes, he's very sweet," she said. "A little tongue-tied though."

"I'm sorry we stood you up. I only just found out about this little gathering. Standing up beautiful women isn't my style, believe me."

"Oh, I know," she assured me. "It's Cam's." She spotted him now across the deck, where he was gulping tequila and conversing with Sean Landeta, the punter of the New York Giants. The glow in her eyes was unmistakable: utter adoration.

"Getting any good shots?" I asked her.

She pushed her glasses up her nose. "A couple. Stuff I might be able to work off of for portraits. Skitsy. Tanner . . ."

I looked around for Tanner Marsh. I didn't see him. Possibly the illustrious critic had fallen overboard and drowned in the Hudson, untreated sewage spilling out of his mouth. There was always hope.

"And you?" she asked. "Have you and Cam been having good talks?"

"I believe so," I replied. "It's still early, of course, but so far he's been candid and cooperative. An excellent subject."

She looked up at me with a quizzical expression. "I hope he doesn't disappoint you."

"Not to worry. It wouldn't be the first time."

She cocked her head slightly to one side now. "I've decided you're going to be a positive influence on him."

I grinned at her. "I've been called many things in my time, but never that."

She giggled. It really was a delicious giggle. Then she went off to say hello to the man she loved.

I worked my way over to the bar and found myself next to Todd, who was getting a Wild Turkey for Boyd.

"He invited most of these people here," Todd volunteered. "Has me check out the gossip pages every morning to see who's in town. If they're hot, Boyd makes it a point to invite them out. Then he tips off the photographers."

"Does he have a publicist?" I asked.

"Doesn't need one. This sort of thing," Todd explained, taking in the yachtful of celebrities with a wave of his hand, "is one of the things he's best at."

Todd seemed much more expansive than he had before. He was, I realized, somewhat drunk.

"And what are you best at?" I asked him.

"Me?" The bartender returned with Boyd's whiskey. Todd reached for it, downed it somewhat defiantly, and ordered another. "Writing is what I really want to do. I've had some short stories going around for a while. Just finished a novel . . ." He trailed off, shrugged his shoulders. "I don't know. It's been years."

"Sometimes it takes years."

He gazed enviously over at McInerney, Ellis, and Janowitz – the Athos, Porthos, and Artemis of Lit Lite – who were yucking it up for Liz Smith. "Not for some people," he said softly.

"Doesn't pay to dwell on that. In the real world there's no such thing as a fairness doctrine. You said you knew Boyd in school."

"I did. Dropped out in my junior year. Some personal problems. Bummed around upstate for a while. Tended bar. Cleared brush. Worked construction. Then I found myself back in the city knocking on his door."

He smiled self-deprecatingly. "And here, for better or worse, I am."

The bartender returned with another Wild Turkey. This time Todd hurried off with it.

We had reached the George Washington Bridge and turned around and started back down the river. The night air was clear and the skyline ablaze now in its fullest glory. I was standing at the rail admiring it, and marveling at how it could inspire such awe and wonder in me even when the city itself no longer could, when a young woman grabbed my arm and told me how much she'd admired the second novel. It was the guest of honor, Delilah Moscowitz, and her cardboard cutout didn't do her justice.

She was a tall, flamboyant peacock of a woman with a wild mane of frizzy red hair, creamy white skin, amused deep-blue eyes, and an upturned petulant upper lip. Her body was sculpted and sinewy, and she was showing it off. She was done up like a Place Pigalle hellcat in a lavender silk blouse unbuttoned to the navel, tight black leather miniskirt, and pink spiked heels worn without stockings. The vibes she gave off were humid enough to peel wallpaper out in Bend, Oregon.

"Glad you liked it," I said. "That makes you, my mother, and that lanky kid over next to Boyd – and him I'm not so sure about."

She swept her windblown hair back over her head. "You're very brave." She had a throaty, challenging voice. "Most men can't deal with their own impotence."

"Who says I can deal with it? I enjoyed your column in today's paper on those ten sexy summer getaways – the elevator to the top of the World Trade Center, the Maurice Villency furniture showroom, air-conditioned cabs . . ."

"I always test them myself personally," she assured me with a mischievous grin.

"I expected nothing less." I grinned back, getting the impression that Delilah Moscowitz, sex therapist, was something of a vampy, good-humored put-on.

Someone began to sneeze like crazy at our feet – Lulu, back from trolling the buffet tables. I looked down at her, then back up at Delilah. Well, well.

"Why is she. doing that?" Delilah asked.

"Your perfume Calvin Klein's Obsession, isn't it?"

"Why, yes," she replied.

"She's terribly allergic."

Delilah pouted. "What a shame if you and I ever have an affair, I'll have to change scents."

"It would be easier than me changing dogs."

"It'd be worth it, you'd find."

"I don't doubt that for a second."

Skitsy Held broke in on us, Cam and Charlie in tow.

"You remember Cameron, don't you, Delilah?" said Skitsy.

"Of course," Delilah said with cordial stiffness. "Nice to see you again." Most discreet. No hint that the two of them enjoyed the odd matinee together.

"Nice to see you, too," Cam agreed, grinning at her with easy, inflamed familiarity. He was a little less discreet. He was a lot less discreet. Still, neither Skitsy nor Charlie seemed to notice. Often, people won't see something right under their nose unless they're expecting to.

Boyd Samuels didn't miss it though. He stood nearby, beaming like the proud breeder of thoroughbred stablemates. I went over to him.

"Enough hi-profile celebs here to keep you busy ghosting for ten years, hey, amigo?" he said pleasantly, his laser eyes scanning the party for available talent. Agents, I noticed, inched closer to their clients when Boyd's eyes lingered on them for more than a second.

"Yes, assuming any of these people will still be celebs in ten years."

He threw back his scarf-clad head and laughed loudly. "Congrats – Cam said you two hit it off fantastically." He took a gulp of his Wild Turkey.

"Yes, and he's told me a lot about your visionary scams," I said. I caught him unprepared with that. I know this because he airmailed his mouthful of whiskey all over my pale-yellow silk tie.

Boyd cleared his throat uneasily. "Scams?"

"Scams. You know, paying kids to take SATs. Selling forged driver's licenses. And of course, your stint as Deerfield campus pharmacist. . . ."

His eyes flickered briefly, registering what I could have sworn was relief. Why? Were there other scams Cam hadn't told me about? "This book is supposed to be about him, not me," Boyd pointed out sharply.

"It is," I assured him. "But you do appear in a featured role – The Friend. Ronald Reagan made a whole career out of it."

He nodded. "True, true, amigo. Only, you gotta protect your people. In case you haven't noticed, drugs aren't exactly a socially approved form of recreation anymore. Christ, you gotta pass a urine test before they'll even let you run a fax machine at a lot of companies nowadays."

"I thought you didn't care about what people thought of you,"

I countered.

"I don't," he assured me. "Only these days I deal with people like senators and Wall Street plutocrats. They think I'm a bad-ass liar, that's chill. They think I'm a crook, that's chill. They think I'm a druggie . . ."

"That's not chill?"

"Leave that part out, okay?"

"You said you wanted a quality book. A quality book doesn't tiptoe around unpleasant facts."

"Kind of a stubborn shithead, aren't you?" he said sourly.

"You noticed," I said grinning. "Look, you asked me to come up with a concept. I did. Cam told me you were crazy about it."

"Thrilled," he insisted. "I'm thrilled."

"Someone certainly isn't."

He leaned closer to me. "Meaning?"

"I've been threatened."

He let out a short, surprised laugh. "By who?"

"Evidently someone who is afraid of what Cam will say."

He mulled that over. "Could just be someone who wants to see him fall on his ass."

"Who would want that?" He glanced over at Skitsy, who was still chatting with Cam and Charlie and Delilah. "I can think of one person right offhand." Then he scratched at his beard thoughtfully. "Know what the best way to handle this is? Liz Smith is standing right over there. Let's go tell her about it. She'll put it in tomorrow's paper, shove the slob right back under a rock. Great publicity, too."

"I'd rather keep a lid on it."

"Why?" he wondered.

"I have my reasons, okay?"

Boyd shrugged, obviously disappointed. I found myself eyeing him. He was a man who'd go to any extreme to promote a client. Had he done this? Had *he* left me that threat as a way of generating publicity?

"Oh, hey," he said, punching me playfully on the shoulder. "A good friend of yours is hanging out down below. Come say hello."

Most of the second deck was a glass-enclosed dining room, where a lot of the guests were busy finding a good home for the lasagna and flank steak and assorted salads on the buffet tables.

A dozen or so senior editors sat together over the remains of their food and drink listening intently to Tanner Marsh hold forth on the subject of mysticism in modern Uruguayan literature, the master pausing only to punctuate each erudite thought with a puff on his brier pipe. You don't run into many pipe smokers anymore, and those you do run into are seldom pleasant. Tanner Marsh wasn't pleasant. He was a gross, fat little man in his late fifties, an alcoholic, and a mean one. *Spy* magazine had taken to calling him the "colorful Tanner Marsh" in snide reference to his nose, which was so red, and his teeth, which were so yellow. He wore a wrinkled, shiny tan poplin suit, a rather greasy blue knit tie, and a white shirt that he'd popped open at the belly button to give his gut some breathing room. It was cool in the dining room but he was perspiring freely, a strand of his thinning gray hair plastered to his forehead.

His piggy eyes turned to narrow slits when he saw me standing there with Boyd. "I remember you," he exclaimed in his booming, condescending voice. "You *were* Stewart Hoag."

That got a few titters from the others seated before him.

"It's true, Tanner – I was," I replied graciously, not wanting to get into a pissing contest with the man. I had matured beyond that. "And on my good days, I like to think I still am."

He drank from the gin and tonic at his elbow and puffed on his pipe. "Perhaps I am being a bit harsh, Stewart," he suggested majestically, eyeing me with amusement. He was trying to provoke me. He enjoyed these little jousts.

"Don't concern yourself," I assured him. "Everyone ought to be good at something. You're good at being a vicious scumbag."

I heard a few gasps. Ah, me, I guess I haven't matured totally.

Tanner bristled. Off came his gloves. "This man," he declared, "should no longer be allowed to own or operate a typewriting machine! His picture should be posted in every business-machine emporium on the island of Manhattan! His pencils and crayons should be confiscated! His – "

"Hey, you can't talk to my coach that way!"

Heads swiveled, my own included. Cam Noyes stood there in the glass doorway, swaying unsteadily. He was quite blitzed now. Boyd hurried over to him and tried to maneuver him back out to the upper deck. Cam brushed him aside and staggered toward Tanner.

"And why not, young Noyes?" Marsh asked his former pupil, obviously relishing this.

"He," Cam replied thickly, "is an artist. An *artist*. You are nothing. *Nothing*."

"Which is what you'll be, amigo, if you don't shut up," Boyd muttered to Cam under his breath.

"Don't tell me to shut up!" Cam snapped belligerently, his eyes never leaving Marsh. "This man . . . ," he went on, referring to me, "this man *exposes* himself in public. That's what he does. What do you do? *Nothing*. What right do you have to judge him? *None*. You sit there on your fucking throne, issuing your fucking edicts . . . And what do you know about writing? You don't understand it. Or him. Or me. You don't understand any of us!"

The dining room was filled with guests now, drawn by Cam's high-decibel harangue and by what promised to be a championship heavyweight bout – in one corner the enfant terrible of American literature, in the other the grand pooh-bah. The gossip columnists strained closer, pens poised. The photographers, Charlie included, crowded in front, cameras aimed.

It was Tanner's turn. Slowly and calmly, he lit a match and held it to his pipe. When he had it going to his satisfaction, he puffed on it until he was sitting in a cloud of blue smoke. "The critic," he lectured Cam, "serves as a guide through the vast and treacherous literary wilderness. He blazes a trail. Without him, some of the great authors in history would have never been found. You, for instance." Marsh glanced at Boyd and showed him his yellow teeth. "Young Noyes seems to have a poor memory."

"No, he doesn't Tanner," Boyd assured him effusively. "Really. Isn't that right, Cam? Huh?"

Was Samuels trying to save his prized client from making a powerful enemy or was he egging him on? I wondered, though not for long.

"Why are you sucking up to him, Boyd?" Cam demanded angrily. "You always suck up to him! All of you people do! What for? Who cares what he thinks?" Cam now stood right over Marsh, who looked up at him with cool disdain. "You haven't got the slightest fucking notion what it takes to create something, Tanner! What it *feels* like. You think you do, but you don't. Know what? I'm going to do you a favor – I'm going to show you!"

With that he grabbed the fat little man by the lapels and yanked him roughly to his feet. Marsh looked pale and frightened now, as if he'd just realized he'd gotten into something his stinging wit might not get him out of. He looked around for a rescuer but none stepped forward. Everyone on board the *Gotham Princess* was much more interested in seeing what Cam Noyes had in mind. I knew I was.

He tore the jacket, shirt, and tie right off Tanner Marsh, exposing his billowing, hairy white flesh. A lot of people gasped. It wasn't a pretty sight. Terrified now, Tanner tried to get away from him. Cam grabbed him by the belt so he couldn't.

"Don't hurt me!" wailed Tanner, wide-eyed and trembling. "Please don't hurt me! Please!"

Smiling now, Cam yanked southward very hard, ripping the waistband of Tanner's trousers and sending them plunging down to his shoes. Tanner stood there now clad only in his baggy, pee-stained boxer shorts. But not for long. Cam ripped those off him, too.

The most important literary critic in America now stood stark naked in front of two hundred of New York's biggest celebrities, most of whose jaws were down near the floor.

No one moved or made a sound, especially Tanner, who was so debased and mortified he seemed frozen there. Flashbulbs went off as the photographers, Charlie included, recorded the moment for posterity.

"There we are, Tanner," declared Cam, standing back to admire his handiwork. "Now you know what it feels like to be an author. Congratulations." With that Cam staggered over to the bar and ordered two more shots of tequila.

Tanner pulled up his ruined trousers with one hand, gathered his torn jacket and shirt around him with the other, and made his way in awkward, mincing strides for the glass door. "You shall be very sorry," he spat at Cam. To Boyd he added, "You shall *both* be."

Then he swept out of the dining room with what little was left of his dignity. Skitsy Held, his hostess and ex-wife, followed him out, horrified. The guests began to disperse, chattering excitedly.

Boyd Samuels slumped down into a chair. "Christ, not one of my clients will ever get a good review from him again." He started chewing on a thumbnail. Abruptly, he stopped. "Maybe I can get Delilah to sit on his face."

"Guess again," she informed him.

Boyd laughed. "Just a figure of speech, honeypot," he called to her. To me he grumbled, "I was told you get results, amigo. I gotta tell you this sure isn't my idea of a solid couple of days of work from you."

Cam was over by the windows now, pulling on a cigarette and gazing out at the Statue of Liberty, which was lit up for the night. Charlie stood next to him with her hand on his arm, speaking to him softly. He seemed not to be noticing her there.

"He's rather impressionable, isn't he?" I said.

"Yeah, he's rather impressionable," Boyd muttered.

"Does he realize how much you manipulate him?"

Boyd frowned at me. "I'm not tracking you."

"You could have stopped that from happening, but you didn't. You wanted it to happen. It'll be all over town by tomorrow. Part of the Cam Noyes legend."

Boyd grinned wolfishly. "You have to admit it was righteous theater."

"He could have strangled the fat bastard with his bare hands," I pointed out. "That would have been righteous theater, too."

"He'd never do something like that," Boyd scoffed. "He's not violent."

"Don't be so sure. Dangerous things can happen when a man starts believing his own clippings."

Boyd narrowed his laser eyes at me. "Sure you're not manipulating him yourself?"

"Me? Why would I want to do that?"

"To get back at the people who made him and unmade you."

I tugged at my ear. "Interesting thought. Total bullshit, but interesting bullshit. You gave me the impression before that Skitsy would like to see him fall on his ass. Why, because he left her for another publisher?"

"That's part of it."

"What's the rest of it?"

He laughed. "Maybe some night when I'm feeling good and loaded, I'll tell you."

"And this thing with Delilah – how long has it been going on?"

He shot me a surprised look. "He told you?"

"Not exactly."

"Then how did – ?"

"I have my methods."

Boyd glanced over at Cam, who was still at the window with Charlie, and then at Delilah, who was by the buffet table chatting with Frank and Kathie Lee Gifford. "They bumped into each other in my office a few weeks ago," he said. "He was smitten on sight – like somebody hit the poor fucker over the head with a tuning fork. But it won't last. Skitsy's putting her on a national publicity tour in a couple of weeks. By the time she gets back, he'll have forgotten all about her – if I know him. And believe me, I do."

Ah, but the evening was still young, and so were we.

No literary night on the town could be complete without a stop at Elaine's, longtime Second Avenue stronghold of bookdom's heavy hitters, and the saloon where Lulu once had her very own water bowl. A few of us roared up there in the Loveboat after the *Gotham Princess* docked a little before midnight – Cam and Charlie, Boyd and Delilah, Todd and me.

John John's mommy, Jackie, was at Elaine's that night with Mike Nichols and Diane Sawyer. So were the usual gang – the Plimptons and Taleses and Vonneguts. Ed Doctorow, Joe Heller. It felt strange being back in Our Place. Elaine was a good sport about it. She made a real fuss over Lulu, who went looking for her bowl, only to come right back, confused, when she couldn't find it.

Elaine flushed with embarrassment. "Sorry, Hoagy. It's been so long since you three . . . I'll put another one down for her right away."

I asked her not to.

We were seated at a big table toward the back. Lulu lay under my chair, sniffling from Delilah's perfume. Delilah made sure she sat right next to Cam. She'd gotten a bit high from all the attention and champagne she'd been lapping up, and somewhat less discreet. She was chattering away gaily to Cam and Cam alone, touching him on the arm, her face aglow, her eyes dancing. He was nodding and smiling. His eyes never left hers. Both of them were oblivious of Charlie, who sat between Todd and me, not missing a thing. Dumb she wasn't. Or inhuman. Maybe she believed she had no right to control her big blond genius. But she sure as hell didn't feel it. She sat there stiffly, her eyes shining like wet stones.

I didn't like this. Not one bit.

We had just ordered our drinks when Tanner Marsh, dressed in a fresh poplin suit, walked in the door with Skitsy Held.

The place suddenly got very quiet. Everyone in Elaine's was staring at them. The evening's news had traveled fast.

Tanner got pale when he spotted us. He and Skitsy began murmuring to each other.

"This should be interesting," observed Todd quietly.

"Hey, should I invite them to join us?" wondered Boyd.

"No, no, let's wait and see what they do," exclaimed Delilah as Elaine rushed over to them.

They didn't walk out. They allowed Elaine to seat them at a table as far from us as possible, Skitsy exchanging grim hellos with the regulars as she passed by them. Slowly, the room's usual level of urbane chatter returned.

Elaine worked her way by our table. "No trouble tonight, Cameron," she pleaded, shooting a nervous look over at Tanner.

Charlie put a fresh roll of film in her camera.

I expected Tanner to retaliate. He was a critic. A critic is someone accustomed to having the last word. But I didn't expect him to retaliate in quite the way he had in mind.

When his drink came, Tanner downed it at once and struggled to his feet. Skitsy put out a hand to stop him, but the fat man shrugged it off and started toward us. Heads turned. The place got very quiet again. When he got to our table, Tanner stopped and stood over us, his eyes on Cam. He said nothing, just stood there staring at Cam, his face an utter blank. Cam stared right back up at him.

Boyd broke the silence. "Evening, Tanner. Care to join us?"

In response, Tanner pulled a gun out of his jacket pocket, pointed it at Cameron Sheffield Noyes, and fired it.

CHAPTER
SIX

I'm quite certain Tanner would have killed his brilliant young discovery if I hadn't taken a swipe at his gun hand a split second before he fired. As it was, the bullet just took off the tip of Cam's left ear before it made a small, neat hole in the wall behind him.

Delilah screamed. Lots of people did. Others, Cam included, froze. Tanner just stood there dumbly, as if in shock. I pried the gun out of his hand and gave it to the bartender, who helped me hustle him out onto the sidewalk, where Tanner immediately threw up. Then he sat down on the curb and began to weep uncontrollably.

"Do you see?" demanded Skitsy Held, who had followed us outside. "Do you see what that boy does to people?"

"Yes," I replied. "And I see what they do to him."

"He's a cancer," she snarled. "He's terrible for publishing. Awful. And so are you for having anything to do with him."

I glanced over at the bartender, who was missing none of this, then back at Skitsy. "That's funny, I thought you said he was still your biggest star."

"You're wrong," she said, shaking her head. "It's not funny at all."

She and the bartender stayed outside with Tanner. Inside, a gynecologist who'd just written a best-selling diet book was bandaging Cam's ear. Elaine was calling the police and Cam was telling her not to.

"No harm, no foul," he said with remarkable calm, seemingly not at all fazed by his narrow brush with death. "The man simply got upset. Quite understandable. Let's just let it drop."

So Elaine put Skitsy and Tanner in a cab, and Cam bought the house a drink, and things went back to what passes for normal around there.

"Get it on film?" I asked a somewhat wide-eyed Charlie Chu as I took my seat.

"Missed it," Charlie replied, her voice quavering. Her glasses slid down her nose. She pushed them back up. "I guess I'm not very cool under fire."

"Who among us is?" I asked.

"You are, coach," Cam pointed out. "You're a genuine man of action. You surprised me."

"Not as much as I surprised myself," I said.

"I still think the dude oughta be put in jail," groused Boyd.

"Me, too," agreed Todd.

Cam shook his head. "Forget about it," he said firmly.

"But he tried to kill you, Cameron!" cried Delilah.

"That's where you're wrong," Cam said, throwing back his glass of tequila and motioning for another. "You can't kill something that's already dead."

After a few more rounds at Elaine's we headed down to Sammy's, the boisterous Lower East Side steak house where everything comes drenched in garlic, and where things got even wiggier.

It was hot and crowded and incredibly noisy in there, even at two a.m. on a weeknight. Waiters rushed about with Fred Flintstone-sized platters of sizzling meat. Patrons took turns at the microphone singing Billy Joel songs off-key to the accompaniment of the house piano player.

We sat around a big round table laden with eggplant salad, pickles, bread, and seltzer siphons. We were one less. Todd, who had to be at work on time, had headed home. Lulu stretched out under me, grunting sourly. She hates it when I eat garlic. My own feeling is anybody who eats canned mackerel has no right to comment about somebody else's breath.

There wasn't much on the menu for Charlie the vegetarian, but she wasn't exactly a woman of appetite by this point. She just picked quietly at some eggplant salad and glowered at Cam and Delilah, neither of whom seemed to care any longer that she was there, or that anyone else was. The two of them were gazing into each other's eyes, cooing into each other's ears, giggling, touching. Maybe it was the sight of Cam's hand resting there upon Delilah's. Maybe it was simply that everyone, no matter how forgiving, reaches a boiling point. Whatever, Charlie Chu turned very human when Delilah Moscowitz got up and flounced off to the ladies' room, twitching her tail. Not that Charlie was obvious about it. She waited a moment before she dabbed at her mouth with her napkin, excused herself, and followed Delilah in there. No one thought a thing of it, including me.

All I knew is one minute everyone in Sammy's was eating and drinking and making merry, and the next minute a horrifying scream was coming from the direction of the ladies' room.

Cam frowned and looked inquiringly over at Boyd, who suddenly got very busy with his steak. Neither of them budged. Not even after the second scream. It was I who paid the call. At full speed. The ladies' room door was locked. I threw my shoulder against it and immediately regretted it. Oh, the door popped open, all right, but so did something inside my shoulder.

The two of them were on the bathroom floor. Delilah was pinned flat on her back with Charlie astride her, clutching her by the throat and brandishing a big, ugly hunk of broken beer bottle before Delilah's terrified face.

"Stay away from him, you hear?" Charlie cried. "Stay away or I'll cut you! He's mine! *Mine!*"

"Hey, Blue Monday," I said softly from the doorway, rubbing my shoulder.

"Back off!" Charlie spat at me. "This is between me and her." She turned back to Delilah, holding the glass directly against her lovely white throat now. "Say it! Say you hear me!"

"I hear you, I hear you, you crazy bitch," gasped Delilah. "He's all yours. Now get the hell off me, will you?"

Charlie relaxed her hold. I immediately grabbed her by the scruff of the neck and pulled her up onto her feet. She didn't weigh much. I tossed her glass weapon in the trash.

By this time the singular object of their affections had come reeling in, jacket rumpled, ear bandaged, blue eyes glazed, a full bottle of beer in one hand, his half-eaten steak in the other. He looked down at Delilah, whose leather miniskirt was hiked up over her hips, then over at Charlie. Then he narrowed his eyes at me, not comprehending. "So what's . . . I mean . . . ?" Before he could say more, Charlie snatched him impatiently by the arm and stormed out, dragging him along like a large, docile child.

"You'll be sorry, you crazy bitch!" Delilah yelled after her from the floor. She lay there a moment, too drained to budge, then looked down at her state of undress and raised an eyebrow at me. "Wanna climb aboard, sailor?"

"That's it, Red. Don't lose your sense of humor. You okay?"

"Just fine," she replied, giving me her hand. "It so happens I love being assaulted on filthy public-bathroom floors."

"Look on the bright side," I said, hoisting her to her feet. "You can get a column out of this – *sharp* advice on how to steal someone else's man."

"He's not someone else's," she retorted, scowling.

"I could have sworn someone else thought so."

She looked herself over in the mirror, tossed her head. "Hey, it's not my fault she can't see the signs."

"Signs?"

"He's unhappy with her. No man who is happy with someone gets as bombed as he does all of the time."

"And you think you can make him happy?"

She turned and faced me, hands on her hips. "No offense, but what business is this of yours?"

"Everything about Cam Noyes is my business now, whether I like it or not."

She thought that over. "You want the truth?"

"Generally."

"If I lose Cam Noyes, she won't have to slit my throat— I'll slit it myself." Delilah took a prescription bottle of tranks out of her purse and threw two of them down her throat. She had several such bottles in there. She had a small drugstore in there.

"Pills are somewhat neater," I countered.

"Not after they get done pumping out your stomach they aren't," she said.

"That sounds suspiciously like the voice of experience."

"Let's just say that this reporter doesn't have it as totally together as her readers think she does," Delilah confided. "And who am I to shatter their illusions." She got her brush out of her purse and went to work on her hair, glancing at me in the mirror. "What, no smart remarks?"

"Not from me. I've spent too much time in too many glass houses."

Her eyes softened. "You're a sensitive man, aren't you?"

"Yeah, I'm an utterly modern kind of guy. What kind is Cam?"

"Everything I've ever wanted – tall, blond, handsome, brilliant, tragic, a bit dangerous. Cam Noyes is the man of this fat, insecure, manic-depressive Jewish princess's dreams."

"You're not my idea of fat."

"I used to weigh a hundred and sixty-four pounds," she informed me. "I work out at a Nautilus club three hours every day to look like I do now. I live on popcorn and cranberry juice and a host of artificial chemicals. You also happen to be looking at somewhat less than half of my original nose. Christ, why am I telling you all of this?"

"I asked."

She admired the curve of her throat in the mirror and swallowed.

"Charlie wouldn't really hurt me, would she?"

"Hard telling. Personally, I wouldn't test her, but I scare easy – all part of the modern-guy thing."

"God, how trashy." She started out of the bathroom, stopped, and looked around. Then she swiveled on one foot in a Tina Turner gyration and cried out, "And don't you just love it?"

The oomph kind of went out of the evening after that. I drove the happy couple home to Gramercy Park in the Loveboat. They rode beside me on the front seat. Lulu snoozed in the back. She was still sniffling, which was not a good sign. It was late. The streets were as quiet as they ever get. Very few cars, aside from the occasional cab whisking late-nighters from one club to another. No one was out walking.

We rode in silence until Charlie said to Cam in a soft, halting voice, "I got so scared when Tanner tried to . . . and then when you and she . . . I don't know what I'd do if I lost you."

"Not going to lose me," he assured her thickly. "Just being nice to her because Boyd asked me to. Strictly business. Not as if I'm planning to bang her or anything."

"Honest?" she asked, wanting desperately to buy into it.

"Honest." He put his arm around her. She cuddled into him, relieved.

"Sorry if I made you mad," she said.

"Mad is not how you made me feel."

"How did I . . . ?"

He took her hand and pressed it due south of his equator. "That's how."

She groaned and climbed into his lap, her arms around his neck. Her mouth found his. They did very little talking after that.

I kept my eyes on the road and my hands upon the wheel. My shoulder ached and I had the taste of garlic and self-loathing in my mouth. I wanted no part of this job. Cam Noyes was a liar and a cheat and a mess. His women were ouchboxes of exposed nerve endings. His best friend was a featured selection of the Reptile of the Month Club. And I was quickly turning into his silent accomplice. I wanted no part of it. What I wanted was out. But I knew I wouldn't get out. Because there was something about Cam Noyes. Maybe it was the fear and vulnerability and torment I saw beneath his golden surface. Maybe it was the kinship between us – of upbringing, of art, of boy wonderdom and the burden that went with it. Maybe it was just that he knew how to make great tables. Whatever it was, I knew I wouldn't get out. Because Cam Noyes desperately needed someone, and that someone was me.

At Eighteenth and Third, Charlie abruptly rolled off his lap and sat there glaring straight ahead, chin raised, mouth drawn tight. I glanced across her at my celebrity – he was out cold, his head back on the seat, snoring softly. All of the tequila and coke had finally caught up with him.

"Sorry," I said to her.

"Don't say another word about it," she snapped.

So I didn't.

The lights were on in the town house.

"Ah, good," I said. "Vic has arrived from Los Angeles."

"How did he get in?" Charlie wondered.

"He has a way with locks," I replied as she started to rouse Cam. "Oh, don't worry about him. Vic will take over now."

"But – "

"Trust me."

We found him in the kitchen unpacking a new microwave oven. A set of dishes, pots and pans, bags of provisions, were piled everywhere. Coffee was perking on a new hot plate. James Mason was reading *The Third Man* by Graham Greene on a cassette player. Vic Early, show biz bodyguard extraordinaire, was getting settled.

He was a balding, sandy-haired giant in slacks and a striped polo shirt. He stood six feet six and weighed 250 pounds, little of it fat. A couple of decades before he'd been a star offensive lineman for the UCLA Bruins. The Rams drafted him in the first round. He chose the Marines instead and went to Vietnam, where he took some shrapnel in the head. He has a plate in his skull. Sometimes it gives him trouble – he sees red. I know this because he once rearranged my face and rib cage. But he hasn't actually killed anyone, as far as I know, and most of the time he's extremely mild-mannered.

Lulu was delighted to see him again. The feeling was mutual. He got down on his knees to say hello and rub her ears with his big football-scarred mitts. She rolled over on her back, her tail thumping, tongue lolling out of the side of her mouth.

"Whew," said Vic, making a face. "Still eating that fish of hers, huh?"

"That she is."

"Got in a little after midnight," he informed me in his droning monotone. "Found an all-night appliance store over on Broadway and Fourteenth. That's one of the great things about New York. Picked up some things I thought we'd need. Receipts are on the fridge."

"Say hello to Charleston Chu, your hostess."

"Quite a place, miss," he observed, gently taking her tiny hand. "I assumed the guest room is for me."

"It is," said Charlie, looking up warily at the hugeness of him. "And welcome."

"Thank you. That art up there yours?"

"It is."

"Keep at it. With some training you could get somewhere. Who knows, maybe even sell some of it."

She smiled. "Thank you."

"Your illustrious host," I advised him, "is in the car."

Vic nodded grimly. "Right." Then he hitched up his slacks and lumbered out the front door.

He returned a moment later dragging Cam Noyes facedown along the floor by one ankle. When he got him into the kitchen, Vic flopped him over onto his back, coughing and gasping. He was wet and muddy head to toe, and he didn't smell too hot.

"My God!" exclaimed Charlie. "What happened to him?"

"I brought him in by way of the gutter, miss."

"The *what?*" she demanded. "Why?"

"He's a drunk," Vic replied simply. "That's where drunks belong."

Charlie crinkled her small nose. "But he smells like – "

"That unpleasant odor is dog dooty, which is what the gutter smells like – no offense, Miss Lulu. Great set of wheels, by the way."

"Wait just one second here," ordered Charlie, glaring up at him, hands on her hips, eyes hard. "Who are you? What are you? I demand an explanation."

Vic ducked his head and scuffed at the floor with a big foot.

"Vic Early," I explained, "is the world's largest nanny."

"Someone please tell me," mumbled Cam from the floor, "why I smell so overwhelmingly like shit?"

"We'll talk about it in the morning, you bum," Vic said coldly.

Cam squinted up at him. "Who're you?"

"He seems to be your new nanny," said Charlie.

"You say nanny?"

"I did," she said, pushing her glasses up her nose.

Cam giggled. "Stupendous – always wanted a nanny."

"Naturally," said Vic, his big square jaw stuck out. "Because you're a big baby."

He went down the steep stairs into the basement. By the time he came back up carrying a painter's drop cloth, Cam was out cold again. Vic rolled him up in the drop cloth, then threw all two hundred pounds of him over one shoulder as if he were a lap rug.

"You'll be wanting to use the guest room yourself tonight, miss," he told Charlie. "I'll sleep down here."

"How come?" she wondered.

"I want him to wake up tomorrow in these clothes," he replied. "I want him to know just what a drunken bum smells like in the morning."

She thought this over for a moment. Then her face broke into a dimply smile. "Whatever you say, Mr. Early. I'll strip the bed—no sense ruining a good quilt." She started up the stairs.

"Good thinking, miss," Vic agreed, following with Cam over his shoulder. "But you'd best step lively. I think he's about to upchuck."

Vic came down alone a few minutes later and poured us coffee. We sat in two of the shell-backed metal chairs in the living room. He fit into his like an elephant in a teacup.

"I didn't know there was a girl," he said unhappily.

"There may not be for long – it's stormy."

"She's a real doll," he observed, sipping his coffee.

"She is. And made of solid steel."

"Really? Wouldn't think so to look at her."

"No, you wouldn't," I agreed, trying to remember the last time a woman had fought for me like she had for Cam that evening. Actually, no woman ever had, unless you count the time Merilee poured that brandy alexander down the back of Sigourney Weaver's dress when she caught the two of us flirting at the *Hurly Burly* opening-night bash. But that was kidding around. Charlie wasn't kidding.

"I've always liked the Asian women," Vic said. "They have a strong sense of loyalty. Clean personal habits, too. Though I can't say much for this one's housekeeping. Place is my idea of a shambles."

"It's called Found Minimalism, I'm told."

"It's minimal, all right." He shifted gingerly in his chair, which shifted with him. "You want him totally clean?"

"As clean as possible. A few more months like this and he'll end up a casualty."

"You can count on that. How far can I go?"

"Try not to disfigure him beyond recognition. His face is his livelihood until he starts writing again. Assuming he ever does."

"He will," Vic said firmly. "I'll get him on a regular schedule starting tomorrow. Up at eight. Run him around the park a few times. Rub him down. Start him on a proper diet."

"Fine. He and I will work here in his study, ten to six. That's when I'd like you to watch Merilee. During the day is when she's most vulnerable."

"Your ex-wife?" asked Vic, frowning. "To what?"

I told him about the threat I'd received. "Probably just hot air," I admitted. "But . . ."

"Can't afford to take a chance," he agreed gravely.

"Don't crowd her. It would be better if she didn't know you were guarding her."

"Not to worry," he assured me. "She'll never know I'm there."

I got wearily to my feet and handed him an envelope.

"For your first week. Glad you're here, Vic."

"This isn't coming out of your end, is it?"

"No chance. I don't like you that much."

He grinned and pocketed it without opening it. "You won't be sorry, Hoag."

"Sorry never entered my mind."

My apartment door was half open.

The lock was untouched. Instead, they'd sledgehammered a fist-sized hole clean through the plaster wall next to the door, reached in, and unlocked it from the inside. A burglary gang had worked its way through the neighborhood a few years before doing just that. The cops called them the Hole-in-the-Wall Gang. I hadn't known they were back.

I stood there on the landing and stared at the hole and the plaster dust heaped there on the floor, my heart pounding. There were no lights on inside the apartment. I looked down at Lulu. Lulu, keen huntress, was looking up at me and sniffling and showing no interest in going in. I really was going to have to get a bigger dog, preferably a meat eater with good sinuses.

I took a deep breath and let it out slowly. Then I pushed the door open all the way and went inside.

The stereo and television were still there.

The leather-and-fur greatcoat that I got in Milan was hanging in the narrow hall closet. My silver cuff links were in their jewelry box in the bedroom.

Nothing of value had been taken. Nothing had even been touched.

Only my Olympia, my beloved late-fifties vintage manual portable, the heavy steel one that is the Mercedes 300 SL Gull Wing of typewriters, and is much, much more than that to me. It is my gallant steed. It was with me in the Périgord Valley when the first draft of *Our Family Enterprise* came. It was with me in Skye and San Miguel de Allende when nothing came. And it was with me in that little stone cottage in the Tuscan hills when I ate pasta drenched in native extra-virgin olive oil and drank Brunello di Montalcino, and *Such Sweet Sorrow* came. It had been through heaven and hell with me, and now it sat there pounded into utter submission – its body smashed, its keys crushed, its workings ruined. You can do a lot of damage to a typewriter with a sledge – even the toughest typewriter in creation. Another magazine picture of Merilee had been left in its dented roller. So had another message written in those press-on letters. *Her face is next.*

I stood there staring down at it and thinking about something someone had said earlier that evening: *This man should no longer be allowed to own or operate a typewriting machine. . . .*

It was Tanner Marsh who had said that. Tanner Marsh, the man who'd said both Cam Noyes and Boyd Samuels would be sorry. Very sorry.

I picked up the phone and dialed Boyd Samuels and woke him up.

"Whuh . . . wha . . . ?" he mumbled.

"I'm not quitting. Put the word out." Then I hung up and went to bed.

Lulu snored on my head the whole night.

CHAPTER
SEVEN

(Tape #3 with Cam Noyes recorded May 8 in his study. Sits at his writing table, one eye swollen shut, lower lip fat and oozing blood. Holds ice bag against lip. Hand shakes.)

Hoag: Small shaving accident this morning, Cameron?

Noyes: That giant oaf made me get out of bed at dawn this morning and go *running* with him. Then he tried to get me to eat a large bowl of *oatmeal.* I was telling him what he could do with his *oatmeal* when suddenly his face got all red and he started rubbing his forehead real hard and breathing in these shallow gasps . . .

Hoag: I told you not to make him mad.

Noyes: Who is this crazy man, coach?

Hoag: Your bodyguard. He's here to guard your body from anyone who might do it harm – including you.

Noyes: He also threw my coke down the drain. Why would he do something so stupid? I'm just going to buy more.

Hoag: I wouldn't if I were you.

Noyes: I thought you weren't going to hassle me about the way I live.

Hoag: I'm not. He is.

Noyes: But you hired him.

Hoag: Actually, you're the one who's paying him.

Noyes: In that case, I want him out of here. He's fired.

Hoag: If you insist. But if he goes, I go.

Noyes: What?

Hoag: You heard me.

Noyes: *(silence)* What are you trying to do?

Hoag: My job, Cameron. You agreed to put yourself in my hands. This is part of the deal. See the newspapers this morning? *(sound of rustling)* Nice little item about you in Billy Norwich's column: "Observers say the association between acid-penned critic Tanner Marsh and his sizzling protégé, Cameron Sheffield Noyes, went out with a 'bang' last night at Elaine's. It seems Marsh was none too thrilled about the eye-opening experience Noyes had treated guests to earlier at the celebrity-studded pub party for Delilah Moscowitz's *Tell Delilah.*" . . . Why did you do it, Cameron? Why did you undress him like that?

Noyes: He was attacking you. You're my friend.

Hoag: That the only reason?

Noyes: What other reason would there be?

Hoag: Your reputation. Living up to it.

Noyes: Believe me, I'm not that calculating.

Hoag: Perhaps you're not. But Boyd is.

Noyes: You don't like him, do you?

Hoag: Tell me about the two of you coming to New York, about Columbia.

Noyes: I had no expectations, no plan. I was vague and roofless. Deep down inside, I'd gotten this feeling of wanting to write, this powerful feeling that I would in some way become a writer and make something beautiful and perfect out of what had happened to me. I didn't really know why I had it, or how to go about doing it, but being in a place that was *alive* seemed important to me. . . . Columbia, well, Morningside Heights is just a polite way of saying Harlem. A student got knifed on our street by a crack dealer the day we arrived. They stashed a bunch of us in a dorm over next to the river on a Hundred and fourteenth, Hudson Hall they called it. An utter hole. Walls were crumbling. My room was so small I had to close the door if I wanted to sit down at my desk. Overlooked the air shaft, which always smelled of garbage. Boyd started moving coke right away. Actually, one of his biggest customers was Todd, who lived in the suite upstairs from us. Shadowy, weird sort of kid. No friends. Used to sit alone in his room and get quietly bombed. Ended up having to leave school. Owed Boyd a lot of money.

Hoag: I guess that's what he meant by "personal problems."

Noyes: The advisers at Deerfield had warned us that college would be so hard. *(laughs)* They were dead wrong. We were stoned free – didn't have to go to class, didn't have to do the reading, didn't have some dickhead corridor master watching over us. We spent most of our time getting a real New York education. Riding the subways through Spanish Harlem at 4 a.m. Hanging out at the Mudd Club and CBGBs. Going to the Museum of Natural History on acid and watching the dinosaurs move. New York is the greatest place in the world for hanging out and collecting experiences. If you want to write, you have to come through here.

Hoag: And had you started?

Noyes: I was keeping a diary of sorts, sketches of our days and nights out that eventually formed itself into a collection of short stories. I submitted them second semester to Tanner to see if I could get into his creative writing class, which is world renowned. The man's a god on that campus. I hoped to learn at his feet. But he turned me down.

Hoag: Were you disappointed?

Noyes: Briefly, but then the modeling thing clicked for me, and that took care of any bruised feelings I might have had. I happened to be balling this black Barnard girl named Stacy who was a model with the Wilhelmina Agency. Lovely girl. She's in a soap now, plays a Rastafarian neurosurgeon. Anyway, one time when I picked her up at her shoot, the photographer asked me if I modeled. When I said I didn't, he said I should, because I had "a very American heterosexual look." Stacy took me up to the agency with her, and they looked me over and shot some tests and signed me up. And that's how I became a model. I started going around town with my portfolio and sitting in a waiting room with two dozen guys who looked exactly like I did. I honestly can't tell you why I got picked over them, but I did. I started doing catalog work, and making righteous bucks. And then Ralph spotted me, and I became a member of his Lauren family, and what a strange, surreal trip that is. It's not just fashion to Ralph. He sees all of it – the clothes, the image, the presentation – as a story. The models are characters in that story. The photographer, Bruce Weber, would take us on location to some estate and we'd frolic about all day in Ralph's clothes before he'd ever start shooting. The idea was to capture the casual spontaneity of family life. Or Ralph's image of family life, which is not, strictly speaking, real. I mean, that whole pseudo-English gentry thing – the models aren't those people. Buying the clothes won't make anyone into those people. It's make-believe. *Ralph* is make-believe – he's really little Ralph Lifschitz of the Bronx. Fashion is a stupendous scam, coach. Maybe the ultimate scam. Boyd quickly got fascinated by it.

Hoag: Somehow that doesn't surprise me.

Noyes: Talked his way into Wilhelmina as a gofer for the summer after our freshman year – watched and listened, fetched coffee. That was his apprenticeship as an agent. He went right from it into publishing.

Hoag: Because you did?

Noyes: Because I did. . . . That was a great summer for us. He'd wangled us an illegal sublet of a great faculty apartment on Riverside. I modeled when I felt like it, wrote when I didn't. That was when I wrote *Bang*. Scribbled the entire first draft longhand in five days and nights on a coke binge. It was unvarnished stream of consciousness. I just let myself go, like cutting the ropes on a hot-air balloon. Who knows where it came from. I sure don't. When I was done, I passed out for twenty-four hours. Then I spent a couple of weeks polishing it and typing it up. The original manuscript came to a little under a hundred pages. I submitted it to Tanner in the fall, hoping once again to get into his class. This time he sent me a note summoning me up to his office. . . . He really is scary the first time you meet him – the antique rolltop desk, the framed correspondence on the wall from John Cheever and Bernard Malamud, the pipe, and the way he looks down his nose at you. I mean, the man can make you feel so incredibly insignificant without even trying.

Hoag: Oh, he's trying.

Noyes: He told me to take a seat. Then he sat down and very deliberately got his fucking pipe going and stared at me. And kept staring at me, not saying a word. Finally, he declared, in that voice of his, "Young Master Noyes, I am not impressed by your little manuscript." Just as I started shriveling in my chair he said, "I am . . . *awed.*" And with that Tanner Marsh fell to his knees before me and kissed my shoes. He really kissed them. And then he clutched me by the ankles and said, "From this day forward, I am your humble servant. Use me."

(end tape)

(Tape #4 with Cam Noyes recorded May 10 in his study. Sips iced herbal tea, fiddles with bowie knife.)

Hoag: You look well rested today.

Noyes: Couldn't help that. Vic insisted on coming to dinner with Boyd and me last night, like some kind of chaperon. I half expected him to cut my meat for me.

Hoag: He would have, if you'd asked him nice.

Noyes: At the stroke of midnight he said to me, "Let's go." I said, go where? He said, "Home." When I refused, he dragged me out of the restaurant like I was some kind of dog. I was still so wide-awake I started reading *The Great Gatsby*. I'm really enjoying it. Thanks for getting it for me.

Hoag: My pleasure.

Noyes: Fitzgerald wrote so gracefully and beautifully. I'm actually kind of surprised he's compared to me.

Hoag: He's not. You're compared to him.

Noyes: You're right. Sorry.

Hoag: Just a meaningless label, anyway. The new F. Scott Fitzgerald. The new Willie Mays. That's the only way the press knows how to deal with someone who's entirely special.

Noyes: I promised Boyd I'd talk to you about . . . Well, he's concerned over what I have to say about Tanner and Skitsy. He thinks some of it might not be so great for my image. You know, not flattering.

Hoag: Candor is always flattering.

Noyes: I know, but he said Tanner and Skitsy could just deny it anyway.

Hoag: Absolutely. I intend to give them that chance.

Noyes: You do?

Hoag: I do. A memoir that acknowledges the other side of the story is always richer and more intelligent for it.

Noyes: I see . . .

Hoag: Look, Cameron. You're an author, not a talk show host. Forget about image. That's how you got blocked up.

Noyes: I know, coach, but what would happen if I . . . if I didn't go along with you on this one?

Hoag: Same thing that would happen if you fired Vic.

Noyes: You're a hard man to please.

Hoag: It's true. Don't ever go to a movie with me.

Noyes: I don't know what to do. *(pause)* I want to please Boyd . . .

Hoag: It's not Boyd's book. It's yours.

Noyes: I know, I know. It's just that I also want you to respect me, and it seems I can't win either way. I lose your respect if I don't tell you what really went on . . . and I lose it if I *do*.

Hoag: As long as you tell the truth, you'll have my respect.

Noyes: You mean it?

Hoag: I mean it.

Noyes: *(silence)* Okay, coach. We'll try it your way.

Hoag: Good man. When we left off, Tanner Marsh was on his knees.

Noyes: Yes, telling me I was a genius. So I said, "You're accepting me for your class?" And he said, "Absolutely not. The last thing a talent such as yours needs is to be polluted by sitting around a table with a dozen pimply kids ranting on about their creative cores. What you need is a great editor. You need me!" He said he wanted us to work together on the manuscript. Focus it, broaden it, take out some of the self-indulgence. And then submit it to a certain publisher who he knew would share his enthusiasm – actually publish it.

Hoag: How did this make you feel?

Noyes: I was flattered, naturally.

Hoag: Not good enough. Dig deeper.

Noyes: (*silence*) As if all of it – the pain, the loneliness, the apartness – had been worth enduring. Because they had forged me. Made me into *someone*. I remember thinking I'd like to send a copy to Kirsten's mother when it came out, inscribed with the words "Fuck you." Is that better?

Hoag: Somewhat.

Noyes: Tanner worked with me every evening in his office for the next couple of weeks, talking over the manuscript page by page. He was incredibly helpful. He knew exactly where I needed to go, even though I didn't know myself. For all of his bullying and grossness, the man really does know a manuscript. The murder-suicide thing at the end was actually his idea. I'd originally left it very vague as to what happens with the gun. He convinced me I was wrong. When we finished going over it, he asked me how long it would take me to rewrite it. I told him modeling was basically how I paid my way, and between it and the occasional class I didn't think I could finish until maybe Christmas. He said that was no good, we had to strike at once because my age was such a plus. He puffed away on his pipe a minute and said, "Young Master Noyes, you've just been named a New Age writing fellow." I was *stunned*. Some of the major authors of the past twenty years had won New Age fellowships. It meant stupendous prestige. More to the point, it meant ten thousand dollars. He said he could arrange immediate residency for me at the Stony Creek Writers Colony in Vermont. He encouraged me to take a leave from school, go up there, and finish the book as soon as possible. So I did. He drove me up there. It was a lovely autumn day. The leaves were just starting to turn. An editor who happened to be visiting one of her authors up there rode along with us.

Hoag: Her name would be Skitsy Held?

Noyes: That's right. Tanner arranged it, of course. Skitsy was the editor he thought would share his enthusiasm for me.

Hoag: What did you think of her?

Noyes: She seemed hard-shell, but nice enough. The two of them spent most of the ride gossiping about people I'd never heard of. I nodded off. Of course, I had no idea then at the extent of their relationship, or how they operated.

Hoag: Let's talk about that.

Noyes: (silence) Tanner and Skitsy go back twenty-five years, back to when she was a blushing Barnard coed and he was an associate English professor. This was long before she had tits. Or at least the same exact pair we know today. *(laughs)* He was still married to his first wife at the time. Skitsy broke up the marriage, actually. His *New Age Fiction Quarterly* was in its infancy. When she graduated, he made her his teaching assistant and put her to work on it. She helped him start the New Age Writers Conference, which he still does for a week every summer in the Catskills. Ever go?

Hoag: Once, a few centuries ago.

Noyes: There are a number of writers' conferences now, but his was the first, and is still the biggest. The idea, as I'm sure you know, is to offer would-be writers from around the country a chance to rub shoulders with genuine New York publishers and hopefully sell them that Great American Novel they've been toiling on in their basement since 1946. He takes over a resort hotel in the Catskills for a week, and for a fee of what is now a thousand dollars, several hundred of these housewives and carpeting salesmen flock to it, manuscript in tow. He invites a dozen or so editors, literary agents, and big-name authors to come, and they do come. It's an excellent opportunity for them to promote their own books, and they usually get laid up there. There are cocktail mixers, seminars, panel discussions. Editors talk about what they look for in a manuscript. Authors say how they made it. The whole thing is a scam – not one new writer has ever been discovered at a New Age Writers Conference. But they keep flocking to it, and Tanner keeps getting rich off of it. He's really quite shrewd. By awarding fellowships to people like me, he's allowed to say the *Quarterly* is published by a nonprofit foundation. That's entirely legitimate, since the magazine never makes any money. But the conference does. Lots of it. He claims that the profits from it underwrite the fellowships. They don't. He pockets them. Keeps an entirely bogus set of books. Walks away with about fifty thousand dollars a year from the foundation, tax free.

Hoag: Which he stands to lose when this is published.

Noyes: Yes. I suppose he will.

Hoag: How do you know all of this?

Noyes: I'll get to that. Eventually, Skitsy became a very successful editor. She and Tanner married and divorced. Though the divorce was ugly, their greed still cements them together. Thanks to the *Quarterly* and to his own horn-blowing, Tanner enjoys an enviable reputation for discovering new writers. He steers a lot of them her way. It's a good deal for her because she knows he'll excerpt them in the *Quarterly*, which is the Good Housekeeping Seal of Hype for a first novel. Guarantees a review in the *New York Times*. If the *Times* review is good – and how can it not be if Tanner's writing it – then the other newspapers and the newsmagazines and the book clubs will fall into line. Then Skitsy can start taking out ads. For another ten grand she can buy her way onto the Walden's Recommended List, which gets her chain shelf-space, and from there it isn't far to the best-seller list. As a payback, she throws a nice finder's fee Tanner's way. See, Skitsy has her own little scam, and it's quite a beauty. She takes kickbacks. In the case of *Bang*, for instance, she offered $35,000. That's good money for a first novel by an unknown. I only saw $25,000 of it. Boyd had to give ten of it back to her, and she split that with Tanner. Not huge stakes, but they can be. In the case of Delilah's book, she offered Boyd $250,000 with the understanding that $50,000 came back to her. She's put away a couple of million tax free through the years that way.

Hoag: Doesn't her company get suspicious?

Noyes: Murray Hill Press is one of the last of the small independent houses, and she's the boss. As far as anyone there knows, the only thing she's guilty of is overpaying, which is no problem since her titles almost always make money. Other publishers hate her because she's inflated prices across the board to accommodate her kickback, though most of them don't really know why she's inflated them. The agents do. Some of them won't stand for it – the older ones in particular. She steers around them, does business with the ones who will, like Boyd, and steers clients their way. She *is* worth it. She makes authors a lot of money. And it's not like they're getting ripped off. Her company is the one that is.

Hoag: I think I understand now how Boyd pried you away from her – he threatened to tell the Internal Revenue Service, didn't he?

Noyes: No, he was much more creative than that. Boyd's an artist, coach. Want to know how he did it?

Hoag: Do tell.

Noyes: Skitsy signed me up for a second book before *Bang* came out. A smart investment on her part. She was able to get me for a modest $50,000. I was able to get an advance. Who knew the book would go through the roof? When it did, I was worth ten times what she'd paid. Naturally, Boyd was dying to get me out of it. But how? She had a signed contract. So what he did was tell her I was suffering from acute anxiety brought on by the sudden success of *Bang*, and couldn't write. He told her I felt incredibly pressured by a signed contract, that I needed to work just like I had before – on spec, no pressure. He proposed that we return the advance to her and that she tear up the contract – all of this strictly for the benefit of my delicate artist's psyche, mind you – and then when I had written a few chapters we'd submit it to her and sign a new deal on the same exact terms. Word of honor. She agreed to it. We gave her back the advance. She tore up the contract. Boyd sold my second book to another house for a million and there wasn't a thing she could do about it. Strictly legal.

Hoag: I wouldn't have expected her to fall for that.

Noyes: Let's say she was somewhat blinded by personal considerations.

Hoag: What kind of personal considerations?

Noyes: (silence) Skitsy Held has . . . she has this itch for young writers. And I was scratching her itch, okay?

(end tape)

(Tape #5 with Cam Noyes recorded May 12 in his study.)

Hoag: I can't believe you did this, Cameron.

Noyes: Were you really surprised?

Hoag: What, to walk into my apartment and find *your* writing table sitting here? Of course I was surprised.

Noyes: Big Vic and I took it uptown in the back of the Olds after work yesterday. He was planning to pick your lock until we discovered that giant hole in your –

Hoag: I can't accept it, Cameron.

Noyes: You said you liked it.

Hoag: I do. But you spent hundreds of hours making it. It's a work of art. It's *yours*.

Noyes: Not anymore. Besides, I can always make another. In the meantime, this old workbench will suit me fine. Your apartment is awfully dreary, coach. Why don't you get a nicer one?

Hoag: I tried once. It didn't work out. Are you sure about this?

Noyes: Positive. I want you to have it.

Hoag: Thank you, Cameron. I'll cherish it.

Noyes: Don't cherish it. Write on it.

Hoag: I'm interviewing Skitsy tonight.

Noyes: Maybe I should come with you.

Hoag: I'd rather you didn't. I'll get more out of her if I'm alone.

Noyes: Whatever you think is best, coach.

Hoag: So when did your thing with her start? At Stony Creek?

Noyes: Yes, it started then. In its own way. *(pause)* Stony Creek turned out to be the former country estate of a railroad millionaire, this huge, gothic mansion surrounded by five hundred acres of sugar maples, and dotted with a couple of dozen little cabins, one writer-in-residence to each. Dinner was a communal affair in the main hall. Breakfast and lunch were delivered to your cabin in baskets. No distractions. No TV. No radio. Nothing to do but work. Tanner headed back to New York after dinner. Skitsy stayed over for the night in the main hall. I unpacked my things, sharpened my pencils, got into bed early, anxious to get an early start the next day. I had just closed my eyes when there was a tapping at my cabin door. I opened it to discover Skitsy standing there with a flashlight and a bottle of wine. Said she couldn't sleep in a strange place and would I invite her in for a drink. So I did. She sat down on my bed and told me how anxious she was to read my manuscript, because Tanner had told her how very talented I was. Naturally, I was thrilled. She was an important editor. We worked our way through the wine, and we talked, and before long I realized her hand was on my leg. I was at Stony Creek to work, not luck around, especially with a middle-aged woman who I wasn't particularly attracted to. I told her so. I wasn't tactful about it. She left in a huff. I tried to sleep, but I couldn't. I didn't like what had happened. I didn't like being there. At dawn I packed up and hitched a ride out of there due south on I-91, all the way down through Connecticut to New Haven, then another one east on I-95 to Old Lyme. There's a general store a few miles up Route 156 where I got provisions and some freshwater lures. Also a small marina where I rented a rowboat. I put it in Crescent Moon Pond and started rowing. I hadn't been to the shack since Smilin' Jack died and it became mine. The mooring was rotted out. I had to tie the boat to a tree. Kids had been using the place for beer parties. There were empties everywhere, windows busted out. There were a few sticks of furniture. A framed, mounted copperhead skin on the wall. Smilin' Jack had found it coiled in one of his wading boots one morning. There's no electricity or running water. Just a well out back with a hand pump. I chopped some wood and made a fire in the stove. Rigged up a makeshift rod and reel and caught myself a perch for dinner. I spent three weeks there in my little shack. Probably the three happiest weeks of my life. I worked all day. Swam for miles at dusk in the cold, clear pond. Fished. Spoke to no one. Grew a beard. When my rewrites were finished, I rowed back out and caught a train for New York. Called Tanner as soon as I got home to tell him I was done, all excited. He wouldn't have been chillier. Told me he'd terminated my fellowship. When I asked him why, he said I'd violated it by running off without submitting a written application. He told me I was uncooperative and obviously not committed to my work, and then he hung up on me. I couldn't believe it. Tanner wanted nothing more to do with me. I told Boyd, and he couldn't believe it either. He said I must have done something else to warrant getting dumped. I told him about the night in the cabin with Skitsy. He looked at me like I was some kind of naive jerk. That's when I kind of realized what Tanner meant by uncooperative. I had been expected to sleep with her. It was part of the deal. A rite of literary passage, if you will, and I'd refused to pay the toll. . . . I don't know, maybe it was all of those weeks alone, but I went into a blind rage. Stormed straight downtown to her office without shaving or changing clothes. Barged fight past the reception desk, locked her door behind me, threw her down on the sofa, and fucked her. There was nothing gentle or quiet about it, and she couldn't have loved it more. Took the rest of the day off. Dragged me up to her apartment, where we did a lot more deliciously nasty things to each other. The next day Tanner asked to see my revised manuscript. A week later Skitsy Held made an offer on it. I asked Boyd to act as my agent. I didn't trust anyone else. *(silence)* I suppose you think less of me now.

Hoag: What would have happened if you hadn't slept with her?

Noyes: I'll never know, will I? All I know is I wasn't going to let sex get in the way of my literary future. It just isn't that important to me. I mean, it's important, but it's not sacred or precious or anything. . . . You give people what they want, the world opens up to you.

Hoag: That's your philosophy of life?

Noyes: That's reality. I gave Skitsy what she wanted. So what if it was sick and perverted and –

Hoag: And is still going on?

Noyes: *(pause)* How did you know that?

Hoag: You just told me.

Noyes: You're awfully slippery. Would have made a damned good lawyer.

Hoag: And my parents very proud. Actually, it's that red lipstick Lulu found under your bed the day we met. Skitsy's color. Hers, wasn't it?

Noyes: You mean you've known about us all along?

Hoag: Let's say I've suspected. So that's how you know about her and Tanner's little schemes?

Noyes: Yes. Pillow talk. She tends to get blabby afterward.

Hoag: Does she know yet about you and Delilah?

Noyes: What about us?

Hoag: Don't kid a kidder.

Noyes: No, I don't think she does.

Hoag: What would happen to their editorial relationship if she found out?

Noyes: It wouldn't be enhanced. Skitsy is definitely the jealous type, and vindictive as hell.

Hoag: Delilah knows about you and her?

Noyes: Yes.

Hoag: She must like to play with fire.

Noyes: She does. She believes danger heightens the intensity of the female orgasm.

Hoag: Does it?

Noyes: *(laughs)* It certainly doesn't reduce it in her case.

Hoag: Why don't you break it off with Skitsy?

Noyes: What makes you think I want to?

Hoag: Something about the words "sick," "perverted" . . .

Noyes: I happen to be into that. The fact is I'm total scum. Don't ever introduce me to your sister.

Hoag: Haven't got one.

Noyes: Good.

Hoag: I repeat, why are you still seeing Skitsy? *(no response)* Does she have something on you?

Noyes: Like what?

Hoag: You tell me. Why does she own you?

Noyes: She doesn't own me.

Hoag: Bullshit. What is it? Tell me!

Noyes: There's nothing to tell!

Hoag: There *is!* You're holding out on me – I can see it in your eyes. What is it? *(no response)* Damn it, Cameron! I *won't* collaborate on a whitewash, you hear me!

Noyes: (silence) I hear you.

Hoag: Then decide what you want. And let me know. Until you do, we have nothing more to say to each other.

Noyes: But coach – !

(end tape)

CHAPTER
EIGHT

Tanner Marsh was naked again, this time on the canvas Charlie was working on in her studio when I came down the stairs from Cam's study. Tanner looked frightened and vulnerable in the painting, like a turtle with his shell yanked off. He had no penis. She had given him a Bic pen there instead.

She worked intently in the late-day sun, often substituting her fingers for a brush. She had on an old, white, paint-splattered shirt, gym shorts, and clogs. There was yellow paint all over her nose from pushing her glasses up with her painted fingers.

"He'll look terrific hanging next to you at Rat's Nest," I observed.

She smiled wearily. "Thanks."

"Here." I took out my linen handkerchief and began to wipe the paint off her nose. "I'm afraid you're making better progress than we are."

Charlie's brow furrowed with concern. "Trouble?"

"The worst kind. He's hiding something from me."

Lulu stretched out between us. Charlie kicked off a clog and rubbed Lulu's ears with her toes.

"Don't take it personally," she said. "He hides things from everyone."

"Even you?"

"Especially me. He *is* getting it on with that redheaded bitch, isn't he?"

I left that one alone. I wasn't going to lie for him.

"I'm leaving him," she announced quietly.

"Sorry to hear that. You want to be the one to tell Barbara Walters or shall I do it?"

"I'll finish these portraits. I won't allow this to jeopardize our project. But I'll finish them elsewhere."

"That's very professional of you," I said. "I don't know if I'd feel the same way in your shoes. In fact, I'm sure I wouldn't."

"I don't blame him," she explained. "He can't change the way he is. He's just making me too crazy. I don't like myself when I'm that crazy." She closed her eyes and shook her head. "God, what I've been through with him. You know one night I found him naked out there in the park, three in the morning, on his hands and knees, face bleeding, babbling incoherently, 'Dead inside. All of us are dead inside.' I had to drag him inside, patch him up, put him to bed. I won't anymore. I won't bring him home so he can go to another woman's bed. I'm not his mother." Her eyes searched my face. "Am I?"

"No, you're not."

"I just don't know what I'll do with myself," she said, her eyes locking onto mine now. "Alone, I mean."

"Oh, I wouldn't worry about that," I assured her.

With that, Lulu got up and went over to the stairs and sat with her back to us.

Charlie watched her and swallowed. "No?"

"No. I'd say you'll be alone for about as long as you feel like it, and no longer."

She reddened, "Are you . . . offering your services?"

"If I were, I'd have to go stand at the end of a long line."

"You could get right up to the from of it if you wanted to," she offered matter-of-factly.

I tugged at my ear. There was no idle flirting with this one. There was only the real thing. "You wouldn't want another writer. We reserve our best qualities for our lead characters. There's not much left over for real life."

"Oh." Disappointed, she pushed her glasses up her nose and got paint all over it again.

I sighed and dabbed at it again with my handkerchief. "What am I going to do with you?"

"You could hold me," she said, her eyes filling with tears.

I put my arms around her. She buried her face in my shirt and sobbed, shuddering violently. I held on to her. I liked holding on to her. When she was done, she held her face up to me, her cheeks wet. She wanted me to kiss her. I wanted me to kiss her, right on that little bud of a mouth. But I didn't. For me, there was still the matter of Merilee. There was also Lulu glowering at me threateningly from the stairs.

"Sorry," Charlie said, taking my handkerchief and wiping her eyes with it.

"No reason to be."

"Could we maybe have a drink sometime? Talk?"

"I'd like that," I replied. "I'll even teach you how to flirt."

"What for?" she wondered, frowning.

"For fun. Beats the hell out of dirty bathroom floors."

She offered me my handkerchief back. It was soaked with paint.

"Keep it," I insisted. "A gentleman always carries two."

Downstairs, Vic was running a vacuum in the parlor. He had on a chef's apron and his Sony Walkman, on which he was listening to Ian Carmichael read *Jeeves in the Offing* by P. G. Wodehouse. A pot of his chili bubbled on the hot plate in the kitchen.

When he saw me, he turned off the vacuum and the tape. "She got to the theater safe and sound, Hoag," he reported, pulling a small spiral notepad out of his apron pocket. "Let's see . . . had a visitor at her place from noon until two. Fellow named Ulf Johansson, former member of the Swedish Olympic bobsled team."

"Oh?"

"Now a personal fitness instructor. A lot of the Broadway stars use him."

"Oh."

Vic chuckled. It wasn't a pretty sound. "Still stuck on her, aren't you?"

"I'll ask the questions," I growled.

"At two she went out to the Fairway Market on Broadway to buy nectarines and skim milk," he droned. "Then she stopped at a newsstand for the current issue of *People* magazine. Also at the cleaners and the liquor store, where she bought two bottles of champagne. Dom Pérignon. Then she returned home. Didn't go out again until she left for the theater." He closed the notepad and put it away.

"Still no hostile contact from anyone?"

"None. Of course, I'm not tapping her phone. I can, if you want me to."

"Let's hold off on that. No reason to invade her privacy. At least not yet."

He went into the kitchen to stir his chili. I followed.

"How do you think our boy wonder is doing?" I asked.

"The man has a definite substance-abuse problem, Hoag. I've got him on two-a-day workouts and a good diet. I'm letting him have two beers at dinner. We've had some episodes, but nothing I can't handle. I may be able to turn around the abuse problem. He's young. His bad habits aren't that deeply ingrained. Discipline and structure will do him a world of good. But . . ." Vic ran a big hand over the lower half of his face. "I get the feeling he may have a deeper problem. He's angry. Self-destructive."

"I've noticed."

"If that's the case, he'll need professional help to get him in touch with it."

"Any idea what it might be?"

"None." Vic tasted his chili, hesitated a moment, added more chili powder. "You?"

"No, but I sure would like to find out."

I walked uptown to Skitsy's apartment. The air was soft and warm. The tulips were blooming in the window boxes, and the spindly little sidewalk trees were beginning to leaf out. Lulu waddled along beside me wheezing slightly. Her sniffles seemed to be moving down into her chest now. A rottweiler. That's what I needed. Name of Butch.

A celebrity's story can keep changing right before a ghost's eyes. That's what was happening to me with Cam Noyes. His had turned faintly sleazy on me, and so had he. I can't say I was disappointed – you have to be expecting something of people to be disappointed by them. I was more puzzled. I couldn't figure him out. He could be an open, sensitive, and very appealing kid capable of fierce loyalty and tremendous generosity. He could also be a total louse, a cynical scam artist who thought nothing of hurting the people who cared about him, or dropping his pants for the ones who could help him. So which Cam was the real Cam? Who was he? What did he believe in? Why was he trying to destroy himself? Why was he still seeing Skitsy? What was he hiding? Questions. I had lots of them. That's the most frustrating part of writing a memoir. Whenever you dig close to a person's core, you begin to face a lot of questions like these and damned few answers. There aren't many when you're trying to figure out what makes another human being tick.

I was anxious to talk to Skitsy. Tanner, too, only he wasn't in for my calls and wouldn't return them.

Skitsy Held lived in the seven-figures district – the penthouse apartment of a fine prewar doorman building on Riverside and Seventy-second. The lady did okay on her fattened editor's salary. She did more than okay.

A bright green awning stretched from the building's front door to the curb, where polished brass posts anchored it to the sidewalk. I was just a few steps from the door when suddenly the awning tore sharply over my head and something exploded on the pavement next to me.

Something that had been a woman.

Skitsy Held had been anxious to talk to me, too. So anxious she didn't wait for the elevator.

They'd thrown a tarp over her, but it didn't hide the stream of blood down to the curb, or the high-heeled shoe lying twenty feet away. Two uniformed cops stood grim watch over the body. Several more had gone upstairs. Their blue-and-whites were nosed up to the curb, along with an ambulance. Passersby were clumped around the front of the building, gawking, talking. In another ten minutes someone would be selling hot dogs and sodas.

A walkie-talkie crackled next to me. One of the uniformed cops, a beefy young Irishman with red hair and a baby face, spoke into it. Then listened. Then looked at me. "You're the friend?"

"We had a business appointment."

"Go on up. Penthouse D."

The front door to her apartment was open. An Italian racing bike was parked in the doorway. I slid past it into the living room, which was done up like a Pennsylvania farmhouse. Antique grandfather clock. Spinning wheel. Quilts on the walls. Oil portraits of dead Pilgrims. A pair of glass doors led out onto the terrace, where there was white wicker furniture and potted plants, and where two uniforms were talking to a short, stocky street kid who was chewing gum with his mouth open. He had on the uniform of a bike messenger – yellow tank top, electric-blue spandex shorts, wristbands, bicycle shoes and gloves.

All three of them looked up at the sight of Lulu and me in the terrace doorway.

It was the kid who said, "Yo, help ya, dude?"

I glanced uncertainly over at one of the uniforms, who nodded encouragingly at me. I turned back to the kid. His hands were on his hips now, his chin thrust somewhat defiantly up in the air.

"They sent me up from downstairs," I said to him. "I had an appointment with Miss Held."

"Oh, right." He came over to me. He was deeply tanned and had a lot of thick black hair and an earring and those soft brown eyes that some women get jelly knees over. I doubt he was more than five feet six, but his biceps and pecs rippled hugely and his thighs bulged in his racing shorts. He stuck out a gloved hand and said, "It's Very."

"It's very what?" I said, frowning.

"Very, *Very*. Romaine Very. Detective Lieutenant. It's my name, dude."

We shook. He had a small, powerful hand and an air of great intensity about him. His head kept nodding rhythmically, as if he heard his own rock 'n' roll beat.

"And you're, like, who?" he asked.

"Stewart Hoag. Make it Hoagy."

"As in Carmichael?"

"As in the cheese steak."

"Whatever." He popped his gum, glanced down at Lulu, back up at me. "Know any reason why Miss Held did herself in?"

"She jumped?"

"What it looks like," he replied, nodding.

"Not offhand I don't."

"Any idea who her next of kin might be?"

"You might try Tanner Marsh. He's in the English department up at Columbia. They used to be married."

Very's eyes shot over to one of the uniforms, who went immediately inside to use the phone.

"Did she leave a note?" I asked.

He shook his head. "We're still looking."

"And no one was up here with her?"

"Doorman says she came home maybe three-quarters of an hour before it happened. Nobody else came or went. Neighbors didn't hear or see a thing. Not that they would – pretty private." He narrowed his eyes at me. "Why, you know something I don't know?"

"Possibly. It depends on what subject we're discussing."

He sighed, exasperated. "You got some reason to believe somebody was up here in the apartment with her?"

"No."

"Stay with me." He headed across the terrace over to the railing.

I stayed with him. The view of Riverside Park and the Hudson wasn't terrible. The sun was getting low now over the Jersey Palisades.

"Was riding my bike down there in the park on my supper break when I heard the commotion," Very explained. "Came on over."

"Hence the outfit?"

"Yeah. Hence the outfit."

"Sound like quite a zealous guy."

He laughed. "That's me. Zealous. Okay, check it out . . . we make it she went over right about . . . here." He positioned himself at the railing. "No sign of a struggle. No fresh scratches in the paint on the railing, which would also tend to rule out any kind of accidental fall. Reads jump to me all the way."

I stood next to him and looked down over the railing.

Twenty-three floors below, Skitsy Held was being loaded into the ambulance. One of the cops was dispersing the crowd on the sidewalk, another was directing traffic.

"Understand she was in publishing," Very said.

I said she was and gave him the name of her company.

"You a publisher, too?"

I tugged at my ear. "I'm a writer."

"Oh, yeah?" he said, nodding. "What kind?"

"Lately I've been ghosting memoirs."

"No shit," he said, impressed. "You do *Vanna Speaks*?"

"She shouldn't have."

"We oughta talk sometime, you and me. I got a million stories I could put in a book. Real-life stories about cases I been on. We oughta talk sometime."

"Now wouldn't be a good time."

"Whatever." He grinned at me, started back inside, stopped. "Stay with me."

I stayed with him. The living room opened into a den, where there were shelves of books and a glass case holding a collection of antique dolls, all of them staring at us.

"Spook the shit outta me," Very said, staring back at them. "If any of 'em says 'Where's mommy?' I'm outta here."

There was one dirty cup in the kitchen sink. Half a pot of coffee in the glass Melitta on the stove. Cold. Otherwise the kitchen was clean, the counter bare. Down the hallway was her bathroom. Very turned on the light. Pink was the dominant color statement. She had used the shower when she got home. It was still damp and fragrant in there. The towel draped over the rod was wet.

He poked open her laundry hamper with a finger. It was empty inside. He closed it and made a face. "Whew, I'd *swear* it smells like fish in here. Is it me?"

"No, it's Lulu." She stood between us in the small bathroom, panting and wheezing. "Isn't it a little odd for somebody to take a shower just before they commit suicide, Lieutenant?"

"Yo, if the lady *had* her act together, dude," he replied, one knee quaking impatiently, "she *wouldn't* a jumped, would she?"

I let him have that one.

Then I let him have my address and phone number and got the hell out of there.

I ordered a boilermaker at the Dublin House bar. Lulu showed me her teeth. I showed her mine. I look meaner. I ordered another.

The liquor didn't help. It didn't make the sight – or the sound – of Skitsy Held hitting the pavement any less vivid. Or troubling.

Romaine Very wasn't wrong. It all pointed the way he said it did. Skitsy came home from a hard day of wresting with authors and agents – enough to drive anyone to suicide. She showered. She strolled out onto her terrace. She did her finest Greg Louganis impersonation. It could have happened that way, only I didn't believe it. The timing was much too convenient. I had been on my way up to talk to her. About her crooked business dealings. About what she had on Cam Noyes. Somebody had shut her up. Somebody had pushed her. The woman hadn't weighed more than a hundred pounds. Tanner Marsh could have done it easily. A good-sized man like Boyd Samuels easier still. There'd be no sign of a struggle, not if he acted quickly and decisively enough. She'd have no time to dig her nails into his arms, or to scream or to . . .

Maybe I was letting my imagination get the best of me. The doorman had said no one went in or out after Skitsy got home. Maybe Very was right.

I got change for a dollar from the bartender and called Cam's house from the pay phone. Vic answered. I told him he'd better put our boy on.

Vic hesitated, cleared his throat. "You didn't get my message?"

My stomach muscles tightened involuntarily. "What message?"

"I left it on your machine."

"What happened, Vic?"

"Cam gave me the slip, Hoag. Took his car and split."

"When?"

"Couldn't tell you exactly. I went up to his study maybe half an hour ago to let him know me and Charlie were going to sit down for chili. I made it vegetarian style, so she could eat it, too, you know? And he was gone. Don't know how he got past me."

"There's the iron veranda outside the studio windows," I suggested. "He might have gone out that way when Charlie was downstairs with you. Jumped down to the sidewalk."

"Could be. I sure feel lousy, Hoag. Like I let you down."

"Don't worry about it, Vic."

"Is there anything I can do?"

"Stay by the phone. I'll call you back." I sat there staring at the phone for a moment, wondering if it was as bad as it looked. Wondering if I was working for a murderer. I dialed Boyd's office. It was past seven but most agents work late hours. Todd Lesser answered.

"It's Stewart Hoag, Todd. Is he around?"

"Sorry, Hoagy. He's at the Algonquin wooing a prospective client. Big one. Anything I can help you with?"

"If you know Delilah's address and phone number, you can."

"How interesting," he said, amused. "I had a feeling you two would be – "

"Business, friend. Strictly business."

"Sure, sure."

He gave me the information. She lived in the Village, on West Twelfth. I thanked him. Then I asked him if he'd heard the news yet about Skitsy.

"Don't tell me she's finally forming her own company."

"Not exactly. She jumped off of her terrace a little while ago. She's dead."

Todd gasped. "Christ, Boyd will be . . . Hey, I'd better get a hold of him right away. Bye."

I got Delilah's phone machine. I hung up on it without leaving a message at the sound of the beep. Now you know I'm that kind of person. I called Vic back and asked him to run down there to see if she and Cam were around. I told him I'd check back with him in thirty minutes.

I thought about heading down to the Racquet Club. My shoulder still ached. A rub wouldn't be the worst thing. But there wasn't anyone there I felt like talking to just now. Or listening to. Instead, I had a cab drop me at Cafe Un Deux Trois, a big, noisy Parisian bistro on the edge of the theater district. I had a Pernod and water at the bar. Then I tried Vic.

"She lives in a real nice brownstone," he droned. "Looks just like the building Kate and Allie lived in. She has the top floor. She didn't answer. Mail's still in the box. No sign of Cam's car. I checked the garages in a four-block – "

"If he were there, it would be parked right out front."

"He's not there. Nobody is. I persuaded her front door to open – just to make sure. You know she has a trapeze in her bedroom?"

"Good work, Vic. How's Charlie holding up?"

"She's in her studio, working with a vengeance."

"Give her some chili. Keep her cool, I'll check in later."

"You're seeing Merilee home?"

"As it were."

I took a table and split some mussels vinaigrette with Lulu. There was a jar of brightly colored crayons at my elbow. The tablecloth was of white paper. I wrote *SSH + MGN* on it in blue, then drew a big red heart around it, and an arrow through that. The middle *S* stands for Stafford. My mother's maiden name. Don't ask me to tell you what the *G* stands for. Merilee's middle name is a deep, dark secret. She hates it. She'd kill me if I told you. It's Gilbert.

After the mussels I tucked away steak frites and a bottle of Côtes du Rhône, and finished off with mousse au chocolat and an espresso. By the time I got over to the Martin Beck, the doors were opening and *The Petrified Forest* audience was starting to spill out. I stationed myself across the street a couple of buildings down and waited like I'd been waiting every night. Several dozen fans crowded around the stage door, along with the autograph hounds and the paparazzi, all of them hoping to catch a glimpse of Sean. And maybe an incident.

The bit players and character actors filtered out first, unrecognized. Then Jeremy Irons, who smiled and signed some autographs before he headed on down the block with his hands in his pockets, alone. Then no one came out for a while. Then Sean did, behind aviator sunglasses. A large male companion was alongside him to ward off the autograph hounds, many of whom yelled and screamed and pushed toward the young star. Sean and friend didn't stop to exchange pleasantries. They hurried off down the block. Flashbulbs popped as the photographers pursued him – taunting him, shouting obscene things about Madonna after him, hoping to get a rise out of him. And a photo they could sell. They were out of luck that night.

The sidewalk got quiet after that, except for the dozen or so faithfuls waiting for Merilee. Her fans are always polite, for some reason. My eyes scanned them. None looked menacing. Or familiar. No prominent New York literary figures, for instance. No one was lurking in the shadows or in a parked car. No one was watching for her. Just me. I waited.

The old guy who worked the stage door hailed a cab for her, as he did every night. When it pulled up, she came striding out, her big Il Bisonte bag slung over one shoulder. Lulu moaned softly. I shushed her. She was casually dressed – sweatshirt, shorts, and moccasins. Of course, this being Merilee, the sweatshirt was cashmere, the shorts pleated lambsuede, and the moccasins alligator. She stopped to sign autographs and exchange gracious pleasantries. Then she climbed in the cab and it started its way down the block in the slow crosstown traffic, Merilee chatting away with the driver. She loves cabbies, provided they don't ride the horn or spit out the window.

I hailed one and hopped in. Mine was a Russian immigrant who spoke just enough English to understand I wanted him to follow her. He did.

We stayed right on her tail until she pulled up in front of our old place on Central Park West. I had my driver wait a few car lengths back as she paid and crossed the street and went inside. She and her doorman had a brief chat, then she gathered up some packages waiting there for her and headed for the elevator. We waited. As soon as I saw the lights go on in the windows overlooking the park, I had him take me home.

Another notice from the Racquet Club was waiting for me in my mailbox. This was a discreet, handwritten one from the club secretary, who wondered if perhaps I was intending to relocate abroad and wished to let my membership lapse. If not, might he bring the matter of my dues balance to my attention?

Why was it I hadn't paid them yet? Or felt like going near there lately? A "gentleman's dinosaur pit," Cam had called it. He had told me how much he wanted my respect. Did I want his, too?

Had he killed Skitsy? Where was he?

My phone started ringing as soon as I opened the door. Vic with some answers, I hoped. I lunged for it.

"It h-hurts, Mr. Hoagy . . . Oh, God . . . !"

"Merilee!"

"I need you, Hoagy," she cried, voice choking with sobs. "I n-need you. Oh, God, it hurts . . ."

"Don't move, Merilee! I'll be right there!"

"Hurry, darling. Hurry . . ."

I hung up and dashed out the door, Lulu scampering on my heel.

CHAPTER
NINE

ulu started whooping in the elevator. As soon as the doors slid open, she went skittering down the tile corridor and hurled her body, paws first, at her mommy's door. The thud brought Merilee.

"Merilee, what – ?"

Sobbing, she threw herself in my arms before I could say another word. I held on to her and smelled her smell, which is Crabtree & Evelyn avocado-oil soap.

"What did they do?" I demanded. "Tell me!"

She wiped her eyes and her nose with my linen handkerchief. They were going fast that day. "They . . . they . . ."

"They *what?*"

"N-Nominated me," she finally got out. "Today, for *Petrified Forest*. For a Tony. Oh, the *pain*."

I breathed for the first time since I'd answered my phone. "Jesus Christ, Merilee . . ."

Lulu was circling around her and moaning for some attention. Merilee knelt and stroked her and cooed at her. Then she stood and we gazed at each other, and I got lost in her green eyes. Merilee Nash isn't conventionally pretty. Her nose and chin are too patrician, her forehead is too high. Plus she's no delicate flower. She has broad, sloping shoulders, a muscular back, and powerful legs. Standing there in her size-10 bare feet, she was just under six feet. Right now her eyes were all puffy from crying and her cheeks flushed. Her waist-length golden hair was tied into a loose bun atop her head. She had on a silk target-dot dressing gown that was identical to my own. In fact, it was my own until she stole it and I had to buy another one. Holding on to my clothes had been tough for me when we were together – she always looked better in them than I did. Under the gown she wore a pair of Brooks Brothers white pima-cotton pj's. Men's pj's, because she insists they're better made. She sews the fly shut.

"Merilee, how could you do this to me?"

She bit her lower lip. "You said to call if I needed you, darling. I did. Need you. And you *came*. It means so much to me that you – "

"Merilee, there've been two threats on your life. My apartment has been attacked by a sledgehammer. My celebrity's onetime editor has jumped off the terrace of her penthouse, or been pushed – that's presently up in the air, so to speak. I don't mean to be unsympathetic, but getting nominated for your second Tony Award simply does not qualify as – "

She put a finger over my lips. "You'll wake the neighbors."

She dragged me inside and closed the door behind us. "I'm sorry, darling. Truly. I simply didn't . . . Merciful heavens, you must have thought I got . . . that I was . . ."

"Yes, I did."

"Poor Hoagy. I feel dreadful now. How can I make it up to you?"

"Depends on how far you're willing to go," I replied, grinning.

"How would a swift kick in the tush be?" she wondered sweetly.

"More action than I've had in over a year."

"That," she declared, "makes two of us."

She had redone the place in mission oak, but not just any mission oak – signed Gustav Stickley Craftsman originals, each piece spare and elegant and flawlessly proportioned. There was an umbrella stand and mouth-watering tall-case clock in the marble-floored entry hall. In the dining room she had a hexagonal dining table with six matching V-backed chairs around it and a massive sideboard with exposed tenons and pins. The living room, with its floor-to-ceiling windows overlooking Central Park, was most impressive of all. Here she had made a seating area out of two Morris armchairs and a matching settee of oak and leather. A copy of the poetry of François Villon lay open on the settee. The coffee table was heaped with fat mailing pouches full of new plays and film scripts that producers and agents wanted her to read. Part of the game. If she showed any interest, the money people would.

I sat in one of the Morris chairs, which was as comfortable as it was beautiful. Merilee curled up on the settee, where Lulu promptly joined her, head in her lap, tail thumping. Me she had forgotten about.

"Congratulations, Merilee. About the nomination. It's wonderful news."

"Thank you, darling," she said softly. "But it's not wonderful. It's dreadful. It means I have to go through the uncertainty and self-doubt all over again, just like when I got nominated before."

"But Merilee, you *won* before."

"That didn't make the waiting any easier." She sighed. "I know I should feel happy, but I don't. I feel empty. I feel as if I have nothing meaningful to show for all the work I've done. I feel as if I don't have a life."

She gazed across the coffee table at me. "Do you ever feel that way?"

"Only most of the time. I take it you're not seeing anyone these days."

She stiffened. "I hate that," she snapped. "Why is it if a man is depressed, it's a weighty existential crisis, and if a woman is, she's just not getting serviced regularly enough?"

"That's not what I meant," I said. "I've missed your quaint little expressions."

"Hmpht." She leaned over to pat Lulu, and frowned when she heard her wheezing. Concerned, she felt her nose. "It's warm and dry. Is she getting sick again?"

"I hope not."

"Did you give her a decongestant?"

"I did not."

Merilee shook her head. "And you call yourself a parent." She got up and hurried off to the kitchen. Lulu watched her.

"Just for that," I advised Lulu, "you get steak for dinner tomorrow."

I reached for the phone on the plant stand next to me and called Vic. There was still no sign of Cam. Damn.

When Merilee came back, she had half of a Sudafed buried in a blob of cream cheese on her fingertip. She'd also brought a chilled bottle of Dom Pérignon and two glasses. "I don't know – maybe we should celebrate the cursed thing," she said grumpily.

"What an excellent idea."

I popped the cork and poured while Lulu daintily licked the cream cheese off Merilee's finger. When she found the pill, she resisted, until Merilee massaged her throat and spoke a lot of baby talk to her. She likes it when Merilee talks that way to her. Me it makes fwow up.

"To you," I toasted, holding my glass up. "And to Gabby Maple."

"To us, and to long ago." She drained half of her glass and made a discreet hiccuping noise. Among her many gifts Merilee owns the world's most elegant belch. "Are *you*, darling? Seeing anyone, I mean."

"I think I could fall into Charlie Chu pretty easily if I wanted to."

Up went one eyebrow. "And do you?"

"She's an interesting woman."

"She's not a woman. She's a girl." Merilee emptied her glass and held it out for me. I refilled it. "As for me, they'll never, ever be suspending me from any canvas – not unless it's fortified with steel mesh and anchor-bolted to the wall. Gracious, look at the roles they're offering me . . ." She snatched a pile of manuscripts off the coffee table and opened one. " 'Approaching middle age.' " She dropped it unceremoniously on the wood floor with a *thwack*, opened another. " 'A handsome, sturdily built, *mature* woman.' " *Thwack*. " 'Spinster.' " *Thwack*. She slumped back against the sofa. "Lord, I'm turning into Betty Bacall!"

"You've never looked lovelier, Merilee," I assured her, sipping my bubbly. "And you know it."

"A gal only knows it if her guy tells her." She sighed. "And I haven't got one. I've been trying the substantial, noncreative type lately. A banker. A dermatologist. Both of them hearty, well-adjusted, content . . ."

"And?"

"They just don't seem to understand me." She gazed at me over her glass. "You look tired, darling."

"Shoulder is bothering me."

"Old javelin injury?"

"New bathroom-door injury."

"Shall I rub it for you?"

"No, that won't be . . . would you?"

She knelt next to me on the floor and began to work her strong fingers into my shoulder. It made me think of when she was in the Sondheim musical. Her legs would cramp up on her in the night, twitch and thump in the bed. I'd rub them for her, then rub the rest of her, then . . .

"Feel good?" she asked softly.

"Better than good."

From the settee, Lulu watched us drowsily. The decongestant was taking effect.

"And how is Cam?"

"Among the missing right now. In more ways than one. I wish I could figure him out."

"He's gotten under your skin, hasn't he?"

"What makes you say that?"

"It has been known to happen."

"Any hint of trouble at this end?" I asked her.

"None," she assured me. "I told you — there's nothing to worry about." She wrapped her arms around my calves and rested her chin on my knee. "Will you take me, darling? To the Tony Awards, I mean."

"Be glad to. Does this mean you've decided to forgive me?"

She gave me her up-from-under look, the one that drove Bill Hurt to madness in the Cain remake. She surprised a lot of people in that movie. She didn't surprise me. "It means I can never pass up a chance to see you in black."

We got lost in each other's eyes for a second.

Abruptly, she went back to work on my shoulder. "I have no idea what I'll wear."

"Talk it over with Cher – I'm sure she'll have some excellent ideas." I cleared my throat. "Perhaps I don't need to say this, Merilee . . ."

"Perhaps you do," she said coolly.

"I never wanted any of this to happen. This rift between us."

"I think . . . I think what hurt me the most was the way you characterized me. Indecisive. Flighty."

"I didn't."

"You *did.*"

"Well, you're not."

"I keep wondering what you'll write about me next. Gracious, this very conversation we're having fight now could end up in some book of yours someday."

I tugged at my ear. "It could."

Lulu was asleep now on the settee.

"Know what I was thinking about tonight, darling, when I was sitting here all alone? How much I feel like retiring from the business. Getting a country place, raising some . . . now this will surprise you . . ."

"Midget human life-forms?"

"Herbs. I'd give anything to just play in the mud all day and never do another sit-up. If someone wants me to come back in a cameo role as, say, the aircraft carrier USS *Chester Nimitz*, fine. Otherwise, I'm perfectly content to hang it up. Buy every spade and cultivator in the Smith and Hawken catalog. Plant bulbs from White Flower Farm, and feed the birds and watch *The Victory Garden* and wear flannel-lined jeans and rubber boots."

"And what would you do with your mink?"

"It gets cold at night there, too. Why, think I'm full of baked beans?"

"I think you need a vacation. Why don't you take a few weeks off?"

"Actually, I was thinking of going to – "

"France?"

"Why, yes. How did you know?"

"Call it a wild guess," I said, glancing over at the volume of Villon on the sofa next to Lulu.

"Oh, I see. It's because Gabby wants to in the play, and you think I take on the characteristics of whomever I'm playing."

"It has been known to happen." The only part of this equation I didn't care for is that Gabby Maple falls for a doomed gentleman writer who is shot dead at the end of the third act by Duke Mantee and buried in the Petrified Forest with the other fossils.

She sat back on her haunches and drank some more champagne. "I can't go to France. France belongs to you."

"To me?"

"To us. You took me there on our honeymoon, when things were so lovely, and I-I can't go anywhere we went together. I made the mistake of going into Elaine's once last year, and Lulu's water bowl was gone and I started to weep." Her green eyes filled up. "Oh, horseradish, I was hoping you'd cheer me up. I suppose no one can." Halfheartedly, she pulled a pile of unopened mailing pouches off the coffee table and began to sort through them there on the floor.

I poured out the last of the champagne and held up the bottle. "Shall I open its friend?"

"Please do." She frowned. "How did you know there was a friend?"

"Masculine intuition."

I found the champagne on the top shelf of the fridge right next to Merilee's most secret, junky passion – Velveeta. I returned with the bottle, sat back down, and began working the cork out as she tore into a fat pouch, pulled out the squat, square box inside, and tossed the envelope away.

I had a delayed reaction. I was busy fiddling with the champagne, and preoccupied with thoughts of Cam Noyes. I must have stared at that discarded pouch for five full seconds before I noticed the press-on letters that spelled out her name and address. And recognized them. And reacted.

I dove for Merilee just as she pulled the lid off the box. I heard a sharp metallic snap as I dove. A glass jar shot out of the box as I landed atop her. It just missed her – splashed its liquid contents all over the floor and the Persian rug and my back. Almost at once the varnish on the floor began to bubble, the rug to smolder and stink. Something hot nibbled at my back. I jumped to my feet and whipped off my silk hounds-tooth sports jacket, which already had several holes eaten in it, and then my shirt, which had just started to go.

Then I fell back on my knees, gasping with relief. I was the only one. Lulu, bless her, was still asleep on the settee. And Merilee seemed more bewildered than frightened.

"What is all of this, Mr. Hoagy?" she wondered as she reached for the jar.

"Don't touch that!" I cried. "It's sulfuric acid. Battery acid."

"But what – ?"

"It was meant to hit you in the face when you opened the box."

Her fingers shot involuntarily to her face. She got very wide-eyed and pale. It was sinking in now. "W-What would it have done . . . ?"

"Put an end to your movie career for real," I said. "Unless they needed someone to play Freddy's sister in a new *Nightmare on Elm Street*."

"And if it had gotten in my eyes?"

I left that one alone.

"Omigod!" She threw herself in my arms, shaking uncontrollably.

"It's okay," I said, hugging her tightly. "It's okay now."

When she had calmed down a little, I gingerly examined the box. The jar had been set inside it on a catapult held in place with a retaining wire. Pulling the top off the box had triggered the catapult, which in turn had snapped back the jar's spring-loaded lid. A simple, monstrous jack-in-the-box. Also untraceable – you can buy battery acid from any hardware supply house.

"I-I don't understand it, Hoagy," she said. "What sort of person would *do* something so . . . so . . . ?"

"Somebody who is really sick," I told her, fingering the envelope it had come in. "How did you get this?"

"It was downstairs waiting for me when I came home tonight."

"Call the doorman, would you? Ask him if he remembers who delivered it."

She went to the house phone by the front door. Lulu finally stirred from her slumber.

"Lassie," I pointed out sternly, "would have barked out a warning. Dragged the pouch off into Central Park with her bare teeth. She *wouldn't* have snoozed through the whole damned thing."

Lulu yawned in response. And went back to sleep with a peaceful grunt.

Merilee returned a moment later. "Ned said he noticed it there earlier this evening after he'd been hailing a cab for a tenant. He didn't see who left it."

"Too bad. Mind if I borrow one of my old shirts back?"

"Not at all, darling. I'll get it for you as soon as I call the police." She picked up the phone, started to dial it.

"Don't do that, Merilee," I said quietly.

She stopped. "Why not?"

"I have my reasons."

"Hoagy, I've been attacked!"

"Don't call the police."

"But you said yourself someone may have been murdered tonight. You said your apartment was trashed. You said – "

"It may be Cam."

"What do you mean it may be Cam?"

"I mean he's a big strong kid, and he's good with his hands and he's violent."

"I see." She bit her lip fretfully. "You don't trust him?"

"I don't know. All I know is he's hiding something from me, and that it may have cost Skitsy Held her life. Only, say it *is* Cam. Why would he go to so much trouble to scare me off of this project – threaten me, try to disfigure you? All he has to do is fire me. I don't get it. I don't know what's going on. Until I do, I owe him the benefit of the doubt. Friends . . ." I trailed off, swallowing.

"Friends what, Hoagy?"

"Friends don't call the police on one another."

She stared at the phone in her hand, then slowly put it down. "Okay, Hoagy. If it means that much to you."

"Thank you."

"Hoagy?"

"Yes, Merilee?"

"Why do you keep getting caught in the middle of such messes?"

"Just lucky, I guess."

Somebody was sleeping in my chair.

My new, easy-opening front door was ajar, my reading lamp was on, and Detective Lt. Romaine Very, the rock 'n' roll cop, was slumped there, snoring. A copy of my second novel lay open in his lap. Another critic. He had changed into a Rangers sweatshirt, jeans, and Pony high-tops. His bike was propped against my bookcase. Lulu sniffed at it, and at him, disagreeably.

"Good and comfy, Lieutenant?" I asked him, my voice raised.

He jumped and sat up blinking, immediately alert. "Yo, saw the hole in the wall, dude. Thought somebody broke in. So I came in to check it out. Waited around for ya."

"Why didn't you just put on my jammies and hop into bed?"

"Sorry, dude. It's this ulcer I got. Used to drink ten, fifteen cups of coffee a day to keep going. Doc won't let me drink any now, so I keep sort of, like, drifting off." He got to his feet, popped a piece of gum in his mouth, and began to pace around my apartment, chomping. "Place is a real dive, y'know?"

"Thanks. It's nice of you to say so."

"What's with the hole?"

"Had a break-in a few days ago. Haven't gotten around to getting it fixed yet." And what was the point? It wasn't as if fixing it would keep out anyone who really wanted in. Besides, I'd always wanted cross-ventilation.

He stopped pacing, started nodding to his personal rock 'n' roll beat. "You report it?"

I shook my head. "Nothing was taken. Must have gotten scared off or something." I put down some fresh mackerel for Lulu, then found some Bass ale in the fridge and offered him one.

"Naw, I'm off beer, too. Also chocolate and anything spicy, which means no pizza, no souvlaki, no hot dogs, no pastrami, no moo shoo pork, no whatever tastes good. Christ, you ever taste that herbal fucking tea?"

I opened an ale and drank some of it. "Kind of young for an ulcer, aren't you?"

"Doc says I have an intensity problem," he replied. "Too much of it."

"Not exactly a calm line of work either," I suggested.

"You got that right, dude."

I glanced at grandfather's Rolex. "I don't mean to be inhospitable, Lieutenant, but it's three a.m. and I'd like to get to bed. Did you want something?"

He flopped back down in my easy chair. "I got a bunch of calls tonight from the press about Miss Held. Seems she was a pretty important lady."

"In certain circles."

"You said ya had some kind of appointment with her."

"I did."

"What about?" he asked.

"Is that important?" I asked.

He popped his gum and narrowed his eyes at me. "Maybe you oughta just tell me, huh?"

"Tell you what?" I shoved aside the newspapers and magazines piled on the love seat and sat down. "Skitsy Held and I were business acquaintances. I had nothing to do with her jumping."

"Who said she jumped?"

"You did." I drank some more of my ale. "Why, have you found something that's changed your mind?"

He shrugged. "Her dirty laundry."

"What about it?"

"There wasn't any. Doorman says she came home in a yellow dress. She died less than an hour later in a blue one. We know she took a shower. But her laundry hamper was empty. No yellow dress. No stockings. No soiled undies. We turned the place upside down. Closets, dressers, everywhere. So, like, where'd the shit go?"

I tugged at my ear. "Laundry room?"

"We checked there."

"Dry cleaners?"

"She used the Empire Cleaners on Broadway. I called the dude at home. He remembered her right away. She was a regular customer for years. He said she hadn't been in for at least a week, and none of his people picked anything of hers up tonight. I also talked to her doctor. He said she had no history of depression or other mental illness, and wasn't seeing a therapist. Not that that necessarily means anything. People can fall off the shelf like that . . ." He snapped his fingers. "But still . . ."

"You think maybe she was pushed?"

"I'm thinking there's something a little bizarre going on. Maybe it's nothing, but sometimes nothing turns into, y'know . . ."

"Something?"

He nodded. "Man, I could tell you stories – "

"Now wouldn't be a good time." I sipped my ale. "To answer your question, I was there to talk to her about my next novel. I was hoping to get her interested enough in it to sign it up."

"What's it about, your new novel?"

"A man and woman who can't stay together but who can't stay apart. I'm hoping it reads better than it lives."

"Why'd you go to her place to talk? Why didn't you meet her in her office during business hours?"

"Common practice. Editors have most of their creative conversations over meals or drinks."

"Sure you weren't involved with her?"

"I told you – I was a business acquaintance."

"Right, right." Very yawned and scratched his stomach. "Got wind of a little scuffle recently at Elaine's," he said casually. "According to an eyewitness, you and Miss Held had some angry words on the curb outside."

"A few," I acknowledged. "You're a busy guy, aren't you, Lieutenant?"

"I liked you better when you called me zealous."

"I liked you better before you started making accusations. I was on the sidewalk in front of Skitsy's building when she hit the pavement. I couldn't have pushed her off her terrace and then made it down to the street before she did. The elevator isn't that fast, and I didn't happen to have my cape with me. I didn't kill her."

"Didn't say you did, dude," he said soothingly. "Just trying to figure out what's going on. Stay with me."

"I'm with you, I'm with you."

"Where were you immediately before you got to her place?"

"Walking."

"Anybody see you?"

"Half of Manhattan."

"I mean, anybody recognize you?"

I sighed inwardly. Maybe they would have in the old days, when it was my picture that was plastered all over the newspapers. Not anymore. "No one."

He nodded. "Hear you're ghosting Cam Noyes's memoirs."

"I am."

"Why didn't you tell me that before?"

"You didn't ask me."

He stuck his chin out challengingly. "You jerking my chain?"

"I am not."

"Dickhead lived in my dorm when he was a freshman."

"You went to Columbia?"

"You sound surprised, dude. Think I'm some kind of Ricky Retardo?"

"Not at all. What did you major in?"

"Romance languages. Did me beaucoup good, too." He belched. "I hear Miss Held was his first editor."

"She was."

"I don't suppose your meeting with her tonight had anything to do with him."

"It did not."

"Just a coincidence?"

"That's right, Lieutenant. Publishing is a small community. Cam and I happened to be at a party she threw recently for another of her writers. She and I got to talking about my new novel. She suggested we get together."

He gave his gum a workout. "Got an answer for everything,

haven't you, dude?"

I left that one alone.

"What else aren't you telling me?" he demanded, scowling at me now.

"Nothing I can think of."

He shook his head. "I'm not supersatisfied."

"Who among us is?"

He stood up and went over to his bike, still shaking his head. "I ran a check on you, y'know? You got no record, but I still keep getting the feeling you been down this particular road before. Why is that?"

I shrugged. "I couldn't say, Lieutenant. Possibly it's the tire tracks across my back."

Romaine Very stood there facing me a minute, his hands on his hips, one knee quaking, chin stuck out. He looked as if he wanted to punch me or say something real nasty. He didn't do either of those things. He just said, "Whatever," in a voice filled with quiet menace. And stormed out the door with his bike, gum popping furiously.

Lulu woke up coughing, her chest rumbling like the aged Morgan Plus-4 I drove in college, the one I couldn't find a replacement muffler for. I fixed her a spoonful of lemon and honey – her old bronchitis nostrum – and after she licked it clean, the two of us took a nice, hot shower together. Lulu hates showering with me. I'm not too crazy about it myself. She slips and slides around, and moans and keeps trying to jump out – all this plus the steamy, enveloping stench of fish breath. It's kind of like bathing with an otter. But she needed the steam for her congestion, and after I warned her it was this or a trip to a vet for a s-h-o-t, she stayed put, withstanding the indignity of hot water beating down upon her head with heroic stoicism.

She seemed to be breathing a little easier when I dried her off. I assured her she was a brave little girl and gave her an anchovy.

Skitsy made the front page of all three morning papers. The *Times* used a file photo of her standing at a cocktail party with her great discovery, Cam Noyes. The *Post* had a picture of her tarp-covered body on the bloody sidewalk in front of her building. If you looked real carefully, you could see me standing there in the background, looking tall and dapper and somewhat nauseous.

I read the stories as I cabbed down to Gramercy Park. They played her death as an apparent suicide. None of the suspicions that Lt. Romaine Very had raised in my apartment were included – no mention of her missing clothes, no hint that he felt somebody may have pushed her. He was being careful until he had something more to go on. After all, there were some important people involved here. There was her ex-husband, noted critic and scholar Tanner Marsh, who was quoted as calling her "the most brilliant editor since Maxwell Perkins." There was that prominent literary agent and gent Boyd Samuels, who called her "a colleague and a friend and a great lady." There was Cam Noyes, who was not available for comment.

Where was he?

Vic was pulling a fresh-baked cranberry bread out of the toaster-oven when I got there. "I checked Delilah's place this morning at seven," he reported. "Again at eight. No sign of either of them. Her mail's still in the box. She never came home last night." He reached into his apron and produced a white envelope. "When I got back, this was under the door. For you."

My heartbeat quickened at the sight of the press-on letters spelling out my name on the outside of the envelope. I ripped it open. Inside it said: *Go to Farmington*. Nothing more. I stared at it, wondering what it meant. Wondering who'd left it.

"Charlie's upstairs packing, Hoag," Vic droned as he poured us coffee. "She sat down here all night waiting for him to come home. He's a real bastard, you know that?"

I couldn't disagree with him, so I didn't.

Vic had moved a white wrought-iron table and a couple of the pastel garden chairs out onto the still-unfinished patio. We took the cranberry bread and our coffee out there and sat in the warm sun.

"Still no sign of that darned contractor," Vic said. "Charlie keeps calling him and calling him. I'm half tempted to go out to Brooklyn and throttle the guy."

"He'll show up when he feels like it and not a moment sooner," I explained. "All a part of the joy of renovating."

I was just starting to fill him in on Very's visit and Merilee's brush with battery acid when Cam Noyes walked in the from door.

CHAPTER
ELEVEN

(Tape #6 with Cam Noyes recorded May 13 in his garden. Appearance is disheveled, eyes bloodshot. Vic brings him coffee, disappears inside, glowering.)

Noyes: Big Vic doesn't seem particularly happy to see me.

Hoag: He's disappointed in you – you broke training. Also wounded his professional pride somewhat. Where were you last night, Cameron? *(no response)* You have heard about Skitsy, haven't you?

Noyes: Saw it in this morning's paper. Couldn't . . . can't believe she did this to me.

Hoag: Did what to you?

Noyes: First mother, then father, now Skitsy. . . . Anybody who matters to me bails out on me. I just . . . I can't handle it anymore, you know? I mean, why does this keep *happening* to me?

Hoag: For what it's worth, Cameron, Skitsy didn't do anything to you. Someone did it to her – she was murdered.

Noyes: But the newspapers said –

Hoag: Forget what the newspapers said.

Noyes: W-Who . . . ?

Hoag: Offhand, I'd have to consider you the top suspect right now.

Noyes: Me?

Hoag: I've done my best to shield you from the police, but I can't shield you for much longer.

Noyes: Damned decent of you, coach, but there's no need for you to get involved.

Hoag: Goddamn it, I *am* involved! Don't pull this shit on me! Where were you last night?!

Noyes: You don't actually think *I* killed her, do you?

Hoag: I think you refused to tell me yesterday what Skitsy had on you. I think before I could ask her, someone made sure she couldn't tell me. I think you can draw your own conclusion.

Noyes: (silence) I went somewhere with Delilah, okay?

Hoag: Where?

Noyes: She gets off on sleaze. It's her thing, you know? We drove out to this adults-only motel in Ozone Park she wanted to go to, the

Galaxy. It's got porn movies on the TV and round water beds and mirrors on the ceiling and complimentary champagne that tastes like carbonated monkey piss. We fucked all night, okay? She has that early-morning gig on *Good Morning America*. Before dawn we drove back and I dropped her at the studio. Then I stopped at an all-night diner on Eleventh Avenue and had steak and eggs and bought the newspapers. That's when I found out about Skitsy. I called Boyd right off. He's totally blown out. *(pause)* I've just been walking and thinking for the past couple of hours. I cried a little. She was kind of a second mother to me, you know?

Hoag: Let's not get too oedipal.

Noyes: Okay, maybe we had a sick relationship. But it was a relationship. I haven't had many.

Hoag: She was killed a little before seven last night. Where were you?

Noyes: On our way to the motel. We got there at about a quarter to eight.

Hoag: Stop anywhere on the way?

Noyes: For hamburgers at a White Castle on Ridgewood Avenue.

Hoag: Kind of an all-around classy evening.

Noyes: Coach, I have no idea what happened to Skitsy, or why it happened. That's the truth. I may be scum, but I'm not a killer. Christ, no. Where's Charlie?

Hoag: Upstairs packing.

Noyes: Good. I'm glad she's over me.

Hoag: I wouldn't say she's over you, but she is leaving you.

Noyes: Any idea for where?

Hoag: She can stay at my place for now, if she wishes.

Noyes: Well, well.

Hoag: It's not like that. I won't be around. Going away for a couple of days on personal business. Strictly an aboveboard offer.

Noyes: It needn't be. On my account, I mean.

Hoag: Duly noted. Why would you want Skitsy dead?

Noyes: I wouldn't. I didn't.

Hoag: Cameron, if I'm going to stick my neck out for you I have to know the whole story. I'll ask you again – What did Skitsy have on you?

Noyes: I already told you, you needn't stick –

Hoag: What was it, goddamnit!

Noyes: Stop yelling at me!

Hoag: I'll stop yelling when you start answering! Why didn't you break it off with Skitsy?! Tell me!

Noyes: (long silence) That's what I've been thinking about all morning, actually. Telling you. It's . . . It's been slowly killing me inside. The horror if it. The guilt. Wanting to get it off my chest. I-I can't stand it anymore. I really can't. And now that she's dead . . . Shit, I didn't kill her. You have to believe me. Do you? *(no response)* She can't tell on me anymore. Can't hurt me. That's a tremendous . . . it's a *relief*. My secret is safe now. I'm safe. Except for you, damn it. You think I'm some kind of liar or killer, and I can't handle that. I want you to know the truth, coach. I'm going to tell you the truth. But only if you promise to leave it out of the book. This is just between you and me. It's personal, understand?

Hoag: Off the record?

Noyes: Yes, off the record.

Hoag: Go ahead.

Noyes: (silence) Do you remember how I told you that Boyd peddled fake driver's licenses at Deerfield?

Hoag: Yes.

Noyes: And that he had to shut down when some kid got loaded and smashed into a busload of kids and –

Hoag: Killed two of them and himself. Yes, yes. Go on.

Noyes: I lied to you about that. He wasn't killed. Didn't get a scratch on him, in fact. Got away clean. None of the survivors saw him. It was early morning, and dark, and he had bailed out of that stolen car a good fifty feet before it slammed into the bus. He chickened out. No guts. He was attempting suicide, you see, and was simply too fucked up to realize that the other people would . . . that the bus would explode when the car hit it. That he would sit there in the ditch hearing their screams. That two of them would die. That he . . . that *I* killed them.

Hoag: Let's try it from the beginning, shall we?

Noyes: Very well . . . Boyd had gone home for the weekend – his mother was ill. He left me some acid. Saturday night I dropped it and went to this dance we had with Stoneleigh-Burnham, thinking it would be a trip. It wasn't. All of those smug, status-conscious people. All of that role playing. Pissed me off. Made me feel caged, like I just had to get out of the place, you know? So I split. Trolled the village for a car with its keys in it. I didn't find one, but as I was walking past the Inn, a guy in a BMW pulled up there to drop some people off. He went inside with them to say good-night, and left his engine running. People do that up there in the winter, to keep the heater going. I just hopped in and took off. Got on I-91 and pointed it south toward Springfield – away. Got it up over a hundred, flying, tripping my brains out. Felt like I was living in some kind of arcade game. I bought a bottle of Jack Daniel's somewhere and stretched out in a farmer's field, just lay there in the snow and drank it and stared up at the stars and the moon. I lay there for hours, wondering if I was doomed like Mother and Father had been. Wondering if life was as awful as it appeared to be. Lying there, I realized that I had no control over my life. Not any of it. That it was simply going to unfold before me, and then it would be over. And that the only real, meaningful control I could ever have was to choose when and how I would die. I felt tremendous power at this realization. *Calm.*

Hoag: Your character in *Bang* felt that calm. You wrote so well about it I felt you must have contemplated suicide at some point.

Noyes: I did more than contemplate it. I got back in the Beemer toward dawn and looked around for how to do it. I was sure it was the right thing to do. . . . I saw that bus sitting there at the intersection. And I said to myself, there it is. Perfect. Just go right into it. Go for it. I didn't know it was full of kids on their way to a ski outing. I didn't know anything. I was still tripping. The bottle was empty . . . I went for it. Picked up speed. Made straight for it. Got closer. Closer still. And then, suddenly, this *force* took over me, this force that yanked me out of the car. I landed in the ditch. I heard the crash, the explosion. Saw the flames. The flames were . . . beautiful. I didn't do the decent thing. I didn't help those kids. I heard them screaming, but I didn't help them. I ran. For miles and miles, until I was near the highway. A trucker gave me a ride north toward Deerfield. I was back in my room early enough Sunday morning that no one even noticed I'd been gone. As the acid wore off that day, I started to pull out of my suicidal depression. And began to realize the enormity, the sheer *horror*, of what I'd done. I'd killed two people! . . . I told Boyd when he came back. I had to tell someone. He shrugged it off. Told me I was lucky to be alive, and a free man, and that I should just forget about it. I couldn't. I thought about turning myself in, of course. But I realized how meaningless that would be, because there was nothing that prison could do to me that would rival the torment I would have to live with – that I *have* lived with ever since. It wouldn't wipe out the screams I hear in my dreams. . . . From time to time, I've thought again about suicide. But the clarity, the *calm*, have never returned. That was a onetime thing. So I suppose you could say I'm doing myself in slowly.

I drink, I snort, I do whatever. To forget. But I don't forget. Not a day goes by when I don't think about it. It's my black pit. Some days, I'm hanging on by my fingertips, trying not to get sucked down into it. Other days, I'm sitting on the edge, dangling my feet into it. I can never, ever walk away from it. It's always there between me and other people, particularly women, who are always so anxious to peer inside of me. . . . One night, when Skitsy and I were drunk and fucked out, I told her about it. She's the only woman I've ever told. This was before *Bang* came out, and she kept wanting to hear all about how wild I was. I guess I was just trying to impress her, I don't know. After the book came out, I started getting bored with her. I'm used to seeing a lot of women, none of them for very long. When I told her I didn't think it was going to work out between us any longer, she said, "Fine. Go off and lay anyone you want. But you're mine twice a week or I call the law on you." She would have, too. She was that tough. So I've been her boy every since. Stuck with her. That's the truth, coach. The whole, ugly truth.

Hoag: I see. Tell me, why didn't she hold this over you when you broke your contract with her?

Noyes: That was something between her and Boyd. That was business. This was personal. She . . . she loved me. I never loved her back, but I didn't kill her. I swear to you I didn't . . . *(silence)* Say something. *Please.*

Hoag: You won't like it.

Noyes: You think that I should turn myself in, don't you? Take my medicine. Am I right?

Hoag: That isn't what I was going to say, though I think a good case could be made for it. You said it yourself – you're killing yourself slowly. You're still young and strong, but soon you won't be. The process will speed up quite dramatically, and that will be the end of you. And what a waste it will be.

Noyes: What *were* you going to say?

Hoag: That aside from the death of your parents, this is the major event of your life. It tells me who you are. Tells me about the pain and intensity of *Bang*. Tells me about the anger inside you. About why you can't write, or have a serious relationship with a woman, or face responsibility. . . . I was going to say, Cameron, that *this* is our book.

Noyes: No, you promised me! You said it didn't have to –

Hoag: Listen to me, Cameron. I can't make you do anything you don't want to do. It's your book. I'm only here to advise you. My advice is this – let this book be your confessional. Come clean. You'll never be able to get on with your life and your work until you do. Confront this thing on paper – openly and honestly. And then face the music. At least this way you've got some control of the situation. Your story will be on the record, complete and accurate.

Noyes: My career will be ruined.

Hoag: And what career is that? A bunch of endorsements? It's your *work* that matters, not some wine-cooler commercial. It's being able to live with yourself.

Noyes: I don't know, coach. I just don't know.

Hoag: I won't pressure you. It's your decision. And your life – you'll have to pay the consequences. Talk to a good lawyer. Talk to Boyd.

Noyes: I know what he'll say – that you're crazy.

Hoag: Don't bet on that. If you do this, you'll get major attention. Maybe even your second *People* cover.

Noyes: Third.

Hoag: My mistake. Sorry.

Noyes: No problem. Could happen to anyone.

Hoag: Think about it, Cameron. Will you do that?.

Noyes: *(silence)* I'll do that.

(end tape)

CHAPTER
TWELVE

I left for Connecticut that night.

I wasn't alone. I talked Merilee into coming along. She needed to get away from her acid-splashed apartment for a couple of days, and I needed to keep an eye on her. It also meant I could drive the red Jaguar XK 150 drophead convertible we'd bought when we were together, and which she got to keep. It's a rare beauty, every inch of it factory original the engine, transmission, black top, sixty-spoke wire wheels, tan leather interior, polished hardwood dash. The damned car only has 31,000 miles on it. Its previous owner had been an elderly East Hampton cereal heiress who'd only driven it to the beauty parlor and the Maidstone. I'd missed how it handled and purred. I'd missed Merilee's riding next to me with the wind in her golden hair.

We left after her curtain with the top down and Lulu in her lap. Merilee wore a baseball jacket and cap of matching suede, a white linen camp shirt, faded blue jeans, and her Converse Chuck Taylor red high-tops. Lulu had her custom-knitted Fair Isle vest on against the night air, and one of Merilee's white silk aviator scarves wrapped around her throat.

"What do you think he'll decide to do?" Merilee asked me when I told her about my breakthrough with Cam.

"Tell all. Take his punishment. Not that it's entirely fair. He'll be judged for the rest of his life over something that he did on a drugged-out suicidal binge when he was sixteen years old. That's tough."

"Not as tough as it was on the children who were on that bus," she pointed out.

"I know that."

"He's not above the law just because he's gifted."

"I know that, too."

"And if he decides *not* to confess?" she asked. "What will you do – turn him in?"

"I don't know," I admitted.

"He's made you into something of an accomplice, hasn't he?"

"I'm afraid I did that to myself."

"Do you think he pushed that Skitsy Held woman?"

"No, I don't." I believed Cam. I wanted to believe him. Still, part of me wasn't so sure – the part that had asked Vic to check out his sleazy-motel story. The part that was making for Farmington without telling him. What I would find there? What was I even looking for? I had no idea. But I had to go.

The late-night traffic on I-95 was light through the commuter towns Greenwich, Stamford, Fairfield. After New Haven it was nonexistent. I let the Jag out to eighty. It seemed happiest at that speed. Lightning began to crackle in the sky when we were outside Guilford, and a light rain began to fail. I stopped and put the top up. It was pouring by the time we pulled off the highway at Old Lyme, the wind gusting sheets of rain before our headlights as we eased slowly through the snug, slumbering little historic village at the mouth of the Connecticut River. The Bee and Thistle Inn there was saving two rooms for us. Old Lyme isn't exactly next door to Farmington, but the Bee and Thistle holds a special attachment for us – it's where we stayed on our first weekend together. Besides, I never claimed we were practical. Just cute.

The inn has been there since 1756. A stand of maple trees shields it from the road, and a broad circular driveway leads to its front door. Inside, a fire blazed in the parlor fireplace. We were greeted like family and shown directly to our rooms. There are eleven of them in all, each furnished in antiques. Ours were across the hall from each other on the third floor. Merilee's had a canopied bed. I unpacked and put down mackerel and water for Lulu, then escorted Merilee back down to the parlor. The kitchen had been closed for hours, but they dug us up some leftover cold sliced duck and crabmeat ravioli, and heated some scones. We devoured it in front of the fire with a bottle of Sancerre while the rain beat down outside and Lulu dozed on the floor. Our hosts served us Irish coffee before they went to bed. We stayed up awhile, sipping it and gazing into the flames.

"I'm glad I let you talk me into this, darling," Merilee said, sighing contentedly.

I glanced over at her. Her face was aglow in the firelight, her hair shimmering. "So am I, Merilee."

"Do you remember what you said to me that first night here?" she asked me softly, her green eyes fixed on the flames.

"Yes. You said, 'Did you ever dream you'd one day find yourself drinking champagne in a bathtub with a glamorous, award-winning actress?' And I said, 'Yes, the very first time I laid eyes on you.' "

She smiled. "That's when I knew I was a goner."

"That's not what you told me later on that night, under the canopy," I pointed out, grinning.

"*Mister* Hoagy, not in front of the child."

Lulu ignored us. She was out. We sipped our Irish coffees.

"Darling?"

"Yes, Merilee?"

"Do you remember everything we said?"

"I'm afraid so. Elephants and writers never forget."

"Who was it that said that?"

I yawned. "I forget."

Upstairs, we lingered in the hall for an awkward, silent moment before Merilee said good-night in a hoarse whisper, darted inside, and closed her door.

I went to bed with Truman Capote, who was my second choice. The storm picked up even more. Lightning lit up the night sky. Thunder rattled the windows. The wind howled. Lulu didn't like it. She jumped down from the bed and scratched at the door, whimpering. She wanted her mommy. I told her to shut up. She wouldn't. I told her to come back to bed. She wouldn't. I got out of bed and put on my dressing gown. The light was still on underneath Merilee's door. I tiptoed across the hall and tapped on it.

"Yes . . . ?" she demanded, instantly suspicious.

I turned the knob. She'd locked the door. "Why, Merilee, don't you trust me?"

"I see I had good reason not to, mister."

"Lulu wants to sleep with you."

"Oh, that's *low*, Hoagy. So, so low. Using a puppy as your Trojan horse. And a sniffly little one at that."

"I'm perfectly serious – she wants her mommy."

Lulu thudded against the door and whimpered.

"Oh, Sweetness!" Merilee cried. "Gracious, why didn't you *say* so, you son of a sea cook."

"I did."

I heard her bedsprings creak and her bare feet on the floor. She opened the door. She was wearing her red flannel nightshirt and a pair of round, oversized tortoiseshell glasses. Those were new.

"I've missed your quaint little expressions," I said.

"Hmpht."

Lulu scampered straight for the bed, where Kazan's memoir lay open on the pillow, and barked. Merilee shushed her and hoisted her up.

"So what's with the new look?" I asked, referring to the specs. "Getting in character to play Annie Sullivan?"

She'd forgotten she had them on. Aghast, she whipped them off and hid them behind her back. "They just get a little tired sometimes," she explained, blushing furiously. "My eyes, I mean. Lately. When I'm reading."

"Uh-huh."

"Oh, *beans*, I hate them!"

"You look cute in them, kind of like a sexy owl."

She softened. "Do I really?" she asked me girlishly.

"Trust me."

Lulu curled up, tail thumping happily. Merilee went over and said some baby talk to her. To me she said, "I haven't had Sweetness with me in ages. I always sleep better when I do."

"She's all yours." I started back to my own room. "Oh, if she starts snoring again in the night, just throw her in the shower for a while."

Merilee's eyes widened. "Just throw her in the *what?*"

"Sleep tight, four eyes."

The rain blew away during the night. It was the sun slanting into my room that woke me. I threw open my window and inhaled. The country air was fresh and clean, and fragrant from the pink and white blossoms on the apple trees. Beyond the thick green lawn, the Lieutenant River sparkled in the morning light.

A plump, giggly teenaged girl brought me fresh-squeezed orange juice, a basket of warm blueberry muffins, and a pot of coffee. I had it in bed while I pored over the transcripts of my tapes with Cam, in particular the material on Farmington the town where he was born and raised, and where he buried his parents. The town he couldn't get out of fast enough.

I was interrupted by a tapping at my door, followed by a woof. And Merilee calling out, "We want our daddy."

"This is *low*, Merilee. So, so low."

"*Mister* Hoagy. Open this door at once."

"It's open."

Lulu scampered in first, snuffling happily, paws and belly soaked. She went right for her mackerel bowl, paying me not the slightest attention. Chomping followed.

Merilee had on a white cotton fisherman's knit turtleneck, gray flannels, and her oiled English ankle boots. Her cheeks were ruddy, her eyes agleam. "It is *glorious* out," she exclaimed. "*We* have been out walking. *We* have devoured flapjacks and sausages. *You*, mister, are a slug-a-bed. A sloth. A potato."

"Am not. I've been working."

"Sweetness didn't snore one teeny bit last night. And her nose is cold again. I think she's *aww* better."

"That's a relief." Her face was still in her bowl. Not so much as a good-morning. "Shall I drop you in East Haddam?"

Some friends of Merilee's were rehearsing a summer production of *Guys and Dolls* at the Goodspeed Opera House.

"Think I'll stick around here awhile," she replied. "I feel like going horseback riding. I can get a lift up there later. May I keep Sweetness for the day?"

"Feel free. She doesn't even know I'm alive."

"Don't be churlish, darling. She's mine too, you know."

"Hmpht."

It took me forty-five minutes to get to Farmington, with its streets of carefully preserved center-chimney colonial houses, its graceful old oaks and maples, its sense of gentility and grace – everything that Cam Noyes despised.

I made my way up Main Street past Miss Porter's and turned onto Mountain Street. High Street, where Cam had lived, ran into Mountain. I tooled along it slowly. Workmen were out battling back against winter. Carpenters were rebuilding rotted front porches. Roofers were reshingling. Tree surgeons were operating. There were a few newer homes set back behind great lawns, but most were old and close to the street. White, with black shutters and little historic plaques, some dating them back to the 1600s. I wondered which had been his. A number of them matched his description of the old Knott house, but none said Knott, at least not that I could make out from the car – several were discreetly hidden behind hedges of hemlock and clumps of lilac.

High ran a half mile or so before it ended at Farmington Avenue. I took this to the outskirts of town where there was a modern complex of antiseptic concrete buildings. The library was directly across from town hall. Its doors whooshed open by themselves.

I was hoping to hook up with the family lawyer, Peter Seymour. I'd had no luck reaching him from New York – information had no listing for him in Farmington or any of the surrounding towns, including Hartford. It had been several years since he'd handled the Noyes estate. Could be he'd retired to Hobe Sound, or died. But if he was still practicing, he was probably still somewhere in Connecticut. Lawyers tend not to leave a state after they've passed its bar exam.

I worked my way through every Connecticut phone book they had there, and they had them all. It's not a very big state. No Peter Seymour, attorney-at-law, anywhere.

The town clerk's office was over in the town hall basement. Small-town lawyers are in and out of the clerk's office filing property deeds and estate records. I figured someone there would know what had happened to him.

The town clerk was a tall, erect woman with blue hair and Marilyn Quayle teeth. She'd never heard of any Peter Seymour, but she'd only been on the job six months. She suggested I contact the local bar association. I did, from a pay phone out in the corridor. They advised me there was no such member of the local bar. I asked them to look back in their records a few years. They did. No attorney named Peter Seymour had practiced law in Farmington in the past twenty years.

Frustrated, I went back across to the library. Again, the doors whooshed.

One entire room upstairs, the Farmington Room, was devoted exclusively to local history – from the town's original settlement back in 1639 right up to the present. There were glassed-in bookcases, framed oil portraits, maps. Quite dignified, all of it. I parked myself in there. I wanted to read up on Cam's fine old family – on his mother, Jane Abbott Knott, on her father and grandfather, both clergymen, on her great-grandfather, Judge Samuel Knott, a chief justice of the state of Connecticut. Maybe it wasn't so fine. Maybe there was something Cam hadn't told me about his Yankee bloodlines. Maybe that was why I'd been sent here.

A local scholar had compiled a nine-volume history of the town, which contained an exhaustive site-by-site account of each home in the historic district – its architectural history, the sequence of its ownership, family trees of those owners, births, marriages, careers, deaths. Nice light reading. The volumes were organized by street name and house number, not by family name, since those changed so many times through the years. I didn't know the house number of Cam's home on High Street, but the Baker and Tilden 1869 Atlas of the Inner Village was included to show me how High Street had looked then. There had been a hotel on the westside corner of High and Farmington, the William Whitman. Four residences had existed on the west side of High, belonging to Hurlburt, Gallager, Manion, and Westcott. The Congregational parsonage was at the other end of the block at Mountain. Across from it was the E. L. Hart Boarding School for Boys, and homes belonging to Whitman, Miles, Badwell, Cahill, and Porter. No Knott residence. Apparently, it had been under a different name then – a Knott daughter who had married. So I plowed through the history of each of those historic homes on High Street. Followed the family trees of all of those families, read of their prosperity, their sickness, their joy, their sorrow. The Revolution. The Civil War. The First World War. The Second. There was enough there to make for a James Michener novel. Certainly the prose was just as turgid. I read and I read. I read until my eyes were bleary and my temples throbbed.

I read until I was quite certain that no home on High Street in Farmington had ever belonged to or ever been associated with the Knott family.

I kept searching. I looked through book after book about the founding and development of Farmington, its prominent citizens past and present. I examined indexes and maps. I stayed in that damned room four hours, and here is what I learned: There had been no local clerics named Knott. There had been no chief justice of the Connecticut Supreme Court named Samuel Knott. There had been no family in the entire history of the village of Farmington named Knott. Period.

Dazed and confused, I reeled back over to town hall and down the steps. It was a discreet town. The town clerk wouldn't let me look at the birth records. Insisted they were confidential. I suggested they were public record. Public record or not, I couldn't see them. I asked if there were any vital records I *could* see.

Deaths.

Through the vault door I went. Into the chilly fireproof records room . . . Noyes, Sawyer, who had hung himself in the cellar of the old house on High Street . . . *Don't take this the wrong way, Son* . . . Noyes, Jane Knott, who had flown off to have dirty fun with Smilin' Jack and crashed in the White Mountains.

There was no record of either death.

I went outside and got in the Jaguar and sat there. Now I knew why the note had told me to come to Farmington.

Cameron Sheffield Noyes didn't exist.

Merilee and Lulu were still out when I got back to the Bee and Thistle. I went straight up to my room and stretched out on my bed. I wanted to get off my feet – the sands under them were shifting too rapidly.

Who was Cam Noyes? Why had he made up his life story? Had anything he'd told me been true? Who had sent me here? What did this have to do with Skitsy's murder?

I phoned down to the bar for a mug of Double Diamond dark English draft. Then I called Cam. Vic answered.

"How is he?" I asked.

"Pretty well, Hoag," Vic replied in his droning monotone. "We did five miles this morning. Attended Miss Held's funeral. I'll put him on. He's been anxious to – "

"Coach!" cried Cam, wrenching the phone away from him. "Coach, I want to do it. I want to tell the truth. All the way, just like you said."

"Glad to hear it, Cameron," I said quietly.

"You were right," he went on, sounding boyish and up. "As long as I hide from what I did that night, I'll never be able to get on with my life and work. I've got to come clean."

"That you do. And what does Boyd say about this?"

"Haven't told him. I'm the one who's in charge of my life, not him. Some cop came by today after Skitsy's funeral."

"Was he short and muscular?"

"Very."

"That's him."

"Huh?"

"What did he want?"

"To know how well I knew Skitsy. Where I was when she died."

"Did you tell him?"

"No."

"Why not?"

"I just didn't feel like it."

I sipped my ale. "I'll be back tomorrow afternoon, Cameron. We have lots to talk about."

"Where are you, anyway?"

"Connecticut," I replied, waiting for his reaction.

"What are you doing out there?" he asked, trying not to sound uneasy. He failed.

I wanted to say who the fuck are you? Why have you been lying to me? I wanted to say that friends don't do that to each other. I stopped myself. I wanted more facts first. I hoped I'd get them in the morning. "Working some things out with my ex-wife," I answered.

"Ah, good," he said cheerfully. "Coach?"

"Yes, Cameron?"

"Are you proud of me?"

"Proud doesn't begin to describe it."

I hung up and called my apartment. Charlie Chu answered.

"Oh, hi," she said warmly. "I was just doing some sketches, and they're going great. It's really helping my head being here, Hoagy. I appreciate it."

"No problem."

"I love your skylight. If you ever decide to move, let me know. It's a darling place."

"That's one word for it." I pictured her there, sitting by the phone with her glasses sliding down her nose. I liked picturing her there. "Any messages?"

"Very."

"Very what?"

"He called a little while ago. Lieutenant Very. He seems real nice. We talked about his ulcer for a while."

"And . . . ?"

"I told him he should eat a lot of rice."

"No, what did he want?"

"For you to call him." She gave me his number. Then she lowered her voice. "I . . . I've been thinking about you, Hoagy. I mean, being surrounded by your things and sleeping in your bed and everything. I feel like I'm getting a special guided tour of you."

I left that one alone.

"I like what I see, Hoagy. A lot."

"Careful, or you'll turn my head."

"What do you think I'm trying to do?" she said. Then she giggled and hung up.

Romaine Very was mad at me.

"What the fuck ya doing in Connecticut, dude?" he demanded harshly when I got through to him.

I could hear the din of the precinct house in the background. "Working. Why?"

"I like everybody at arm's length, that's why."

"I had no idea, Lieutenant. I still have a book to turn in, you see."

"Ya shoulda said something to me about it."

"I apologize. I had no idea I'd be hurting your feelings."

"You're not hurting my – "

"I understand you phoned."

"Yeah, I phoned," he replied, popping his gum. "Your honeypot sounds supernice."

"She's not my – "

"A lot of ladies, they find out you're a cop, they talk to you like you're some sack of shit. Not her. Said she's an artist. Doesn't Cam Noyes live with an artist, too?"

"What was it you wanted, Lieutenant?"

"We found Miss Held's dress this morning. The yellow one."

"Where was it?"

"Stuffed in a trash bin three blocks away with her bra and panties. That makes it official – it's now a murder investigation. Thought you'd wanna know."

"Thank you. That wasn't very smart, was it? Ditching the clothes nearby like that."

"No, it wasn't," he acknowledged. "They were wet."

"It rained last night," I pointed out.

"I know, but they were inside a plastic bag and the trash bin had a lid on it. None of the other trash around it was wet. Lab's checking 'em over. We'll see. Coroner's office thinks she died from the fall, period. They didn't find nothing to indicate a struggle. No scratches or finger marks, nothing under her nails. You got anything for me?"

"Me?"

"Thought maybe you was tracking something down out there."

"Nothing to do with this, Lieutenant."

"I don't know about you, dude," he grumbled. "I really don't. I mean, my head hears ya but my stomach don't." He burped. "And my stomach's usually right. When you coming back?"

"Tomorrow."

"See that ya do," he ordered. "Connecticut. I went there once."

"Oh?"

"Didn't like it. Stay with me, dude."

Merilee still wasn't back yet. It was nearly seven. I didn't know whether to be concerned or not. I decided not to be. I'd been careful not to tell anyone where we were staying.

I had another glass of draft outside on a bench by the river. The sun was setting over the tidal marshes. I watched it, and found my thoughts straying to someone fresh and cute and talented. Someone Chinese.

When the sun fell, I went inside. Miss Nash had returned. I made a dinner reservation and went upstairs. Her shower was running. Lulu was waiting for me in my room, incredibly happy to see me. Of course it was dinnertime. I put down her mackerel, had a quick shower, and stropped grandfather's pearl-handled straight-edge razor. After years of going through packages of disposable razors, I'd decided there was already enough plastic waste in the world. I now make less of it, and the shave isn't terrible as long as the blade is sharp and my hand is reasonably steady. I dressed in my double-breasted white Italian linen suit, a lavender broadcloth shirt, and a woven yellow silk tie. After I'd doused myself with Floris, I headed downstairs, where I was shown to a candlelit table on the dining porch.

Merilee joined me a few moments later. I could tell the second she entered the dining room – heads everywhere turning at the sight of her that something was very wrong. She looked beautiful enough. Her hair was up, and she had on a high-throated Victorian silk blouse, a cameo brooch, paisley skirt, and her Tanino Crisci shoes. When she sat, her cheeks glowed in the candlelight. But her back was stiff and she was chewing on her lower lip. Her eyes carefully avoided mine.

I ordered dry martinis with extra olives, and asked her if everything was okay. She said everything was absolutely, totally fine. I let it go. I learned long ago that I couldn't dig anything out of Merilee. She spills only when she's good and ready to spill. So we ate our baby lamp chops and new potatoes and pecan pie in sphinxlike silence. As soon as we were done, she said she was very tired and went directly up to her room. Lulu joined her. I had a large calvados before I headed up, too. When I got to my door, I could hear Merilee weeping behind hers. I tapped lightly on it. She told me to please go away. I went away.

Her time to spill was three a.m. That's when she and Lulu came in my room and got on my bed, and she said, "I bought a Land-Rover today."

"A Land-Rover?" I yawned and rubbed my eyes. The moonlight was slanting through the window and across the foot of the bed. She looked lovely in it as she sat there in her red flannel nightshirt, hands folded neatly in her lap.

"A dear, battered old one. It looks like something out of a Stewart Granger movie. Super for hauling things and it runs like a – "

"Hauling what things, Merilee?"

Her forehead creased. It does that when she's trying not to cry. "I-I bought an eighteen-acre farm today."

"You did what?"

"In Hadlyme. The house was built in 1736." Her words tumbled out quickly now. "It has nine rooms. Exposed beams. Wide-oak floors. Seven fireplaces. The one in the dining room has a baking oven. There's a three-story carriage barn and a duck pond and an apple orchard and the dearest, sweetest little chapel with stained-glass windows and . . ." She came up for air. "I took one look and said I'm home."

"But when did you – ?"

"I got to talking this afternoon with the folks at Goodspeed about how much theater there is around here now – them, the Ivoryton Playhouse, the National Theater for the Deaf in Chester . . . and I started thinking how nice it would be to be involved in something so decent and non-Hollywood. I could teach, direct a little. And I've always adored this area. So I drove around with a local realtor and she showed me this place and I bought it. I was afraid to say anything about it at dinner because I knew you'd tell me how impulsive and impractical I am."

"I wouldn't."

"You would. You'd get all male on me. Want to go out and survey the place yourself, strut around with your hands on your hips and – "

"I don't strut around with my – "

"And cluck at every little – "

"I don't cluck."

"And try to talk me out of it. You can't. I'm going through with it. I got a good price, and before I did a thing I checked it out first with my lawyer and my agent and my manager and my accountant and my psychic, and they all told me to go ahead." She sighed. "It's *time*, darling. To settle down, and live, and not worry anymore about meaningless things like Tony Awards." Her eyes found mine in the moonlight. "I thought the chapel would be lovely for you – in case you ever wanted to come up and . . ."

"Pray?"

"Write, you ninny. It's wonderfully quiet, and has a wood stove, and you could stay as long as you like."

"Thank you, Merilee. That's very kind."

She took my hands. "Please tell me I'm not a fool."

"You know you're not. It sounds . . . well, it sounds fantastic. Truly."

We sat there holding hands a moment on my bed.

"I have something to tell you, too," I said. "It's about Charlie."

Merilee dropped my hands. "Charlie?"

"I may start seeing her."

Merilee frowned. "I thought she was living with – "

"Moved out on him. She's staying at my place while I'm gone."

"And when you get back?"

"I don't know," I admitted. "All I know is she's the first woman I've felt something for in a long, long time. Present company excepted, of course."

"I see," she said very quietly.

"Do you have a problem with it?"

"Of course not, darling."

"Would you tell me if you did?"

"Of course not, darling." She stretched out across the bed with her head on my feet. "Oh, God, are we through?"

"Our divorce pretty much meant that, didn't it?"

"In name only."

"I thought one *married* in name only."

"I mean truly through." She gazed at me, her eyes shimmering pools. "In our hearts through."

"Do you want us to be?"

"I don't think I could stand it, darling," she confessed. "I hated it when we weren't speaking. There were so many times I reached for the phone. So many times I wanted you."

"Me, too, Merilee."

"But I also don't think I could stand *us* again, either. You have this way of making me feel like an awkward thirteen-year-old girl again, all vulnerable and misty-eyed. I'm sorry, true love just isn't for me anymore, darling. It hurts too much."

"Not if you let yourself go."

She shook her head. "I'm no longer that young or that foolish."

"Sure you are. We both are."

She smiled. "Cam Noyes has been good for you, hasn't he?"

"I seriously doubt that."

She looked over at the window dreamily. "When I was looking at the farm today, the very first thing I thought of was how . . . how nice it would be if only . . ."

"If only what, Merilee?"

She shuddered. "Nothing. Just turning into a sentimental fool, I guess."

Then she said good-night and went back across the hall to her own room.

I was already up and dressed when the plump, giggly teenager tapped on my door at dawn with my muffins and coffee. As soon as I'd eaten, I took off in the Jaguar with Lulu.

I drove north along the Connecticut River on Route 156, through marshland and forest, past the old Yankee dairy farms with their colonial farmhouses and lush green pasturage dotted with cows. There was early-morning fog, but it was lifting. I found the small marina at Hamburg Cove and rented a rowboat. It fit nose-down in the Jag with the top down and Lulu in my lap. Sort of. The state forest turnoff wasn't far. It was a dirt road, heavily rutted and still muddy from the rain. I took it slowly. After a mile or so it dead-ended at Crescent Moon Pond, which wasn't what I'd call a pond. It was a good half mile across to the dense forest on the other side. I saw no shack there. No one was out fishing.

I got the boat into the water and Lulu into her life vest. She's the only dog I've ever met who can't swim – she sinks to the bottom like a boulder. Then I pushed off and started rowing. It was very quiet out there aside from the birds and the sound of the water lapping gently against the boat. Lulu sat stiffly in the bow, weight back on her butt, front paws splayed awkwardly before her. Her large black nose quivered at the unfamiliar smells.

It wasn't until I got halfway across that I realized how Crescent Moon Pond got its name – it had a severe crook in its middle. I hadn't been looking at the other side at all, merely the bend. As I rounded it, the other side now came into view. And so did the shack, set back in the trees.

The mooring was rotted out, the footpath up to it overgrown. The wooden steps to the from porch were wobbly. So was the porch. The front door swung open and shut in the breeze off the pond. I heard something scurrying around inside. This time Lulu took charge

– tore headlong into the shack, snarling ferociously. She flushed out an entire family of field mice. Then came strutting back to me, immensely pleased with herself.

"Good work, Lulu."

Inside there was a black cast-iron wood stove, scarred pine table and chairs, an empty oil lantern, a few kitchen rudiments, piles of empty beer cans. Cigarette butts had been ground into the bare wooden floor. The tiny bedroom off the main room had a stained, mildewed mattress in it, and a pine dresser. Out back I could see a well with a hand pump, and an outhouse.

I had seen enough already, but when I went back into the main room and noticed what was hanging on the wall over the table I was convinced: It was the framed, mounted snakeskin. The one Smilin' Jack had found in one of his wading boots.

It was just as Cam had described it to me.

The shack was real.

Old Lyme's town hall was a stately old white building down Lyme Street from the Bee and Thistle. It being Saturday, they were open until noon. Locals were lined up at the front desk for their summer beach permits.

The town clerk here was round and white-haired, and a lot jollier than the one in Farmington. She told me all property deeds were recorded and filed by index number. To find out the index number you looked it up in the index book under the deed holder's name. Not surprisingly, I found no deed holder named Cameron Sheffield Noyes. I asked the clerk what to do if I knew where the property was but not who owned it. She sent me to the assessor's office to find out who'd been paying taxes on it.

The town assessor was a gruff, impatient old Yankee with two hearing aids and a white crew cut that he'd no doubt had since before they staged a comeback. I had barely begun to describe the shack at Crescent Moon Pond when he cut me off, pulled a surveyor's map book down off a shelf, and began searching through it, licking his thumb as he went. When he found what he wanted, he dove into his files, harrumphed, and presented me with a name: Ferris Rush, Jr., c/o the Boyd Samuels Agency in New York, New York.

Hello, Ferris. Wish I could say I was pleased to meet you.

Back in the clerk's office I tried the name Ferris Rush, Jr., in the index book. This time I got a number, and a look at the deed. Ferris Rush, Jr., of New York City had taken title to the shack on Crescent Moon Pond a little less than two years before, when he turned twenty-one. The property had been held in trust for him for the previous eight years by Ina Duke Rush of Port Arthur, Texas, received from the estate of John Rush of Essex, Connecticut, for no financial consideration.

I still didn't have a lot of the answers. But now I did know something I hadn't known throughout this whole damned collaboration.

I knew what questions to ask.

CHAPTER
THIRTEEN

Charlie had brought in my mail. Bills. Yushie gadget catalogues. And another, even sterner, handwritten note from the secretary of the Racquet Club. I was really going to have to do something about that.

The bed was neatly made. Her clothes were folded in a wicker, rope-handled trunk that she'd stashed in the closet. An extra toothbrush and a tube of Tom's organic toothpaste were in the bathroom. A gauzy nightshirt hung from the hook on the back of the door.

A most unobtrusive little roommate. Hardly knew she was there, aside from the cloying smell of oil paint in the air. And from the kitchen. An easel stood in the middle of it on a drop cloth, directly under the skylight. Her paints and brushes were crowded onto the counter, along with spray cans and cements and rough charcoal sketches. Boxes of broken crockery and old bottles and magazines were piled up against one wall, her portfolios stacked against them. This invasion of her turf made Lulu uneasy. She nosed warily amongst the stuff, tail between her legs, as if she expected to encounter a cache of Mexican jumping beans.

Another nude was in progress on Charlie's easel – this one a study of a young man. Her style was primitive. So was her subject. He was heavily muscled and exuded a raw, crude power. From the neck down, that is. She'd pasted the head of the Gerber's baby on his shoulders.

It was Cam Noyes, or Ferris Rush, or whatever the hell you wanted to call him. I had a few choice names in mind myself. So, evidently, did she.

She'd left me a note by the phone, her handwriting square and careful. *H – I'll be hanging around Rat's Nest till six. Call me when you get back. We'll go to lunch on my break at two. Hope I haven't messed up your kitchen too much. I've missed you – C*

I was really going to have to do something about that, too.

I glanced at grandfather's Rolex. It was just past one. I called Rat's Nest and left word with the clerk at the desk that I'd be there at two. Then I showered and dressed and called Vic.

"He's taking his nap now, Hoag," he reported. "We did our five miles and our errands and now he's out cold. That contractor actually showed up while we were out. Put some dry wall up in the kitchen, then split. Nervy bastard was in and out before I could give him a piece of my mind."

"They have an uncanny instinct for that," I said. "They flit from job to job all day long, keeping as many as four customers unhappy at once."

"I checked out that adult motel Cam said he went to the night of Miss Held's death. He was there, all right, he and Miss Moscowitz. From eight until four the next morning. I found two White Castles on Ridgewood Avenue they might have stopped at on their way out, when Miss Held was pushed. Nobody remembered them at either place. That's not a good sign. They're both recognizable celebrities."

"That car of his doesn't exactly whisper, either."

"She was with us last night – Miss Moscowitz," said Vic. "She's some kind of handful. A little strident for my own personal taste, but – "

"She stay the entire night?"

"She'd already left for the studio when I got up at six," he replied. "I figured it was okay, her staying here. She's encouraging him to stay off the coke. And better they're here together under this roof than out who knows where."

"I agree."

"He's starting to make some progress, Hoag. The last couple of days he's had a real sparkle in his eyes. He's practically a new man."

"I'll say he is."

"Excuse me?"

"I think we should keep up our guard on Merilee."

"I'll leave right now, stay with her until tonight's curtain. Can you get down here and take over Cam?"

"There's a lunch date I'd like to keep first, unless . . ."

"No, no, go ahead," Vic insisted. "He's fast asleep. She didn't let him get much rest last night, believe me. He'll be fine here by himself for an hour or two. And of more use to you afterward. Enjoy your meal, Hoag."

I caught a cab downtown.

Charlie was up there on her canvas waiting for me, blue from head to toe. Blue Monday. All except for the red stain where the bowie knife had been plunged into her stomach right up to its brass hilt.

Two blue-and-whites and some unmarked sedans were parked out from. The steel door was wide open with a yellow police cordon across it. A uniformed cop stood guard. Gawkers crowded the sidewalk.

At the reception desk a plainclothesman was interviewing the clerk with the Buddy Holly glasses. She was shaking her head and sobbing.

A half dozen cops were fanned around Blue Monday, staring, murmuring grimly to each other. They could have been admirers at an exhibition, except for the one who was dusting the handle of the knife for fingerprints.

I stood there staring, too. At the blood. At the eyes that didn't move or blink. My chest felt heavy. I was thinking about that extra toothbrush in my bathroom and those neatly folded clothes in the wicker trunk. I was thinking about what might have happened that was never going to happen now. Not ever.

I stood there staring at the bowie knife. His bowie knife.

Lulu shifted restlessly at my feet.

One of the cops was watching me. It was Romaine Very. His bike was leaning against the lumpy fifteen-thousand-dollar statue. They hadn't sold it yet, for some reason. He motioned for me to step outside with him. I took one more look at Charlie. Then I did.

"Yo, like, how come you keep showing up at murder scenes, dude?" he demanded, gum popping, one knee quaking. "I mean, it's getting a little *funny*."

"It's getting hysterical."

He belched and made a face. "I hate looking at dead chicks. Especially pretty ones."

"Can you tell me what happened?"

He looked up at me, head nodding rhythmically, eyes narrow slits. He took his time. Finally he shrugged, yanked a pad out of the back pocket of his jeans, and opened it. "The clerk, one Rita Gersh of Great Neck, Long Island, stepped out for a break at two. Went to hit the cash machine at her bank, get herself a sandwich and coffee. Miss Chu, the victim, usually went out for the sandwiches, on account she liked to get out and stretch her legs, y'know? But today she was expecting someone for lunch."

"That was me. We had a date."

"I know. Miss Gersh said you called. I was kinda hoping you'd volunteer it – fact is, we was just about to come looking for you, dude."

"I didn't do it."

"Maybe not," he conceded, working his gum with a hard tightening of his jaws. "But you look real good for it."

"Please tell me the rest."

"Before she left, Miss Gersh helped Miss Chu down so she could use the powder room before her date arrived. Before *you* arrived. Miss Gersh hung a sign on the door saying she'd be back in ten minutes. She left the door unlocked. Whoever did it worked fast. He was most likely watching the door for his chance. When he saw Miss Gersh split, he took it. Stuck her with a vintage bowie. The genuine article. Don't appear to be any prints on it. It was wiped clean. No sign of forced entry at the front door. Someone knocked and Miss Chu let him in."

"So it was someone she knew?"

"Pretty much had to be. Miss Gersh says she wouldn't have let any customers in."

"Did the surveillance camera record anything?"

He shook his head. "No tape in it. It's just a monitor."

The local TV news crews were showing up now, crowding the front door, barraging the cop there with questions. We stepped farther away from them.

"How did she get back up on the canvas?" I asked Very.

"Her killer put her up there."

"Before or after he stabbed her?"

"After. We found blood in the middle of the room. We're assuming it's hers. Gotta check it."

"Why did he do that – put her back up?"

He shrugged. "Make some kind of statement, maybe. Who the hell knows?"

"You'd have to be pretty strong to lift up a body like that, wouldn't you?"

"About as strong as you'd have to be to toss Skitsy Held off of her terrace."

"You think it's the same person?"

"Don't know, dude. I did get the lab test results on those clothes of hers we found."

"And?"

"They had Wisk on 'em."

"Wisk?"

"It's a liquid detergent. Y'know, ring around the collar?"

"I know what Wisk is, Lieutenant. What does it mean?"

He shifted uncomfortably there on the sidewalk. "It means her killer was downstairs in the laundry room doing a load of wash while we was there. It means the fucker left *after* we did."

"You didn't check the laundry room at the time?"

"We had no reason to," he replied sharply. "It read suicide, remember?"

"But how did he get in?"

"We don't know," he snapped, nostrils flaring. "We blew it, okay! That what you wanna hear? You happy?"

"Not particularly."

He shoved the notepad back into his jeans, softened. "She was the one I talked to on the phone at your apartment, wasn't she?"

"She was."

"Seemed real nice."

"She was."

"Lived with Cam Noyes, didn't she?"

"Until recently."

He nodded away. "How'd you figure in that?"

"I didn't. I let her use my place while I was away. That's all."

"So she dumped him?" he asked, smelling a motive.

"He's been seeing someone else."

"That'd be Delilah Moscowitz, huh?"

"Why, yes. How did you – ?"

"I staked out his house last night for the helluv it. She stayed over. Noyes wouldn't by any chance own a bowie knife, would he?"

I hesitated. It didn't make any sense. He'd *wanted* Charlie to leave him. Or so he'd said. *Had* he killed her? Killed them both? How much more did I owe him? How much farther out on the limb was I prepared to go for this man who'd done nothing but lie to me?

Very was staring up at me, eyes narrowed. "A bowie knife?" he repeated.

"I wouldn't know," I finally replied.

"I see," he said doubtfully, popping his gum. "Been doing some more checking on you, dude. Your other ghosting gigs."

"Learn anything interesting?"

"Yeah. People have this way of dying around you."

"You noticed."

"Of course I noticed. I'm a detective. Noticing things is my business. You got something against me?"

"Absolutely not, Lieutenant."

"Then how come you're not being straight with me? You haven't been straight with me from the start."

I left that one alone.

Very shook his head. "I oughta take you in. I really oughta. Only you're a paddle. You'll do me more good out here, stirring up the water. I'm putting you on a tight leash, understand? If I feel like yanking, I yank. Hard."

"Thanks for the warning, Lieutenant. Anything else?"

He belched. "Yeah, don't leave town again."

"I wouldn't think of it."

I looked around for Lulu. I didn't see her. I found her inside with the cops. They were ignoring her. They shouldn't have been. She was sneezing.

The Loveboat wasn't out front, and he wasn't in the house. His clothes had been cleared out of his closet. His suitcases were gone.

He was gone.

I sat down on his bed, took a deep breath, and let it out slowly. I had no choice now. I had to believe it. The man I'd been working with these past weeks was a murderer.

I reached for the phone on the nightstand to call Very and tell him. But I couldn't make myself dial the phone.

I had to find him myself first. Had to ask him who he really was. Had to ask him why. Only then could I turn him in. Step away. Lick my wounds. I never said I was smart. In fact, when it comes to getting involved with my celebrity subjects, I definitely am not.

The contractor had shown up again. The new kitchen sink was in now. Out back, the bluestone patio had finally been laid in its bed of cement. It came out real nice.

Too bad there wasn't anybody living there anymore to appreciate it.

When all else failed me there was still Bobby Short. I took in his midnight show at the Hotel Carlyle. It's what I do when I can't see life's bright side no matter how damned hard I look for it. There's just something about the way Bobby has with Cole Porter, about the sharp brine of the caviar and the tart cold of the champagne that cures what ails me. Usually. Not tonight. Tonight I kept thinking about how he shouldn't have done it. Any of it. Tonight I kept thinking about how big a jerk I was. I should take out an ad: *This friend for hire. Give him*

a table and he'll follow you anywhere. Tonight I kept thinking about Charlie, and the way her glasses slid down her nose.

Bobby was playing "I Get a Kick Out of You" when there was a rustle next to me, and the scent of avocado oil. It was Merilee, in a shimmering white strapless dress. Her hair was brushed out long and golden and she had on one of her old trademark white silk headbands. She slid into the banquette across from me.

"What are you doing here?" I asked as Lulu whooped and licked her fingers.

The waiter brought her a glass and poured her some champagne. She heaped some caviar on a wedge of toast, ate half of it, and fed Lulu the rest, almost losing a finger in the process. Lulu has mighty expensive taste for someone who eats canned mackerel.

"I'm taking in the rest of this show and this caviar with you, darling," she said, sipping her champagne. "Then I'm taking you to the Cat Club on East Thirteenth, where they have a dance floor and a seventeen-piece swing band that's as loud and hot as they come. If you're still on your feet after that, and if you're good to me, I'll take you down to Ratner's and buy you a large plate of lox and onions and eggs before I deposit you at your door." She poured herself some more champagne. "But first I'd switch to single malt if I were you. I understand the barman has a fine old Glenmorangie."

"Merilee . . . ?"

"Yes, darling?"

I got lost in her green eyes for a moment. "You're not the worst person I've ever known."

She smiled and took my hand. "That's positively the second-nicest thing you've ever said to me, Hoagy."

"What's the nicest?"

" 'I felt that one all the way down to my toenails.' "

"Why, Merilee, you're getting awfully frisky in your gender years."

"It's true, I am. Isn't it odd?"

I got the waiter over and ordered a double Glenmorangie. I downed it in one gulp when it came, and ordered another.

Lulu didn't growl at me.

C H A P T E R
F O U R T E E N

(Tape #1 with Delilah Moscowitz recorded May 16 in her apartment on Twelfth St. Decor is modern, expensive, impersonal. Wears black sleeveless jumpsuit, sweat socks, no makeup. Hair is tied in a tight ponytail.)

Moscowitz: You look like you were out all night drinking.

Hoag: Only because I was, Red.

Moscowitz: I didn't sleep a wink either, thinking about Cam. The police were here asking me all sorts of questions, like they think I know where he went or something.

Hoag: Was it Very?

Moscowitz: Very what?

Hoag: Lt. Romaine Very.

Moscowitz: Is he gorgeous? *(no response)* Has an ulcer?

Hoag: Yes.

Moscowitz: It was Very. They know it was Cam's knife now. They dug up a *Rolling Stone* photo of him cleaning his fingernails with it. Same markings and everything. Can I get you more cranberry juice?

Hoag: This will be fine.

Moscowitz: Sorry I don't keep anything else in the house. I'm a compulsive eater – whatever's here I go through. Where's your little dog?

Hoag: My ex-wife gets her on Sundays.

Moscowitz: Just like child custody. How cute.

Hoag: Do you?

Moscowitz: Do I what?

Hoag: Know where Cam went.

Moscowitz: How would I know?

Hoag: Look, I'm not the police. I'm on his side. If you want to help him, tell me what you know. Have you heard from him?

Moscowitz: No, damn it. All I know is he's gone and they're after him and . . . promise you won't tell the police this?

Hoag: We don't pool information.

Moscowitz: I'm pissed as hell that he didn't take me with him.

Hoag: You'd have gone?

Moscowitz: Are you shitting me, jack? The man I love is a hunted desperado. He's *front page news.*

Hoag: He's a murderer.

Moscowitz: I don't care. I'd give anything to be on the run with him.

Hoag: Just like Bonnie and Clyde?

Moscowitz: Better. My parents wouldn't shit bricks over Bonnie and Clyde.

Hoag: I guess you got to know him pretty well.

Moscowitz: I guess.

Hoag: Did he ever talk to you about his childhood?

Moscowitz: Never. He's peculiar that way. Most men I've known like to unload after they unload. Not him.

Hoag: Does the name Ferris Rush mean anything to you?

Moscowitz: Ferris Rush? Is that a man or a woman?

Hoag: A man.

Moscowitz: No. Never heard it before. Look, I don't mean to rush you, but I have to finish packing.

Hoag: Going out on tour, I understand.

Moscowitz: Yes, I'm doing the Carson show on Tuesday. Local L.A. TV and radio. Then San Francisco. Then I work my way back across the country. Twenty-one cities in eighteen days. A major grind.

Hoag: Any chance you're meeting up with Cam somewhere along the line?

Moscowitz: Only if he gets hold of me and says come.

Hoag: And you will?

Moscowitz: I will.

Hoag: Even if it hurts your career?

Moscowitz: I couldn't care less about my career.

Hoag: He told me the two of you went to Ozone Park the night Skitsy was killed. Got to the Galaxy Motel at about eight. That part checks out. What doesn't is where he was an hour earlier when she was thrown off her terrace.

Moscowitz: We were eating at a White Castle.

Hoag: So he said.

Moscowitz: It's the truth.

Hoag: You're claiming he didn't kill Skitsy?

Moscowitz: Look, maybe he killed Charlie. It sure looks like he did. But he was with me when Skitsy died. I swear it.

Hoag: I see. You know, it's funny how alibis work. You're his for the time of her death. But you can also turn that equation around – he's *yours.*

Moscowitz: What's that supposed to mean?

Hoag: Pretty strong, aren't you?

Moscowitz: My coach at the club said I bench press more weight than half the men he has.

Hoag: You'd do anything for Cam, wouldn t you?

Moscowitz: Yes, I would.

Hoag: Would you kill for him?

Moscowitz: (silence) I didn't throw Skitsy off of that terrace.

Hoag: Were you happy with her as your editor?

Moscowitz: Of course.

Hoag: No creative differences?

Moscowitz: Skitsy Held put this reporter on the best-seller list. That has a way of smoothing over all sorts of creative differences – not that I'm saying we had any.

Hoag: You would have if she'd found out about you and Cam.

Moscowitz: That's true.

Hoag: Had she?

Moscowitz: Not that I know of.

Hoag: What did Cam tell you about the two of them?

Moscowitz: Very little, except that she liked to be tied up.

Hoag: Nothing about why he continued to see her?

Moscowitz: I guess he liked doing the tieing. I wasn't thrilled about her, but I didn't consider her any sort of rival. It was Charlie who was his main squeeze. You already know how she and I got along.

Hoag: I guess you were pretty happy when Charlie gave up on him.

Moscowitz: Sure I was.

Hoag: Any idea how Skitsy felt about her?

Moscowitz: Cam said she never found her particularly threatening.

Hoag: You she would have found?

Moscowitz: Me she'd have freaked over. But what's the point in going on about it? It never happened.

Hoag: Just thinking out loud. It's kind of interesting how the three of you were all involved with the same man, and how the two of them are dead, and you're not.

Moscowitz: You don't actually think *I* did away with them, do you?

Hoag: I think you were at Rat's Nest yesterday. I think you were there right around the time Charlie was murdered.

Moscowitz: I-I wasn't. I've never even been near the place.

Hoag: Don't kid a kidder, Red.

Moscowitz: What makes you so sure I was there?

Hoag: I have my methods.

Moscowitz: *(silence)* Do the police know?

Hoag: Not from me they don't.

Moscowitz: All right . . . Cam trusted you. I'll trust you. *(pause)* I went to see her.

Hoag: What for?

Moscowitz: So there'd be no hard feelings. She and Cam still had to work together on their book, and I wanted it to go well. I did it for his sake.

Hoag: It had nothing to do with her threatening to cut you if she ever caught you near him again?

Moscowitz: She didn't scare me.

Hoag: How did your visit go?

Moscowitz: Shockingly well, though I must admit it was a little weird having this serious conversation with a blue mannequin. I told her how sorry I was it had happened, and how I'd never meant to hurt her. She said she understood and that she was fine. That she'd already met someone else who she really liked. She thanked me for coming by, and apologized for what happened in Sammy's. And then I left.

Hoag: What time?

Moscowitz: I don't remember exactly. I got there about one. She was alive when I left. The clerk saw me go. Ask her. Go ahead.

Hoag: That's for the police to do. Not my concern.

Moscowitz: What *is* your concern?

Hoag: Cam Noyes.

Moscowitz: Why?

Hoag: I work for him.

Moscowitz: That's all?

Hoag: He's a friend. He's in trouble.

Moscowitz: I think I'd like to have you as a friend myself.

Hoag: We wouldn't stay friends for long.

Moscowitz: Meaning we'd become enemies or meaning we'd become lovers?

Hoag: One of the above.

Moscowitz: Agreed. . . . Charlie didn't seem at all upset when I left. I really don't know what happened between them to set him off. I guess she made him mad about something and he lost control.

Hoag: I don't buy that. He took the knife there with him from home.

Moscowitz: So?

Hoag: So that's what they call premeditation – he went there

planning to kill Charlie. What I can't figure out is why.
(end tape)

(Tape #1 with Boyd Samuels recorded May 17 in his office in the Flatiron Building.)

Samuels: This place has been a frigging madhouse. Cops, reporters, TV. Everybody wants to know where he is. How the fuck should I know? He's gone. Wigged out, the poor fucker – don't say it. I know you warned me. And I didn't listen to you, and I feel like shit about it, okay? *(pause)* Think he did in Skitsy, too?

Hoag: So it would appear.

Samuels: Man, when he breaks it off with a chick he makes it permanent, huh?

Hoag: Possibly he did it to keep her from talking to me about how he'd hit that busload of kids. That makes some sense. But then he went ahead and told me about it himself the next morning. That doesn't.

Samuels: You know about the bus?

Hoag: I encouraged him to put it in the book.

Samuels: You *what?*

Hoag: He couldn't stand holding it in anymore. He was prepared to go to jail for it if he had to.

Samuels: Why the fuck didn't he mention any of this to me?

Hoag: Doubtless because he thought you'd talk him out of it. I don't suppose *you* did Skitsy in. To protect him, I mean.

Samuels: Me? *(laughs)* I'm an agent, amigo. The telephone is my bayonet. I'd swear the law was following me though. Maybe I'm just being paranoid.

Hoag: You're not,

Samuels: You, too?

Hoag: Yes.

Samuels: Well, they can forget it. I'm not making it easy for them to catch him. They're getting zilch from me.

Hoag: Meaning you know something?

Samuels: (silence) Turn off that recorder a second.

Hoag: (rustling noise) Okay, it's off.

Samuels: Okay . . . We have heard from him.

Hoag: Where is he? What did he say?

Samuels: Todd talked to him. I was talking to Ovitz on the coast. By the time I got off the line, he'd split. He was at a gas station somewhere in Mount Vernon.

Hoag: What's he doing there?

Samuels: How should I know? He's on the run. He called to say he was sorry to bring all of this down on me. And on you, too. He mentioned you.

Hoag: He's doing himself no good. He should turn himself in.

Samuels: You and I know that, amigo. But it's his life. His decision. I'm not turning him in. They keep asking me if I know where his financial records are, since they turned up zilch at the house. I told them no. I didn't tell them that everything – tax records, bank statements – is kept right here. Let 'em search the place. Nail me for obstructing justice. I don't care. I owe him that much.

Hoag: Mind if I turn the recorder back on now?

Samuels: Sure. Go ahead.

Hoag: (rustling noise) I want to talk about Ferris Rush.

Samuels: (silence) Shit. You know about that, too, huh?

Hoag: I know very little about anything. All I know is that Cam Noyes doesn't exist. Nor does his family tree.

Samuels: Okay . . . Ferris Rush is his real name. I guess you figured out that much already. The two of us made up the name Cameron Sheffield Noyes in college when he started modeling. We thought it suited his look better. Give him the right sort of image, you know? And gradually, he's sort of invented a past to go with the name.

Hoag: All of it?

Samuels: The Farmington part, for sure.

Hoag: That explains why he doesn't have any family photographs.

Samuels: My favorite part is the bit about the father hanging himself. That weird suicide note and everything. He's a born storyteller.

Hoag: He certainly is. And to think he told me he was suffering from writer's block. Hell, he and I have been writing his second novel all along, haven't we?

Samuels: Hey, look, it's not such a big deal. He's no different than a million other performers with stage names and made-up backgrounds, is he?

Hoag: I suppose not. Only, I don't do windows or heavy cleaning or bogus memoirs.

Samuels: I know. That's why we didn't take you into our confidence. We knew you wouldn't do it, and we wanted you. No hard feelings, huh?

Hoag: What did you guys think, that I wouldn't check any of his stories out? That I'd accept it all at face value?

Samuels: You would have if the shit hadn't hit the fan.

Hoag: And if somebody hadn't tipped me off. Sent me to Farmington.

Samuels: No shit? Who did that?

Hoag: The same person who's been trying to get me off of this project from the beginning. I wish I knew who it was, and how it fits in with him killing Skitsy and Charlie.

Samuels: I don't know anything about that, Hoag.

Hoag: You wouldn't be scamming me now, would you, amigo?

Samuels: I'm not, I swear. Listen, Cam's publisher called me first thing this morning, salivating. They want to get the book into print fast. Are you in?

Hoag: Only if you give me the whole story – his real background, how you made him up and marketed him. I can put it together with the tapes I already have, and with Charlie's illustrations. It should make for interesting reading.

Samuels: Interesting? Shit, we'll nuke the best-seller list! You want the real story, crank up your recorder. I'll give it to you. No point in hiding it now. It's all going to come out at his trial – assuming he's caught, and he will be.

Hoag: Good point. And this way you get fifteen percent of the action, right?

Samuels: You're wrong about me. I'm his friend. Always have been. . . . Ferris Rush is poor white trash. Grew up an only child in a run-down shack on the outskirts of Port Arthur, Texas. His dad, Ferris senior, is an itinerant oil rigger, sign painter, carpenter, drunk, and full-time douchebag. Killed a guy once in a bar fight. Spent some time in jail for it when Ferris was a baby. Grandpa Rush did some time, too, for robbery. That bowie knife was his. Probably stole it off some rich guy . . . His mom is a beautician. She and his dad got married when they were sixteen, for the usual reason.

Hoag: That would be Ina Duke Rush?

Samuels: Yeah. He sort of likes his mom. Stayed in touch with her after he ran away from home. Not anymore, I don't think. But for a while there she remained his legal guardian. He ran away when he was twelve. Headed north with cowshit between his toes and an accent you could cut with a knife – sorry, poor choice of words. He ran because his father beat him. He ran because all he could see down the road was him ending up no different. His dad's brother, Jack, had been in the Navy a long time, working on submarines at the Groton sub base. When he got out, he took a job repairing pleasure boats at an Essex boatyard. Jack wasn't much more of a bargain than his brother – he drank, too, and didn't have any money. But he could put Ferris in touch with people who did. So Ferris moved in with him and set about finding his future. That's something he's never had much trouble doing. Even when he was barely into his teens he was six feet tall and well built, with the wavy blond hair and blue eyes. Older women have always taken a hands-on interest in him. Two, in particular, have had a major impact on his life. The second, Skitsy, you already know about. The first was a woman named Maude Champion. Thanks to Uncle Jack, who had contacts around the Essex Yacht Club, Ferris landed himself a summer job crewing on a sixty-footer owned by a wealthy Farmington banker named Harrison Champion. Champion was in his early sixties. His second wife, Maude, was forty and a very proper Yankee lady – the kind who think their shit tastes like Häagen-Dazs. Former deb with lots of free time and no children of her own. The model for Jane Abbott Knott. She immediately took a quasi-maternal interest in Ferris, who was so bright and handsome and eager to improve himself. She tutored him. Helped him lose his accent. Taught him how to dress and act like a young gentleman.

Hoag: So that explains it – that self-conscious, mannered way he has. His gestures, his speech.

Samuels: Right. It's all acquired, from Maude. She taught him everything. Gave him spending money. Bought him clothes. And on or around his thirteenth birthday, she also started fucking him. . . . Now, less than a year after Ferris moved in with him, his Uncle Jack died. Liver failure. The last thing Ferris wanted was to go back to Texas. That was the last thing Maude wanted, too. She had some family money of her own that her husband didn't know about. She used it to send Ferris to Deerfield for a proper education.

Hoag: Which is where you met him.

Samuels: Yes. He was the only member of the freshman class who was already a professional gigolo. *(laughs)* Actually, Ferris was a truly amazing guy to me at age fourteen. I mean, I had some wild instincts, but I still came from a conventional suburban environment. Not Ferris. He lived strictly by his own wits and his own standards. He was like some kind of modern-day adventurer. Not that he ever bragged about it. I was his best friend. I knew he was fucking Maude, and that she, not his parents, was putting him through school. But none of the other guys knew.

Hoag: Where did he tell them he was from?

Samuels: He didn't.

Hoag: How much of what he told me about your Deerfield days together was true?

Samuels: Aside from his background, almost all of it. Him getting kicked off the football team . . .

Hoag: The suicidal binge? Did he hit that busload of kids?

Samuels: Yes, he did. But it was no profound suicidal binge. He was just loaded, that's all.

Hoag: You talked him out of turning himself in?

Samuels: It never came up. Ferris didn't even consider it. Guilt wasn't something he knew much about then. He's acquired that along the way. Now what he did eats away at him – though I guess he has some fresh sins on his mind these days. Summers he stayed in the guest room over the garage of the Champions' historic home in Farmington – the house he described to you as his own. Most of his time was spent in Essex taking care of the yacht and Maude while her husband was busy working in Hartford.

Hoag: He mentioned a Dana Hall girl named Kirsten who he fell for one summer. He said her mother broke it up.

Samuels: Half true. He met Kirsten the summer before our senior year. Her parents sailed from the Essex Yacht Club. I think it was the first and only time he's been seriously in love. Anyway, he got permission from Maude to stay overnight alone on the yacht instead of at the house. And as soon as he did, he started slipping it to Kirsten. You can't keep secrets around a small-town yacht club – everybody knew Maude was fucking Ferris behind her husband's back, and before long everybody also knew Ferris was fucking Kirsten behind Maude's. She got wind of it soon enough. Freaked out. Total jealous rage. Told him he was low-class trash. Told him he and Kirsten were through or else. He refused. She said fine, then I'm pulling the plug on you – no place to live and no Deerfield . . . Poor little Kirsten never knew what hit her . . . Ferris was never the same after that. He was very bitter. Despised Maude for what she'd made him do. And made him realize about himself. Still, he let her keep him. She paid his way into Columbia. It wasn't until he was making enough modeling to support himself that he finally, once and for all, told her to fuck off. But I think he's always had this need for a mother figure, because it wasn't long before he'd found himself another Maude in Skitsy. . . . He did well at modeling. Made righteous bucks at it. Could have become a superstar if he'd wanted. Gone into acting even. The ladies loved him. But he didn't like it. Kept saying he felt like some kind of show dog. To keep himself sane he started keeping a journal of all the weird, strange shit we came in contact with freshman year instead of going to class – the clubs, the models, the coke. He made me read them. Asked me if they were any good. I honestly didn't know. I was no literary scholar. I'm still not. I told him he ought to show them to Professor Tanner Marsh – if someone like Tanner Marsh says you have talent, then you have talent. I mean, literature is not like the hundred-yard dash. There's no stopwatch. There's only the master opinion-shapers like Tanner. If he says you're a genius, then you are one. I swear if you got him to call a book of completely blank pages a "major redefinition of abstract minimalism in modern American literature," you could sell fifty thousand copies at $17.95. It's all bullshit – I'm the first to admit it. But you need people like Tanner if you want to get a book off the ground. That and the right image. Like with Cam Noyes and *Bang*. I wanted people to think reading it was synonymous with a hip, dangerous good time. And they did, not so much because of its content but because of the public life Cam Noyes leads the people he hangs out with, the women he fucks, the clothes he wears, what he eats, drinks, smokes. I wasn't selling literature. I was selling *attitude*.

Hoag: In other words, you promoted it like a bottle of cologne with him as its spokesman: The Man from *Bang*.

Samuels: Go ahead and laugh. Until we came along, a publisher's idea of publicity was to take out an ad in the *Times*. I put Cam Noyes in jeans commercials. I put a wine cooler in his hand. I put him on MTV. And why not? He's not just an author. He's a spokesman for an entire generation. I know the old fucks in tweeds think that it isn't dignified, that it cheapens literature. To me it's bringing publishing into the modern age. It's bringing new readers to your product. I'm doing it with Delilah now. Starting next week she's national TV spokeswoman for a new feminine hygiene spray – sassy but tasteful. There's nothing undignified about it at all. It's good, sound business.

Hoag: And the way you got Ferris out of his contract with Skitsy – was that good, sound business, too?

Samuels: I don't apologize for that. I needed a loophole so I manufactured one. And hey, there were no hard feelings between Skitsy and me. She took her hat off to me for outsmarting her. That's why I let her have Delilah. That was me taking my hat off to her. Her company's going to make millions off of Delilah. You just watch that chick take off.

Hoag: We were watching Ferris Rush take off.

Samuels: Right. Where was I? Oh, yeah, so he took some of his stories to Tanner Marsh,

Hoag: Using which name?

Samuels: Cameron Sheffield Noyes, because it sounded so dignified. Tanner turned him down cold, but that didn't stop him. He kept at it. Wrote his novel. And this time Tanner went apeshit. Why, I'll never know. Personally I didn't see that much difference between the diary sketches and the novel. But Tanner did, and more power to him.

Hoag: How much did he know about Ferris's real name and background?

Samuels: He knew only what Ferris told him, which was zero. Since the lead character in *Bang* was privileged, Tanner assumed he was, too. I told Ferris – encourage the guy. Drop some names like Farmington and Deerfield and the Essex Yacht Club.

Hoag: Why? What was the point?

Samuels: *Image.* Tanner had to like the book even more if he thought he had a real live blue blood on his hands, an author with rich friends and relatives. People like Tanner, with their little nonprofit snob magazines, they suck up to money like nobody's business.

Hoag: He did eventually find out the truth though, didn't he?

Samuels: Oh, sure, from Skitsy. Ferris couldn't keep anything from her. When she told Tanner, he got a little pissed at us for misrepresenting Ferris's background, but hey, by then Cam Noyes was a household name, and *Bang* a national best-seller. How pissed could he be?

Hoag: Ferris told me he hit something of a snag with Tanner because of what happened with Skitsy in his cabin at Stony Creek. Or should I say didn't happen.

Samuels: What do you mean?

Hoag: He said he blew Skitsy off, and that as a result Tanner blew him off. He said you had to set him straight.

Samuels: Never happened. Forget that wide-eyed innocent bit. It's total fiction. Ferris Rush had been kept since he was thirteen. He didn't need me to tell him the score. He fucked her that very night in his cabin at Stony Creek. Fucked her without hesitation because he knew she could do him a lot of good. Then, the next morning he was so overcome with self-loathing he ran off and hid. I think he must have realized he was embarking on another Maude-type relationship, and he didn't like himself for it. Didn't like seeing himself for what he is – a hustler. See, that's always been his problem. He's always wanted to be somebody dignified and classy. He's always wanted to be Cameron Sheffield Noyes, the poor wigged-out bastard.

(end tape)

(Tape #1 with Tanner Marsh recorded May 17 in his office at Columbia University. Wears rumpled corduroy suit, smokes pipe. Books, papers, are heaped everywhere. Room hasn't been tidied or aired out since the Truman administration.)

Marsh: They said you were there just after it happened, Stewart. That you saw my Skitsy.

Hoag: I did.

Marsh: Tell me, did she know what was happening to her? Did she suffer.

Hoag: It was over very fast.

Marsh: I feel so much better now that she is in the ground. These past few days and nights all I have been able to think of is, where is she? Is she in a plastic body bag somewhere? In some refrigerator? Now I know where she is. . . . We divorced, of course. But I-I never stopped loving my Skitsy.

Hoag: I'm sorry, Tanner.

Marsh: Thank you, Stewart.

Hoag: Make it Hoagy. The only person who calls me Stewart is my mother.

Marsh: Skitsy was not perfect, Stewart. She had her insecurities. She was capable of ruthlessness, cruelty. But she knew talent and how to handle it. She was the best. *He* was the best. Young Noyes. What a tragedy . . . She felt so strongly for him. Not like the others. And there were others. She collected them, just like she collected her antique dolls. My writers are just like my dolls, she said to me once – childlike and rare and extremely breakable. . . . Skitsy wasn't shy. If she saw someone she wanted, she took him. But none of them meant a damn to her – until he came along, that cold-blooded, murdering bastard.

Tell me, Stewart, how does it feel to be collaborating with a man who has killed two women? Two women who loved him?

Hoag: I can't say it's the most fun I've ever had.

Marsh: Why do you do this crap, Stewart?

Hoag: Everybody ought to be good at something.

Marsh: I suppose I was awfully hard on your last novel. It was only because *Our Family Enterprise* led me to expect so terribly much. You're the most gifted of them all, Stewart. You do know that, do you not?

Hoag: Careful. My ego swells easily. How did you feel when Skitsy eventually revealed his real background to you?

Marsh: (pause) I felt, I suppose, a bit used. Duped. Angry . . . I imagine I felt just like you are feeling right now yourself, Stewart.

Hoag: Possibly. Would it have mattered to you if you'd known it from the start?

Marsh: Let us put it this way . . . There is a great deal to be said for Texas authors – provided they write about Texas. Actually, my first impression of him was that he did not seem the writer type at all. By that I mean he was so robust and handsome and charming. Looked me right in the eye. Smiled. I found myself wondering what on earth this beautiful boy would be writing about. I suppose that was why I agreed to look at his stories, even though I do not generally accept freshman submissions.

Hoag: And?

Marsh: They were crude and juvenile, aswim in run-on sentences, wild mood swings, shifts in tense, voice. I did not understand half of his references. More significantly, I did not want to. I told him so. I was not particularly tactful.

Hoag: How did he respond?

Marsh: He did not get defensive or huffy, which is what they generally do. He simply thanked me for my time, shook my hand, and told me with utter conviction that he would be back in the fall with new and better material. I expected never to see him again, or if I did, to receive more of the same. . . . Undaunted, he did return a few months later, now clutching the manuscript for a novel. Inasmuch as he had shown no talent before, my inclination was to refuse to read it. But again, I was intrigued. Who was this boy? What drove him to work so hard? I glanced at his manuscript that evening. It was . . . It was nothing like what he had shown me before. He had grown so tremendously, both as a talent and as a man. He had his own voice now, a voice filled at once with self-assurance and with self-doubt, with strength and with hurt, with cynicism and with idealism. There was a sense of wholeness and purpose, a *vision*. Rereading the first page of *Bang* never fails to give me goose bumps, Stewart. . . . I sat here in my chamber until well past midnight until I finished. And when I did, I put down my pipe and wept. I wept because only once in a lifetime – and only then if he is very lucky – does someone in my position have the privilege to discover such a great talent in its very infancy. To be allowed to refine it, shepherd it. The manuscript was not perfect, mind you. There were numerous spots where his pacing faltered, the quality of his observations diminished. The ending was not nearly momentous enough. But all of this was minor. All that truly mattered was this robust young sophomore, this magazine cover boy, was a genius.

Hoag: He told me that the ending was your idea.

Marsh: At best, I pointed our conversations in a certain direction. Toward a fuller, more dramatic climax. It was he who came around to the suicide idea. . . . Working with him was a most interesting experience. The boy simply did not *get* what he had done. I had heard of writers like him – totally instinctive – but I had never worked with one before. If I were to ask him about a particular sentence or observation, what it meant, he would simply reply, "It means what it says." Not disagreeably, mind you. He simply did not know how to talk about his work. . . . I arranged a fellowship and residency at Stony Creek for him so he could complete his revisions at once without distraction.

Hoag: And you introduced him to Skitsy.

Marsh: Yes. I had called her in a daze that first night upon reading the manuscript. Told her I had come upon a brilliant young pupil who I felt certain would shortly have a manuscript she would agree was more than worthy of publication. She was, naturally, anxious to meet him.

Hoag: I'm a little vague about what happened up there between them.

Marsh: I do not trade in bedsheet gossip.

Hoag: Nor do I. I'm simply trying to understand their relationship. I have to, considering what has happened.

Marsh: Very well. . . . I knew the instant she set eyes on the boy that she wanted him. She acted nervous and girlish the entire ride up there, chattered incessantly. I left them up there that evening fully aware that by dawn they would become lovers. And they did. They made passionate love for the entire night in his cabin. Ferris is an inexhaustible and violent lover, she advised me.

Hoag: Did she always fill you in on the details of her conquests?

Marsh: Yes, she did.

Hoag: Didn't that bother you?

Marsh: Far from it. I insisted upon it.

Hoag: I see.

Marsh: Then at dawn, without warning, he suddenly became abusive and cruel toward her. Called her the vilest names. Yanked her from his bed by her hair and pushed her out the door into the woods, naked. He would not let her back in, or even give her her clothing. She had to return naked to the main house in the semidarkness, debased and humiliated. After she had bathed and dressed, she returned to his cabin, determined to have words with him. Only he was gone. Packed up and left the place without a trace. Disappeared for weeks. To this day, I do not know where he went. Skitsy told me all of this as soon as she returned to New York. She also told me that if I ever so much as uttered the name Cameron Sheffield Noyes in her presence, she would have me disemboweled. When he resurfaced with his finished manuscript, I let him have it. I told him that I had gone to an extraordinary amount of trouble to introduce him to the finest editor in New York, and that the stupidest thing a boy in his position could do was make an enemy of her. I told him that to make an enemy of her was to make one of me. I told him to get out of my office and to take his manuscript with him. He left with his tail between his legs. . . . Their romance resumed almost at once. I used that word advisedly, Stewart. For it was a romance. Stormy. Emotional. It was love.

Hoag: That's not exactly how he described it.

Marsh: I am not surprised. For him to be so attached to a woman twice his age does not fit with his public image. The rest of the story you know. The book was published nine months later to excellent notices.

Hoag: You yourself wrote the most important one, the one in the *Times*.

Marsh: I did.

Hoag: Didn't you regard that as a conflict of interest on your part?

Marsh: Absolutely not. I regarded it as my due. I had discovered him. I was entitled to present him to the publishing community. Besides, it is not as if the boy *needed* my help. He has a unique gift for drawing attention to himself. People *wanted* to read him, and to read about him. Meet him at parties. Be seen with him.

Look like him. Talk like him. From the outset he has been, quite simply, a star. It is his gift and, I believe, his curse. Nothing about his celebrity has helped him as a writer. I have always believed the writer is a marathon runner. His eyes must remain focused on the long distance, and shielded from the easy diversions – the movie deals, the cocktail parties, the women. Boyd Samuels, alas, does not happen to share my belief. He proceeded to turn him from a budding literary talent into a marketable commodity. I wanted nothing but the best for Ferris. I had the highest of literary ideals. Samuels wanted bucks. Such a waste. Think of his potential, Stewart. Given time and nurturing, he could have been among the giants of this century. Instead, he is a drugged-out, burnt-out, angry young mess. A murderer. I hope he rots in jail for a long, long time. After all Skitsy did for him.

Hoag: She did a lot for herself, too, according to Ferris.

Marsh: (pause) Meaning what?

Hoag: Her little kickback scheme. He told me she did mighty well by it. He didn't slight you, in case you're wondering. He told me all about how you skim off the profits from your writers' conferences. I never got a chance to ask Skitsy for her response. I'd like to ask you for yours.

Marsh: (silence) She warned me he might try to rattle the cage.

Hoag: And how do you respond?

Marsh: Allow me to assure you his charges are utterly false and groundless. I do not know the source of his information, but –

Hoag: Skitsy. He got it all from her – pillow talk.

Marsh: I must say I find it vile and reprehensible to discuss this matter for the purposes of a book that Skitsy's own murderer intends to profit from. I will not. And if I have to take legal action against your publisher to prevent you from doing so, I shall. Do I make myself clear?

Hoag: Your power must mean a lot to you. After all, you're the ayatollah of American lit. It would be awfully tough on you to get taken down, wouldn't it?

Marsh: What are you – ?

Hoag: Ferris's charges stand to raise a few eyebrows. People just might look at you a bit differently. Certainly the IRS will. The *Quarterly*, the Conference, will suffer. Maybe even die. It's pretty understandable that someone in your position might take some pretty drastic steps to hold on to what he has.

Marsh: I do not know what you are –

Hoag: Delilah Moscowitz's pub party. Perhaps you recall it. We were aboard the *Gotham Princess*? It was a rather warm evening . . . ?

Marsh: I recall it, as you well know.

Hoag: You said in from of a number of adoring listeners that I should no longer be allowed to own a typewriter.

Marsh: A figure of speech. What of it?

Hoag: Are you sure you didn't back it up – with a sledgehammer? Are you sure you haven't been trying to get me off of this project ever since you got wind of what we were up to? That you didn't send me those threats? Try to blind my ex-wife?

Marsh: This is preposterous. I did none of it.

Hoag: You didn't send me to Farmington to expose him – this boy who humiliated you in from of all those famous people? Who you tried to shoot at Elaine's?

Marsh: (*silence*) I-I was in a state of shock. Traumatized. I did not mean to. Kill him, I mean. I meant to defend myself. He had left me so . . . so defenseless, you see. I lost control. A momentary thing. I regretted it at once. I would not . . . could not willingly hurt him, or anyone.

Hoag: Possibly you "lost control" again the evening that I was to visit Skitsy. Possibly the two of you disagreed over how much, if anything, to reveal to me.

Marsh: This is outrageous! I will not sit here and listen to these groundless accusations! The police are quite certain who killed Skitsy. Just as they are quite certain who killed Charleston. You have no right to interrogate me like this. None. This interview is terminated. Turn off your recorder. Shut your notebook.

Hoag: I get the feeling you want me to leave.

Marsh: At once! (*sound of rustling*) No, wait. Not yet, Stewart. Before you go, there is one thing . . .

Hoag: Yes, Tanner?

Marsh: I am a fair man.

Hoag: I've always said so.

Marsh: I know you are doing this out of loyalty to Ferris. Out of friendship. I understand that. I want you to write another novel, Stewart. A grand, glorious novel. I hope with your gifts you will. And when you do, Stewart . . .

Hoag: Yes?

Marsh: I will be anxiously waiting to review it.

Hoag: Wonderful.

(*end tape*)

CHAPTER
FIFTEEN

T he day of Charlie's memorial service was the first hot, muggy one of spring. The air was so moist and rank it felt as if someone were holding a plastic bag over the city's head.

The service was held at Rat's Nest. Not many people showed up for it. A couple of grand poohbahs from the Whitney and MOMA. Some gallery owners, critics, and fellow artists. Vic Early, who wore a navy-blue suit and sat stiffly with his hands folded in his lap like a good, huge boy. Me. Boyd Samuels wasn't there. Charlie wasn't there, either, in spirit or body. Her only relative, an older sister in San Francisco, had requested the body be shipped out there for burial. I had made the arrangements.

My police tail waited discreetly outside after following me there from my apartment, just as I'd been followed the previous two days wherever I went. Very was taking no chances. I was on a leash, all right, for as long as my celebrity was on the loose. That morning's papers had reported no new leads in the manhunt, other than a story in the *Post* that a witness claimed he had seen Cameron Noyes enjoying lunch at a Pizza Hut in Clinton, Iowa. The claim had been discounted when the witness turned out to be someone who'd previously spotted Elvis having coffee there. Reporters were calling me constantly now for quotes and tips. I was hanging up on them. It gets easy after the first dozen times you do it.

It was a short service. A couple of people got up and said some words about how important an artist Charlie could have become, and how her death was such a terrible waste. I didn't pay close attention. I was getting sick of hearing about waste.

Afterward, I headed uptown to my apartment with Vic and my tail to pack up Charlie's things for her sister. There really wasn't much, and I was fully capable of boxing it myself, but the big guy insisted. When he does that, you give in. We worked in silence. Neither of us felt particularly chatty.

Lulu watched us from under the bed, trembling. Packing upsets her. Some trauma buried deep in her early puppyhood. What, I don't know. But I do know I'm not putting her in therapy.

We didn't pack up Charlie's personal papers. Very had said he might want to look through those. We also left the portraits, photos, and sketches she'd done for the book. Those belonged to the publisher.

When we were done, I helped Vic carry the boxes downstairs. Then we put them, and him, in a cab bound for United Parcel.

"I wish I could give you a reason to stick around, Vic," I said to him through the open cab window. "But I'm afraid I can't. So if you want to be heading back to L.A., you may as well. Your end of this job is history."

Vic sat there in the backseat, rubbing his forehead. "I don't feel like I did much good, Hoag."

"I don't feel like I did either."

In the front seat, the cabbie, who wore a turban, began drumming his fingers impatiently on the steering wheel. He stopped as soon as he saw Vic glowering at him in the rear-view mirror.

"I'll be sticking around his place until they catch him," Vic informed me. "I'd like to be here. I'd like to ask him why he did that to that nice little girl. You don't mind, do you, Hoag?"

I patted his heavy shoulder. "Not even a little."

Lulu was still cowering under the bed, her eyes glowing in the darkness. I was trying to coax her out with promises of bouillabaisse and coquilles St. Jacques when the phone rang. It was Very.

"How's the belly, Lieutenant?" I asked him as he popped his gum in my ear.

"Sour, dude. Just got a sweet break, though – his wheels turned up."

"The Loveboat? Where?"

"Trenton. Low-income housing project. Cruiser spotted it there early this morning. Bunch of homeboys were breaking into it. Plates and registration still on it. Suitcase full of clothes in the trunk. He wear real preppy shit? There's a Ralph Lauren suit, white. Bunch of Brooks Brothers shirts and boxer shorts . . ."

"That sounds like him."

"Nobody saw him – at least nobody says they saw him. It's not one of your more cooperative neighborhoods. FBI is in on it now, which is about egos and territorial bullshit and stomach acid that I can live without. They began canvassing the people on the street. All anybody will tell 'em is they think the car was left there sometime last night. Any idea what he'd be doing around Trenton?"

"None."

"He have any family or friends there?"

"Not that I know of."

"Okay if I try a theory on you, dude?"

"Go right ahead, Lieutenant."

"What it is," he began, giving his gum a workout, "I was eyeballing this book of his, *Bang*, and his character in that, when things get real crazed for him psychologically – when he starts to, like, crack up – he runs to Atlantic City for a blowout. You think Noyes could be headed there like in his book? Or is that too wigged-out?"

"I can't tell you if he's headed there or not, Lieutenant," I replied. "I can tell you that with Cam Noyes the line between fact and fiction is extremely fuzzy. I'd say it's worth pursuing."

"Me, too. Trenton's a little off course between here and A.C., but not much. I figure he's taking an indirect route in case we're watching the Garden State Parkway and Route Nine. We're checking the buses in case he took one there from Trenton. Also limo services, taxis, car rentals. You got any addresses for him down there?"

"No, but if your theory holds true, he's probably heading for the hotel were the movie was made. That's where I'd try."

"Good thinking. I gotta run now. Dude?"

"I know, I know, Lieutenant – stay with you."

"Not what I was gonna say."

"Oh. What were you going to – ?"

"Dude?"

I sighed. "Yes, Lieutenant?"

"We're gonna nail his ass."

"Yes, I believe you will."

Then he said, "Stay with me," and burped and hung up.

I immediately got my Il Bisonte overnight bag out of the closet, stuffed some clothes and shaving gear and mackerel cans in it, and told Lulu we were leaving. She still wouldn't budge from under the bed. I had to grab her by the front paws and slide her out, shaking, covered with dust balls. Then the two of us headed out.

A cab dropped us at the garage on West Sixty-seventh where Merilee keeps the Jaguar, my police tail hovering a careful half-block behind in an unmarked navy-blue sedan. I gassed it up, put the top down, and headed out. I didn't have time right now to ask Merilee for permission. I worked my way down Broadway, making no effort to beat the sluggish flow. My tail stayed his same half-block behind. There was the usual bottleneck at Columbus Circle before Broadway became all one-way and the flow opened up. I cruised through what was left of the theater district and then the trashy splendor of

Forty-second Street before I made a right at Thirty-ninth and headed west toward the Lincoln Tunnel, which is how you go under the Hudson into New Jersey, especially if you're heading south to Atlantic City. My tail stayed with me.

The tunnel traffic choked up just before it reached Ninth Avenue. Truckers, cabbies, delivery-van drivers, were stuck there honking and cursing at each other hotly. I casually inched ahead of a cab and then not so casually cut him off as I swung left onto Ninth and tore downtown. The Jag is a phenomenal darter – it's almost as swift and elusive in traffic as Merilee is in the shoe stores of Milan's Montenapoleone. By Thirty-seventh, I was losing sight of my tail in my rearview mirror. I made a right there on two wheels and shot through the crosstown traffic to Eleventh, where I made a left and then sped down to Thirty-fourth, no tail in sight. I took Thirty-fourth back across town toward the East Side. Certain I was alone now, I got on the FDR Drive and made my way up the East River toward the New England Thruway. And Connecticut.

Ferris Rush was many things. Brilliant. Disturbed. Tragic. One thing he wasn't was stupid. If he was headed for Atlantic City, there was no way he'd abandon the Loveboat there in Trenton for everyone to find. That was to throw the police off. He knew Very would draw precisely the conclusion Very had drawn. He knew they would spend days combing the hotels and casinos for him.

They would find nothing. Ferris Rush had gone in the direction I was going now – the opposite direction. He was making a run for his shack on Crescent Moon Pond, just as he had run for it after that night with Skitsy in his cabin at Stony Creek. Every man, Smilin' Jack told him, needs his secret place. The shack was his. He was headed for the pond. And so was I. To have it out with him.

The shack was dark.

No light came from its busted windows as I rowed around the bend in the dusk, Lulu seated stiffly before me in her life preserver, nostrils aquiver. What had been sticky haze in the city was cool dampness here. The pond gave off a fetid, yeasty smell. It was very quiet. No sound except for the soft plop the oars made as they broke the glassy surface. It was completely dark by the time I reached the shack, dark like it doesn't get in the city. I couldn't even see Lulu in the other end of the boat. I needed my flashlight to guide me to the remains of the mooring. No other boat was tied up there. The kid at the boatyard said no one besides me had rented one in days. Was I wrong? I couldn't be. He was here. Had to be here.

Lulu remembered where we were. She guided me up the shack's rickety steps to the open front door. The oil lantern was sitting there on the rough table as before, only it had oil in it now, and a box of kitchen matches next to it. I lit it, bathing the room in golden light.

The wood stove had been used in the past day – the heavy cast iron was still warm to the touch. Fresh firewood was piled before it. Cans of chili and soup were piled up over with the kitchen things. A tin of crackers. A crumpled pack of Marlboros. His brand. A half-empty bottle of tequila. His drink.

I carried the lantern into the tiny bedroom. Lying there on the stained mattress was the copy of *The Great Gatsby* I'd given him a couple weeks before. I know it was the same one because it was my own cherished copy, the autographed first edition I'd found hidden among the old Dartmouth yearbooks in grandfather's attic one hot summer day long ago.

I went back out onto the front porch and called out his name as loud as I could, in every direction. I waited. After a moment, I heard footsteps off the brush. Coming toward the shack. Closer. Closer still. I shone the flashlight – it was a raccoon. Lulu growled at it but didn't budge from the porch. Raccoons fight back.

It had gotten cold out. I made a fire in the stove and sampled the tequila. Out back I pumped some water into a pail from the well. I put a bowl of it down for Lulu along with a can her mackerel. I opened one of the cans of chili and heated it in a pan on the stove. When it was hot, I ate it with some crackers and washed it down with tequila and well water. Then I stretched out on the mattress with the lantern and F. Scott Fitzgerald and wait for Ferris Rush to come home.

I waited for a long time. I waited the whole night, sleeping fitfully with my old leather jacket and Lulu over me for warmth. I waited through the long next day, a day I spent skipping stones on the pond and sitting on the porch in the sun thinking about Ferris Rush and his story, the story I was about to write. It was a story of genius, ambition, and greed. Of sex, drugs, fame, fraud, and murder. A lot your basics.

It was not a pretty story, and there was no happy ending to it – at least I sure couldn't see one coming. One question still nagged at me. Was Ferris Rush the villain of this story or the victim? Was he responsible for what had happened or were those around him responsible – Boyd Samuels, Tanner Marsh, Skitsy Held, and all of their machinery of literary celebrity? I still didn't know the answer to that question. I would have to face him to know it.

Toward late afternoon I put Lulu back in her life preserver and rowed us across to the Jag. I left the boat there and drove to the general store a few miles up the road from the boatyard. No one there remembered selling any canned goods to a blond guy in the past few days. I bought some ham sandwiches and a six-pack of Guinness and used the pay phone out front to call Merilee.

"Why, it's Mr. Hoagy," she exclaimed warmly.

"Just wanted to let you know I borrowed the Jag from the garage," I told her. "It was an emergency, and I didn't have time to ask if you – "

"Quite all right, darling," she said mildly. "I still think of it as half yours anyway. Hoagy?"

"Yes, Merilee?"

"Hello."

"Hello yourself," I said, pleased she was being such a good sport about my stealing her car. "Listen, there's one other thing. If Very happens to call, don't tell – "

"If a very *what* happens to call you what?" she broke in, confused.

"Romaine Very. He's a short, muscular cop with an earring and bad stomach. If he calls you in the next day or so, and he will, tell him I've been writing in seclusion and that I cannot be disturbed by anyone for any reason. Tell him I'm always this way when I write. Tell him I'm weird. Tell him anything. Just don't tell him where I am, okay?"

"Okay," she agreed. "And where are you?"

"You don't want to know."

"Horseradish."

I tugged at my ear. "I'm in Connecticut. I've found him. At least I think I have."

"But half of the police in the Northeast are looking for him in – "

"The wrong place."

"Hoagy, may I remind you that this man has already killed two people?"

"I'm well aware of that fact."

"What's to stop him from killing you, too, if you get in his way?"

"I have my methods." I glanced down at my protector, who lay curled at my feet, daintily licking her soft white underbelly. "Besides, all I want to do is talk to him. As a friend. I care about what happens to him. Face it, there aren't a lot of people around now who do."

"That's because he's murdered the others. Hoagy, Hoagy, Hoagy. You loyal fool."

"You got that half right. Merilee, will you tell Very what I said?"

"Of course, darling. You can always count on me."

"Thanks. And thanks for being so understanding about the car."

"It's true, I am being terribly understanding. It must be because you let me see Sweetness on Sundays. She'll come stay with me in the country sometimes, won't she? She loves the outdoors so."

"Of course. But you have to remember that deep down inside she's still a city dog. She likes the hubbub, the ballet, breakfast in bed . . ."

"She's not the only one."

"I remember. Champagne and fresh-squeezed orange juice for starters. A slice of muskmelon, followed by a caviar-and-sour-cream omelet, followed by – "

"*Mister* Hoagy. There are laws against discussing *that* on interstate phone lines."

"No law against remembering though, is there?"

She was silent a moment. "No. None," she admitted softly. "Hoagy?"

"Yes, Merilee?"

"Be careful. Lulu is much too young and innocent to lose you. And so is her mommy."

I took the long way back to Crescent Moon Pond. Up the winding country road into Hadlyme, then onto a narrower one that twisted its way through a forest before it dead-ended at a small farm set behind old stone walls encrusted with lichen. I stopped there and turned off the engine. The house was set way back behind fields of wildflowers and green grass and fruit trees and a pond, where I could hear the ducks quacking. It was a snug old house, creamy yellow in the late-day sun, with white shutters and trim. The carriage barn was red. It was a lovely place, a safe haven, a refuge. She was right – it was home.

I sat there gazing at it, wondering if it would ever be *my* home. It would never have lasted with Charlie. It would have turned up Merilee again. She and I were destined for each other. Or doomed, depending on how you want to look at it. And maybe it *was* time for this. Time to surrender what was left of New York to the Yushies. I didn't belong there anymore. Maybe I never had, but when you're the center of attention, you tend not to notice. Was this the ending for novel number three? Hoagy the country squire – scribbling in his chapel in the morning, shoveling manure in the afternoon? I sat there gazing at it and thinking it didn't sound too terrible. Of course it didn't. Daydreams seldom do.

Ferris Rush wasn't the only one whose line between fact and fiction was awful damned fuzzy.

I started up the Jag and floored it out of there, cursing myself.

I ate the ham sandwiches and drank the Guinness and spent another night on that sour-smelling bare mattress. And another day on the porch, where I reread *The Great Gatsby*, and enjoyed it more than I ever had. And still one more night. And with the dawn came the reality – he wasn't coming back to his secret place. I had gotten close, closer than anyone else had. But I'd missed him. He was gone, and this time I didn't know where.

I had no choice now. It was time to go back to the city and get out my mukluks.

CHAPTER SIXTEEN

Mr. Adelman had nearly wept when I'd shown up at his shop on Amsterdam with my hammered, ruined Olympia. It was he who had sold it to me and lovingly maintained it through the years. I'd begged him to save it. He'd said he was a typewriter man, not a magician.

He *was* a magician. It shone like new there now on his counter, straining for action. He shone, too, a proud craftsman of the old, old school. Before he would let me take it home, he made me swear I'd never run over it again with a Jeep, or whatever I had done to it – he didn't want to know. I made him swear he'd never let Benetton or The Gap push him out on the street. We shook on that.

When I got home with it, I made a pot of coffee and arranged the transcripts of my interviews in piles on Ferris Rush's writing table. I had mixed feelings about his table now. Part of me wanted to saw it in half and throw it in the street. For now, I intended to keep it. I'd earned it.

I got my mukluks out of the closet and put them on. I wore them when I wrote the first novel. I've worn them every single time I've sat down in from of my typewriter since. They're starting to get a little ragged, but so am I. After I poured myself a cup of coffee I sat down at the table and got started. Lulu stretched out under me with her head on my foot, swallowed contentedly, and dropped off.

I am not who you think I am. I am not Cameron Sheffield Noyes. My name is Ferris Rush, and I am a murderer.

I took it from there. My opening approach was to weigh the privileged, made-up Farmington upbringing of Cam Noyes against the gritty, real Port Arthur childhood of Ferris Rush. I gave him a sardonic, slightly weary voice, the voice of his *Bang* storyteller. His voice. Quickly, I realized that this would be my hardest memoir to get down on paper. Unlike the other celebrities I'd written for, this one happened to be an acclaimed novelist. His prose, his observations, would have to have some kind of literary merit. The words couldn't just come tumbling out onto the page any old way. In fact, they soon wouldn't come tumbling at all. I got stuck in deep mud after three pages, my wheels spinning, and I couldn't get out.

Something was wrong.

It wasn't writer's block. That's a void, a fear. The stomach muscles tighten. The hairs on the back of the neck stand up. No, this was the nagging itch I get when a scene I've written doesn't work. Oh, it seems fine on the surface. But deep down inside I just know something is wrong with it. Only I don't know what it is. It's an itch I can't get to. Not until I've analyzed the scene from every possible angle, taken it apart piece by piece, turned it inside out. Eventually, if I keep at it long enough, I find the flaw. But I can never rest until I do. Because my itch is never, ever wrong.

I didn't have the whole story. I thought I did but I didn't. I was wrong. That's why I was stuck. I was still missing something. Something crucial. But what?

I got up and paced from one end of the living room to the other. It's not very far. I paced, the floor of the old brownstone creaking under me. Lulu watched me, her eyes darting back and forth, back and forth. I went over my approach. I went over everything that happened from the beginning, step by step. What was I missing? Was it something he'd said to me once, something that didn't fit? Something somebody else had said? What?

I took Lulu for a walk in Riverside Park, a man possessed now. I turned the soil over and over as I walked, my hands shoved in my pockets, lips moving. That's one big plus about living in New York. No one in the park paid me any attention—their lips were moving, too. I got nowhere. I stopped at a Greek coffee shop and ate a cheeseburger that tasted like flannel. I climbed back up to my apartment and made another pot of coffee and started working my way through the transcripts, line by line, searching for I didn't know what. I read all of them. It was nearly four in the morning when I was done. I found nothing. Nothing that took care of my itch.

Lulu was fast asleep now on the love seat. I opened a Bass ale and fell into my chair and drank it. I went over my Farmington trip notes. Nothing there either.

It was only out of utter desperation that I started looking through the carton full of Charlie's papers, the one Very had asked me to hold on to. He still hadn't had a chance to sift through it yet – the manhunt was keeping him busy. There were sales records in there for work she'd sold. Some pretty prominent collectors involved. . . . Letters. One from her sister in San Francisco, who was going through a difficult pregnancy and wondering whether the baby would save her marriage. Another from a man named Alan Berger, who lived on East Sixty-third and whom she'd evidently dumped for Ferris. I set this letter aside. . . . Clippings – rave reviews for her work from the *Times*, *Newsweek*, *Artnews*. . . . Tax returns for the past two years. Passport. Checkbook, bank statements, canceled checks. I leafed through her checkbook. She'd evidently taken care of their domestic life in Gramercy Park—New York Telephone, Con Edison, Allstate. Each entry was in her square, careful handwriting. I yanked the rubber band off the canceled checks and rifled through them. She was organized. In the lower left-hand corner of each check she'd detailed precisely what service had been rendered. Phone service, April. Home insurance, first quarter . . .

And then I saw it. One particular canceled check. And a bomb went off in my head. That odd fact. Here it was. And here was the key that unlocked the door. Maybe. I glanced at grandfather's Rolex. It was six-thirty now. What better time to catch someone in. I reached for the phone and dialed the party whose name was on that check. Someone who was rather surprised by my call, especially at this hour, but who was not at all uncooperative. We talked briefly. But plenty long enough to confirm my worst suspicions. I hung up shaking, my mouth dry.

It all made sense now. Horrible, ugly sense. Worse than I could have imagined, and I have a vivid imagination. Now I knew why I couldn't write Ferris Rush's story yet. I was wrong. About all of it. We were all wrong.

But I'd need Very's help if I was going to make it right.

He was waiting for me with his bike out in front of the building on Fortieth and Lex where Skitsy's company, Murray Hill Press, had their offices. The secretaries in their summer dresses and Reeboks were eyeballing him standing there in his tank top and spandex shorts as they went through the revolving door. He was ignoring them. He was too busy glowering at me.

"Yo, what's this all about, dude?" he demanded coldly, muscular arms crossed in front of his chest.

"A theory I want to test out, Lieutenant," I explained. "Can't do it without you."

"Seem you can do *plenty* without me," he said, jaw working his gum.

"I can?"

"You purposely slipped your tail outside of the Lincoln Tunnel, disappeared for two whole fucking days. I wanna know where."

"Didn't you speak to my ex-wife?"

"Sure, I spoke to her. Got my chain jerked about how sensitive an artist you are, how you require seclusion. . . ."

"You didn't believe her?"

"Show me some respect, huh!" he exploded. "I'm a person! You *talk* to a person! You don't jerk chains! I want to know where you were! Was it Atlantic City?"

"No, it wasn't."

He waited for me to tell him more. When I didn't, he started nodding to his own personal beat, the muscles of his neck and shoulders bunched tightly. "Okay. That's cool. You wanna fuck around, we'll fuck around – in a interrogation room. Let's go."

"Wait, Lieutenant. Hold on. All I'm asking of you is – "

"Too fucking much, dude. I'm trying to find a guy who blew away two ladies. The trail's cold. My stomach is in involuntary spasms. You're holding out on me. And *now* you expect me to play along blind with you. Uh-uh. No way. I'm coming down on you – suspicion of aiding and abetting. You are under arrest. You have the right to remain silent. Anything you say may be – "

"Okay, okay, Lieutenant. You win. What do you want to know?"

"Everything. Until I get it, you get nothing from me, except a cell."

"And if I tell you, you'll help me?"

He didn't answer me. Just stood there glaring at me and popping his gum.

So I told him. I told him all about Ferris Rush of Port Arthur, Texas, and how he'd slammed into a busload of kids and gotten away with it, and how Skitsy Held had owned him because of it. I told him about the shack on Crescent Moon Pond, and how I'd been there, and thought he had, too. I told him all of it, because it didn't matter anymore. All that mattered was that I get into Skitsy Held's files upstairs, and I couldn't do that without him.

When I finished, he closed his eyes a second and made a face and rubbed his stomach, mulling it over. "Okay . . . okay . . . and now you got some theory involving Murray Hill Press."

"Correct."

"What's this theory got to do with Rush?"

"Everything and nothing."

He frowned. "I don't follow."

"Do you trust me, Lieutenant?"

"No."

"Look, just do this one thing for me and I promise I'll make it up to you for having been so uncooperative."

"How?"

"I'll take you to Ferris Rush."

His eyes widened. "Wait, you know where he is?"

I started for the revolving door. "Stay with me, Lieutenant."

He stayed with me.

CHAPTER
SEVENTEEN

(Tape #2 with Boyd Samuels recorded May 20 on the patio of Ferris Rush's Gramercy Park town house. Also present are Lt. Romaine Very, Vic Early, and Samuels's assistant, Todd Lesser.)

Hoag: Thanks for coming here like this in the middle of the workday. I know it was short notice.

Samuels: You said it was an emergency, amigo. Whatever we can do, we'll do. To tell you the truth, I'm not exactly thrilled about the police being in on this. . . .

Hoag: It has to be this way. I'm sorry.

Samuels: (pause) If you say so. Go ahead.

Hoag: I wanted to talk to you about one of your scams – your biggest scam, in fact. I really have to hand it to you. You're an artist.

Samuels: Thanks, but I'm not sure I know what the hell you're talking about.

Hoag: Your freshman year at Columbia, Boyd, when you and Ferris were hanging out a lot at the clubs, and he was modeling, and getting bored with it. He started writing stories about your scene, and he submitted them to Tanner Marsh under his modeling name, Cameron Sheffield Noyes. Tanner told me he was really knocked out by him. His looks, breeding, personality. The kid had star written all over him, except for one small problem – his writing.

Samuels: Yeah, Tanner didn't like the stories. So Ferris went back to work, and the novel was a whole different thing. Tanner loved the novel.

Hoag: Yes, he said it was nothing like what Ferris had shown him before. That he'd grown tremendously, blossomed. But that isn't what really happened, is it?

Samuels: (silence) Meaning what?

Hoag: Want to tell us how it happened, Boyd? *(no response)* Or perhaps Todd can fill us in.

Lesser: Me?

Hoag: You. You told me at Delilah's party that you left Columbia because of personal problems.

Lesser: Yes, I did.

Hoag: According to Ferris, your personal problem was that you

170

were one of Boyd's biggest cocaine customers.

Samuels: Hey, no need to get into that, amigo, especially in front of —

Very: Shut up, Samuels.

Samuels: Yessir.

Lesser: It's true. I-I had trouble being away from home for the first time. Fitting in with new people. Couldn't seem t-to talk to anybody. So I started spending more and more time alone in my room. And getting deeper and deeper into coke.

Hoag: How much did you owe him, Todd?

Lesser: J-Just under two thousand dollars. But I paid it back before I left school. I paid back all of it.

Hoag: I know you did. Want to tell us how? *(no response)* Come on, Todd. Tell us what were you doing there in your room with the door closed.

Lesser: I . . . I . . .

Hoag: You were writing a novel, weren't you? The story of one sensitive young man's breakdown. Your breakdown.

Lesser: Yes.

Hoag: You were desperate. No money to pay Boyd back. No money to get more coke. So when Boyd came to you with a small proposition, you listened. You had to listen. Isn't that right, Boyd?

Samuels: I'm thinking to myself, whoa, this Marsh guy smells class and money on Ferris. Can maybe turn him into a major celebrity. I'm thinking what a shame it is we don't have a book the fat slob can run with.

Hoag: So you bought yourself one. You erased Todd's debt and fed him some more coke, in exchange for which he gave you his manuscript. No big deal, was it, Todd? No different from getting paid to do a term paper for somebody. You were just a college kid, a strung-out, fucked-up college kid. All you cared about was getting Boyd off your back and your nose filled. How could you possibly have known what was going to happen? How could anyone?

Very: Yo, you're saying *this* guy wrote *Bang*?

Hoag: I'm saying Ferris Rush has never published a word in his life. Or even read a word, for that matter. He's a front. A face. A personality. A scam. Tanner told me how strange he found him when they worked together on the manuscript. How Ferris seemed not to grasp what he had written. Of course he didn't — he hadn't written it. That's the real reason why he ran away from Stony Creek. He was afraid if he spent too much time around there with all of those real writers, somebody might get wise to him. So he hid out at his shack. You met him there, didn't you, Todd? The two of you went over Tanner's suggestions together. Then you did the rewrites while Ferris fished. When you were done, he resurfaced with his finished manuscript. And sold it. You freaked out at this point, didn't you, realizing that your book was actually going to get published and that someone else was going to get the credit for it. Pretty tough to handle. You couldn't. You dropped out of school. Took off. Why did you let them get away with it, Todd? Why didn't you speak up?

Lesser: Because I had no real proof that I wrote it. No handwritten manuscript. No contract. It was just my word against theirs, and nobody would have believed me – Boyd assured me of that. He also assured me he'd go to any length to ruin me if I fucked this thing up for them.

Samuels: Toddy and I made a legitimate business deal. He *sold* me the manuscript. Besides, I've always taken care of him. I gave him a job, didn't I? I didn't have to do that.

Hoag: You've taken care of him, all right. Because of him Ferris Rush became a world-famous literary luminary and a millionaire. In exchange for that you let Todd get your coffee for you. You're a gent, Boyd. A real gent. . . . The secret of *Bang* has stayed a secret. No one has ever found out. Not Tanner. Not even Skitsy, did she?

Samuels: Correct.

Hoag: Naturally, Ferris couldn't deliver a second novel. He became more and more angry and self-destructive – partly because of the schoolbus business, but mostly because he's been a complete fraud. He's been able to fool other people, but not himself. You cooked up your bullshit memoir idea to keep the money flowing in. Charlie's art was a nice bonus. And you brought me in. Why? Why not just have Todd write it? Why take the chance your secret might get out?

Samuels: To succeed it had to be prestigious. People around town had to know a name writer was involved, even if uncredited. You were the ideal candidate.

Very: Yo, if I could jump in here . . . ?

Hoag: Go ahead, Lieutenant.

Very: It's not that I'm not finding this a stimulating literary discussion, but where is it taking us, y'know?

Hoag: Be patient, Lieutenant. We'll get there.

Very: Yeah, but you told me you knew were Ferris Rush is.

Hoag: I do.

Very: So where is he?

Hoag: We're sitting on him.

Very: (silence) We're what?

Hoag: Ferris Rush is dead. Has been since the day Charlie died. He was murdered by the same person who stabbed her and pushed Skitsy. His body is hidden under this nice new bluestone patio the contractor laid down. Except it wasn't the contractor who laid it – was it, Todd?

Lesser: I-I don't know what you mean.

Samuels: Toddy?

Early: You killed that nice little girl? *You!*

Hoag: Sit down, Vic. Stay cool.

Samuels: Jeez . . . what's the matter with him? He looks like he's going to –

Hoag: Vic, can you hear me? *Vic?*

Early: (silence) Yeah . . . Sorry, Hoag. I'm okay. Sorry. Go ahead.

Hoag: I found something when I was going through Charlie's canceled checks, Todd. Something that clicked. You told me that after you dropped out of Columbia you drifted around upstate for a while. Worked odd jobs. Worked *construction.*

Lesser: I did. So?

Very: Who was this canceled check to, dude?

Hoag: One Michael Mordarski of Sheepshead Bay, Brooklyn. He's the contractor who's been renovating this place. I spoke to him first thing this morning. Asked him if anyone had been around in the past few days to put in a little dry wall here, a little patio there. He said no one had. He apologized, promised he'd finish up here as soon as he could. *(pause)* He's down there, isn't he, Todd?

Lesser: (silence) The sleazy bastard got what he deserved. He didn't deserve his success. He was a fraud, like you said. A fraud! His very existence demeaned the world of literature! He didn't deserve her, either. Charlie. She was so sweet, so lovely. And he used her. Cheated on her. Hurt her.

Hoag: Want to tell us about it, Todd? *(silence)* Okay, feel free to stop me if I miss anything. . . . You wanted me off of this project from the moment Ferris called Boyd and told him what our plan was – a plan for a book that might actually have some value. You didn't want that. You wanted him to keep sliding down, down, down, this pretender who had achieved the success that rightly belonged to you. So you came to my apartment that first night, by way of my roof, and you left me a threat. When I didn't quit, you played it a little tougher. Sledgehammered your way in. Destroyed my typewriter – only another writer could know how much that would hurt. Then you tried to blind Merilee with that little jack-in-the-box. Except I still didn't quit. Neither did you. You sent me to Farmington so that I'd find out the truth about who Cameron Sheffield Noyes really was. What were you hoping I'd do?

Lesser: Quit. Tell everyone in town. Embarrass him. Humiliate him.

Hoag: Skitsy's murder really threw me. I kept thinking she was killed so she couldn't talk to me. She wasn't. Her death had nothing to do with our book, or with her crooked business dealing or any of that. *(rustling noise)* It had to do with this, didn't it?

Samuels: What is that?

Hoag: A rejection letter. Lieutenant Very and I found it this morning in her files at Murray Hill Press. That's something else you mentioned to me at Delilah's party, Todd. You told me you'd just finished writing a novel.

Samuels: I didn't know you were writing another book, Toddy.

Lesser: I wouldn't let you get your filthy scheming hands on it! You'd steal it! Make me say Ferris wrote it!

Hoag: What's it about, Todd?

Lesser: A brilliant young writer. His rise to fame and fortune. His burnout. It's called *Boy Wonder*. I-I'm very proud of it. I submitted it on my own to Skitsy. She was the best in the business. She had made Ferris. Now it was my turn. Time for the success I deserved. That's all I wanted – what I deserved. What I had earned. It was only fair.

Hoag: And she turned you down.

Lesser: She dismissed it. Said it was . . .

Hoag: "A small, predictable story about small, predictable people. The writing is flat and undistinguished. Sorry I can't be more enthusiastic, Toddy. Maybe next time."

Lesser: "Maybe next time." *Maybe next time!* I'm the man who wrote *Bang*, damn it! They've compared me to F. Scott Fucking Fitzgerald! But she didn't smell money on me. I wasn't hot. So it was sorry, Toddy. Tough shit, Toddy. I-I couldn't accept that. I just couldn't. It wasn't fair. I deserved more. I called her and she agreed to see me for a few minutes at her apartment after work. I went up there at six. Boyd had already left the office for a drink date. One of the other kids covered for me. I said I was getting my teeth cleaned.

Hoag: How come no one saw you go in her building?

Lesser: No one ever sees me. I'm part of the wall. The doorman was busy flirting with somebody's maid out on the sidewalk. He ignored me. I just walked in. I didn't sneak in. I-I never went there intending to *kill* Skitsy. It's just that she made me so damned mad. She *patronized* me. Treated me like I was some kind of untalented amateur, some *loser*. Didn't even offer me a drink. So I-I told her the truth. I told her I wrote *Bang*. I told her that Cam Noyes was a fraud. That she'd been taken in. Know what she did? She laughed at me. She was so damned sure of herself, and of her right to dictate who gets into the charmed inner circle and who doesn't. I just couldn't stand it, her laughing at me like that. So I pushed her. It was an impulse. Blind rage. And then . . . then I realized if I got out of there fast, if no one saw me, it would look just like a suicide. I ran into her bathroom and grabbed the clothes in her hamper. A yellow dress, some other things, detergent. I took the stairs down two flights in case anybody was coming up in the elevator. Then I caught the elevator down to the laundry room in the basement. I did a load of wash while the shit was hitting the fan. No one looked for me down there. When I left, there was still a lot of confusion out front and no one noticed me. By now, I'd been away from the office an hour. I was in a hurry to get back. I had the wet laundry with me in a shopping bag. It wouldn't have been smart to leave it there. And I didn't have time to drop it off at my apartment – I live way the hell out in Park Slope. It's all I can afford. So I dumped it a couple of blocks away in a trash can. I guess that was a mistake.

Very: It was.

Hoag: Still, you managed to turn it to your own advantage, didn't you, Todd? Everyone assumed Ferris killed Skitsy. You certainly made it look like he killed Charlie. . . . You loved Charlie. More than you could stand. It was incredibly painful for you to see them together, her and Ferris – the man with the career, the woman, the *life*, that should have been yours. You were elated when she left him. You thought this was your chance. Only it wasn't, was it? She left a note for me at my apartment Saturday morning saying she'd meet me for lunch if I got back from Connecticut in time. A somewhat romantic note. You saw it when you let yourself into my apartment that morning by way of my easy-opening front door.

Lesser: I-I wanted to see if the two of you were . . . if she was . . .

Hoag: You freaked. Decided if you couldn't have her, no one could. You'd already killed one person. You decided to kill two more, especially because it all fit together so very neatly – at least it did if you moved quickly and carefully, and you did. You're very good with plots, Todd.

Lesser: Thank you.

Hoag: You hightailed it right over here and waited for your opportunity. You got it when Ferris and Vic went out for a nice long run. The second they left you slipped inside the house. Spare key?

Lesser: Boyd had one made for me in case I ever needed to drop anything off to be signed or whatever.

Hoag: You went upstairs and stole the bowie knife. You knew there were photos of Ferris with the knife, that it would be traced to him. Then you laid your groundwork for later on by doing some dry-wall work in the kitchen. What with New York contractors being so notoriously unreliable, you knew no one would question it, and that it would draw attention away from your main intention. You slipped out before Ferris and Vic got back. Went to Rat's Nest with the knife and waited across the street for the clerk to leave on her break. You knew Charlie would be alone in there waiting for me. You knew the setup there – you'd picked her up there a few times when Ferris was running late, or forgot her. You also knew you had to work fast. You buzzed the second the clerk left. Charlie let you in.

Lesser: She died in my arms. No more pain. I was the one who could make her happy, you know. I was the only one. But she wouldn't have me. She was blind. All she knew was the pain. So I freed her from it. It was an act of mercy, don't you see? It was beautiful. I put her back up on her canvas when she was gone. She deserved to be up there. She was a great artist and *Blue Monday* was her greatest statement. Her last statement. I gave it to her. It was from me to her. Something we'll always have. Together. No one can take it away from us. No one.

Hoag: You ducked out before the clerk got back, before I arrived. You came directly here and let yourself in. Ferris was asleep upstairs. Vic was out guarding Merilee. That was a stroke of luck for you – he left Ferris here all alone. Tell me, what would you have done if he hadn't?

Lesser: That's easy – I'd have killed him, too.

Early: Kill me? Just exactly how, pal?

Lesser: Mind if I take off my raincoat, Lieutenant?

Very: Whatever.

Lesser: With *this*.

Hoag: (silence) What is that you're pointing at me, Todd?

Very: It's a Mossberg pistol-grip pump-action .22-caliber shotgun, dude. Current weapon of choice among drug enforcers. Can be concealed along the leg and whipped out like a pistol. But it packs the punch of a longarm. Nice toy. Where'd you get it, Lesser?

Lesser: Bought it from a drug dealer I know.

Hoag: Is it loaded, Todd?

Lesser: Yes, it is.

Hoag: Just checking. Shall I go on? *(no response)* I'll go on. You went upstairs and murdered Ferris in his sleep. Did you use that?

Lesser: No, too messy. I wanted no traces to be found. I strangled him. It was so much more . . . *personal.* Intimate. I felt so powerful, so *right* as I held that sleaze there in my hands, knowing I was not only choking the life out of him but *ruining* him, too. His reputation, I mean. No one would ever think of him as a great writer now. He'd just be a murderer. A common murderer. I dragged him down here in the sheet and dug a hole and buried him. Then I smoothed it over and laid the patio. Then I went back upstairs and remade the bed and packed up some of his clothes, cigarettes, the book he was reading, anything that he might take with him if he were on the run. I stuffed it in the trunk of the Olds and drove off. I couldn't disappear for a long time – I knew Boyd would start calling me as soon as he heard about Charlie – but I wanted to get the car past the tollbooths before the police put out the word on it. I stashed it in a twenty-four-hour garage in Hoboken. Then I took the train home.

Hoag: And so began the manhunt. That was a nice touch, telling Boyd that Ferris had just called from a gas station in Mount Vernon. Boyd believed you. I believed you.

Lesser: People tend to. It's because I'm so nonthreatening. They think only winners know how to lie. After work I went back out to Hoboken, got the car, and drove it to Trenton, where I left it. I wanted the police to think he was heading for Atlantic City.

Very: Score one for you.

Lesser: From Trenton I caught a bus to New Haven. I hitchhiked the rest of the way to Crescent Moon Pond. I assumed the police would eventually find out about the shack after they struck out in Atlantic City.

Hoag: And you wanted it to look like he'd been hiding there. Another nice touch. Convincing. I waited two whole days there for him to come back. How did you get out to the shack without a boat?

Lesser: There's a trail through the woods behind it that runs into a road after a couple of miles. I backpacked in and out. I had a flashlight. When I got there, I made a fire and lit the lantern and unpacked the stuff I'd brought with me – the package of Marlboros, copy of *Gatsby*, food, half-empty bottle of tequila . . .

Samuels: That sounds like an excellent idea. *(sound of chair scraping)*

Lesser: Where do you think you're going, Boyd?

Samuels: Nowhere. Just raiding the liquor cupboard.

Lesser: Sit down. Now!

Samuels: Okay, Toddy. If that's what you want.

Lesser: And don't call me Toddy! I hate that name. It's a name for an ineffectual wimp.

Hoag: Which you are not.

Lesser: You've always used me, Boyd. Treated me like a nothing. Maybe you've changed your opinion of me now.

Hoag: I think we all have, Todd. You're no wimp. You're the boss whatever happens now is up to you.

Lesser: Nice to see that you know it. I guess this is what it takes. I guess you have to point a gun at people to get their respect.

Very: You got it, Lesser. But what are you gonna do about it? Kill all four of us? You're gonna have to, because if even one of us survives this – and I don't think you can take out more than two of us before the other two jump you – you're smoked. We got your whole confession right here on tape. Don't make it any worse for yourself, Lesser. Just hand over the gun.

Lesser: What have I got to gain? My life is over no matter what I do.

Hoag: Maybe not, Todd. Everyone's going to know the truth about you now, about how you wrote *Bang*. You're going to be famous, and there's going to be a great deal of interest in your new manuscript. Don't you think so, Boyd?

Samuels: Give me ten minutes on the phone and I'll get you seven figures. Guaranteed.

Hoag: You've *made* it, Todd. Ferris is gone. It's *your* time now. You wanted to be a great author, not a mass murderer. Don't blow it.

Lesser: *(silence)* Maybe you're on to something . . .

Hoag: Sure I am. Hand over the gun, Todd. Just hand it over. That's the spirit. No, don't, Todd! Not that! No! *(sound of explosion, indistinguishable curses)*

(end tape)

CHAPTER
EIGHTEEN

They had to wait awhile before they could dig up the patio. The photographs had to be taken. The body had to be bagged and carted away, the blood and brains hosed off. It wasn't a neat job. You don't get a neat corpse when you blow your own head off with a shotgun.

Two of them moved the patio furniture aside and started in on the bluestone with picks and shovels while Very talked to the FBI on the phone inside. I watched them work. Boyd Samuels sat in a garden chair next to me gulping a large whiskey. He was trembling and quite pale.

It was a warm day, and heavy work. The diggers offered no resistance when Vic returned from the basement with a sledgehammer and joined them. Soon they were standing back, watching in awe as the big guy ferociously attacked the stones and mortar. The ground shook from each thundering blow. His chest heaved. The sweat flew from him. He had failed Ferris. Now he was atoning.

"Thought you had him there for a second, dude." Very was standing next to me now, popping his gum.

"Had him?"

"Talked him out of pulling the trigger. He seemed to be wavering there for a second, y'know?"

I shook my head. "Never. He had to do it."

"How come?"

"His hero had."

The stones and mortar were broken up now. Vic and the diggers began to shovel it aside.

"Felt kinda sorry for him, actually," Very said, eyeing Boyd Samuels, who was staring morosely into his glass. "He did get pretty royally screwed. That didn't give him the fight to take out three people. No way. But still . . ."

I tugged at my ear. "Yeah. I think I know what you mean."

"Lieutenant!"

They'd found the shallow grave. A corner of white sheet stuck out of the bare, dark earth now.

Very nodded to them. They started digging.

"What will you do with him, Lieutenant?" I asked.

"Take his remains over to the coroner," he replied. "See that he's given a proper burial."

"Couldn't you just leave him here? He's dead and buried. Why disturb him? We know what happened."

Very narrowed his eyes at me. "Procedure, dude. Gotta be followed. Besides, this is a private residence. A body can't be buried here."

"He belongs here."

"In his backyard?"

"In Gramercy Park, with all of the other major figures in American literature. In his own weird way, he was one of them."

They lifted the body out by the sheet and laid it on a stretcher. Then they unwrapped it. It was him, all right. They carried him through the house to the ambulance out front.

Boyd Samuels followed them, barking at them to be careful. "That's my friend there," he cried. "My best friend."

Very's jaw worked on his gum as he stared at the empty grave. "Gotta admit I doubted you there for a while, dude. Thought you were jerking me around, and you were. But I see where you were coming from now." He stuck out his hand and burped. "Take care of yourself, dude."

I shook his hand. "Likewise, Lieutenant. And take care of that stomach."

"What I gotta do is find a less stressful line of work," he said, nodding. "But hey, what else is there that's so much fucking fun, huh? Sometime we gotta get together. Like I told ya, I gotta million stories to – "

"Now wouldn't be a good time."

"Whatever," he said easily as he left.

Vic was sitting in the shade, mopping his face with a towel. I sat down next to him. Neither of us spoke for a while.

"There was nothing you could have done, Vic," I finally said. "If you *had* been here to protect him, Todd would just have killed you, too."

"I could have tried," he said softly.

"He had a shotgun."

"I could have tried," he repeated. "It's what I'm paid to do."

"No, you're not. You're not paid to die."

He shrugged that off, hung his head.

I went inside and found two beers in the refrigerator and came back out with them. He took one from me and drank some of it.

"Listen, Vic. Merilee is going to need a live-in caretaker at her new farm. Someone handy and reliable and self-sufficient. Might be a good situation for you. Nice area. Fishing's good."

"Don't know, Hoag. I was thinking about heading back out to L.A. It's where my friends are."

"You have friends here."

He ran a big hand over the lower half of his face. "To tell you the God's honest truth, I hate L.A. Always have."

I patted his meaty shoulder. "Good deal. I'll tell her you're interested."

"Thanks, Hoag. And you don't have to worry. I wouldn't make a pass at her or anything."

"I know you wouldn't."

"When are you two gonna get back together again, anyhow?"

"Hey, mind your own business."

He chuckled. It wasn't a pretty sound, but it beat silence.

It took me twenty minutes to find Lulu. She was upstairs cowering under the bed in the master bedroom. Gunfire is not one of her favorite things. Skitsy's red lipstick came sliding back out from under there with her. I picked it up and looked at it.

This time it was my turn to throw it against the wall.

I spent most of my time after that in my mukluks. The writing went smoothly now. I had the whole story. And another bestseller. Surefire.

In my free time I thought a lot about Ferris Rush, and how he'd scammed me and how I just couldn't seem to make myself hate him for it – no matter how hard I tried. I thought about Todd Lesser, whose hunger for respect twisted and ultimately devoured him. I thought about Charlie Chu, who was done in by both men through no fault of her own, and about what might have been. I thought about all three of them, and Skitsy Held, too, and felt no anger. Just sadness.

I don't ever want a kid brother again.

Boyd Samuels phoned me one evening while I was working, sounding immensely pleased with himself. "I did a beautiful thing today, amigo."

"Quit the business?"

He laughed. "Sold Toddy's book, *Boy Wonder*. It's brilliant, and it's going to be a major success. Maybe even bigger than *Bang*."

"Too bad he won't be around to enjoy it."

"I'm not keeping my commission though. Tanner's helping me set up a scholarship fund at Columbia with it in Toddy's name."

"You're all heart."

"Can't just keep taking, you know? Sometimes you have to give a little something back. That's what's wrong with this world – not enough people do." He shifted gears – into grave. "Hear about Delilah?"

"What about her?"

"Bitch tried to kill herself. Slit her wrists just before she was gonna appear on a local talk show in Seattle. They had to rush her to the hospital. They said she'll be okay. Why would she do something crazy like that?"

"She loved him. Or the man she thought was him. Sorry to hear about it."

"Not as sorry as I am, amigo. It means her tour is off, and so are her sales. Fuck it, that's the business for you – win one, lose one. So listen, what are your plans after you finish up?"

"Why?"

"Got an anorexic prima ballerina I'm dying to put you together with. Seven-figure advance."

"I don't think so."

"How about the college basketball coach of the year? It'll sell two hundred thousand copies hardcover in the Southern states alone."

"Not interested."

"Okay, I hear you. We'll talk again after you've had a chance to chill out. I want us to cook up some more scams together. You're family now, understand?"

"You could do me one favor, amigo," I said. "It's not a big one."

"Anything. Name it."

"Disown me."

After I hung up, I called the hospital out in Seattle. Miss Moscowitz wasn't taking any calls. I left my name and number. I never heard from her.

Merilee wore a bare-shouldered black silk chiffon dress to the Tony Awards with her pearls and a heavy white silk shawl that had belonged to her great-grandmother. Her face was made up and her golden hair was up in a bun. She looked utterly gorgeous as I let her into the limo that was to whisk us off to the Minskoff Theatre for the show – gorgeous and nervous. She was nibbling on her lower lip, and she started wringing her hands the second she settled into the backseat, Lulu whooping and snuffling hello.

As our driver pulled away from the curb, I noticed Merilee staring at me with her big green eyes.

"Something wrong?" I asked.

"Nothing, darling," she said, reddening. "I just never get tired of looking at you in a tux."

"I never get tired of looking at you, period."

"Bless you, darling," she said, wringing her hands some more. "Oh, God," she groaned. "Why are we doing this? I hate these things."

"Nonsense. It'll be fun."

"That, mister, is easy for you to say."

I stirred the iced pitcher of martinis I'd brought, filled two glasses, and held one out to her.

She shook her head. "I'd better not – I'll forget my acceptance speech." Then she lunged for the glass. "Oh, what the hay, I'm not going to win anyway."

"That's the spirit." I held up my glass. "To the woman of everyone's dreams, particularly my own."

Her eyes got all soft for a second. She took my hand and squeezed it. Then we drank, and she stole my olive. She's always claimed mine tastes better than hers. I wouldn't know. She's never let me near hers.

"Ask me what I did today," I commanded.

"Okay – what did you do today?"

"Resigned from the Racquet Club."

"Really?" She tilted her head at me. "How come?"

"Dinosaurs belong there. I don't."

"Good for you, darling," she said approvingly. "That place always struck me as some kind of eerie throwback to the days of Chester Arthur and cigars and port. I've always hated it."

"I never knew that."

"Sometimes it's best to keep one's opinions to oneself." She sipped her martini. "And now what? Is there another novel?"

"I think so."

"Good," she said, pleased. "Yes, there's nothing quite like a good strong dose of reality to send you running, screaming, back to the comforting world of fiction." I refilled our glasses. "Vic will be ready to take over for you out there tomorrow, if you like."

"I like. He seems so sweet and loyal, almost like a big St. Bernard."

"Just don't let anyone ever get him mad."

"Why, what happens?"

"You don't want to know."

Limos were backed up all the way down the block from the theater. We had to wait our turn for our grand arrival, which was fine by me. Gave us enough time to finish our pitcher of martinis. When we finally did inch up to the front of the theater, blinding TV lights and plenty of commotion were waiting there for us. Cameras were rolling. Flashbulbs were popping. Hundreds of onlookers were shouting and crowding the police barricades.

Our chauffeur hopped out and opened the door. Merilee groaned and squeezed my hand again. Then she took a deep breath, gathered her shawl and her star presence around her, and stepped out onto the curb, smiling radiantly at the crowd, which gasped and applauded at the sight of her. I took her arm and we strode inside, blinking from the lights, Lulu waddling along behind us.

The theater had been converted into a television studio for the night. A giant teleprompter was set up in front of the stage. Cameras and monitors were everywhere. Most of the seats down front were already filled with nominees and producers and angels. We said hello to Meryl Streep and Don Gummer as we passed by them. David Mamet and Lindsay Crouse. Joe Papp.

We were just about to take our seats when Merilee suddenly stopped and grabbed me by the shoulders. "Say yes, Hoagy."

"Say yes to what?"

"Just say it," she commanded urgently.

I shrugged. "Okay . . . yes."

"Good."

With that she took my hand, turned, and dragged me back up the crowded aisle, politely elbowing people aside to make way for us.

"Merilee, where are we going?" I called after her. We were going out the front doors to the street again, and back to our limo, which was double-parked halfway down the block.

"Merilee, where are we – ?"

"To JFK, please," she told our driver as she jumped in, heaving a huge sigh of relief.

Lulu and I got in after her.

"What did I just say yes to?" I asked her, mystified, as we pulled away from the theater.

She threw her arms around me and kissed me. It was some kiss. We were halfway to Queens before she pulled away, gasping, reached inside her evening bag and produced our passports. "The question, mister, was will you run away to Paris with me."

"Is that what we're doing?"

"Uh-huh. No luggage. No reservations. No mackerel. No nothing. We're just hopping on the Concorde and going. What's to stop us?"

"Only sanity, and we've never let that stand in our way before. But what about the Tonys?"

"*Fuck* the Tonys."

"Merilee Gilbert Nash!"

"I've asked you never to use my middle – "

"I'm going to tell your mother you invoked the F-word!"

"She'd never believe you," she huffed.

"You're right, she wouldn't." I stroked her face, got lost in her green eyes for a moment. "Maybe we'll be able to find that same little hotel in the seventeenth arrondissement, the one with the bed that sloped in toward the middle."

"Where, I seem to recall, we spent most of our time," she added, giving me her up-from-under look.

"Merilee, you really are getting awfully frisky."

"You mind, darling?"

"Nope. I just hope I can keep up with you, so to speak."

"I'll make sure you do," she whispered, her lips brushing mine.

"And what happens afterward?"

"Usually you fall asleep with your mouth open."

"I meant – "

"We're not going to think about afterward," she declared. "Afterward is the sort of thing that middle-aged people worry about, not people like us. Now shut up and kiss me."

I took her in my arms and did just that.

Lulu wriggled around between us, tail thumping. She'd always wanted to go to France. The tricky part would be finding a beret that fit her.

The Woman Who Fell From Grace

the fourth
Stewart Hoag & Lulu Mystery

For Stella
who has been nice enough
to stay behind

It's being hailed as the ultimate American novel, and maybe it is. It's huge, loud, sentimental, and its pants are on fire. It's also a rollicking good time. I devoured it in greedy bites and would happily come back for seconds.

—from Dorothy Parker's review of *Oh, Shenandoah* in the Sunday *New York Times*, June 2, 1940

CHAPTER
ONE

I was standing in the lobby of the Algonquin Hotel seeing double. Two utterly distinguished, utterly identical elderly gentlemen sat there before me sipping on martinis at one of the small, round lounge tables. They had the same handsome, patrician face – eyes blue, brows arched, nose long and rather sharp, chin cleft, hair silver and wavy. They wore the same double-breasted navy blazer, white cotton broadcloth shirt, yellow-and-burgundy-striped silk tie. They looked up at me at the same time. They smiled at me at the same time. Same smile. Same teeth. White.

I had to blink several times to make sure I wasn't having an acid flashback from the summer of '70, the one I can't remember too much about, except that I wanted to move to Oregon and raise peaches. I even shot a glance down at Lulu, my basset hound, who was looking uncommonly pert that season in the beret Merilee had bought her in Paris. Lulu was blinking, too.

"Frederick, Mr. Hoag," said one, as I dumbly shook his long, slender hand.

"Edward, Mr. Hoag," said the other, as I shook his.

"Won't you please join us, sir?" they said in perfect harmony.

Harmony because their voices were different. Each spoke with the gentle, courtly accent of the Southern aristocrat. But while Frederick's voice was husky, Edward's was softer, higher pitched. A small distinction, but I had to grab on to something, anything, to keep from hooting. I joined them. Lulu turned around three times at my feet and curled up with a contented grunt. She likes the Algonquin. Always has.

It was after five and the place was filling up with the pasty-faced English tourists and assorted New York literary fossils and bottom feeders who usually hang around there. Peter Ustinov was giving a radio reporter an interview on the sofa next to us, and a whole new meaning to the words *couch potato*. Rog Angell was busy demonstrating the hitch in the Straw Man's swing to two other owlish *New Yorker* editors. Pretty much everybody else in the hotel was staring at Eddie and Freddie, who might have been retired diplomats or rear admirals or a new set of Doublemint Twins for the Depend-undergarment set, but who were actually the Glaze brothers of Staunton, Virginia, the exceptionally shrewd keepers of the *Oh, Shenandoah* flame. It was the Glaze brothers who had just engineered the record-shattering $6.2-million auction for the most eagerly awaited literary sequel of all time, the sequel to *Oh, Shenandoah*, the epic romance novel of the American Revolution penned in 1940 by their mother, Alma Glaze. *Oh, Shenandoah* wasn't the greatest novel in the history of publishing, but it certainly was the most popular. More than 30 million readers in twenty-seven different languages had gobbled up the thousand-page saga through the years. Ten times that many had seen the Oscar-winning movie, which in the opinion of most critics ranked as the greatest Hollywood blockbuster of all time, greater than *Gone With the Wind*, than *Citizen Kane*, than *Yes, Georgio*. For decades, fans had been clamoring for a sequel. Now they were going to get one.

"So glad you could make it, Mr. Hoag," Frederick rasped as he rang the bell on our table for our waiter.

"My pleasure. And make it Hoagy."

"As in Carmichael?" asked Edward softly.

"As in the cheese steak."

"Would that be the one they serve in Buffalo?" Frederick inquired.

"Philadelphia. It's chicken wings they do in Buffalo."

"And I'm sure they do them exceedingly well," said Edward graciously.

Our waiter, Frank, hurried over and said how nice it was to see me again. The Glaze brothers ordered another round of martinis. I tagged along, heavy on the olives. Lulu had her usual. After Frank went off, Edward leaned over and scratched her belly roughly, as if she were a hunting dog. She's more the champagne-and-caviar type. She snuffled in protest.

He immediately made a face. "My goodness. Her breath is somewhat . . ."

"She has rather strange eating habits."

Frank returned with our drinks and a plate of pickled herring and raw onion for Lulu. She attacked it at once. The brothers watched her. They sipped their drinks. They glanced at each other. I watched them, beginning to detect the subtle differences. Frederick had a more relaxed set to his jaw and shoulders, an easier manner. Edward appeared more formal and reserved. The shy one.

It was Frederick who began. "Exactly how much do you know about this project of ours, Hoagy?"

"Very little. I've been away."

He leaned forward eagerly. "With Merilee Nash?"

"Frederick, please," scolded Edward. "You're being nosy."

"It's okay," I assured him. "I'm used to being a public laughingstock. It's kind of a nice feeling, after a while."

"I shall bring you up to date, if I might," said Frederick. "As you may know, our mother, in her last will and testament, specified that no sequel to *Oh, Shenandoah* would be authorized until some fifty years after her death, which is – "

"Which is to say *now*," interjected Edward.

Frederick shot him a cool glance, then turned back to me. "Sometime before her death, Mother had in fact outlined the plot for a second volume, which was – "

"Which was to be called *Sweet Land of Liberty*," Edward broke in.

Frederick shot him another cool look. He clearly didn't like it when Edward interrupted him. Something told me that Eddie had been doing it for sixty years. "*Which*," Frederick went on, "she then tucked away in the safe in the library of Shenandoah, our family's estate, where it has remained, sealed, until – "

"Until a few weeks ago," Edward said. "When it was, at long last, opened."

Frederick calmly pulled a slim gold cigarette case from the inside pocket of his blazer, removed a cigarette, and lit it with a gold lighter. He politely blew the smoke away from me. He blew it directly toward Edward, who scowled and waved it away, irritably.

"The safe's opening," Frederick continued, "took place live on national television. That Geraldo Rivera person. Perhaps Mr. Rivera is a friend of yours . . . ?"

I popped one of my olives in my mouth. "Not even maybe."

"Horrible little man," sniffed Edward.

"Garish display," agreed Frederick. "Mave's idea, naturally."

"Naturally," said Edward.

Mave was their younger sister, Mavis Glaze, the socialite who wasn't quite so famous as their mother but who was damned close. Ever since the late seventies, when the PBS affiliate in Washington, D.C., asked her to host a little half-hour, weekly show on social graces called *Uncommon Courtesy*. Something about the stern, matronly way she said "Courtesy is most decidedly *not* common" had tickled Johnny Carson's funny bone. He began to make her the butt of his nightly monologue jokes, and then a frequent guest on *The Tonight Show*, and before long her show had gone national and Mavis Glaze had become the Jack Lalanne of manners with a chain of more than seven hundred etiquette schools. To get Mavis Glazed was to emerge civil and poised, the perfect hostess, the perfect guest. "Civilization," declared Mavis over and over again in her endless TV commercials, "starts here." She ran her empire from Shenandoah, the historic 5,000-acre estate that had been in the Glaze family since the days when Virginia was the jewel of the colonies. Shenandoah was where Alma Glaze's epic had been set. The movie had been filmed entirely on location there. Part of the time now it was open to the public, and the public came by the busload to see it. They felt a special kind of love for the place. Shenandoah was America's ancestral home. It was even more popular with tourists than Monticello, Thomas Jefferson's home, situated across the Shenandoah Valley outside of Charlottesville. Jefferson was only our nation's most brilliant president. He never won an Oscar.

"Given Mave's own prominence," Frederick went on, "we all felt that she – "

"*We* being my brother and I," Edward broke in, "as well as the publisher and Mave . . ."

"That Mave should author the sequel." Frederick casually brushed some cigarette ash from the sleeve of his blazer onto the sleeve of Edward's. Edward reddened and flicked it onto the floor. "It seemed only natural," Frederick concluded.

I nodded, wondering how long it would be before one of them had the other down on the carpet in a headlock, and which one I'd root for.

"The understanding," explained Edward, "was that we find a professional novelist to do the actual writing. Someone gifted enough to meet Mother's high literary standards, yet discreet enough not to divulge their association with the project."

"Or the contents of Mother's outline," Frederick added. "Just exactly what happens in *Sweet Land of Liberty* is a well-kept secret, Hoagy. We've planned it that way to heighten reader anticipation. The tabloids would happily pay one hundred thousand dollars to steal our thunder."

I nodded some more. It's something I'm pretty good at.

"We all felt a novelist successful in the romance field would be most appropriate," said Edward. "The publisher came up with a list of several." He rattled them off. Two were milion-plus sellers of historical bodice-rippers in their own right – Antonia Raven and

Serendipity Vale, whose real name was Norman Pincus.

"Unfortunately," lamented Frederick, "none of them has worked out."

"How many have you gone through?" I asked. You can only nod for so long.

"Five of them left the project after one day," replied Edward. "Amply compensated for their time, of course. To assure their silence."

"Three more didn't make it to the end of the first day," added Frederick.

"Pretty surprising that any red-blooded writer would walk away," I said, "considering how much money is involved."

"They didn't walk, sir," said Edward. "They ran."

"Mavis," explained Frederick, choosing his words carefully, "is, well, *Mavis*. She's . . . She can be, perhaps, a bit . . . high-strung. Demanding. Magisterial . . ."

"She makes Nancy Reagan look like Little Red Riding Hood," Edward blurted out.

"A prize bitch," acknowledged Frederick. "But she's our baby sister and we love her."

Edward nodded emphatically. At least they agreed on that.

"Sounds like what you need," I suggested, "is someone who's used to being screamed at. Why don't you ask around up at Yankee Stadium?"

"What we need," said Edward, "is someone who can retain the flavor and spirit of *Oh, Shenandoah*. Otherwise, Mother's fans will be terribly disappointed. Unfortunately, Mave has, well, some ideas of her own. Ideas that are nowhere indicated in any of Mother's notes, though she insists they are indeed Mother's very own." He glanced uneasily over at Frederick, colored slightly, and lowered his voice. "Ideas she says Mother has personally communicated to her. While she sleeps. In her dreams."

I tugged at my ear. "What kind of ideas are we talking about?"

"Queer ones," Edward replied gravely. "Very, very queer."

"According to the terms of our contract with the publisher," said Frederick, "the estate has final say on the contents of the manuscript. We insisted upon it. If Mavis gets her way, Hoagy, and she always does, I have no doubt that the publication of *Sweet Land of Liberty* will rank as one of the greatest embarrassments in the history of American publishing. Not to mention a major financial disaster."

"You're her brothers," I said. "Won't she listen to you?"

"Mavis doesn't have to listen to us if she doesn't choose to," replied Edward. "And she generally doesn't choose to. You see, Hoagy, Mother believed in a system of matriarchy. We three children took her family name, Glaze, not father's, which was Blackwell. And when she died, she left Shenandoah and the entirety of her fortune to Mave and Mave alone. Frederick and I merely serve her in an advisory capacity. I happen to practice law. Frederick is an investment counselor. Protecting the financial and legal interests of Shenandoah and Mavis does occupy much of our time, and Mave does pay us quite generously for it. But it is she who has final say in all estate matters."

"And when she dies," added Frederick, "Shenandoah will pass on to her own first daughter, Mercy. Mave's husband, Richard, the gallant Lord Lonsdale, gets nothing."

"What does he do with himself?" I asked.

"Come when Mavis calls him," Frederick replied drily. "Tail wagging."

"Do they have any other children?"

"Just Mercy."

"And you gentlemen?"

"We are both bachelors," Edward said. "Without issue."

I drained my martini. Another appeared at my elbow instantly. "Sounds like one big unhappy family."

"Just like any other," agreed Edward pleasantly.

"Does your publisher know what's going on?"

"Only that we're having a bit of trouble finding a writer," replied Edward. "Not why. They are, however, getting nervous about our deadline. They expected the book to be well under way by now. They impressed upon us yesterday the amount of pressure they are under. Huge sums of money have been committed. The paperback publisher is waiting impatiently in line, as is the movie studio."

"They recommended you," said Frederick. "As a sort of specialist."

"I suppose that's one word for what I am."

"They said there isn't a celebrity alive, including Mavis, who you can't lick."

Edward shuddered. "What a horrible image, Frederick."

Frederick stared at him a moment. Then turned back to me. "You're our last and best hope, Hoagy. We're desperate. Will you fly down to Shenandoah and talk to Mavis?"

I sat back in my chair. "I should warn you there aren't many people who are good at what I'm good at. It's a rare talent. In fact, I'm the only one who has it."

"Not exactly bashful, are you, sir?" said Edward stiffly.

"You want bashful, get J. D. Salinger. He'll cost you a lot less money than I will."

"Certainly we can hammer something out," Frederick ventured. "We're all reasonable men, aren't we?"

"You might be. I'm not."

Frederick cleared his throat. "Frankly, money happens to be the least of our worries right now. Get Mave to stop communicating with the dead. Deliver a novel that Alma Glaze would have been proud to put her name on. Do that and we'll meet your price, no matter how unreasonable. Satisfied?"

"Every once in a while, if I try real hard." I sipped my martini. "Okay, we'll fly down there."

"Excellent," exclaimed Frederick, pleased.

Edward frowned. "By 'we' I trust you're not referring to Lulu here."

A low moan came out from under the table. I asked her to let me handle it.

"I am," I replied. "I tend to do most of the heavy lifting, but we always work together. We're a team."

Edward smiled. "Like Lunt and Fontanne?"

"I was thinking more of Abbott and Costello."

"I understand," said Frederick, "but there is the matter of the Shenandoah peacocks. Our trademark. They've lived on the north lawn for more than two hundred years. Their wings are clipped to keep them from flying away or – "

"Or crapping on anyone's head," Edward broke in.

Frederick lit another cigarette and blew the smoke Edward's way. Those boys were at it again. "That makes them exceedingly vulnerable to predators – dogs, cats, raccoons, foxes. The grounds are kept carefully guarded, and no animal of any kind, no matter how well trained, is ever allowed on the property. I'm sure you can appreciate that."

"Gentlemen, the sole predatory act of Lulu's life was a growling contest she got into in Riverside Park with a eight-month-old Pomeranian named Mr. Fuzzball. She needed eighteen stitches when it was all over."

They mulled this over a moment, lips pursed. They looked at each other. A silent message passed between them. "We have your word, as a gentleman, that she'll not harm the peacocks?" asked Edward.

"You have my word, as a gentleman, that she'll be deathly afraid of them."

"Very well," said Frederick reluctantly. "We'll finesse Mavis on this particular point. Just try to keep Lulu under cover, if you can."

"That's no problem. In a rainhat and sunglasses she easily passes for Judd Hirsch. When do we leave?"

CHAPTER TWO

We left early the next week. I had stuff I had to do first. It was nearly April. My Borsalino was due for its 30,000-mile overhaul at Worth and Worth. I had to take the wool liner out of my trench coat and put my winter clothes in storage and fill the prescription for Lulu's allergy medicine. I had to read the damned book, all 1,032 pages of it.

Partly, *Oh, Shenandoah* was the story of how the American Revolution shattered forever the privileged lives of colonial Virginia's landed British gentry. But mostly it was a love triangle, heavy on the violins. Flaming-haired Evangeline Grace, the beautiful, headstrong young daughter of a wealthy tobacco planter, was torn by her love for two men. John Raymond, handsome son of the colonial governor in Williamsburg, was a brilliant law student, a sensitive poet, a budding statesman. The other, a dashing, hot-blooded Frenchman named Guy De Cheverier, was a fearless adventurer, a ruthless brigand reviled by polite society. It was their story. It was the story of the great Virginia plantations – of colorful horse races and grand balls, of velvet waistcoats and powdered wigs, and smiling, happy slaves. And it was the story of the Revolution. De Cheverier would become a daring war hero who time and again led his brave, loyal men into victorious battle against the Redcoats. Raymond would break with his English father to become an architect of the Revolution at the side of his William and Mary law classmate Tom Jefferson. Real figures from American history were sprinkled throughout the novel – George Washington, Benjamin Franklin, James Monroe, James Madison. Alma Glaze did her homework. She drew her portrait of Shenandoah Valley plantation life from local historical records and supposedly, her own family's illustrious past. Still, it was the love triangle, the battle between Raymond and De Cheverier for Vangie's hand that carried the reader's interest across so many pages. Which one would she marry? In the end, she couldn't decide, and since neither was willing to bow out gracefully, the two of them fought a duel for her hand, Vangie to marry the winner. Who won? Alma Glaze never told us. All she left us with was that famous closing line: "As one man fell, Evangeline stepped forward, eyes abrim, breast heaving, to embrace both the victor and the new life that surely promised to be her grandest adventure." For fifty years, readers had been arguing over what the hell that meant. That's why there was so much interest in the sequel.

Naturally, it's hard to read it nowadays without seeing the faces of the actors who played the roles in the lavish Sam Goldwyn production, the only movie in Hollywood history ever to sweep Best Picture, Best Director (William Wyler), Best Screenplay (Robert Sherwood), as well as Best Actor and Actress. Warner Brothers loaned Goldwyn Errol Flynn to play De Cheverier. For the coveted roles of Evangeline Grace and John Raymond, Goldwyn cast the gifted young British stage performers Sterling Sloan and Laurel Barrett, who also happened to be husband and wife in so-called real life. Neither had appeared in an American film before. Sloan was fresh off his acclaimed Hamlet in London's West End and bing touted as the new Olivier. The fragile, achingly beautiful Barrett, the woman who beat out every top actress in Hollywood to play Vangie, was a complete unknown. Both won Oscars for *Oh, Shenandoah*. Sloan's, of course, was awarded posthumously. He dropped dead of a ruptured brain aneurysm only hours after wrapping the film on location in Virginia. His death at age thirty-two destroyed Barrett. She suffered a nervous breakdown soon afterward. She was in and out of institutions for depression right up until she died in 1965 at the age of fifty-two, her life made, and seemingly unmade, by her *Oh, Shenandoah* triumph. She wasn't alone in that.

Alma Glaze herself encountered outrageous swings of fortune, good and bad. A small, rather flinty woman given to wearing orthopedic shoes and severe hats, she was the only child of the Shenandoah Valley's most distinguished old family, and wife to a successful local banker. She began work on her first and only novel one summer while she was recovering from pneumonia. She spent seven years on it. When she finally finished it, she gave it to a childhood friend who taught literature at Mary Baldwin, a small, proper nearby women's college. The friend sent it on to his brother, an editor for a New York publishing house. The rest is publishing history. *Oh, Shenandoah* sold an incredible one million copies in its first six months, sometimes as many as sixty thousand copies in one day. Still, Alma Glaze wasn't able to savor its success for long. The day she was awarded the Pulitzer Prize for literature was the same day her husband died of tuberculosis, leaving her a forty-two-year-old widow with three children. She sold the film rights to Sam Goldwyn for the then-whopping sum of $100,000. And though the movie's success would surpass even that of the book, she was again unable to enjoy it. The week after it premiered, she was run over by a hit-and-run driver while she was crossing a street in Staunton, Virginia, her hometown. She died instantly.

And now it was a raw March morning fifty years later, and I was squeezed into a tiny, stuffy De Havilland Dash four-prop that was riding the turbulence on down to Charlottesville from New York, by way of Baltimore. My complimentary honey-roasted peanuts and plastic cup of warm orange juice were bouncing around on the tray before me. Lulu was on the floor under me, making unhappy noises. My mind was on how I never expected things to turn out this way. This wasn't me. This was someone else sitting here getting airsick. Not me. Never me.

If you're a serious fan of the gossip columns, and of American literary trivia, you may remember me. It's okay if you don't. It has been a while since the *New York Times*, upon reading my first novel, *Our Family Enterprise*, labeled me "the first major new literary voice of the '80s." Ah, how sweet it had been. The best-seller list. The awards. Fame. Marriage to Merilee Nash, Joe Papp's hottest and loveliest young leading lady. The eight art-deco rooms overlooking Central Park. The red 1958 Jaguar XK150 convertible. The gaudy contract for book two. But then there was this problem with my juices. They dried up. The creative kind. All kinds. Merilee got the apartment and the Jag, the Tony for the Mamet play, the Oscar for the Woody Allen movie. Briefly, another husband, too, that fabulously successful playwright Zack something. I got Lulu, my drafty old fifth-floor walk-up on West Ninety-third Street, and my ego, which recently applied to Congress for statehood.

My juices did come back. Somewhat. There was a slim second novel, *Such Sweet Sorrow*, which managed to become as great a commercial and critical flop as my first was a success. Merilee came back, too. Somewhat. These days we're two intelligent semiadults who are content not to ask questions anymore and to just go ahead and make each other miserable. Actually, we get along fine as long as we're not together. I still had my apartment. She still had her eight rooms on Central Park West and her eighteen acres in Hadlyme, Connecticut, where right now she was busy playing in the mud while the offers rolled in. No plans for a merger. We know better than that.

I'd just spent the last three months in a small boat on the Aegean, subsisting on grilled fish and iced retsina and fasting from the neck up–no books, no magazines, no newspapers. No ideas, except my own. Slowly, a third novel had begun to take shape. But it would take me a good three years to write, and I had no publisher for it and no money left. That meant I had to fall back on my second, decidedly less distinguished calling – pen for hire. I've ghosted three celebrity memoirs so far. Each has been a best-seller. My background as a writer of fiction certainly helps. Good anecdotes are vital to the success of any memoir. The best way to make sure they're good is to make them up. It also helps that I used to be a celebrity myself. I know how to handle them. The lunch-pail ghosts don't. That's why the Glaze brothers had turned to me.

On the downside, ghosting has proven hazardous to my health. Not to mention the health of others. People have this way of dropping dead around me. Consider yourself warned. Also consider this before you get any ideas: If you're in trouble, if you need help, if you don't know who to call, don't call me. I'm not a hero. Besides, you can't afford me.

We left the storm behind as we flew further south. There was nothing but blue skies over Virginia. I was one of four men who got off at Charlottesville, and the only one who wasn't wearing mint-green golf slacks. The air was softer and more fragrant than in the North, the sun bright and hot. I was halfway to the small cinder-block terminal when I suddenly realized I was alone. Back across the runway I went and up the steps into the plane.

She was still under the seat, trembling as badly as she does when she's about to get a s-h-o-t. She flat out didn't want to get off the plane. She does like to fly. In fact, she's already amassed enough frequent-flyer miles to qualify for a free coach flight all the way from New York City to Lansing, Michigan. This, however, was a little much. I asked her what the problem was. All I got in response was whimpering. I told her to come. She refused. I'm bigger. I dragged her out from under the seat, hoisted her up, and carried her, thrashing and moaning in protest, out the cabin door.

"Terrible twos," I explained to the stewardess.

My rented Chevy Nova smelled as if somebody had once stuffed it full of Styrofoam peanuts. I stowed my gear in the trunk, tossed my trench and Borsalino in the backseat, and took off the jacket of the gray cheviot-wool suit I'd had made for me in London at Strickland's. I shoved the driver's seat back to accommodate my legs and rolled down the windows so Lulu could stick her large, black nose out and wail unhappily at the parking lot. I reminded her I'd gone to a lot of trouble to get her invited along, and if she wasn't going to behave, she could spend the next three months in a kennel with a lot of strange, mean pit bulls. She shut up.

I worked the Nova out of the airport and through the outskirts of Charlottesville, seat of Albemarle County, lush Eden where Jefferson built Monticello and Monroe built Ash Lawn, and where the haves still breed horses and cattle and themselves in plush country comfort.

Spring came earlier here. The cherry trees were already blossoming a gaudy pink. The tulips and daffodils were open, the grass was thick and green, and the forsythia bushes were explosions of mustard yellow.

I picked up Route 64 outside of town and coaxed the Nova up to eighty, where it handled smooth as a Maytag in the spin cycle. The highway climbed through the Blue Ridge Mountains. Then it tumbled down and before me spread the valley with its gently undulating patchwork quilt of fertile green farmland and red clay soil, its tree-shaded brick manor homes, its calm. Clumps of cattle munched away on the grass and the Alleghenies rippled endlessly across the sky. There may be prettier places on earth than the Shenandoah Valley, but I haven't seen one.

I got off the highway at Staunton, the historic little town where they don't pronounce the *u* and where two world-famous celebrities, Alma Glaze and Woodrow Wilson, were born. It's a gem of a place – steep, hilly streets of turreted Victorian mansions shaded by magnolias and redbuds, a restored turn-of-the-century business district, and a pleasing absence of the Yushie influence. Nary a sign of the young urban shitheads in their spandex workout togs. No take-out stir-fry emporium called Wok 'n' Roll. No singles Laundromat called *dirtysomething*. The tallest building in town was the Hotel Woodrow Wilson, and it was built in 1925. Eleven stories, not counting the neon sign on the roof.

It was just past five. Workers were streaming out of the office buildings and the Augusta County Courthouse for their cars. They were smiling and laughing. No scowls. No snarls. No one was riding on my tail. No one was blasting his horn. They must put something in the water.

The Glaze brothers' directions took me through town on Beverley Street past the Dixie Theatre, the vast, fabled, old silent-picture palace where *Oh, Shenandoah* had its original worldwide premiere. Workmen were busy sprucing the place up. A newly restored 70mm print of the film classic was being screened there in a few weeks as part of the fiftieth anniversary celebration. It was going to be a major deal. Surviving cast and crew members were even going to be flown in. Not that very many biggies were still around. The three stars and Goldwyn and Wyler were long gone. So was most of the all-star supporting cast. Raymond Massey, who played Thomas Jefferson. David Niven, who was the smug British colonel, Edgerton. Ethel Barrymore, Donald Crisp, Walter Huston, Linda Darnell. About the only surviving cast member I could think of was Rex Ransom, who played James Madison. I was hoping Rex came. I wanted to meet him for reasons that had nothing to do with *Oh, Shenandoah* and everything to do with my childhood.

I turned onto a narrow country road outside of town that twisted its way back through poultry farms and fenced pasturage. Fields of winter rye were being plowed under for fertilizer. The air was redolent of loamy soil and cow pies. Some black Angus grazed alongside the road. Lulu barked gleefully at them, secure in the knowledge they couldn't catch her as we sped past. Such invincibility did not, however, extend to her sinuses. Her hay fever was already making her sniffle. I'd have to give her a pill when we got there. I didn't want her developing breathing problems again. She snores when she has them. I happen to know this because she likes to sleep on my head.

Occasionally, a blue sign assured me I was on the right road for Historic Shenandoah. After about ten miles, the road came to an end at a white paddock gate, which was closed, and another blue sign, a big one. I had arrived. Historic Shenandoah was open for guided public tours Mondays, Wednesdays, and Fridays from nine to three and all day Saturday. The public was not welcome at any other time, such as now. The closed gate and the six-foot brick wall topped with electrified barbed wire made that quite clear. So did the surveillance camera. There was a phone at the gate. I picked it up and got a recording that told me everything the sign told me, then told me that if I had any other business to please hold on. I held on. The stirring Muzak version of "Vangie, My Love," from Max Steiner's *Oh, Shenandoah* movie score, began tickling my ear.

Until there was a click and a woman's voice: "Help ya?"

"Stewart Hoag. I'm here to see Mavis Glaze."

"Y'all want to drive right on up past the gift shop to the main house. Somebody'll be there to meet ya."

The gate swung open. I drove through. It closed behind me automatically. Evenly spaced ash trees lined the drive on both sides as it snaked up through fenced pasturage for several hundred yards before it arrived at a parking lot. There were picnic tables here and rest rooms and a log-cabin gift shop, where the people who were willing to spend five dollars a head to see the house where *Oh, Shenandoah* was filmed could spend even more on *Oh, Shenandoah* picture postcards, pens, pins, plates, peacock feathers, place mats, paintings, and posters, on *Oh, Shenandoah* cuff links, candlesticks, cookie molds, and cookbooks, on the many different renditions of "Vangie, My Love," which had been recorded through the years by everyone from Bing to Burl to Billy. Idol, that is. The parking lot was empty now, the gift shop closed. A pair of black custodians were sweeping up. They didn't look up at me as I drove past. The drive worked its way through some dense forest now, climbing as it did. Then the trees opened out in a huge semicircular forecourt of crushed stone, and there it was before me, up on a terraced rise so it could look down on the valley. Shenandoah was a mid-Georgian mansion of red brick built in the 1750s in the Palladian style. In fact it was considered the finest Palladian mansion of the British Colonies still intact. The main house was two stories high with a two-tiered portico and a mansard roof. Smaller, matching two-story dependencies flanked it in the forecourt and were connected to it by covered arcades. Broad stone steps led up to the front door, the one where a sobbing Vangie embraced De Cheverier after his bloody triumph over Edgerton. A short, massively built woman in her sixties stood there waiting for me in a pastel-yellow pantsuit that wouldn't have looked good on Elle Macpherson. On her the effect was that of a banana that had two Bosc pears stuffed inside it. She had curly white hair and Popeye forearms and so many jowls her chin seemed to be melting into her neck. She came down the steps to greet me, her skin flushed with perspiration. She was squinting at me.

"Welcome to Shenandoah, Mistuh Hoag," she said, her voice surprisingly high-pitched. She stuck out her hand. "I'm Fern O'Baugh, the housekeeper, cook, whatever."

We shook hands. She nearly broke mine. A lot of her may have been fat, but her forearms weren't.

"Make it Hoagy."

"As in Carmichael?"

"As in the cheese steak. The one they don't do in Buffalo."

She squinted up at me curiously. Then a big jolly laugh erupted from her and she began to shake all over. "My, my," she gasped. "I do love a man with a sense of humor. Y'know, I've read about you many times, Hoagy, in *People* magazine. All about your stormy marriage to Miss Merilee Nash, the woman who has everything except love."

"More fiction than fact, I assure you."

"Glad to hear it," she said brightly. "Because, honey, you come across in print like a real beanbag."

"Fern, I think we're going to get along just fine."

She erupted into another laugh. Then she took two steps toward my suitcases, tumbled right over Lulu, and sprawled heavily to the ground with an "Oof." I gave her my hand to help her up. My knees buckled but somehow held.

"My, my, I'm sorry, darlin'," she said, squinting down at Lulu. "I'm blind as Mistuh Magoo without my glasses. Should be wearing 'em, but they're such a bother." They were on a chain around her neck. She put them on and peered down at Lulu, who peered back up at her. "I do declare," Fern cried, astonished. "You're a little puppy dog! I thought you just had to be a big ol' puddy cat. Sure do smell like one."

"She has rather strange eating habits."

"But what's that there blue pancake she's got on her head?"

Lulu snuffled, insulted.

"A present from her mommy," I explained.

"Now, Hoagy, I must have your word she'll stay off the north lawn. She riles the peacocks and Mavis'll shoot her and me both."

"Not to worry."

"Good." Fern snatched up my suitcases as if they were empty and started up the steps with them. She was quite light on her feet for someone so round. "Too bad you didn't get an earlier flight," she said to me over her shoulder. "You just missed her."

I stopped. "What do you mean I missed her? We have an appointment. That's why I'm here."

"I know, but she flew up to Chicago to appear on the Miss Oprah Winfrey television show. Special program on the death of politeness in the modern American family. Last-minute thing. Mave felt sure you'd understand."

"Oh, I do," I said stiffly. "And when will she be back?"

"Sometime after midnight. Give you time to get settled. Now don't you go getting heated up about Mavis. She's the duchess. Anybody wants to get along with her learns that right off, or gets chewed up and spit out. That's the way it is." She glanced at me uneasily from the doorway. "Now I can just *tell* what you're thinking. You're thinking, 'That's the way it *was*, ma'am.' You're thinking, 'She hasn't met *me* yet.'"

"My thoughts don't tend to be that hard-boiled, generally. Runny is more like it."

"Well, you just stick that business in your back pocket and sit on it. No offense, but you don't look nearly tough enough to me. In fact, you don't look tough at all." She checked me over. "Got a nice tall frame on you, but they ain't been feeding you enough up there in New York. How you stay so skinny?"

"Good breeding."

"I'll have to start putting some meat on your bones. I can do French tonight, Italian, you name it."

"Southern will more than do."

"Fine. I'll fry us up a few chickens. It's just you and me. Richard went with Mave, and Mercy has a late class. You allergic to anything I should know about?"

"Only assholes."

She grinned up at me. "We *are* gonna get on fine."

We went inside.

The broad entrance salon extended straight through the center of the old house to the glass doors at the back, which were thrown open to let in the late-afternoon breeze. The north lawn out back was being cut by a gardener on a tractor mower. The aroma of fresh-cut spring grass spiced with wild chives wafted in the doors, finer than any perfume. The salon was paneled in tulip poplar with crown molded-wood cornices. The floor was irregular, wide oak boards. A narrow staircase with a walnut railing led up to the second floor. The furnishings were spare – a tall clock, a Chippendale table, a deacon's bench. Glaze-family oil portraits hung from the walls along with old maps and documents. One was the original royal land patent from the 1700s.

Two pedimented doorways on either side of the entrance salon opened into the four downstairs rooms. Fern led me through them. They were large, airy rooms with twelve-foot ceilings and tall windows overlooking the gardens. The walls were painted eggshell white throughout, with raised plaster molding and colonial-blue chair rails, except for in the library, which was paneled like the entrance salon. All four rooms had stone fireplaces. Again, the furnishing was spare, and Chippendale. The two front rooms were parlors, one formal, the other a sitting room. The sitting room was where John Raymond proposed to Vangie in the movie. The two rear rooms were the dining room and the famous library, where Alma Glaze wrote *Oh, Shenandoah* in longhand seated before the windows at a small writing table. There was a velvet rope in front of the table to keep visitors from touching it and the writing implements arrayed upon it. Her original manuscript lay there in a glass case in the middle of the room. Aside from this, and the obvious presence of electricity, the downstairs was just as it had been more than two hundred years before.

"The main house is only used for formal occasions nowadays," Fern declared. "Mostly, it's here for the tourists. They see the downstairs, the master bedroom upstairs, and Miss Alma's own room from her girlhood, which they used for Vangie's in the movie. The rest of the upstairs is still in need of historical restoration. The Glaze family was still living up there until the 1920s, when they remodeled the east wing and moved out there. That's where they live now. Keep their privacy that way. We lead visitors from here over to the old kitchen wing, and then the historic service yard and then on out. C'mon," she commanded, smacking me in the shoulder with the back of her hand. "I'll give ya the quick tour."

Lulu and I followed her through a narrow door off the dining room and down a short wooden stairway to a damp, cellar passageway.

"They'd bring the food from the kitchen along here to the table," she explained, puffing as we made our way down the long, dark corridor, passing the wine cellar and then the root cellar. "Quite a trek, but they always had the kitchens a distance away from the main house in the old days, on account of the heat and danger of fire."

The sunken corridor eventually came up outside the old kitchen. A low railing kept people from going inside. The kitchen ceiling was very low and soot-blackened. There was a vast open hearth with a baking oven and a cast-iron crane with heavy cast-iron pots hanging from it. A pine table sat in the middle of the room heaped with antique kitchen implements. Dried herbs hung from pegs. The floor was dirt.

"Whole lot of sweaty, hard work," observed Fern. "But believe me, the food come outta here tasted a sight better than what you get outta one of those microwaves. The cooks slept upstairs. Kitchen fire heated the whole place." She smacked my shoulder again. "C'mon."

I followed her, rubbing my shoulder. I'd have a welt there by morning. Outside, eight or ten rough, old, wooden outbuildings were clustered around a big kitchen garden. A gaunt old man in baggy, dark-green work clothes and a John Deere cap was slowly turning over the garden soil with a spading fork.

Fern pointed to the buildings. "That was the toolhouse, cobbler's shop, counting house, smokehouse, joinery, blacksmith . . . They didn't have no shopping mall to run down to in those days. Had to do everything themselves on a plantation this size. Be resourceful. That's what's wrong with people today – don't have to use our brains anymore. Nothing but a mess of jelly up there now."

"That would explain prime-time television."

She let out her big, hearty laugh. "Want y'all to come meet Roy. He's caretaker, head gardener."

"It must take a big staff to run this place," I said as we started over to the old man with the fork.

"All of it's day help from Staunton," she replied. "Custodians, housekeepers, gardeners, tour guides – everybody except for me and Roy. He has an apartment over the garage. Does his own cooking. Is good for maybe three, four words a year. Roy? Say hello to Hoagy. He'll be living here awhile. The short one's Lulu."

Roy was close to eighty, and mostly bone and gristle and leather. His face and neck were deeply tanned and creased, his big hands scarred and knuckly. He had a wad of tobacco in one cheek.

"Glad to meet you, Roy," I said, sticking out my hand.

He gave me a brief glance. His eyes were deep set and pale blue and gave away about as much as the ones you see on a sea bass under a blanket of shaved ice at the fish market. He spat some tobacco juice in the general direction of my kid-leather ankle boots, the ones I'd had made for me in London at Maxwell's. Then he went back to his forking. My hand he ignored.

Lulu growled at him from beside me.

We chose not to linger.

"Don't mind Roy," advised Fern as we started back to the main house. "At first, I thought he was rude. Then I decided he was slow. He ain't neither. He just hasn't got anything to say. Been working here forever, and I never have figured out why, since he's not exactly what you'd call competent. Of course, one thing you're gonna discover is things don't always make sense around here."

"Sounds not dissimilar to everywhere else."

We took the covered brick arcade back to the old house. Six of the Shenandoah peacocks were out on the lawn now, strutting and preening.

One of them honked at us, a flat, derisive Bronx cheer of a honk.

"That's Floyd," declared Fern. "He's the biggest."

Not that any of them were exactly small. They were big as tom turkeys. Their electric-blue necks were nearly three feet long, and their train of tail feathers was twice that. They were aware of us watching them. They watched us back. They didn't look very friendly. One of them spread his fan of plumage for us to see. It was not unimpressive.

"That's Wally. He's all ham."

I felt something at my feet. Lulu was crouched between my legs, trembling.

Fern looked down at her and laughed. "I guess we don't have to worry about her at that."

The great lawn sloped downward from the back of the house. A circular footpath ringed it, the border beds planted with tulips and daffodils. Beyond were orchards, a pond and gazebo, the family cemetery, where Alma Glaze was buried. For a backdrop there were the Alleghenies. The sun was setting over them.

"If you're going to live in a museum," I observed, "this isn't a terrible one."

"Mavis, she feels America has a right to see Shenandoah," Fern said with more than a trace of pride. "After all, it's a national treasure. Family doesn't make a nickel off the proceeds, y'know. All goes to the Society for the Preservation of Virginia Antiquities, of which Mavis happens to be president."

"Been here long, Fern?"

"Thirty-five years," she replied. "Longer, if you figure in the movie. I was in it, y'know. What's wrong, honey? Don't I look like your idea of a movie star?" She laughed hugely. It had been a long time since I'd met anyone who laughed so easily and often. "Fact is, damned near everybody in town was in it, with all them crowd and battle scenes. But me, I was picked out of fifteen other girls in the tenth-grade class to play Vangie's little sister, Lavinia. Had me one whole line of dialogue, too: 'Why, thank you, Mistuh Randolph,' " she declared with a dainty curtsy. "Miss Laurel Barrett, she was a fine actress and lady, and very, very kind to me. I sure felt sorry she had so much misery in her life. . . ." She looked up at me very seriously for a moment as if she wanted to tell me something. But then she changed her mind and went and got my suitcases.

There was less grandeur in the east wing. The ceilings were lower, the floors carpeted, the decor 1950s English country estate, complete with chintz-covered furniture and flowery wallpaper. Lots of peacock art, too. Framed peacock watercolors. Vases of peacock-feather arrangements. Peacock needlepoint pillows. You'd be surprised just how little it takes to make a really powerful peacock statement. A short hallway led to the kitchen, which was big and modern and cluttered. A round oak table piled with papers sat in the middle of it. Fern's bedroom and a suite of offices were off the kitchen.

"This here's kind of the nerve center of the estate," Fern explained. "Though I reckon you'll find wherever Mavis happens to be at the moment is the nerve center." She laughed. "She and Charlotte do their business here. Charlotte is her assistant. Nice quiet girl. Handles her correspondence, her schedule, and so forth. She's up in Chicago with Mave and Richard right now."

We went out the kitchen door to an L-shaped brick courtyard that was the modern service yard. There was a three-car garage, a garden shed, a workshop. The tractor mower was parked here next to a pair of battered pickups. At the far end of the courtyard was a row of low, attached, wood-framed cottages that looked quite old.

"Guest rooms," Fern informed me as we headed toward them.

"Converted carriage houses?" I asked.

"Slaves' quarters," she replied matter-of-factly.

"Perfect."

Mine had a small sitting room that faced onto the courtyard. There was a pine student's desk, matching easy chair and love seat, and a fireplace. Lulu promptly tested the easy chair for fit. It passed.

"I put in that little fridge you asked for," Fern pointed out. It was over next to the desk. "Stocked it with milk, imported mineral water, and anchovies, like you wanted. What y'all do with cold anchovies anyway?"

"You don't want to know."

A spiral staircase led up to the bath and sleeping loft. The bed had a skylight and ceiling fan over it, and a fine old quilt on it.

"We'll be more than comfortable here," I assured her.

"Y'all need anything, just let me know," she said. "I'll be in the kitchen. Come on in and eat when you're ready."

The place was a bit stuffy. I left the screen door open while I got settled. Lulu busily cased the place, large black nose to the floor. She wasn't crazy about the spiral staircase. The steps just weren't made for someone with her body and her nonlegs. She had to descend sort of sideways, with a *hop-thump-thump, hop-thump-thump*. She sounded like a bowling ball going down. Before I did anything else I opened up a tin of chilled anchovies and wrapped one tightly around one of her allergy pills. She devoured this with a single chomp. She prefers them chilled – the oil clings to them better. Then I unpacked her bowl and spooned a can of her Nine Lives mackerel for cats and very weird dogs into it and set it by the front door. While she dove in, I opened the bottle of aged Macallan single malt I'd thoughtfully brought along, and I poured two fingers in a water glass. I sipped it as I unpacked my faithful late-fifties-vintage, solid-steel Olympia manual portable, my electric coffeemaker, my tape player, my tapes. I'd brought Erroll Garner with me. Something had told me it was going to be his kind of project. Then I went upstairs and hung up my clothes and changed into a polo sweater of black cashmere and a pair of old khakis that were soft as flannel.

Lulu was waiting for me at the bottom of the staircase with a mournful expression on her face, mournful even for her. When I asked her what her problem was, she whimpered and glanced over in the direction of her supper dish, greatly distraught.

A kitten was finishing her mackerel.

"Well, what do you expect me to do about it?" I demanded. "You're the huntress, not me. Defend your turf."

She did try. She growled at the kitten. Even bared her teeth, a sight known to throw sheer terror into the hearts of more than a few baby squirrels. The kitten just ignored her – it was pretty pathetic – while it licked the mackerel bowl clean.

It was maybe four months old and on the scrawny side. Its ears stuck straight up and made it look a little like a bat. Gray mostly, with white belly and paws and a gray-and-black-striped tail. Its eyes were a yellowish green. I suppose it was cute, if you happen to care for cats. I don't. I've never understood the strange power they hold over people. All they ever do is sleep or hide behind the furniture. People who live in apartments even let them shit in the house.

There weren't supposed to be any cats around Shenandoah. I wondered whom it belonged to.

Its meal completed, it arched its back and leisurely came over to me and attempted familiarity. Rubbed against my leg. Bumped my ankle with its head. Made small motorboat noises. This business got Lulu growling again. I reached down and picked the damned thing up and showed her – it was a her – the screen door. I latched it behind her. I'd have to remember to keep it latched in the future, or Lulu would starve.

This kitten didn't know how to take a hint. She tried to push the screen door open again. When she failed, she started yowling out there in the growing dark. I had to shoo her off. She darted under one of the pickups, her eyes glowing.

I poured myself another Macallan. I was unpacking my briefcase when someone tapped at the screen door. I went over to discover a midget human life-form, type male, standing out there looking warily up at me. I opened the door. He was maybe eight years old, with a mess of dirty-blond hair and freckles and narrow shoulders. He wore a blue sweatshirt cut off at the elbows, soiled khakis, and high-topped sneakers.

"Thorry to bother ya, mithter," he said. He was missing a couple of front teeth. "Can I . . ." He looked nervously over his shoulder at the house, then turned back to me. "Can you keep a theecret?" he whispered urgently.

"I doubt it," I replied. I ought to tell you right off – I like cats a lot more than I like kids. Kids I rate dead even with large, spiny reptiles. "What kind of secret?"

He hesitated, swallowed. "Y'all theen Thaydie?" he asked gravely.

I frowned. "Thaydie?"

"Not Thaydie," he said, shaking his head. "*Thaydie.*"

"Sadie."

"Have ya?"

"That all depends," I said, tugging at my ear. "Is she small and furry? Has a tail?"

He nodded eagerly.

"Under that pickup over there."

He scampered over to the truck, knelt, and talked her out softly. Then he carried her back to me, hugging her tightly to his small chest. "Thankth, mithter. Thankth a whole lot."

"No problem. I'm a big believer in happy endings."

He glanced inside at my sitting room through the screen door. "Y'all have a *dog*? Wow!" Thrilled, he barged inside, handed me Sadie, and bounded over to Lulu.

"Sure thing," I muttered. "Come right on in."

"What'th her name?"

"Lulu."

"Hey, Lulu." He fell to his knees and began stroking her.

She suffered this quietly. She isn't crazy about kids herself. Most of them tend to tug on her ears and call her Dumbo. Sadie, meanwhile, began wriggling in my arms. When I tightened my hold on her, she bit my thumb. Her teeth were razor sharp. Wincing, I put her down on the sofa.

"I thought cats weren't allowed here," I said as she made herself at home.

"She's *mine*!" he cried, suddenly terrified.

"Okay, okay. She's yours."

He relaxed. "She'th a thtray. I found her. Been hidin' her, feedin' her from my plate. Don't tell the witch, okay? She'll take her off to the pound to get murdered, for sure."

"The witch?"

"That ol' Fern."

"Seems pretty nice to me."

"I *hate* her."

"I'm Hoagy by the way."

"I'm Gordie. Live in the cottage next to ya, Mithter Hoagy."

"Make it plain Hoagy, seeing as how we're neighbors."

He gave Lulu a final pat and jumped to his feet. "Wanna play catch? I can throw a thpitter."

"Darn. I didn't think to bring my mitt down with me."

"Wanna watch a movie? Got me a tape with my favorite actor in it."

Before I could reply, someone outside called out his name. It was Fern.

"Oh, no!" he gasped, shoving Sadie at me. "Hide her, quick! She'll *kill* her!"

"Gordie?" called Fern from my doorway. "You in here?" She put her glasses on and saw he was and came in after him.

I hid Sadie under my sweater, wondering just how I'd gotten myself into this.

"Gordie, you're supposed to be taking yourself a bath," Fern barked, every inch the drill sergeant. "You ain't supposed to be bothering Hoagy here."

"He wasn't," I assured her.

Gordie said nothing. Just stood there stiffly.

She pointed a finger at him. "Bathe yourself, Gordie. Or I'll be in to do it for ya, hear me?"

He still said nothing. His manner had changed noticeably in her presence. He'd withdrawn into himself. His face was now a mask, betraying nothing.

Exasperated, she grabbed him by the shoulders and shook him. "You hear me!"

"Yeth'm," he finally said softly and obediently.

"That's better. C'mon, Hoagy." *Thwack.* "Dinner's waiting."

"I'm right behind you."

Gordie relaxed as soon as she left. I gave him Sadie back.

"Thankth, Hoagy," he said. "*You* take baths?"

"Frequently."

He shrugged, disappointed. "Well, 'night."

"Good night, Gordie. Who is your favorite movie star, anyway – Arnold Schwarzenegger?"

"Naw. *McQueen.*"

"That makes two of us," I said.

"Really?" he cried.

I nodded approvingly. "You're okay, Gordie. You're definitely okay. Too bad you're a kid."

The big round kitchen table was heaped with a platter of fried chicken, bowls of coleslaw, macaroni salad, mashed potatoes, black-eyed peas, stewed tomatoes, a basket of corn bread.

Fern was filling two chilled mugs with beer. She squinted at me blindly when I came in. "That you, Hoagy?"

"Looks good," I said, partly to identify myself, and partly because it did.

"Well, sit and get at it, honey. Just save a little room. I made an apple pie this morning, and there's vanilla ice cream. We make our own. Vanilla, strawberry . . ."

"Licorice?" I asked, daring to hope. It's my favorite, and damned hard to find.

"Licorice? Why would anyone want to eat that?"

"I can't imagine."

I sat and got at it. We both did. The chicken was crisp and moist, the salads homemade, the corn bread fresh baked and laced with hunks of bacon. It wasn't a common meal. I told her so between bites.

"Got a husband, Fern?"

"That a proposal?" She erupted in her big jolly laugh. "Naw. Never have."

"Gordie. Who is he?"

"He's the VADD poster boy," she replied. "Picture's plastered up all over the state. Them public service posters for Virginians Against Drunk Driving. Poor thing's parents were killed by one a few months ago. Local working people. Gordie had no other living family, so Mavis decided to adopt him. She feels very strongly about drunk drivers. They've never known for sure, but it's generally believed her own mom, Alma, was run over by one. Mavis helped start VADD. The proceeds from the golden-anniversary celebration are going toward it."

"She sounds mighty into her causes."

"Mavis don't know how to do things halfway. And she's got a darned good heart, too, deep down inside. People around here thought it mighty kind of her to take Gordie in as her own. I kinda like having him around to fuss over, you want to know the truth. I'm just sorry there isn't more for him to do around here. No other kids to play with. He gets bored. Real quiet, too. Can't hardly get a word out of him."

"Could have fooled me."

"He talked to you?" she asked, surprised. "Wonder how come."

"Just my good fortune, I guess."

She got us a couple of fresh beers from the fridge and filled our mugs.

"If he's a member of the family," I said, "how come he's living out there in a guest cottage?"

"No room for him in here," Fern replied, cleaning her plate. "Mavis has got her gymnasium in the spare bedroom upstairs. She works out like a demon. I offered to give up my room down here for him. She wouldn't hear of it. But, hey, he bothers you, let me know. I'll move him somewheres else." She drank deeply from her mug, then she sat back with a contented sigh. "So it's not true what they say about you in all them articles?"

"What do they say?"

She narrowed her eyes at me shrewdly. "That you solve murders."

"Oh, that. Not true. I attract them. A flaw of some kind in my character. I wish I knew what." I had some of my beer. "Why do you ask?"

Fern took a deep breath and plunged ahead. "Cause I think somebody was murdered here. Sterling Sloan, the star of *Oh, Shenandoah*. I think he got himself murdered here fifty years ago next month, and that whoever did it to him got away with it."

CHAPTER
THREE

"**S**terling Sloan," I pointed out, "died of a ruptured aneurysm in his brain."

Fern puffed out her cheeks. "That's what they *said*, to sweep the whole mess under the rug. But I know otherwise."

"What do you know?"

"I know I was there on that set," she said, leaning forward anxiously. "I know I saw something. Something I've never dared tell another living soul about."

"Why tell me?"

"Because I think I can trust you. And because it has to come out now. Don't you see?"

I tugged at my ear. "I'm afraid I don't."

"Other people know what really happened. She knew. Miss Laurel knew. Why do you think she went so nuts?"

"She was an actress. Kind of goes with the territory."

Fern shook her head. "The others, they'll be coming here for the fiftieth anniversary. Aren't many of them left. Most of 'em are gone now, the secret buried with them. Don't you see, Hoagy? It's now or never. This is the last chance to see the plain truth come out."

"The truth is anything but plain," I said. "It's a very confusing business, and the closer you get to it, the more confusing it gets."

"But you'll help me, won't you?"

I hesitated. "Well . . ."

"Don't say you aren't intrigued," she said, grinning. "I can tell you are by the way you look."

"And how do I look?"

"Profound. Disillusioned. Bored."

"I always look this way. That breeding thing again."

"Look here," declared Fern. "I ain't no crank from down on the farm thinks she seen flying saucers shaped like cigars. I ain't crazy."

"I didn't say you were, Fern. It's just that – "

A car pulled up outside in the courtyard. Fern stiffened, raised her index finger to her lips. The engine shut off. The car door opened, closed. There were footsteps. Then the kitchen door opened and in walked a tall young blonde clutching a pile of books. She was pretty, in a neat, correct, Laura Ashley flowered-print-dress sort of way, complete with lace collar and puffed sleeves. She would never exactly be willowy. She was a bit sturdy through the legs and hips. But there was a healthy pink glow to her cheeks, a youthful brightness to her blue eyes, a clean lustrousness to her hair. And there was what is, for me, the most attractive quality any woman can possess – she knew who she was. She was Mercy Glaze, the girl who would inherit Shenandoah.

"Say hello to Stewart Hoag, Mercy," said Fern as she dished up our pie. "Goes by Hoagy."

Mercy looked me over briefly and offered me her hand. "Pleased to meet you," she said, manner forthright, grip firm. No Southern coquette this.

"Likewise," I said.

Mercy dropped her books and purse on the counter, grabbed a leftover drumstick from the chicken platter, and started to bite into it.

"Get yourself a plate and napkin and sit down," commanded Fern. "You're a lady, not a field hand."

"Tastes better this way," Mercy insisted, attacking it happily.

"Mavis would kill you if she saw you," Fern said.

"So don't tell her," Mercy said.

Fern promptly whipped a Polaroid camera from a drawer and aimed it at her.

Mercy froze, genuinely alarmed. "You wouldn't."

"I *would*," Fern vowed.

Mercy rolled her eyes and flounced over to the cupboard, every inch a suffering teenager now. She got a plate and napkin and sat across the table from me. "You're the writer who's going to get along with Mother?"

"That's the idea. Any advice?"

"Yes," she replied, nibbling at the chicken leg. "Place your foot firmly on her neck and keep it there."

"That'll work?" I asked.

"I honestly couldn't say," she replied. "But it sure would be fun to see someone try it."

"Polk Four phoned for you a while ago, honey," Fern told her, setting my pie and ice cream before me. For my benefit she added, "Polk's her fiancé."

"He is not," Mercy said petulantly. "He just thinks he is."

"Polk Four?" I inquired, tasting my dessert. I was not disappointed.

"Polk LaFoon the Fourth," Fern explained. "He's Augusta County sheriff like Polk Three and Polk Two before him. Handsome as Mistuh Bob Stack in his uniform. And he's smart, too. Got his law degree from Duke. Gonna be our attorney general someday. Maybe even governor" – she winked at me – "if he marries right."

"I swear, Fern," declared Mercy. "You are getting absolutely senile, the things come out of your mouth." She turned to me, frowning. "You're not the same Stewart Hoag who wrote *Our Family Enterprise*, are you?"

"I am.

She looked a bit awestruck now, poor child. "I-I read you in modern lit."

"You don't say. Large class?"

"I guess there were about eighteen of us. Why?"

"Just calculating my royalties."

"You're a real distinguished American author," she pointed out.

"Careful. My head swells easily."

"To tell you the truth," she confessed, "I didn't realize you were still alive."

"That's more like it, though you could bring me back down a little easier in the future."

She giggled. Fern busied herself at the sink, noisily.

"So you do this sort of work, too?" Mercy asked, fascinated.

"Yes. I'm kind of the Bo Jackson of publishing."

"But isn't this, well, beneath you?"

"Nothing is beneath me," I replied, "with the possible exception of screenwriting."

"I guess I don't understand why you bother."

"Just finicky, really. I won't eat out of garbage cans."

"Oh." Chastened, she poured herself coffee. "You must think I'm awfully sheltered and insensitive and stupid."

I gave her a frisky once-over. "That's not what I'm thinking at all."

She blushed and lunged for her books. "Well, I've got a paper due tomorrow," she said, starting for the stairs with her coffee. "Know anything about Spenser's *Faerie Queen*?"

"Yes. Understanding it won't come in handy later in life."

"That's not what this little girl needs to hear," Fern cautioned.

Mercy sighed. "I'm not a little girl, Fern. I'm twenty-one years old."

"Don't remind me," said Fern. "I was a middle-aged woman when you was born. I hate to think what that makes me now.

"Enjoy your Spenser," I said.

She smiled and said it was nice meeting me. Then she went off to her room.

"Seems like a nice girl," I observed.

"Keep your hands off or Mavis'll cut 'em off," Fern warned. "With a hatchet."

"Not to worry, Fern. I'm not looking these days."

"Look all you want. Just don't touch."

I brought my dessert plate to her at the sink. "Thanks for the best meal I've had in a long time."

"You don't believe me about Sterling Sloan, do you?" she demanded, peering up at me. "You think I'm some crazy old lady."

"That's not the case at all, Fern," I replied tactfully. "I'm flattered that you confided in me. I'm just not your man. I came through the gate in a Chevy Nova, not on the back of a white horse. You need someone with a square jaw and fists of stone and a resting pulse rate of fifty-six. You need a hero."

"I reckon so," she said, crestfallen. "I just don't know who . . . I mean, you were my best hope."

I sighed inwardly. One hundred percent marshmallow, through and through. "I'll sleep on it. How's that?"

She brightened considerably. "That's more like it!" *Thwack*. "Only don't sleep too late. You got an audience with Mavis at nine o'clock sharp in the old library. She has fits if people are even a minute late."

"I thought the old house was only used for formal occasions."

"Believe me, honey, meeting Mavis Glaze *is* one."

Her phone rang several times before she finally picked it up. My heart began to pound at once when she did. It always does when I hear that feathery, dizzy-sounding, teenaged-girl's voice that belongs to her and no one else.

"Did I wake you?" I asked.

"No, I'm sitting up with Elliot."

"Something serious?"

"I don't know, darling. He simply wouldn't touch his food all day."

"Maybe he just wasn't hungry, Merilee."

"Hoagy, pigs are *always* hungry. No, I'm afraid Elliot's not himself, the poor dear."

She had named him after her first agent. And people say there's no sentiment in show business.

"Call me old-fashioned, Merilee, but I still don't believe in giving a name to someone you intend to eat."

"Mr. Hoagy! How could you be such a-a *barbarian*!"

"Merilee . . ."

"Elliot happens to be a member of this household, sir! And he's certainly more of a gentleman than you'll ever be."

"Merilee . . ."

"What!"

"Hello."

"Hello yourself. Did you find out yet?"

"Find out what?"

"Who Vangie marries at the end of *Oh, Shenandoah*, silly."

"Not yet. Do you really care?"

"Are you serious? I've only read that book eight times and wept uncontrollably every single time. And the movie, merciful heavens . . . Now listen, Hoagy, when you do find out, don't tell me who it is. I'm serious. I'm such a blabbermouth I'll spread it all over town and get you in deep doo-doo."

"Okay," I said.

Stunned silence. "What did you say?" she demanded.

"I said okay."

"*Mister* Hoagy!"

"Just agreeing with you, Merilee."

"I'm not so sure we can be friends anymore."

"Is that what we are?"

"How's sweetness?" she asked, neatly slipping my jab.

Lulu whimpered from next to me on the bed. She always knows when her mommy is on the phone. Don't ask me how.

"Her usual obnoxious self. Have you called the vet about Elliot?"

"Not yet. I don't want to be one of those overprotective city slickers who they all hoot at. I will if he isn't better in a day or two."

"Well, look on the bright side."

"Which is . . . ?"

"He could stand to take off a few hundred pounds."

"Very funny."

"What do you remember hearing about the filming of *Oh, Shenandoah*?"

Merilee is a big fan of show-biz gossip, as long as it isn't to do with her, of course. She often befriends elderly fellow cast members and eagerly soaks up their reminiscences of Hollywood's golden age.

"Way over budget," she replied. "Tons of pissy fits, bad weather, last-minute rewrites. First two directors got fired by Goldwyn in preproduction before Wyler finally took it over . . . Or are you more interested in who was doing the big, bad naughty with who?"

"I've missed your quaint little expressions."

"It seems to me," she recalled, "it was one of those shoots where everyone was hopping into the feathers with everyone else. Of course, that always happens on location, particularly with a love story."

"Why is that?"

"We can't tell the difference between real and make-believe, darling. That's what makes us actors."

"Which am I?"

"I like to think of you as a bit of both."

"Why, Merilee, that's the second-nicest thing you've ever said to me."

"What was the nicest?"

"'You're not the sort of man who I can see wearing anything polyester.'"

"As I recall," she said, "neither of us was wearing anything, period, at the time."

"Merilee Nash! You've been getting seriously ribald since you started hanging around with farm animals."

"So that explains it."

"Anything about Sterling Sloan?"

"Well, he died."

"I know that. I was wondering if there was any chance it didn't happen the way they say it did."

She was silent a moment. "Oh, no, Hoagy . . . You're not getting into something weird again, are you?"

"No chance. Housekeeper here just has some crazy idea."

"I certainly don't remember hearing anything." She mulled it over. "I'm skeptical, frankly. *Oh, Shenandoah* has commanded so much attention through the years. If there'd been even a hint of scandal about Sloan, the sleaze-biographers would have been all over it by now."

"That's kind of what I was thinking."

"Of course, I could ask around for you. Some of the old-timers might remember if there was scuttlebutt. Want me to?"

"If you don't mind."

"Not at all. It'll give me an excuse to call them. Comfy down there?"

"Aside from a lousy set of rental wheels."

"Possibly you're a bit spoiled in that department."

"Possibly that's not the only department I'm spoiled in."

We were both silent a moment.

"I'd better get back to Elliot," she said softly. "Hoagy?"

"Yes, Merilee?"

"What was her name?"

"Whose name?"

"The girl you met tonight."

"I . . . what makes you think she was a girl and not a woman?"

"A woman can tell."

"Why, Merilee, if I didn't know you better, I'd swear you were jealous."

"I'd swear I was, too."

"You never have been before."

"I wasn't forty before," she declared, sighing grandly. "And more important, neither were you. Sleep tight, darling." And then she hung up.

I undressed and climbed into bed. I was working my way through a collection of James Thurber stories, which is something I do every couple of years to remind myself what good writing is. I had just gotten settled in when I heard a car pull up in the courtyard outside. I turned out my bedside lamp and pulled back the curtain.

A big Mercedes 560 SEL sedan was idling out there in the moonlight with its lights on.

Two women got out, one tall, almost regal, the other short and thin. The driver pulled the Mercedes into the garage while the two women spoke briefly. Then the tall one went in the kitchen door of the east wing, closing it behind her. The other woman got into a red Pontiac LeMans that was parked there and started it up. The Mercedes's lights went off in the garage. A man got out and closed the garage door and went over to the LeMans. He was stocky, with a heavy torso and short legs. He said something to the woman in the car, gestured for her to roll her window down. Instead she began easing the car out of the courtyard toward the driveway. He was insistent – ran out in front of her, waved his arms for her to stop. She wouldn't. In fact, she floored it and made right for him. She wasn't kidding around, either. He had to dive out of the way or she'd have run him over as she sped on down the drive. He landed heavily and lay there a moment. Slowly, he got to his feet and brushed himself off. He stood there watching the driveway for a long moment before he went in the house.

I turned over and went to sleep, Lulu comfortably ensconced in her favorite position. I didn't stay asleep long. She woke me at three, pacing the bedroom floor, whimpering like she had on the plane. I told her to shut up and come back to bed. She wanted me to let her out. These things happen. I did, after reminding her to stay away from the peacocks. Then I went back upstairs to sleep.

I dreamt I was being smothered by peacock feathers.

A steady tapping at the cottage's front door woke me. Grandfather's Rolex said it was seven-thirty. I padded downstairs and opened it. A covered breakfast tray was waiting there for me on the doorstep. So was Sadie, my new friend, who sat poised on her haunches a foot away, staring at it intently. Lulu was stretched out a few feet from her, staring at her staring at it. Lulu and the tray came inside with me. Sadie did not.

There was a copy of that morning's *Staunton Daily News Leader* to go with my scrambled eggs, country ham, grits, toast, juice, and coffee. The food was excellent. So was the news. Crime in Augusta County was down 11 percent over the past three months, according to Sheriff Polk LaFoon the Fourth. And veteran Hollywood actor Rex Ransom was definitely planning to attend the *Oh, Shenandoah* fiftieth-anniversary gala. Already my day was made. When I finished eating, I climbed into a hot tub and lolled there. I was still there at nine, when I heard someone pounding on my front door, and at nine-fifteen, when someone pounded on it again, louder. When I got out, I stropped grandfather's pearl-handled straight edge and shaved and doused myself with Floris. I dressed in my charcoal silk-and-wool tickweave suit with calfskin braces, a white Turnbull and Asser broadcloth shirt, lavender-and-yellow bow tie, and my brown-and-white spectator balmorals. I emerged with my breakfast tray a few minutes before ten. That damned cat was still there on my doorstep. Gordie was sitting on the ground nearby tossing a ball against a wall and catching it in his mitt on the comeback. The red LeMans from the night before was parked by the kitchen door.

"Mornin', Hoagy," Gordie said glumly.

"Something wrong?"

"Thaydie's awful hungry," he replied. "Jutht wish I had a little milk to give her . . . I mean, she'll *thtarve*." His lower lip began to quiver.

I sighed. This was turning into a miserable job. Truly miserable.

"I have some milk in my fridge," I said grudgingly.

His face lit up. "Really?"

I went back inside and filled my empty coffee cup with milk and put it out for her. She lapped it up hungrily.

"Gee, thankth, Hoagy," Gordie exclaimed.

"No problem."

"Wanna play catch?"

"Don't you have school or something?"

"I'm on thpring break. Throw me one? Jutht one? Huh?"

"All right, one fly ball. Go deep."

He tossed me the ball and dashed across the courtyard toward the lawn. It was an old hardball, worn and frayed. The sight of it in my hand triggered a memory. Of another worn, frayed hardball, another little boy, another tall, distant man. A powerful and most unexpected wave of nostalgia crashed over me. Nostalgia isn't generally my style. Especially for that time and that tall, distant man.

Gordie was waiting for me, pounding his mitt. I waved him deeper. Then I wound up and aired out the old javelin shoulder. I sent the ball high in the air, way over his head. The little guy went after it. He was quick. He was there waiting for it when it came down, mitt held high.

"Wow," he hollered, trotting back to me with it, "I ain't never theen anyone throw a ball tho far in my whole life!"

"It's all in the mechanics," I said, wondering just when the pain would stop shooting through my shoulder. "Not a terrible grab, by the way."

"Thankth. Throw me another?"

"Later. Maybe."

Inside, Fern was doing the breakfast dishes. Someone was typing in the adjoining office.

She squinted at me disapprovingly when I handed her my tray. "Honey, Mave's been waiting over there for you nearly one hour. I knocked on your door twice. You deaf or you just got a death wish?"

"None of the above."

She shook her head sadly. "Been nice knowing you."

"Care to place a wager on that?"

"What kind of wager?" she asked, grinning at me.

"You have to make me licorice ice cream.

"And if I win? Because I don't plan to lose. And honey, I sure don't eat nothing gray."

"Ten bucks?"

We shook on it. Then I headed for the old house to meet Mavis Glaze.

CHAPTER
FOUR

She was smiling.

Mavis Glaze always smiled. Her face was frozen that way. It happens sometimes when you have one lift too many. The skin was drawn across her cheekbones tight as Saran Wrap pulled over a bowl of leftover fruit salad. There was, however, no smile in the hard blue eyes that stared out at me from behind the writing table where her mother had created *Oh, Shenandoah*. The eyes were cold steel. She sat stiffly, her hands folded tightly before her on the desk, knuckles white. Every muscle in her tall, lean body seemed taut. You could have plucked an F-sharp off the cords in her neck. The lady wouldn't bend in the wind – she'd snap. Even her copper-colored hair was drawn into a tight, *tight* bun. She had the same long blade of nose and cleft chin her brothers had. On them it looked better. She was not a pretty woman, though she was, for sixty, a handsome one. She was elegantly dressed in a double-breasted pantsuit of cream-colored raw silk with a white silk blouse. Her nails were painted salmon, as was her mouth. She wore no other makeup.

She glanced down at her wristwatch, then back up at me. "You are precisely one hour late, Mr. Hoag." She enunciated every syllable as if she were speaking to a small, slightly deaf native boy. "My brothers led me to believe that you were a professional. Sadly, they were mistaken. Your behavior is anything but professional. It is unacceptable."

"That makes us even.

She glared down her nose at me. "I seriously doubt that," she said witheringly.

"We had an appointment yesterday afternoon," I said. "You didn't keep it. You didn't have the courtesy to reschedule it or to contact me so I could make other arrangements. You just kept me hanging around here, wasting my time. You're lucky I'm here at all. And if you don't start talking to me like your collaborator instead of the guy who pumps out your septic tank, I won't be."

Her blue eyes widened slightly. Otherwise she didn't react. Until she abruptly grabbed one of the tulips out of the vase on the desk and snapped its stem in half. "Get out, Mr. Hoag. Get off my property at once. If I find you anywhere near Shenandoah in one hour, I shall call the sheriff and have you arrested."

"You'd better call your brothers, too, while you're at it. They'll have to break it to your publisher that we didn't hit it off. I'm afraid it won't go down too well, since I was kind of your last shot."

"Last shot?" She bristled. "Whatever do you mean?"

"You're the laughingstock of the entire publishing industry, didn't you know? You're blowing the biggest sequel in history, and dragging your publishing house down with you. They're very unhappy. And they're going to be even more unhappy about this. But that's your business, not mine. Nice meeting you, Mavis. Actually, it wasn't, but it's important to be gracious to one's hostess. I learned that from your show."

I started for the door, not particularly fast. She let me get all the way to the knob before she finally said, "Perhaps . . . perhaps we got off on the wrong foot. I-I apologize about yesterday. I assure you it won't happen again. Sit down. Please."

I sat down, round one mine.

She treated me to her frozen smile. It was starting to bring to mind Nicholson in *Batman*. "People have always misunderstood me," she stated. "I've never cared about which fork they used for their salad. Simple, human consideration is what matters to me. Respect for your neighbor. Saying 'please' and 'thank you' and 'excuse me.' No one does anymore. It's all 'Me first' now. They cut each other off on the highway. They give each other the finger. They urinate in the street. They gather in sports arenas for the express purpose of chanting obscenities at visiting players."

"In New York we chant them at the home team as well. We like to think of everyone as the enemy."

The blue eyes flicked over me suspiciously. "I understand you brought some form of animal with you."

"Using the term loosely."

"My brothers were extremely vague about it. It's not vicious or something, is it?"

"I'll have to tell her that one – she can use a good laugh."

Mavis pursed her lips and frowned at me. "You've no notebook? No tape recorder?"

"Not to worry. If anything memorable is said, I'll remember it. Chances are I'll have said it."

Her eyes flashed at me. "Are you always this unpleasant, Mr. Hoag?"

"Generally. And it's Hoagy."

"Well, I am not impressed by your attitude, Hoagy," she said imperially.

I tugged at my ear. "My mother used to say that. Still does, come to think of it."

"Are you close to your parents?"

"I make sure I call them at least once every decade."

She stood up and moved over to the window and looked outside at the gardens. The peacocks were strutting around near one of the tulip borders. She watched them. "You may as well know this about me from the start – I never learned how to suffer weak willies or fools or mediocrity gladly. Or how to hold my tongue. I stand up for what I believe in, and what I believe in is doing one's best and tolerating nothing less. If I were a man, I'd be held in high esteem. Since I'm a woman, I'm called a bitch." She turned away from the window and faced me. "I respect talent. From what everyone says, you have it. Lord knows you don't get by on your charm. A lot of men can't work for a strong woman. Can you?"

"I'm here, am I not?"

She nodded, satisfied, and went back to the desk and sat down behind it. "James Madison was married in this room in 1794 to Dolly Payne Todd. This was a parlor in those days. They were all here to drink Madeira wine and dance the minuet and pay their respects to the Glazes. Washington, Jefferson, Monroe. My family's history is Virginia's history. The Glazes settled this valley, sat on the House of Burgesses, served in the Continental Congress. And this house is history, as well. John Ariss, the most important architect of the Virginia Palladian style, designed and built it in 1756. Jefferson himself designed the portico addition in 1767 to improve the upstairs ventilation."

"You can document that?"

She stiffened. "Pardon me?"

"I understood that virtually no documentation of Jefferson's designs existed from prior to 1770. They were all obliterated when Shadwell, his birthplace in Albemarle County, burned to the ground."

"Ah." She raised her chin at me. "I assure you we rely on a more accurate form of history, Hoagy. *Oral* history. You seem . . . well versed in the revolutionary period."

"Not really."

"It was the most exciting time in our nation's history," she declared. "A time of boldness and daring and risk. Not like today. Today we're afraid of our own shadows. Afraid of salt, of caffeine, of good, red meat. Afraid of the air we breathe, the water we drink. *Afraid.* All we want now is a life *without* risk. Guarantees – as if there are any in life. Our forefathers knew otherwise. They're the ones who made America a great power. We're nothing but a bunch of neurotics now, weak willies who sit cowering before our television sets wondering why our influence in the world has dwindled." She sat back in her chair, made a steeple of her fingers. "I suppose that is why *Oh, Shenandoah* remains so popular with readers. It evokes that boldness Americans like to believe we still have. And why there is so much interest in *Sweet Land of Liberty*."

"Tell me what happens."

She moistened her lips. "Vangie marries John Raymond, Hoagy," she revealed. "De Cheverier dies at his hand. It is Raymond who lives. Flourishes at Jefferson's side. Helps author the Articles of Confederation. Becomes a great leader. Only Vangie doesn't love him, Hoagy. Not in her heart. She is miserable. She cries herself to sleep at night for the memory of Guy De Cheverier. In 1785, Raymond is posted to London as an aide to John Adams. She goes along at his side. She detests London. Despondent and lonely, she carries on a flirtation with a handsome young stableboy. Still, she remains true to Raymond. Until he is named minister to France two years later. It is in France, during the time of its own revolution, that Vangie's passion is rekindled beyond her ability to control it. It is in France that she meets Napoleon. She has a passionate love affair with him, Hoagy. An affair that must end when Raymond is recalled to America. She is devastated. Upon their return to Shenandoah, he becomes governor of Virginia. When Jefferson is elected president in 1800, he names Raymond secretary of state. And then, Hoagy, as the war of 1812 beckons, mother intended that John Raymond, husband of Evangeline Grace, himself be elected president of the United States. A truly magnificent story, is it not?"

"It is. How detailed are her notes?"

"Not very," she confessed.

"I understand you also have some ideas of your own."

"They are *not* my own," she insisted. "They are Mother's. Mother speaks to me."

"Want to tell me what she says?"

"That Vangie should have an illegitimate child with Napoleon," she replied firmly. "A beautiful girl."

"Good idea," I said.

"Do you really think so?" she asked, pleased.

"I do. She could arrive in America as a young woman toward the end of the story. Cause her mother no end of problems."

"Excellent, Hoagy," Mavis exclaimed. "You impress me right off. You *breathe* narrative."

"Yeah, I'm full of it. What else?"

She hesitated. "There's a certain . . . perspective that is missing. I feel – that is, Mother and I both feel – *Oh, Shenandoah* and *Sweet Land of Liberty* are but a small section of a much larger, more *cosmic* canvas."

"Cosmic?"

"Evangeline Grace is not merely a figure of the American Revolution, Hoagy. She is a woman of the ages, one who has led many lives. She was Cleopatra and Lucrezia Borgia and Anne Boleyn. She was Joan of Arc. Fictionalized, of course – "

"Of course."

"And before all of this, before she led these many fascinating lives, Vangie came here from far, far away."

"How far away?"

"Venus, before the greenhouse effect poisoned its atmosphere several million years ago and made it uninhabitable."

"So you're saying . . . ," I said slowly, "that Evangeline Grace, the heroine of *Oh, Shenandoah*, is actually an alien?"

Mavis nodded. "And that I intend – that is, Mother intends – to reveal this now, in *Sweet Land*. The entire story. It is vital. I insist upon it."

No wonder the lunch-pail writers had quit on her. The wonder was how they'd kept this giddy little literary morsel under their hats. Their silence must have cost the Glaze brothers plenty.

Mavis leaned forward now, anxious for my reaction. She was just like every other celebrity I'd ever met. Armor on the outside, tender, mortal ego underneath.

I waited her out. I sat back and took off grandfather's Rolex and rubbed at a scratch on its crystal. I put it back on, checked the time, and calculated what it would be in Greece, in Fiji, in Kokomo, Indiana. And then, with just a hint of awe in my voice, I finally said, "It's my turn to be impressed, Mavis. I didn't realize you had such a rich, bold imagination."

"Mother," she countered. "Not me. Mother."

I shook my head. "No, Mavis. Alma Glaze would never dare dream this big. This isn't Alma talking. This is your own voice crying to be heard. This is the you that no one knows. The primitive you.

The sensual you. People fear you. They think you're some sort of tight-lipped martinet. They're wrong. I see that now. You're someone who has poetry inside her."

She gulped. The woman positively gulped. "Do you . . . do you really think so?" she asked breathlessly.

"I do."

"My brothers think I am mad."

"Naturally. They're businessmen. Earthbound, so to speak. You can't expect them to comprehend you."

"But *you* do?"

"I do."

"And you agree that this belongs in *Sweet Land*?"

"May I speak frankly, Mavis?"

"Please. Hold nothing back."

"I think it's powerful stuff. Too powerful. I see *Sweet Land* as a traditional, old-fashioned American vehicle – a Schwinn one-speed with foot brakes. Strap a jet engine onto it and you'll only total it."

"But – "

"This is another book, Mavis. Your own book. Not your mother's. *Yours*. And you will write a book, a book even bigger than *Oh, Shenandoah*. I believe that. And I think you do, too, deep down inside. But *Sweet Land*, I think you have to leave it be. This book is hers." Mavis said nothing. "Vangie and Napoleon. What an idea." And just think of the casting possibilities – Hoffman, Pacino, Michael J. Fox . . . "What a child they'll have."

"A girl," she insisted. "It's a girl."

"Perfect."

Mavis tapped the gleaming surface of the writing table impatiently with her fingernail. "I don't know . . ."

"I do," I said. "Trust me. I'm on your side."

She let out a short, humorless laugh. "That would be a first. It has been me against everyone else for as long as I can remember."

"No longer. You have me now."

She gave me her steely stare. I met it. Then she turned away and took a deep breath and let it out slowly. "You'll be taking over the writing?"

I nodded. "Just leave everything to me.

"What shall I be doing in the meantime?"

"Thinking about your own book. Let those ideas percolate. Let yourself go. We'll go over what I'm doing chapter by chapter. I'll be around if you need me."

Again with the stare, a bit more wide-eyed now. This was new for her – being bossed. She wasn't sure how to respond. "Very well," she finally declared airily. "I place myself in your hands."

"You won't be sorry."

She gave me her frozen smile. "When you get to know me better, Hoagy, and you shall, you will learn something about me."

"And what's that, Mavis?"

"I am never sorry."

Frederick and Edward were waiting for us in the east-wing peacock parlor wearing matching gray flannel suits and apprehensive expressions. Frederick was chain-smoking. A man and woman I didn't know were also in there. All four of them looked up at us when we came in. Mavis's eyes went directly to the man's and flickered a message his way. He then turned to the brothers and relayed it. They both exhaled with relief and came toward me with their hands out, beaming.

"So nice to see you again, Hoagy," exclaimed Frederick.

"Glad everything seems to have worked out," added Edward. "Thrilled. May I introduce you to Charlotte Neene, Mave's treasured assistant?"

Charlotte was a thin, anemic-looking little woman in her thirties, complexion sallow, short brown hair lank, dress drab. She wore no makeup or lipstick or jewelry. Her hand was bony and gelid. "Mr. Hoag," she murmured, careful not to make eye contact.

"Miss Neene," I said. "Would that be your red LeMans out there in the courtyard?"

"Why, yes," she replied, chewing nervously on her lower lip. She had pointy, rather feral little teeth. Her lip was pulpy from being chewed on. "Why do you ask?"

"I've been thinking of getting one. How does it handle?"

"Okay, I suppose," she replied vaguely.

"Glad to hear it."

"And this fine gentleman," interjected Frederick, with more than a hint of derision in his voice, "is Mave's husband, Lord Lonsdale."

"*Richard* Lonsdale, Hoagy," Richard said heartily, after he'd shot Frederick a quick, dirty look. "Do ignore the title bit. Freddy's just having you on. Welcome, and so forth. Damned decent of you to make it down."

Richard went at the ruddy English country-squire bit a little much for me, though I must admit it doesn't take much to be too much for me. He had the clipped, regimental voice, the brush mustache, the robust vigor. He had the tweed Norfolk jacket, the leather-trimmed moleskin trousers, the wool shirt, the ascot. He didn't completely pull off the ascot, but then no one has since Orson Welles died. His hair and mustache were salt-and-pepper. His shaggy brows were coal black and in constant motion. He had an involuntary blinking twitch that kept them squirming around on his forehead like two water bugs pinned to a mat. Evidently his drinking didn't subdue it, and he did drink. The red-rimmed eyes and burst capillaries in his nose said so. He was a big-chested man, so big he looked as if he were holding his breath all the time. But he wasn't tall. His legs were unusually short. His hands were big and hairy. They were also bandaged.

"What happened to your hands?" I asked.

"Tripped in the courtyard last night after I'd put the car away," he replied, twitching at me. "Those bricks get damned slippery. Fell flat and scraped them both raw. Stupid, really."

Edward leaned in toward him and softly inquired if perhaps Mavis would like a sherry before lunch. Richard glanced at her. She raised her chin a quarter of an inch.

Richard immediately flashed his large white teeth at me. "Sherry, Hoagy? To celebrate your undertaking?"

I said that would be fine and watched him fill a set of cordial glasses from a cut-glass decanter, marveling at the fine, civilized heights to which the Glazes had elevated sibling loathing. It was a subtle business, really, but it was undeniable – Mavis and her brothers never actually spoke to each other, or even made eye contact. They communicated only through Richard. He was their go-between, their envoy. He kept the peace. Or perhaps "truce" was a better word for it. Whatever, they had it down so pat they must have been existing this way for years.

Mercy breezed in the door from school as Richard was handing out the glasses. She sang out, "Hello, all," and started up the stairs.

"You're just in time to help us celebrate, Mercy," Mavis called after her. "Come."

She did, though Richard didn't fill another glass for her. I got my own special hello and smile. I could almost feel Mavis's eyes boring into the back of my head. We raised our glasses.

"Hoagy and I," began Mavis, "it is my great pleasure to announce, have arrived at a creative meeting of the minds. . . ."

"And here, ladies and gentlemen," Mercy cracked brightly, "we go for the ninth time."

"Mercy, either hold your tongue or leave this room at once," snapped Mavis.

"Now, Mave . . . ," said Richard consolingly.

"Quiet, Richard!" she ordered. Mercy started out of the room. "Mercy, *stay!*" There was no need for the lady to have dogs around. She had her family.

Mercy stayed, her eyes twinkling with amusement. Richard stood there twitching. Everyone else seemed quite used to this.

"Let us drink to *Sweet Land of Liberty*," continued Mavis. "And to Mother."

"To Mother," toasted Frederick.

"Mother," toasted Edward.

We drank. It wasn't very good sherry. It tasted like children's cough syrup. When mine was gone, I turned to Charlotte and said, "Do we throw our glasses into the fireplace now?"

"Why, no," she replied, a bit goggle-eyed. Whimsy obviously wasn't her forte. Or maybe I was just losing my touch. She excused herself and scurried off to the kitchen.

"Best of luck to you, Hoagy," said Edward genially.

"You'll need it," added Frederick under his breath. "And if there's anything you need – information, advice, a horse whip – just let us know." He went over to refill his glass.

Edward lingered. "I certainly do envy you, Hoagy," he said wistfully.

"You wouldn't if you knew me better."

"I would. You do something creative. I always wanted to. As a young man, I even dreamt of following in Mother's footsteps. But it was never meant to be. No talent – of any kind. I've come to accept it. One of the last stages of maturity, I suppose, is coming to grips with one's own lack of uniqueness."

"Writing is the least amount of fun you can have with your clothes on. You're really a lot better off practicing law."

He shook his head. "No, I'm not, Hoagy. Believe me."

The dining table was set for seven.

Mavis, high priestess of American home entertaining, immediately took charge of the seating. "Richard, you're at that end, I'm at the other. Let's see, that leaves us with an odd man out."

"That would be me," I said.

"Charlotte, you will sit on Richard's left." Mavis gripped her assistant by the shoulders and gave her a firm shove in the right direction. "And next to you . . . no, that's no good. We'll have two men sitting next to each other. You'll have to sit between my brothers, Charlotte, with Hoagy and Mercy across from you. Yes, I believe so. No, wait . . ."

"I appear to be fouling up the seating somewhat," I suggested to Mercy.

"No, you're just giving her an excuse," she murmured.

"To do what?" I asked.

"Move me to a different chair. Mother won't allow me to sit in the same chair for very long for fear I'll get comfortable. She thinks comfortable people are soft people."

Mercy seemed to accept this with good grace. I found myself thinking how sorry I was she had Mavis for a mother.

The lady was still playing musical chairs. I started for the kitchen.

"Wait, Hoagy," she commanded. "Where are you going?"

"I want to tell Fern to start churning," I replied, smacking my lips. I could practically taste that homemade licorice ice cream.

"Churning? Churning what?"

"She's not in there," Charlotte informed me. "She went to the old house for a second."

I went to the old house after Fern. I had my priorities. I found her in the entrance salon. She was lying there on the floor at the bottom of the stairs. Her neck was at a very funny angle. At least I thought it was funny. She thought it was funny, too. She was grinning up at me. She hadn't lost her jolly sense of humor. Just her life.

Polk Four was so clean you could eat off him.

There wasn't a wrinkle in his crisp khaki uniform. There wasn't a smudge on his wide-brimmed trooper's hat. His black leather holster gleamed. His square-toed blucher oxfords gleamed. He gleamed. Polk was in his late twenties and stood several inches over six feet and didn't slouch. He had the trim athletic build and flat stomach of a high school basketball star. His hair was blond and neatly combed, his eyes sincere and alert and wide apart over high cheekbones, a thin, straight nose, and strong, honest jaw. He had no blemishes on his face. I doubted he'd ever had any, or ever suffered from excess stomach acid or insomnia or the heartbreak of psoriasis. I hated him on sight.

He got there in ten minutes in his shiny-gray, sheriff's-department Ford, a deputy trailing behind him in another just like it. He took charge right away. There was nothing youthful or indecisive about Polk Four. He was the sheriff of Augusta County. The deputy kept himself busy taking photographs of Fern's body. The paramedics came, but there wasn't much for them to do except stand around. The body couldn't be moved until a doctor looked her over and signed the death certificate.

We all waited for him in the old parlor. Mavis was exceptionally still and composed. If there were tears in her, she would not allow them out now. Mercy wept openly into one of my white linen handkerchiefs.

The brothers had sharply contrasting reactions. Frederick was in total command – it was he who had called Polk Four and herded us into the parlor. Edward was unconsolable.

He rocked back and forth in his chair, sobbing and moaning. "I keep thinking of the night Mother died, Fred," he cried. "I was at Fern's when I got the news, remember? She was the one who actually told me."

"Let's not go into that, Ed," Frederick said sharply. "Come on, now."

"She was a rock, Fred, is all I meant."

"That she was." Frederick patted his brother gently on the shoulder. "That she was."

Richard had gotten himself a large brandy and sat there sipping it and furtively trying to make eye contact with Charlotte, who sat in a corner wringing her hands, her own eyes firmly fastened to the floor.

The doctor arrived in half an hour. He was weary and elderly. He examined Fern where she lay. Cause of death: broken neck. Then Fern O'Baugh was lifted onto a stretcher – it took three strong men to do that – and wheeled out.

Polk joined us in the parlor. "My deepest condolences, Mavis," he said, hat in hand. "It's a terrible loss. Just terrible."

"Thank you, Polk," she said softly.

"She was a real fine old lady," Polk went on. "Almost like another mother to Mercy." He looked over at her, coloring slightly. "Hi, Mercy."

"Hello, Polk," she said, sniffling.

"She was family, Polk," declared Mavis. "Family."

"Speaking of which . . ."

"We'll be handling the funeral arrangements," Frederick informed him.

"Fine, sir," Polk said. "We'll need some additional information for the certificate. Date and place of birth, social security number, parents' names . . ."

"Of course, Polk," Frederick said, lighting a cigarette. "Whatever you need."

Richard got up and started out of the room with his empty brandy glass.

"Sit, Richard," commanded Mavis.

He stopped. The muscles in his jaw tightened. "I merely wished to – "

"I *know* what you merely wished. Sit!"

He drew himself up, steaming. But he didn't erupt. He submitted. Sat back down, twitching.

"What do you think happened, Sheriff?" I asked.

Polk's clear blue eyes took me in for the first time. "We haven't met, sir."

"He's Stewart Hoag, the author, Polk," said Mercy. "Going to be living here for a while."

Polk Four looked me over, measuring me unsurely. I guess he didn't meet many fizzled literary icons. "Welcome to the Shenandoah Valley, Mr. Hoag," he said, "though I suppose this isn't what you'd consider a nice hello. She fell, in answer to your question. Those stairs are quite steep and narrow. That's how they built them in the old days. If you're not real careful on your way down, it's easy to take a tumble. Fern was a big lady. She tumbled hard."

"The guides always have to warn the tourists to watch their step," pointed out Charlotte.

"She must have gone up and down them a million times," I reasoned.

"That's true," Polk agreed with a reassuring smile. "But accidents do happen."

"Oh, Polk, must you be so banal?" demanded Mercy.

He reddened. "I realize you folks are upset. I'll not intrude on your privacy any longer."

"Thank you for everything, Polk," said Mavis. "And you're not intruding. You've been most kind. Hasn't he, Mercy?"

"Yes, Polk. You're always *most* kind," Mercy said hotly.

He walked out, singed at the ears. I followed him.

The ambulance and the doctor were gone. Polk's deputy was lingering.

"Any chance Fern's fall was something other than an accident, Sheriff?" I asked him.

Polk stopped and stood there looking at me with his hands on his hips. "Such as?"

"Something other than an accident," I repeated.

He frowned and scratched his chin. He had the closest shave I'd ever seen. It looked as if his whiskers had been surgically removed. "You mean like was she pushed or something? Everyone here loved Fern, Mr. Hoag. She was a fine old lady. And this is a fine old family. Mavis, her brothers, Mercy, they're not that sort of people."

"We're all that sort of people, Sheriff."

He narrowed his eyes at me. "You have some mighty strange ideas, Mr. Hoag. Where are you from?"

"New York City."

He nodded, as if this told him all he needed to know. Everyone from New York was crazy. Not like here, where the valley's biggest luminary wanted to turn her lead character into an alien. "You'll find things are a little different here, Mr. Hoag. This is a county where justice still has the upper hand. Fern O'Baugh's death was an accident, plain and simple. Take my word for it." He started for his cruiser, stopped. "I hope you won't be upsetting these good people."

"I wouldn't think of it, Sheriff."

"Good." He squared his shoulders, not that they needed squaring. "Mercy . . . she's a spirited lady, like her mother."

"She is."

"She and I . . ."

"I wouldn't think of that either, Sheriff."

He tipped his big trooper's hat to me. "Good day, Mr. Hoag."

"See you later, pardner."

He stuck his chin out at me. "Don't call me pardner." Then he got in his car and drove away, his deputy on his tail.

The man was right. Fern's death gave every appearance of being an accidental fall. Except to me. She'd told me Sterling Sloan was murdered. She'd told me she knew something about it. And now she was dead. That's how it looked to me.

I took the driveway around back to my guest quarters. Lulu was out cold in her easy chair, paddling her paws in the air, whimpering. Bad dream. I roused her. She woke with a start. Grudgingly, she followed me back to the old house. It was empty now. Everyone had gone back to the east wing.

We went up the stairs. They were steep. Creaky, too. There was a short central hallway on the second floor. Two bedrooms were open for public view, both of them furnished with lovely old canopy beds, washstands, wardrobe cupboards. One was the master bedroom, the other the room that had been Vangie's in the movie. There was a definite air of familiarity to it. The brocaded-silk bedcover upon which lay Vangie's most trusted confidante – Miss Penelope, her porcelain doll. The mirrored dressing table where Vangie sat each night combing out her wild mane of red hair. The vast double-doored wardrobe from which she chose her most tempting outfits. There was also a definite air of weirdness. Because Vangie wasn't a real character out of history. Vangie was fiction. And this was a movie set.

The room next to Vangie's was locked. So was another door across the hall. I stood there in the hallway, wondering what exactly Fern was doing up here in those seconds before she died. She was about to serve lunch next door. Why had she come up here?

Lulu was sniffing the floor at the top of the stairs. There was a carved banister post on either side of the top step, painted white to go with the hallway decor. Lulu looked up at me when I approached. When she did, I noticed she had white particles stuck to her wet black nose. I knelt beside her and wiped them off.

The particles were tiny flecks of white paint.

There were more of them on the floor at the base of each banister post. I ran a finger along one of them. The wood was hard and smooth with several coats of glossy paint over it. Except about three inches from the floor, where a set of thin grooves had been made in the paint. All the way around. On both posts. Fern hadn't been pushed. Nothing so crude as that. Someone had tied a trip wire across the top of the stairs after she'd gone up. She was easy prey – blind as a bat without her glasses. They'd lain in wait for her to go down – and down she went. Then they'd removed the wire and returned to the house. It could have been anyone in the family. Anyone could have slipped out for a minute while we were having our sherry. That's all it would have taken. One of them had shut her up. Made sure she'd never tell what she knew about Sterling Sloan. What was it she'd seen? What had been covered up? And how could it possibly matter now, fifty years later?

But it did matter. That much I knew for damned sure.

Mercy and Charlotte were in the kitchen getting our belated lunch together.

"I managed to drop a paper clip in my typewriter," I said. "Need a piece of wire to get it out."

"You'll have to ask Roy for it," said Mercy as she took a tray of food into the dining room. "I have no idea where you'd – "

"Bottom drawer there under the toaster, Hoagy," broke in Charlotte. "With the tools."

There was a flashlight in there, a pair of pliers, a hammer, screwdrivers, twine. There was also a spool of wire and a pair of cutters. I cut myself a length of wire.

"What's in those closed rooms upstairs in the old house?" I asked Charlotte.

She took a pitcher of iced tea out of the refrigerator. "They keep the vacuums and cleaning supplies in the room next to Vangie's. That used to be the sitting room. There's still a door connecting them. They moved the big wardrobe in front of it so the tourists would stop asking if they could go in there. The other room is a bathroom, from when the family still lived up there."

"I was wondering what Fern was doing up there."

"Getting something, I suppose," Charlotte said, chewing on her lower lip.

"Makes sense," I agreed. "Only she was empty-handed when I found her. Odd, don't you think?"

She looked at me strangely. Clearly, she thought I was being morbid and weird. "I can't imagine what difference it makes," she said brusquely. Then she sped out with the tea.

I put the wire and cutters back in the drawer and closed it. I turned to find Frederick standing there before me. I was getting good at telling the brothers apart now – as long as Frederick had a cigarette in his hand.

"I wonder," he said, "If you could drop by my office later this afternoon. We have business."

Frederick Glaze, investment counselor, did his business in Staunton on the top floor of the Marquis Building, a three-story, turreted, red-brick Romanesque on Beverley Street. I took the stairs. I was by myself. Lulu had shown more interest in her chair than a trip to town.

His offices were large, bright and hi-tech. No cobbler's shop, this. Modular cubicles filled with modular young brokers working the phones and the terminals. The place smelled of money. His own private office was located in the round turret, and the past. He had an old rolltop desk in there, and a pair of worn leather armchairs and no computer. There was also an old freestanding steel safe, the kind that fall out windows and flatten people on the street below in cartoons. His windows offered a panoramic view of the business district and the Victorian houses climbing up the steep hills beyond it.

Frederick's jacket was off. The sleeves of his white broadcloth shirt were turned back to reveal a silver wristwatch on one wrist and an ID bracelet on the other. He seemed profoundly weary under his smooth, genteel exterior. "Thank you for coming, Hoagy. Sit down, please. Ed won't be joining us. This Fern thing hit him pretty hard. Ed, Fern, and me . . . we all grew up together. We were classmates. Friends."

"I didn't realize that."

He coughed huskily, drank from a glass of water at his elbow. "When you get to be my age, you get used to losing your friends. But you don't get to liking it. You keep wishing you'd treated them better."

"Did she confide in you?"

He raised his eyebrows. "Confide in me?"

"Personal things. Doubts, fears."

"She had none. Fern O'Baugh was the happiest soul I ever met. Why do you ask?"

"Just curious."

He got up and went over to the safe. "Mavis certainly seems taken with you. She even seems willing to keep her queer notions out of Mother's sequel just because you said she should." He spun the tumbler on the safe and began to work the combination from memory. "I take my hat off to you, sir. You do indeed work miracles."

"Everyone ought to be good at something."

He opened the safe door wide, reached inside, and pulled out a loose-leaf, three-ring notebook and a legal document. He closed the safe and carried these back to his desk. He held on to the document. The notebook he handed over to me.

"Your copy of Mother's notes for *Sweet Land of Liberty*," he explained. "In her own hand, but quite legible. You'll find a lot in there to do with plot and character, and not a lot to do with the sights and sounds. We've the resources of the Staunton Historical Society should you need anything checked out. Girls at Mary Baldwin would be only too happy to help out. Just turn them loose. No sense you getting bogged down, I mean. Speed is of the essence at this point."

"I understand."

He lit a cigarette and sat back in his chair. "Mother's notes are in the form of a diary. As it happens, she was keeping it while *Oh, Shenandoah* was being filmed out at the estate. A lot of what you're going to be reading is her impressions of what was going on around her. How she felt the actors were doing, bits of gossip, things like that."

I found myself leaning forward. "Oh?"

"You may find it interesting reading. Not that it has anything to do with this project. It's more of a literary artifact, really. We plan to publish it as an introduction to the special golden-anniversary edition. You'll find the notes for *Sweet Land* scattered throughout. Fairly complete, except for the ending."

"The ending?"

"We have no idea how Mother intended to end the book," he confessed. "She evidently didn't like what she'd done because she tore it out. All we know is that John Raymond is elected president." He chuckled uneasily. "We don't know what is supposed to happen after that."

"Not to worry. Endings are easy. It's beginnings that are hard."

"Fine," he said. "We leave it to your capable hands. I simply didn't want to think you were missing something."

"I generally am, but it's okay. I'm used to it."

"The notebook is yours for the duration of the assignment. Please guard it with your life." Frederick buzzed his secretary, then picked up the document he'd pulled from the safe and examined it. "Anything else I can do for you while you're down here?" he asked.

"What did you have in mind?"

"Brokerage assistance. Investment opportunities. We're putting together some very exciting tax shelters."

"I usually shelter my earnings in the nearest cash register."

"Suit yourself. Never hurts to ask." He buzzed his secretary again, impatiently. "I'd like you to sign this, Hoagy," he said, passing me the document. "It states that I have delivered to you on this day a copy of Mother's notebook, and that you will not reveal its contents to anyone without the prior written consent of the estate. To do so will constitute a breach of contract and leave you liable for a suit. Understood?"

I said it was.

He smiled. "Just a formality, really. Something Ed drew up. You know how lawyers are."

There was a quick tapping at the door. A heavy, plain-faced young woman with curly black hair came trudging in.

"Ah, here you are, dear," said Frederick brightly. "Come on over here beside me, Melinda. I need you to notarize this."

She waited next to him obediently, stamp in hand, while I read over the document and signed it. When I looked up, I noticed there was something odd about the way she was standing. Her entire body seemed frozen there. She was staring straight ahead, stone faced, deathly pale.

Frederick Glaze's right hand was on the desk before him. His left was clamped around Melinda's ample right buttock like a barnacle.

He had a blissful, elfin smile on his face. He looked like a beatific little boy. It was the happiest I'd seen anyone look in a long time.

They picked me up the second I hit the sidewalk with Alma's diary. There were two of them. One had a flattop crew cut, the other a ponytail. It was nice, I reflected, to see ponytails staging a comeback. They both wore flannel shirts and jeans. They both looked as if they ate meat three times a day, not necessarily cooked.

Now I knew why Lulu hadn't wanted to come with me.

They stayed a steady two storefronts behind me as I made my way down Beverley Street. When I paused to window-shop, they paused to window-shop. They weren't particularly cool or professional about it. Maybe they just didn't care if I spotted them.

A sharp, cold wind was cutting into the soft spring air. Big gray clouds were blowing across the valley from the Blue Ridge Mountains. Winter wasn't gone after all. I turned up my collar and moved on down the block. They moved on down with me. I was loitering at the window of a bookstore, weighing my options and not liking them, when I spotted Charlotte inside there browsing. My lucky day. I went in.

She was over in paperback fiction with her nose buried in a copy of my second novel, the one with the cover that belonged on something by Sidney Sheldon. Both of my novels were well represented. There's no telling where you'll find exceptional little bookstores.

"In case you're wondering," I said to her, "the big sex scene is on page seventy-four, such as it is."

She clapped the book shut, blushing. "I-I came in for some stationery," she blurted out, hurriedly returning the book to the rack. "I was just sort of curious . . ."

I retrieved the book from the rack and handed it to her. "My treat."

"Oh, no, I couldn't," she said, her eyes darting nervously for the floor, for anywhere.

"I insist. Feel free to take it home and not enjoy it. Of course, I do expect something in return."

She frowned at me, suspicious. "Such as?"

There were some Mary Baldwin sweatshirts and bookbags over in the next aisle. I picked out a canvas portfolio with a zipper and slid Alma's diary inside it and tucked it under Charlotte's arm. "Would you take that back to the estate for me?"

"Oh, I'd be happy to," she said, relieved.

We went outside together after I paid. My two tails were waiting patiently for me beside a brass memorial plaque stuck in the sidewalk to mark the spot where Alma Glaze had been run over. Their arms were crossed, their eyes fastened on me. They really didn't care if I spotted them.

"How's the iced tea in that cafe across the street?" I asked Charlotte.

"Real good. They make it from scratch."

"Care to join me for a glass?"

She thought it over. "Well, only if you'll let me pay for both of us. So we'll be even." She tried to smile, but it never quite caught up to her eyes. "Okay?"

"It's a deal."

The Beverley Cafe was deep and narrow and dark. Hard wooden booths were set against the walls. We took one. A fat little kid was buying a candy bar at the cash register. Two old men in work clothes were having pie and coffee and muttering to each other. Otherwise it was empty.

Charlotte had put a drab coat on over her drab dress. She kept it on. Shifted uncomfortably there in the booth. Chewed on her lower lip. She seemed grateful when the sulky waitress shuffled over to us and said, "Hey, Charlotte."

"Hey, Luanne. Iced tea for two, please."

Luanne looked me over, lingered for an introduction, didn't get one, sighed, and moved slowly off.

"Were you and Fern close, Charlotte?" I asked.

"Not really. She was a meddlesome old thing. Always pestering me to change my hair and stand up straight. I guess she meant well, but I wasn't looking for another mother."

I glanced out the window at the street. No sign of my friends. "And you and Mavis?"

"What about us?"

"How long have you been working for her?"

"Two years.

"Like her?"

Charlotte clasped her hands primly on the table before her. "I despise Mavis Glaze more than I ever thought it was possible to despise another human being," she replied calmly.

Luanne came back with our iced tea. Charlotte dumped three spoonfuls of sugar in hers before she took a sip. "You don't know about Mavis and my father, do you?"

I tasted my tea. It was already sweetened. Plenty sweetened. "What about them?"

"I may as well tell you myself, since you'll be hearing it before long anyway. There've always been two fine old families that ran things in the valley. Owned the land. Owned the LaFoons. One was the Glazes, the other the Neenes. Franklin Neene was my father, and the end of the line. I'm an only child and the family money is long gone. About the only thing left was the name – my father was judge of the Staunton Circuit Court, and a fine, respected man. Honest. Fair. Gentle. Sensitive. Too sensitive for his own good, really. When Mother died four years ago of ovarian cancer, he had a real problem bouncing back from it emotionally. He . . . He began to drink. I did my best to take care of him. Quit my job over at the high school – I was a secretary in the administration office. Kept house for him, watched over him. But he got worse and worse. Pulled away from his friends and his activities, resisted any kind of help. He was never drunk on the bench. Never. He was much too conscientious for that. He just sat in his room alone and drank, night after night. Until one night he suddenly jumped in his car and drove off. I didn't even hear him leave. He showed up at a local restaurant, the Golden Stirrup, drunk out of his mind. Rammed a couple of cars in the parking lot. Made quite a scene. Got himself hauled into jail." Charlotte drank some of her tea, gripping the glass tightly with her short, stubby fingers. "Mavis heard about it, of course, and she happens to be head of Virginians Against Drunk Driving."

"So I've heard."

"Well, she decided his behavior was unbecoming to a public servant of a judge's stature and launched a campaign to get him thrown off the bench. She urged people to write letters to the governor. She made it into a big story in the newspapers. And she wouldn't let go. She hounded him and hounded him. The poor man was ill. Everyone knew that. There were decent, humane ways it could have been handled. Medical leave, early retirement – something to save him his dignity. But she'd have none of that. She wanted his scalp. You see, Mavis always hated that there was another family name in the valley that rivaled her own. And this was her big chance to make sure there no longer would be. She forced him to resign in disgrace. He had no other choice. Two mornings later I found him inside his car in the garage, the garage door closed and the engine running. It was suicide, and Mavis Glaze drove him to it." Charlotte took a deep breath and let it out slowly. "We had a big old house here in town, heavily mortgaged, and not much else. I sold it and rented an apartment. And came to work for her."

"How can you stand to?"

"I need the job," she replied simply. "Besides, if you live in a small town, you get used to hating people and not being able to do anything about it, except leave. I can't. This is my home. I've never lived anywhere else. I'm too old to start over now, and too much of a coward."

"How do you feel about the rest of the family?"

She glanced furtively around the cafe, turned back to me with a conspiratorial gleam in her eye. "Well, Frederick's got a real problem keeping his filthy hands to himself," she said in a hushed voice.

"I noticed."

"I try not to be alone in a room with him if I can help it. He's never actually attacked anyone, as far as I know. But he did get in some trouble when he was younger. They say he made phone calls."

"Phone calls?"

"Dirty ones. You know, to women. They all knew it was him. Polk Two had to go out and talk to him about it. They were going to press charges if he didn't quit it." She shook her head in amazement. "He and Edward couldn't be more different. Edward's such a fine, considerate man. He always makes a point of asking me how I'm doing, and he listens to what I say. A lot of people never listen."

"Odd that neither of them ever married."

"Edward was once. A long time ago, to a French girl he met in Washington. He doesn't like to talk about it. I think she left him for another man."

"And Richard?"

She swallowed and looked away. "What about him?"

"He's in love with you, isn't he?"

"Who told you?" she demanded angrily. "Did he tell you?"

"He didn't have to."

She gave her lower lip a workout. "He thinks he is. Don't ask me why. Maybe because Mavis strips him of his self-esteem. Of course, he lets her do it. He never pushes back. Maybe that's what it's all about. Maybe he needs to feel . . . manly or something. I don't know. I've never encouraged him. If anything, I've discouraged him, y'know?"

I nodded. Trying to run a guy down with your car was certainly my idea of discouragement.

"But he keeps pestering me," she went on. "I've never had a married man pursue me this way before. Actually, I've never had any man pursue me this way. I don't know what to do."

"Do you love him?"

"I don't know. It's not as if we've ever . . . I mean, he and I haven't . . . I do know he drinks too much. He's not a very happy man."

"Who among us is?"

"He's actually offered to divorce her. He wants to take me home to England with him. He says he's about to come into money of his own over there. Lots of it."

"Oh?"

"Family money of some kind."

"I see. Does Mavis know about any of this?"

Her eyes widened. "You wouldn't . . . ?"

"She won't hear about it from me."

She smiled gratefully. She looked somewhat vulpine when she smiled. "I assume she doesn't know. If she did, she'd fire me in a second, figuring I'd somehow engineered the whole thing to get back

258

at her. Believe me, I don't have revenge in mind. I just want to do my job. I guess the smart thing to do would be to find a new one." She finished her iced tea and reached for the check. I let her have it. A deal's a deal. "Still, I sometimes wonder if it would serve her right."

"If what would?"

She showed me her pointy little teeth. "If I wrecked Mavis Glaze's proper, perfect, civilized little kingdom for her."

They were lounging against my rental car in the public lot around the corner, jeans riding low on their hips, trying to look tough. And succeeding. No one else was around. Unless you count Gordie, who watched over us from the giant VADD billboard by the hardware store next door. There was a black-and-white photo of him looking as if he were about to cry. And underneath: *If people didn't drive drunk, he wouldn't still be waiting for Mommy and Daddy to come home.*

"Hey, mister," the crew cut said, grinning at me crookedly. "Y'all help us out?"

"Be happy to," I replied, unlocking the car and tossing my jacket inside. Good tailoring is hard to find. It's a sin to waste it. "What did you have in mind?"

"Couple of bucks for something to eat?" suggested the ponytail.

"Okay," I agreed. "Provided you fellows do a stranger a kind turn yourself someday."

"We'll sure try," the crewcut promised, enjoying this. He was certainly enjoying it more than I was.

I took my wallet out of my trousers. Before I could open it he knocked it from my hands to the pavement. I looked down at it, then up at him, then over at the ponytail. "I have to hand it to you fellows – you've got real panache."

They stared at me blankly, waiting. There was a script to follow, and they expected me to follow it. They also didn't know the meaning of the word *panache*.

I looked back down at the wallet and sighed. "Okay, here goes . . . You want to pick that up?"

The crew cut scratched his stubbly chin and thought it over. "You go ahead and do it."

"Okay. But just so you know for the future – this is not my idea of a kind turn."

I bent down for my wallet, bracing myself for the first one. It was a punch to my right kidney from the ponytail. It made my insides feel as if they'd exploded. I crumpled to my knees, gasping, and got a work boot to the shoulder, another to the neck, and then, as I pitched over onto my side, one smack in my bread basket. That one put me into the fetal position, fighting for breath. I hate getting hit. It hurts a lot. Besides, it really shouldn't be part of my job description. I wondered if Bill Novak and Linda Bird Francke ever got stomped. Probably not.

They patted me down roughly. Finding no notebook on me, they began searching the car, cursing to each other impatiently while I lay there, helpless.

"Shit, where is it?" growled crew cut when they came up empty.

"Musta passed it to the lady."

"Shit." Frustrated, crew cut kicked me again—this time behind my right ear.

This time things started spinning around. Then they went black.

Lulu was standing over me, sniffing at my face. I tried to say her name. Nothing would come out. My hand reached for her but she pulled away from me.

I opened my eyes. I was trying to pet Polk Four, who was crouched over me on the pavement sniffing at my breath to see if I was drunk. He'd already decided I was crazy. His sheriff's vehicle idled there behind him in the lot, radio squawking.

"You okay, Mr. Hoag?" he asked, brow furrowed with concern.

My stomach ached and my shoulder, neck, and head throbbed. But I could breathe okay. No broken ribs. "Fine. Just banged my head on a steel-toed boot."

"How many of them were there?"

"Four. Two to a man."

He handed me my car keys and wallet. They had taken my cash.

"What did they get?" he asked.

"Fifty, sixty bucks."

He shook his head, disgusted, and stood up and looked around, hands on his hips. He looked about eight feet tall standing there. "Heckuva thing, this happening in the middle of Staunton in broad daylight. Heckuva thing. You must not think too much of our little town now."

I sat up, groaning. "Oh, I wouldn't go that far, Sheriff."

"Drive you to the hospital? That's a nasty welt by your ear. Might have a concussion."

"I don't hear any bells, two and two is four, and my name used to be Stewart Hoag." I offered him my hand. "You could help me up."

"Fair enough." He gripped my hand and hoisted me up onto my feet. I think it was better for him than it was for me. "Feel well enough to follow me?"

"I don't know. Where are you going?"

"You should fill out a report. This'll be a Staunton City Police matter. Be happy to run you over there."

"Maybe some other time."

"It's the right thing to do," Polk Four said firmly. "You should do it."

I limped over to my car and dropped slowly in behind the wheel. My jacket lay on the passenger seat. The stupid clods had torn the lining out of it. "It was murder, Sheriff."

"I can imagine it was pretty painful," he said gently.

"Fern O'Baugh. It was murder."

He leaned in through the open window, rested his elbows on the door. "Now look, Mr. Hoag," he said patiently. "We've already been over this."

"I found some grooves in the banister posts at the top of the stairs. Flecks of paint on the floor. Somebody used a trip wire."

"Find the wire?" he asked skeptically.

"Well, no. But I did find some wire in the kitchen. Anyone could have gone in there and – "

"Listen to yourself, Mr. Hoag. You've got nothing. There's no telling how long those flecks of paint have been there, or how they got there either. Posts could have gotten bumped with a vacuum cleaner or a piece of furniture."

"It was a trip wire."

He bristled. He didn't like my stirring it up. Or maybe he just resented that I'd tried to pet his head. "I warned you about this once already, Mr. Hoag. I care about these people. I won't stand for you upsetting them. Understand?"

"Fully. You don't want to step on any fine old corns."

"Now that's uncalled for, mister!" he snapped. "I don't deserve that! No way!" He stopped and paused a moment to collect himself. "You've been knocked around some. You're not yourself."

"No, I am. That's the depressing part."

"Be careful driving back to Shenandoah, okay?"

"Will do, pardner."

"And don't call me pardner!"

He got back in his car and waited there, fuming. I edged the Nova out of the lot and started for the outskirts of town. He peeled off with a screech in the other direction.

I headed back to Shenandoah, wondering. How was it that Polk Four had happened along? Was he keeping an eye on me? Why? Who had hired the clods to get Alma's diary from me? One of the more enterprising supermarket tabloids? A trashy television newsmagazine? It didn't matter. Not really. What mattered was that whoever it was had good information. They knew I'd be picking up the diary at Frederick's office, and they knew when. They had very good information. They had inside information.

CHAPTER
SIX

Mavis Glaze liked to patrol her realm twice daily on a hot-pink dirt bike, I guess to remind all of the birds and the bees just exactly who was in charge. She was zipping across the front pasture when I pulled the Nova through the gate. The sight of her perched regally atop her motorcycle, back stiff, nose high, smile frozen, gave a whole new meaning to the words *bitch on wheels*.

Roy, the talkative old gardener, waved her down when she got to the ash-lined drive. He pointed to the outer wall over by the souvenir stand, where he'd left a shovel and wheelbarrow. She started over there with him. When she saw me, she indicated she wanted me to follow them. I did. Who was I to let her down?

The two of them had their heads together by the wall. Roy was kneeling on the ground, one knobby hand scratching fretfully at some fresh soil there.

"Roy seems to feel some form of animal life is getting in under the wall at night," Mavis informed me. Her biker outfit consisted of a trim white cotton jumpsuit and belted suede jacket, with a flowered scarf over her head. "A fox, or perhaps a coon."

Roy gave me his blank stare, worked the chaw of tobacco in his cheek.

"Not a matter we can afford to take lightly," Mavis added. "It's after the peacocks, you see."

"What will you do?" I asked.

"We prefer not to put down traps," she replied. "One of them might wander into it. Roy will have to hunt it down and shoot it."

He got to his feet and leaned over and murmured something to her, his lips barely moving.

She nodded. "Your dog," she said to me. "Keep it on a leash after dark, for its own safety."

"Thanks for the warning, Roy," I said. In response he spat some tobacco juice at my feet. Maybe it was just his way of saying you're welcome.

Mavis didn't care for it one bit. She turned her hard blue pinpoints on him and breathed fire. "Roy, I have told you innumerable times that if you *must* partake of that *disgusting* habit to please have the courtesy not to expectorate in my presence! Since I obviously have *not* made myself understood, perhaps docking you one day's pay will make my point clear. I will *not* be spat at! Do you understand!"

Roy bowed his head and nodded penitently.

"See that you do!" She turned her back on him and marched briskly toward her motorcycle. I followed. "There was a delivery for you about an hour ago," she said to me over her shoulder. "I had him leave it outside your room."

"Thank you."

She stopped and looked me over. "You look terribly pale. You're not ill, are you?"

"Nothing a short single malt and a half dozen tall ice packs can't handle."

"Excuse me?"

"Don't mind me."

She hesitated. "I've been thinking about the book. *My* book. I can't think about anything else, really. I'm just so alive with ideas and sensations. I-I feel like an exposed nerve. Is it that way for you? When you write, I mean."

"On my good days."

"They're coming so fast I can barely keep up. It's thrilling. I can't wait to tell you about them."

"And I can't wait to hear them, Mavis. In the meantime, write them down in a notebook as they occur to you."

"That's just what Mother did. She even kept a notepad by her bed at night. Father would tease her about it." Briefly, her face softened at the memory. Then it abruptly hardened again. She climbed on her little pink motorcycle.

"Nice little machine," I observed.

"It was a Christmas present from Richard."

"I'd have thought a horse would be more your style – strong, proud, classical." I also couldn't help thinking if she had a horse to kick, she'd do it less to people.

"I never go near them. I was thrown by one as a girl. Rather badly – I broke my collarbone."

"I'd have thought you'd climb right back up."

"People often say that to me, mistakenly. It's not that I am afraid. Fear doesn't enter into it."

"What does?"

"A horse failed me, Hoagy. Failure is a habit. I don't believe in giving in to it." She started up the motor and revved it. "I'm terribly upset about Fern. Such a loyal, dependable friend.

Irreplaceable, as well. I've spent the entire afternoon on the phone with a host of agencies trying to find someone who can take over for her. They've checked Southampton, Palm Beach, Pasadena. No one seems available anywhere right now. I can't imagine why." She let out a long sigh. Then she turned the tiniest bit schoolgirlish on me. "Actually, that's not true. I *can*. I don't know how to lie to you. I wonder why. Perhaps because you're not afraid of me."

"Why should I be afraid of you?"

"The truth," she confessed, "is that I am not considered a desirable employer. I am too hard on people."

A car came zipping up the drive from the gate. Charlotte in her red LeMans. She stopped beside us and rolled down her window and handed me the zippered canvas portfolio with Alma's diary in it. Before I could thank her she'd floored it and was off for the house.

"Interesting woman," I observed. "I understand her father – "

"Franklin Neene was a weakling," Mavis snapped.

"Still, you must have felt pretty awful about what happened."

"Why should I? I didn't tell him to climb into his car and shut the garage door. I didn't tell him to give up. That was his decision. His *cowardice*. Only a coward quits on life."

"It's true, you know."

She gave me her frozen smile. "I'm glad we see things – "

"You *are* too hard on people."

Her eyes flashed at me. "I can't help being who I am. I've tried to be easygoing, accommodating. Someone who has lots of friends to laugh with, confide in. Someone who isn't so . . . isolated . . ." She looked away uncomfortably. "It's not in my nature. A person must be true to his or her nature. I simply cannot tolerate weakness. There's no place for it in my life – with one notable exception, of course. We all have our flaws. Richard happens to be mine. I'm afraid we can't all be lucky in love."

"Careful. You'll spoil what few illusions I have left."

"Maybe the reason you're not afraid of me," she suggested, "is that you don't give a damn."

"Maybe the reason I'm not afraid of you is that I *do*."

She narrowed her eyes at me challengingly. "You puzzle me, Hoagy. I'd like to get to the bottom of you."

"Careful, I'm semispoken for."

"I meant," she said sharply, "I'd like to figure out what makes you tick."

"Feel free. And let me know if you do – it would be nice to know myself after all these years.

The sky was becoming dark and threatening now, the air raw. Rain wasn't far off.

Mavis looked up at the clouds and shivered. "I never learned how to cook. At Mother's insistence – she feared I'd be made a slave to some man. Thank goodness Charlotte volunteered to make little Gordie dinner tonight."

"Will she tuck him into bed, too?"

"Gordie is a very, very lucky boy," she pointed out.

"I'm sure he reminds himself of that on a daily basis." I tugged at my ear. "I happen to know a gifted, mature woman who has managed several prominent British estates. Hasn't got a weak bone in her body. Also happens to be quite discreet." As well as a born ferret for inside information, and just what I needed right now. "If my friend Pamela's available, you couldn't do any better."

Mavis pursed her lips. "I know Richard would adore having a fellow countrywoman. . . . She's good, you say?"

"She's the best."

"I'd need references."

"She'd have them."

"Could she start right away? Time is of the essence. I'm expecting a thousand guests here for my VADD costume ball the night of the golden-anniversary premiere. The Quayles are flying in. Senator and Mrs. Robb. The Kissingers, the Buckleys. Patricia Kluge. Gore Vidal, Bill Blass, King Juan Carlos. Barbara Walters is taping a three-hour special for ABC. . . . I don't know what I'll do if – "

"Shall I call Pam?"

"I'd love for you to call her." She placed her long fingers on my arm and left them there. "And thank you, Hoagy," she said warmly. Or what was warmly for her.

"All part of the service," I assured her, glancing down at her fingers. She removed them, coloring.

I only hoped Pam wouldn't mind standing in for someone who had just been murdered.

It was the Jag that was waiting for me outside the door of my guest cottage, the red 1958 XK150 drophead Merilee and I had bought when we were together, and which was hers now. It is a rare beauty, every inch of it factory original. Seeing it sitting there in the courtyard with its top down, sixty-spoke wire wheels gleaming, almost made me forget I'd been used as a soccer ball that afternoon. There was an engraved Tiffany note card on the tan leather driver's seat: *I wouldn't want you to forget me, darling.*

I couldn't forget her if I wanted to, and I didn't want to.

A few fat raindrops were starting to fall. Quickly, I put the top up and went inside. Next door, Gordie's TV was blaring. There was, I was pleased to note, no sign of his goddamned cat.

Lulu growled at me.

Sat there in her chair and growled at me as if I were a stranger who'd barged into the wrong room.

"Excuse me, miss," I said. "I don't mean to intrude, but I happen to live here. At least I did the last time I looked."

She stopped growling. Now she was just glowering at me.

I went over and sat on the arm of the chair and patted her. Or tried to. She pulled away from me, as if I'd sprayed my hand with some kind of doggy repellent.

"For your information," I pointed out, "Hoagy could use a little sympathy. Possibly a lick on the face."

No response.

"Lassie would have been right there by my side," I said. "Chased those two off. Or at the very least raced over to Polk's office and barked. 'Hoagy's in trouble! Hoagy's in trouble!'"

She continued to glower at me from under her beret.

"Are you feeling all right?" I grabbed her nose. Cold and wet. "Want to go back to New York or something?"

She hopped down and waddled over to her bowl. She wanted her dinner or something.

I gave it to her. She ate mechanically, like a middle-aged husband chewing on his wife's pot roast for the thousandth time. I watched her, concerned. She wasn't herself. She seemed very far away to me. I couldn't imagine why.

I made a fire in the small fireplace and put some ice in a towel and laid it against the throbbing welt on the side of my head. I was pouring myself a Macallan when I heard it. Softly at first. Then louder.

Meowing.

I ignored it. I sat and enjoyed the fire and my single malt and ignored it. It got louder. And then she began to yowl, loud enough to be heard across the valley. Certainly loud enough for Roy to hear her. Roy and his shotgun.

Disgusted, I went to the front door and opened it. Sadie sat there in the doorway in the rain, all bright-eyed and perky and wet. She'd brought me a token of her affection. A dead mouse. At least, I think it was dead. I didn't look too close. I told her to go away and take her friend with her. I closed the door. She promptly started yowling again. I threw it open. Now she was hanging from the screen door by all fours, eye to eye with me. I went out there and yanked her from the screen and set her down on the ground. She immediately leapt up onto my right shoulder, scampered around the back of my neck, down the other shoulder, and into the crook of my left arm, where she nestled moistly and began making small, comfortable motorboat noises. At least someone seemed happy to see me.

"Tell you what," I said to her grudgingly. "If you'll shut up, I'll bring you out something. But just this once. Never again." I put her down. "Wait out here. And don't ever bring me a rodent again."

Lulu was still eating and still giving me the cold shoulder. I spooned the leftover mackerel from her can into a saucer and took it back out to Sadie. The rain was really coming down now. Not that she was complaining. She was waiting just as I asked her to, quietly getting wetter and wetter. I sighed and held the door open. She came right in. The mouse she left on the doorstep. Lulu eyed her from her bowl but didn't seem to mind. Whatever was bothering her it wasn't Sadie. I put the saucer down inside the door and Sadie went for it, starved.

I sat back down before the fire with the telephone. I talked the rental agency into hauling away their Nova and a florist into delivering a dozen long-stems to the farm in Connecticut. I tracked down Pam through her brother in Croydon. She was being a woman of leisure at a residential hotel in Bournemouth, and bored stiff. She'd be at Shenandoah as soon as the airline schedules allowed.

I fed the fire and my whiskey glass. I put on a Garner tape and let the little elf and the rain have their way for a while. Then I opened up the notebook. Alma Glaze had kept her diary on unlined paper. Her writing had a tendency to go uphill as she got to the right edge of the page. No curlicues or flourishes. Her handwriting was small, tight, and no-nonsense. Just like the text. Just like the woman.

CHAPTER
SEVEN

June 9

I sit in the gazebo, gazing out at the North Lawn, trying to stay out of everyone's way. They have begun their filming today. The very last scene, the duel, is being filmed first. I'm told they do everything out of sequence in Hollywood. How can they? How can the actors know what to feel if the preceding scene has not yet been filmed? Curious. The lawn is filled with their modern equipment — cameras, lights, trucks, trailers. Amidst all of it stand the duelists, Errol Flynn and Sterling Sloan, in their costumes and powdered wigs.

Mr. Flynn cuts such a tall, dashing figure as De Cheverier. He is an utterly charming, devilish man. Last evening he kissed my hand and pronounced me "the loveliest writer I've ever laid eyes on." He is so full of life, so eager to embrace its challenges. . . . Mr. Sloan is in many ways his opposite. He is a small man, five feet six at most. He must stand on a platform to see eye to eye with the strapping Flynn. He has such tiny hands that the costumer told me he must wear boy's gloves. His forehead is unusually high, his skin fair, his mouth delicate, hair a lovely ginger color. But that voice! So rich and baritone! Were it not for that he would seem too small and frail to project John Raymond's inner strength. Sloan is a very quiet man. There is an air of deep suffering about him, of dark inner torment.

Laurel Barrett is an exquisite, fine-boned creature. She has the loveliest, purest white skin I have ever seen. However, she is very arrogant and high-strung. When I told her how pleased I was she had been chosen to play Evangeline, she said, "I can well imagine you would be." I gather she is not well liked by the cast and crew. Certainly she makes no attempt to be cordial. There seems to be more than a little marital strain between her and Mr. Sloan. Or perhaps I simply do not understand performers.

Mr. Wyler, the director, certainly seems to. Willy is very much in charge. He asked the gentlemen to perform one small part of the duel scene over and over again this morning. They did so without question. I suppose they are used to this, since so much of moviemaking seems to be mindless, painstaking repetition. . . . Happily, Mr. Goldwyn has returned to Hollywood for the time being. What a vulgar, horrid snake! What a total figment of his own imagination! And what does he actually do? His sole interest here seemed to be in trying to bed any living, breathing woman he could get his hands on. Briefly, he even pursued the "dahlink" widowed author of "Old" Shenandoah, as he insists upon calling it. We were not amused.

June 10

The children are in heaven. They consider this entire enterprise their personal playground. The twins are enamored of the cameras and lights and of the men who handle them. Particularly Edward, who, with the typical verve of a man with one entire year of college under his belt, has pronounced himself bound for a career in the theatrical arts. He is terribly underfoot, I'm afraid. . . . Little Mavis has taken to worshiping Mr. Flynn with every ounce of her ten years. She follows him about and constantly seeks to dominate his attentions. He's been quite charming about it. Her main competition is Miss Barrett, who appears to be terribly smitten by him. I can only hope the filming will not be highlighted by a real duel between these two gentlemen.

Mr. Flynn has liquor on his breath at nine in the morning. Still, he is a perfect professional and the crew adore him. They do not care for the moody aloofness of Sloan and Barrett, whom they have dubbed Himself and Herself. Mr. Niven is most ingratiating. Miss Barrymore intelligent and convivial. I believe she and I shall become friends.

Seeing my characters come to life this way, I cannot help but think of their continuing on after Oh, Shenandoah. *Of Evangeline's going forth to live the joys and the sorrows of this sweet land of liberty. John Raymond must win the duel. For it is he, a statesman, a man of peace, who is destined for greatness in the new land. De Cheverier, the eternal rebel, is a man of war. He is a flame, burning brightly in Evangeline's heart, but his time has now passed.*

And on it went. Alma's notes for *Sweet Land* were, in fact, rather sparse. There was little here that Mavis hadn't already told me. Mostly, there was gossip. Pretty good stuff, though, if you're interested in that sort of thing. It so happened I was.

June 14

Everyone is talking about how Mr. Niven and Linda Darnell are sleeping together. Neither of them has bothered to be discreet about it. I do not understand these people.

My poor Frederick is hopelessly in love with Helene Bray, the fast young actress who plays Evangeline's best friend, Abigail. Helene curses like a sailor and flirts with most of the young men on the set. She also happens to be sleeping with Rex Ransom, the handsome young actor who plays James Madison. I don't have the heart to tell Frederick. . . . Edward has the acting bug now. But he's so enthusiastic and genuine that he's actually managed to befriend Himself, the moody Mr. Sloan, who has consented to discuss his craft with Edward in his free time. Quite an unexpected privilege.

Little Fernie O'Baugh, the daughter of that fellow who fixes cars in town, looks simply lovely in her costume as Evangeline's sister, Lavinia . . . . I wonder if perhaps Mavis is spending too much time around Mr. Flynn. He made the oddest, crudest remark today about how much he enjoyed having her sit in his lap. I do believe I will start keeping her away from him.

June 25

Willy drove Miss Barrett to utter hysterics this morning. They were filming the scene where Donald Crisp, the fine actor who plays her father, tells Vangie he despises De Cheverier and would never countenance their marriage. Willy wanted Miss Barrett to break down in response and was not satisfied with what she was giving him. He made her film it over and over and over again, tormenting her, driving the poor woman to such a state of frenzied exhaustion that she genuinely was breaking down. She was not acting. Only then was he satisfied. It did not seem to bother him in the least that she then had to be given a sedative and put to bed. Mr. Sloan got into a violent quarrel with Willy because of it. I thought the two would come to blows. An aide had to separate them. Mr. Sloan then refused to come out of his trailer after lunch. He said he had a severe headache. Willy instructed the crew to pound on the trailer with hammers, creating such an unbearable amount of noise within that he simply had to emerge. The shooting went surprisingly smoothly after that. . . . Actors are children. Willy is their father.

I must say I am appalled at how casual they all are about altering my dialogue. Mr. Sherwood was most faithful in his script. Not so Willy and the performers. They keep changing a word here, a phrase there, and in the process destroying its authenticity. When I sell the film rights to Sweet Land of Liberty, *I will make sure they cannot do this. It shall be in the contract.*

June 29

Whispers about Mr. Flynn and Miss Barrett. They have filmed several love scenes together, and the passion they are generating appears to be quite genuine. She has been seen coming out of his trailer. Such a lovely creature. How could she? And with her own husband right here! I do not understand these people.

July 12

Quite a scare today. Little Mavis didn't turn up for lunch and no one seemed to know where she was. Toward late afternoon she was found across the road in the Appleby pasture, which they've rented for the battle scenes. The little fool had taken off on a horse and had a nasty spill. Dr. Toriello rushed her to the hospital, where it was discovered she had broken her collarbone. She's in a great deal of pain, but she'll live. I must remember to thank Mr. Sloan. The crew said it was he who found her.

July 16

The rains came again today, washing away all of Willy's best-laid plans. He is under increasing pressure from Mr. Goldwyn to finish on time. The strain is beginning to show on him.

The bad weather did give me an opportunity to lunch with Miss Barrymore. She is a lovely person, hardworking and professional and very proud of the fine theatrical tradition of the Drews and the Barrymores. She is deeply concerned about her dear brother John, whom she calls Jake, a darling boy but so troubled by drink and demons. She believes he will soon die. She has noticed the same sickness in a member of this cast. I assumed she meant Mr. Flynn, but she meant Mr. Sloan, who, like John Barrymore, achieved greatness in his portrayal of Hamlet. Ethel believes certain men are born to play the Sweet Prince, and that these men are also born to be destroyed young by the poisoned cup just as he was. . . . If Mr. Sloan drinks he hides it well. I have never noticed him intoxicated.

July 27

Newsreel cameramen came today to fan the flames of publicity. Went away with the impression that everything was going well. Nothing could be further from the truth.

The love affair between Mr. Flynn and Miss Barrett is quite evident now. So is the effect her brazen infidelity is having on Mr. Sloan. He is pale and drawn and complains of constant migraines. Frequently, he is unable to leave his trailer. The doctor has been attending him. Miss Barrett dismisses his condition as a display of martyrdom and refuses to yield to it. This has resulted in a frightfully juvenile battle of wills. If he will not come out of his trailer to do a scene, then she will not come out of hers. This afternoon they kept the crew waiting for hours before they would appear. Everyone, I must say, seemed quite unconcerned about it. Stars will be stars, or some such thing. . . . Willy's reaction was the most surprising. While he is upset at the delays, he actually seems pleased that Miss Barrett is involved with both men, for it mirrors my story and consequently makes the scenes among them all the more genuine. I told Miss Barrymore I thought this was rather inhuman of him. She said it was always a mistake to think of a director as a human being.

Mr. Niven told me it is best not to take sides in such matters. Most of the crew have taken Miss Barrett's, partly because they adore Mr. Flynn, partly because Himself, when he does emerge from his trailer, is so snappish and unpleasant. There is something about that man I don't like. My Edward believes he is a genius and terribly misunderstood. Edward *thinks Miss Barrett is a witch. Actually, he used a stronger word than that. College man.*

August 10

Mercifully, they finish today. A party is planned in town tonight. I suppose I shall have to go.

Something rather strange happened this morning. They had been shooting the last bedroom scene upstairs in my old room, the scene in which John Raymond bursts in on Vangie while she is dressing to demand once and for all whether she loves him or De Cheverier. Her sister, Lavinia, little Fern O'Baugh, happens to be in the room at the time, as is Bessie, Vangie's wise old personal maid. Pearl Blue plays Bessie and is a dear. It being rather cramped and narrow up there, I stayed out of the way during filming. When they were done, I went up to see Fern. I was at the top of the stairs when I heard a scream, and then Fern came flying out of the sitting room, her face white, her wig cockeyed. The poor child practically knocked me over in her haste to get down the stairs. I wondered, naturally, what had happened. When I went in there, I found only Pearl and the makeup girl, Cookie Jahr, finishing up. I asked them what on earth had frightened Fern so. They had no idea. They said she had been chatting gaily away when suddenly, without warning, she had screamed and run out of the room. Mystified, I went next door into the bedroom. The crew had cleared out. However, I did find Mr. Sloan in there with one other –

That was it. Alma's notebook ended here. The rest had been torn out.

C H A P T E R
E I G H T

Why had Fern O'Baugh screamed?

What had she seen? Whatever it was, someone had made damned sure there'd never be anything on paper about it. Alma Glaze hadn't changed her mind about how to end *Sweet Land of Liberty*, as Frederick had advised me. I knew better. She, or someone else, had torn out those last pages of her diary because of what they had to say about Sterling Sloan, and how he died. But what? Who had been there in Vangie's room with him? What had been going on? How was I going to find out? Fern had told me time was running out. She'd mentioned the golden-anniversary celebration. Did a survivor from the cast or crew know something? Cookie Jahr, the makeup girl? No telling. I only knew that something had been covered up just like Fern said. And that somebody wanted it to stay that way. Real bad.

I put the notebook down and yawned and knuckled my eyes. It was past one. The rain had let up. The fire was just a glow of coals. Lulu was asleep in her chair, Sadie in the kindling box. Across the courtyard, the east wing was dark. The Glazes were asleep, too.

I carried Sadie next door. Gordie's light was on. So was his TV. He was fast asleep before it on the love seat in his Washington Redskins knit pj's. I turned off the TV and picked him up off the sofa. He didn't weigh much. I carried him up the spiral staircase to his room and got him into the bed without waking him. Or so I thought.

I was reaching for his bedroom light when he opened his eyes. "Had me a looth tooth, Hoagy. Bottom tooth."

"Oh, yeah?"

"Fell out. Kept it though." He sure did. He had it clutched right there in his clammy little hand.

"That's swell, Gordie. Real nice."

"There a tooth fairy here?" he asked gravely.

"I seriously doubt it."

Out came the lower lip. He rolled over and faced the wall, crestfallen.

Don't look at me that way. I never claimed I was good with kids. Just that I don't like them. "Uh . . . actually, I'm pretty sure there *is* one, Gordie. Has to be one. I mean, this is the planet earth, isn't it?"

He turned back to me, brightening considerably. "Hoagy?"

"Yeah, Gordie?"

"G'night, Hoagy."

I turned out his light. "Good night, Gordie."

I slipped across the courtyard and into the east wing, which was left unlocked at night for Gordie's sake. I closed the kitchen door softly behind me. It was dark in there, except for a light over the stove, and quiet aside from the hum of the refrigerator and the growl of my stomach. Charlotte's meat loaf at supper tasted as if it had been made from remnants of the Berlin Wall. As sandwich makings, however, it might do. I found its remains in the fridge, cut a slab, and slathered two pieces of bread with mayo and ketchup and Fern's homemade pickle relish. I took a bite. Not terrible. I opened a beer and drank from it. I went into Fern's bedroom off the kitchen and turned on the light.

It was a small, narrow room. Single bed with rock-maple headboard and woven white cotton spread. Matching maple dresser and nightstand. *Oh, Shenandoah* memorabilia crowded the walls. Autographed photos of a fifteen-year-old Fern, costumed and bewigged, standing on the set with Sloan, with Barrett, with Flynn. Framed pages from her shooting script. A review from the local paper that singled out her fresh beauty and fine performance. It had been the high point of her life. I wondered, as I ate my sandwich, if it had been on her mind as she tumbled headlong down that stairway.

There was a paperback copy of a Jackie Collins novel on the nightstand next to an old-fashioned windup alarm clock. One drawer, shallow, containing two pairs of eyeglasses, a prescription bottle of high blood pressure pills with her doctor's name on it, two rolls of pennies, a small tin of Bag Balm antiseptic ointment, and a snub-nosed, .38-caliber Smith & Wesson Chief Special, loaded. There were no personal papers of any kind. None in any of the dresser drawers either.

I found them on the top shelf of her closet in a shoebox, a big fat wad of them wrapped in tissue paper and bound up in rubber bands. Love letters, all of them written by the same strong hand on plain white stationery and dated during June and July of the year the movie had been made: *Fern, my darling, I cannot eat or sleep for the pain and longing of thee. I cry out in the night for your touch* . . . And so on. Each letter was signed *Thine Sweet Prince*. No other name. He wrote her poetry, too, with no apologies to either Emily Dickinson or Hallmark:

O beauty, whose name be Fern
She who comes to me whilst I sleep
It is for her lips, pouting blossom, I yearn
And for her pure, pure heart I weep.

There were dozens more of them. I wrapped them back up and pocketed them and put the shoebox back up on the top shelf of the closet. I turned around to discover Mercy standing there in the bedroom doorway, blond hair tousled, blinking from the light. She wore a sleeveless white cotton nightshirt and nothing over it. The material wasn't quite sheer but it wasn't exactly flannel either. I could see the curve of her hips beneath it, the ripe fullness of her breasts and thighs. On her feet she wore a pair of fuzzy slippers fashioned to look like giant bear paws.

"What are you doing in here?" she wondered, yawning.

"Got hungry," I replied. "Wandered in and started looking at all of Fern's pictures. Sorry if I woke you."

She ventured into the room a few steps. "Fern was so proud of that," she said softly, gazing at the wall. She turned to me and swallowed. She didn't seem quite as confident as she usually did. She glanced at the bed, hesitated. She sat down on it, hands folded in her lap. "You didn't. Wake me, I mean. I've been tossing and turning."

"Thinking about her?"

"More about Polk, to tell you the truth."

"What about him?"

She shrugged her shoulders. Her bare arms were smooth and strong. I offered her my beer. She reached for it and took a small sip.

"Kind of hard on him, aren't you?" I suggested.

"Maybe I am," she conceded. "There's just something so solemn and perfect about him that sometimes I can't help myself, y'know? I mean, there's no trace of the man after he leaves the room – he's odorless, colorless, tasteless . . ."

"He's a politician," I pointed out. "To the bone."

She helped herself to more of my beer. "I really do like him. He's kind and fair. It's just that mother *loves* him, and I feel like she's pushing me into it. I'm used to that. Mother has never given me much freedom. Most of the time that's okay. I know she wants what's best for me. But this . . ." She trailed off, stabbed at the braided rug with her giant slipper. "Sometimes I think I'd like to buy a ticket to somewhere, anywhere, and just go and not tell a soul. And never come back." She looked up at me. "I know what you're going to say – never is an awfully long time."

"No, that's a little Manilowish for me."

"All I've ever done is go to school. There are so many places I still want to go, so many things I want to experience. I can't even begin to think about settling down and marrying Polk. I mean, how can I know if I even want to stay here until I've been somewhere else first?"

"You can't," I replied. "I took a year off when I got out of school. Bummed my way through Europe. Scribbled in a notebook. It was something I needed to do before I settled down."

"And were you glad you did it?"

"I don't know yet. I still haven't settled down."

She looked at me seriously. "How come you seem to understand me and no one else here does?"

I left that one alone, very aware of her there on the bed. Her soft young mouth, the smell of her. She smelled like baby powder. Merilee smelled like Crabtree & Evelyn avocado-oil soap, though I can't imagine what made me think of that just now. "My parents didn't understand me either," I said. "Still don't."

"Does that bother you?"

"Only if I think about it."

"Fern sort of did," Mercy said. "But she never did have the nerve to leave here. Do things on her own."

"How about your uncles?"

"My uncle Edward has traveled a lot. But he's a guarded sort of person. He and I have never found it easy to talk to one another. It's easier to talk to Uncle Frederick, only he still treats me like I'm a little girl."

"He mentioned that someone at your school might be willing to track down period detail for me."

"How about me?"

"You?"

"I'd love to help you. It would be an honor, really. I'm really good at library work. Just let me know what you need and I'll find it for you. Okay?"

She stuck out her hand. We were in the process of shaking on it when Mavis appeared in the doorway wearing a blue silk robe, her tight copper ponytail brushed loose. She didn't like any of it – her daughter sitting there on the bed in her see-through nightshirt. The empty bottle of beer. The two of us holding hands. She didn't like it one bit. She turned her icy blue eyes on me, jaw clenched under her permanent smile. "You're fired!" she snapped. "Get out!"

"But nothing is going on, Mother!" protested Mercy.

"I came in for a snack, Mavis," I exclaimed. "I'm afraid I woke Mercy and she – "

"We were just *talking*," insisted Mercy.

"Go upstairs, Mercy!" Mavis ordered.

"But Mother, nothing was – "

"*Go upstairs!*"

Mercy rolled her eyes and got up. "We were just talking, Mother." Then she padded out the door.

Mavis watched her go, her arms crossed. Then she turned back to me. "I hate you for this."

"Mavis . . ."

"I feel betrayed. I feel violated. I feel used. You are no longer welcome here. I expect you to be gone by morning."

"Mavis, I assure you it was entirely innocent – "

"Don't insult me any more than you already have."

"She just needed someone to talk to. It happens. However, if you insist, I'll be out in the morning." I started for the door. She stepped aside so I could pass. "Naturally, you have my word I'll divulge none of the contents of your mother's diary. And I'll try to set aside the fact you've insulted me, though I'm not sure I can."

"*I've* insulted *you*?" she cried. "How?"

"By not believing in me. By thinking I'd ever do something sleazy. Something to hurt you."

She lowered her eyes, unclenched her jaw. She went over to the bed and yanked on the spread until it was good and taut. She sat down on it. "Perhaps I . . ."

"Perhaps you did."

"You . . ." She cleared her throat. "You read Mother's diary?"

"I did. I'd like to take a look at the original."

"It's in the safe in Mother's library."

"May I see it?"

Mavis frowned. "Right now?"

We took the covered arcade, her slippers clacking on the bricks. There was an electronic security panel at the back door. She entered a numerical code to disarm it. Then we went in, and she turned on the lights in the library. The safe was hidden behind a hinged section of raised paneling next to the fireplace.

"Father installed it," she informed me. "He had it done in the early thirties, when the local banks began to fail. Including the one he himself ran." She spun the tumbler once, then be gan to work the combination. "There's no money in it now, of course."

"Who else knows the combination?"

"My brothers."

"Not Richard?"

"Richard is not privy to private family matters."

The safe clicked open. She reached inside, pulled out a worn old leather-bound writing tablet and handed it to me. Blobs of red wax remained where it had been sealed shut. I opened it to the end. Alma's writing left off where my copy did – just before she identified who was in Vangie's room with Sloan. There was nothing but blank pages after that. I held the first blank up to the light to see if any impression from her pen had been left on it. It hadn't. I examined the gummed binding. Slivers from the pages that had been ripped out remained stuck in it. Several pages. I closed it and looked at the traces of sealing wax.

"This seal was unbroken when you opened the vault on *Geraldo*?" I asked.

"It was," Mavis replied.

"So these pages were torn out fifty years ago? There's no way it could have been done after that?"

"Not that I can imagine." She looked at me, puzzled. "Why do you ask?"

"Could someone other than your mother have done it?"

"I seriously doubt it. None of us knew the notebook existed at all. Not until after she'd died and her will was read. She'd told no one she was working on it."

"Not a soul?"

Mavis mulled this over. "Her lawyer must have known. He had to. He drew up the codicil to her will. Yes, Polk LaFoon knew. Old Polk One. He's long dead, of course."

"Why did she insist on the fifty-year delay?"

"Mother was not a haphazard or arbitrary person. Whatever she did she did for a reason."

"And what was that reason?" I pressed.

"I can't say."

"Can't or won't?"

"Can't. I honestly don't know, Hoagy. None of us do." She took the notebook from me, put it back in the safe, and closed it. "Nor do I understand what you are getting at."

"I'm getting at this, Mavis. Those pages were torn out because they revealed what made Fern O'Baugh scream. Fern knew something. Whatever it was got her killed. She was murdered."

Mavis's eyes widened in shock. "Fern *fell.*"

"She had help."

"But Polk Four said she – "

"Polk Four doesn't agree with me. In fact, he thinks I'm nuts."

"And why shouldn't I?" she demanded.

"No reason. Except for the fact that I'm not. Did Fern ever say anything to you about what she saw?"

"Not a word. I did wonder about it myself when I read the diary."

"Any ideas?"

"I know she worshiped Laurel Barrett. Possibly she found Sloan in there embracing another woman. Evidently a great deal of that sort of thing went on. I wouldn't know myself. I was only a child then."

"But would that send her fleeing down the stairs?" I wondered aloud. "Screaming hysterically?"

Mavis sat in the chair behind her mother's writing table. "I've figured it out, you know. It's been bothering me. It's why I was awake at this hour, heard you and Mercy."

"Figured what out, Mavis?"

She reddened. "Why I can't lie to you," she replied, going schoolgirlish on me again. "I think it's because you see inside me. No one else can. Richard . . . he sees only my strength, not my vulnerability. But you do. I don't know why, but you do. I sensed it the very first time we met. I-I apologize about before, Hoagy. About not trusting you. I do trust you. And I don't think you're crazy."

"Thank you, Mavis."

"Only, answer me this, Hoagy – why would someone want to kill poor Fern now, all these years later?"

"Fern believed that Sloan's death was covered up," I said. "She'd decided to stir up the waters. Someone didn't want her to."

"Why?"

"I haven't figured that part out yet. Tell me something, Mavis. Did Fern have a boyfriend at the time the movie was being made? An admirer? Some guy who carried a torch for her? Was there anybody like that?"

She thought this over. "There was someone."

"Who?"

"He was a few years older than Fern, and already engaged to

another girl, whom he eventually married."

"Who was it, Mavis?"

"It was Franklin Neene," she replied. "Charlotte's father."

Lulu was no longer asleep in her easy chair. She was sitting just inside the door, scowling at me.

Richard had taken the chair. Also a glass of my single malt. He sat there waiting for me, comfy as can be. He and his gold-inlaid Browning twelve-gauge, which was pointed right at me.

CHAPTER
NINE

"**H**andsome little piece you've got there, Richard," I observed.

"Isn't it, though?" he agreed, draining his scotch. His navy-blue cashmere robe had fallen open to reveal his bare, exceptionally simian legs. The barrel of the Browning was resting on one of them, setting it on a course due south of my equator. "A Christmas present from my Mave," he added thickly.

"Would it happen to be loaded?"

"Yes, it would, lad," he replied, shaggy eyebrows squirming.

"Can I talk you into pointing it, say, somewhere else . . . ?"

"I'm afraid you can't, lad. Sorry."

"Quite all right. Pour you another?"

He held his empty glass out to me. "Damned gentlemanly of you."

He'd gone through about half of my Macallan. I poured us both some, then sat on the love seat. We drank. The Browning never left me.

"You're messing with trouble, lad," he said.

"I generally am, in spite of myself."

"Sniffing about my henhouse in the wee hours. My women tiptoeing up and down the stairs, their little hearts aflutter. Bad business this, a young rooster about."

"Your description is most flattering," I said, my eyes on the shotgun, "but I assure you I – "

"Can't tolerate it. Won't. Expect you to stay out here at night."

"I got hungry."

"Then I expect you to starve." He puffed out his deep chest. "Got it?"

I said I did.

"Excellent. Knew we'd understand each other. Now that I've spoken my mind we can relax and enjoy your fine whiskey." He stood the gun on the floor against the sofa and sipped his drink. "Do you hunt, lad?"

"No, I'm too good a shot. I might actually hit something."

"But that's the sport of it."

"I've never considered murder a sport."

He twitched at me. "I've not yet made up my mind about you – whether you're good for Mave or not, I mean. She's spoken of little else since you arrived."

"I do have that effect on some people."

"Still," he said, "I think you and I are more than a little alike."

"Oh?"

"Saw it about you from the start. Way you carry yourself. You're a gentleman, lad. We speak the same language. Live and die by the same code. It's in our blood. They haven't got it in theirs, you know. The brothers Glaze. That's why they've never understood me."

I got busy with my drink, wondering who else was going to open up to me tonight. Roy? One of the peacocks? I only wished Lulu would. She was still giving me the Greta Garbo from under the coffee table. Maybe she just needed more fiber in her diet.

"They've never shown me an ounce of respect," Richard went on. "Think I checked my balls at the altar. Think I've no proper job. Not true, any of it. Someone has to do what I do — make sure Mave is contented. Because if she's not, she makes bloody well sure no one else is. That's my job, twenty-four hours a day, seven days a week. Tricky as brain surgery."

"How long has it been since Mavis and her brothers have actually spoken to each other?"

He grinned at me from behind his mustache. "At least as long as I've been around, lad, and that's twenty-six years."

"Any particular reason?"

"It's the money. Of course it is. Alma gave Mave complete control of the family purse strings. The brothers, they're merely glorified bean counters. Resent it terribly. Despise Mave for it."

"They both have professions of their own," I said. "Why didn't they ever move on, start fresh? Why hang around here and torture themselves?"

"They can't help it, lad. They're pampered little babies, and Shenandoah, it's their mum's golden tit. Besides, this way they can try their damnedest to make Mave miserable. It's bats, all of it. Of course it is. Plenty here for everyone. But you know about families. . . ."

I tugged at my ear. "Yeah, I suppose I do."

"As do I. Why I came to North America as a young man. And why I've never been back. I'm second son, you see. Kenneth, my older brother, he got it all. The lordship. The property. Master of all he surveys. I got nothing. That's how it's done. Kenneth offered me a position. But I wasn't about to have that bastard ordering me about. The brothers Glaze, they like to ride me about it. They know it's a sore spot with me. Know it because it's their own damned sore spot as well, isn't it?" He chuckled to himself. "As it happens, I merely traded one chain of succession for another, but this one's tilted a bit more in my favor. I've a fine life here. A grand life." He sipped his whiskey.

"And yet you're willing to give it all up."

He narrowed his eyes at me over his glass. "Am I?"

"Charlotte seems to think so."

He smoothed his mustache, turned ultracasual on me. "What did Charlotte say? I mean, strictly out of curiosity . . ."

"That she's tried to discourage your advances."

"And?"

"And that you don't discourage easy."

He winked at me. I think. It might just have been his tic. "Man to man, she's nothing more to me than a bit of bed fluff."

"Not exactly the description of her that leaps to my mind."

"That's where you'd be wrong, lad. Take an older man's advice – it's the quiet ones are the best. They appreciate your attention. Do anything for you. Unfortunately, they also happen to be the toughest to catch. So I've been feeding her a bit of line about running off with her. But I've no intention of actually doing so. I'd never leave Mave. Never."

"Charlotte told me you were coming into money."

"That little bitch," he said tightly. He hesitated, then said, "I am. That's the truth. And perhaps I *have* thought about running off. Being my own man again. Being . . . needed. A man has to be needed by someone. Makes him feel alive. Mavis, she needs no one. Always has everything her way. Never gives an inch. Don't get me wrong, lad. I'm happy being with a woman who fights back. I'm just not happy being with one who wins *all* the time. . . . I've thought of running. Taking someone with me. Sure I have. But it's only idle fantasy. I know I'll never do it. That's what makes me different from other men."

"No, that's what makes you just like other men. Tell me, how much are they paying you?"

"Who?"

"Whichever sleazy tabloid you tipped off about me picking up Alma's diary yesterday."

"Whatever do you mean?" He sounded genuinely baffled.

"Fifty thousand? A hundred?"

He shook his head. "You're wrong, lad. Couldn't be more wrong. My brother, Ken, he's on his deathbed with cancer. Ken never married. When he dies, I inherit the title and all that comes with it."

"I see."

"It's the truth. I'm not in contact with the press. I'd never sell

Mave out like that. Never." He drained his glass and reached for his Browning. Slowly, he got to his feet. "I've kept you up long enough."

"A word of advice?"

"By all means."

"I wouldn't keep stringing Charlotte along. Because if she decides to take you up on your offer, and then discovers you weren't serious, you'll need more than that Browning. You'll need a bazooka."

Lulu woke me in the night again.

She was crouched on the pillow next to my head, whimpering. When I asked her what she wanted, she jumped down off the bed and skittered over to the spiral staircase. Down she went . . . *hop-thump-thump* . . . *hop-thump-thump* . . .

She wanted me to let her out.

I started to, until I remembered Roy's warning. "Are you sure about this?" I asked her.

She was sure about this.

I got into my trench coat and aged pair of Timberlands. Then I dug her leash out of my Il Bisonte bag. She hates the leash. Considers it an affront to her dignity. But she'll usually submit to it if I insist. Not this time. She changed course on me the second she spotted it. Went back upstairs. Jumped up onto the bed with a grunt. She didn't want to go out now. At least not with me.

I went to the bottom of the stairs. "Lulu, I am getting a little tired of this moody, high-handed tyranny. You're starting to make me feel like a goddamned cat person. There happens to be a man with a gun out there. A man who has been ordered to shoot anything with four legs. If you want to go out, you go with me and go on a leash. Take it or leave it."

She took it. Most sourly.

The sky had cleared. The stars were brighter than I'd seen them since I was out on the Aegean. I stopped to get the flashlight from the Jag's glove box. Then I flicked it on and we set out. We walked alongside the historic service yard until we picked up the path that rimmed the great north lawn along where Raymond and De Cheverier fought their climactic duel. There was only a sliver of moon. It was black out there beyond the flashlight's beam, and silent except for the occasional rustling of night animals in the brush. I found myself thinking about the Glaze family as we walked. I thought about Mavis and how afraid she was underneath her armor. Afraid she wasn't as perfect as she expected everyone else to be. I thought about Mercy and how she was chaffing at the narrowness of the life Mavis had laid out for her. I thought about Frederick and Edward – their bitterness toward Mavis, their highhandedness toward Richard. I thought about all of them. And as I did, I began to feel that same sense of melancholy I always feel when I'm getting pulled into my celebrity's family troubles. Not that I ever want to. I don't. But I can't seem to help it. Hazard of the profession, at least it is for me. I'm not the answer man. I've never solved my own problems, let alone somebody else's. I'm no healer. But it's hard to tell somebody that when they're begging you to heal them. Especially when it has gone as far as murder.

I wondered if there was more to the rift between Mavis and her brothers than their mother's will. I wondered if something else had happened a long time ago – fifty years ago – to turn them against each other. I wondered.

A narrow path plunged into the woods just beyond the cemetery. We took it. We hadn't gone far when I started to hear a scuffling sound of some kind, steady and rhythmic. Then I saw the flicker of a lantern through the trees. We started through the brush toward it.

"That you, Roy?" I called out, so he wouldn't blow our heads off.

It wasn't. It was Gordie, hard at work in a small clearing digging a hole in the damp earth with a shovel. He still had his pj's on, with a pair of sneakers. He was covered with dirt. He worked so intently that he didn't even hear us coming.

"Hey, Gordie," I said. "What are you up to?"

He looked up in total panic at the sound of my voice and started to run. I grabbed him by the arm. "It's okay," I assured him as he squirmed in my grasp. "I'm not going to tell anybody. Just wondered."

He swallowed and took a deep breath, relaxing. "Nothing. Not doing nothing."

I released him and went over and checked out his hole. It was narrow, about three feet deep. "I'd say you're digging a tunnel." No response. "Where to?" Still no response. "Come on, you can trust me."

"Out," he confessed solemnly.

"Out where?"

"The other thide of the wall." He cocked his head toward the six-foot brick wall that was beyond the trees where we stood.

I nodded. I understood perfectly. I dug holes myself when I was his age. Straight down through the earth toward Europe – my sense of geography wasn't much. Only, I dug in daylight.

"Kind of late, isn't it?" I suggested.

He shook his head. "Betht time. You can be detected during daylight."

"Hard to argue with that," I admitted. "Well, I guess I'd better let you get back to it. Onward and downward."

He nodded and grimly resumed digging. Strange little guy. If he wasn't careful, he might grow up to be a writer.

"Hey, Hoagy," he called after me.

"Yeah, Gordie?"

He grinned. "Tooth fairy came."

"Yeah, I had a funny feeling he might."

"Only left me a quarter though. Got me a dollar before."

"I'm afraid they don't make anything like they used to, Gordie," I informed him. "Including fairies."

Lulu led me back through the woods, straining at her leash. She now seemed to have a firm idea of where she wanted to go and was anxious to get there. She led me across a muddy pasture in the direction of the souvenir building, then steered me past that to the exact spot in the outer wall where I'd seen Mavis and Roy conferring. The spot where the peacock predator was getting in.

About twenty feet short of the wall she pulled up abruptly, black nose quivering in the flashlight beam.

Roy was sitting there on a folding chair behind a tree, a shotgun in his lap, motionless. The consummate hunter.

"That you, Roy?" I called out, so he wouldn't blow our heads off.

He didn't respond. Not that he's a particularly verbal kind of guy, but he didn't so much as move. I started toward him. I was leading Lulu now. She wanted nothing to do with this.

There was a good reason why Roy wasn't moving. He was fast asleep on the job, breathing slowly and deeply like an old draft horse. There was a thermos at his feet. I opened it and smelled its contents. Equal parts coffee and bourbon.

Lulu moseyed over to the burrow under the wall and sniffed at it delicately. Then she snuffled at me, pronouncing herself ready to move on. We started back. We hadn't gone far when I heard an animal crashing through the brush alongside us. Lulu froze and let out a soft, low growl. It was met with an answering growl. Then she relaxed and whooped softly, tail thumping on the ground. And out of the brush it came, eyes glowing in the flashlight beam. It was a mutt, part terrier, part collie, male, with a dirty-gray muzzle and a busy stub of a tail. They greeted each other in the way dogs will do. Then Lulu yapped in a manner I can only describe as girlish and tumbled over onto her back, dabbing at him playfully with her paws while he sniffed at her in an extremely personal manner. I stood there holding the flashlight and watching them. My chest felt heavy, my knees weak. The signs had all been there, but I'd been too dumb to read them. They do say a father is always the last to know.

Lulu was in love.

"Your daughter has a boyfriend."

"How cute." She yawned. It was five in the morning.

"It is not cute, Merilee. He is a mongrel, a cur. He looks like a Butch or a Bowser. Definitely a Bowser. And who knows where the hell he comes from?"

"I'm sure he comes from a very fine – "

"He had his nose in her bum."

"And what did you do?"

"Chased him back under the wall, the no-good mutt. I *knew* something was up. She's been acting weird ever since we got here. I think this calls for prompt, decisive action, Merilee. I'm putting her on the first plane to New York tomorrow morning."

"Hoagy, she's a big girl now and there's not a thing you can do about it," she said lightly. "Face it, darling. Your little one hears the call of the wild."

"Then I'm getting her a pair of earmuffs – shearling."

"Hoagy?"

"Yes, Merilee?"

"Hello."

"Hello yourself. How's Elliot?"

"Mr. Hewlett, the cranky old farmer down the road, came and looked him over. Said he was all stopped up."

"Elliot or Mr. Hewlett?"

"Elliot, you ninny. So we rolled him over onto his back and – "

"Elliot or Mr. Hewlett?"

"*And* dumped two ounces of caster oil down his throat. He squealed in protest but – "

"Elliot or – "

"If you don't stop that, I'm going to hang up. . . . Anyway things seem to be moving along smartly once again. I was going to call you in the morning, actually. It seems your housekeeper there *is* on to something."

"Make that was."

"Oh, dear. Hoagy . . . are you okay?"

"Just dandy. What did your aged chums say?"

"There were some very hush-hush whispers around the lot about Sterling Sloan."

"What about him?"

"Apparently he was a rather serious morphine addict."

"Oh?"

"Hollywood drug of choice in those days, I'm told," she said. "Goldwyn made sure it stayed a deep, dark secret because of all the major drug scandals in the twenties. And it has pretty much stayed that way, actually. None of Sloan's biographers have gotten on to it."

"That's not too surprising. Most show-biz biographers would rather make up the dirt than dig for it."

"They also said Rex Ransom has been going around town for years bragging he knows something nasty. It seems he had the hotel room next door to Sloan's. And he was there when Sloan died."

"Excellent. I'll talk to him when he gets here. I'm dying to meet him anyway."

"Rex Ransom?" she said, surprised. "Whatever for?"

"It so happens, Miss Nash, that Rex Ransom was my very first hero."

"Your *hero*? Why on earth was he . . . Oh, wait, didn't he do one of those fifties kiddie serials on TV?"

"Not just any serial, Merilee. He was the Masked Avenger, he and his faithful steed, Neptune. When I was five, I had a Masked Avenger mask, a lunch box, time-traveler ring. I walked like him. I hitched up my trousers like him . . ."

"And I'll bet you were cute as a bug's ear."

"That's not for me to say."

"I hope he doesn't let you down," she said vaguely.

"Why would he let me down?"

"Some things a little boy has to find out for himself."

"You've been a big help, Merilee. How can I repay you?"

"Well, I do have something in mind. . . ." She hesitated. "I-I had a nice chat on the phone with your parents last night."

"Why, what did they want?" I demanded.

"Don't shout at me. They didn't want anything. I called to wish your father a happy birthday. It was his seventieth yesterday, you know."

I left that one alone.

"They've been in Hobe Sound," she said.

"Naturally. It was winter."

"He sounded so sad, Hoagy."

"Price of brass must be down."

"That's not it at all. He *misses* you. You're his only child. He knows he made mistakes, tried to turn you into someone you're not. He understands that now. He doesn't know what else to say to you, except that he's sorry."

"This all sounds a lot more like your dialogue than his."

"You can repay me by calling him. It's been so many years since you have."

"What's your second choice?"

"He's an old man, Hoagy. He won't be around much longer."

"He'll never die," I assured her. "He'll simply stare death in the face and say, 'I am very, very disappointed in you.'"

"You have to settle this, Hoagy, or you'll be sorry for the rest of your life."

"I've prepared myself for that. Look, Merilee, I'm – "

"You're a grown man, and I can't make you call him if you don't want to, nor should I try to. Does that cover it?"

"Thank you for being so understanding. I knew there was a reason we were friends."

"Oh, is that what we are?" she asked sweetly.

"Good night, Merilee."

"Be kind to Lulu, darling. She needs you now more than ever. This is a grand adventure she's embarking on."

"So to speak."

"Hoagy?"

"Yes, Merilee?"

"She's a Virgo, Hoagy."

"Oh, God. I hate this."

The morning was bright. So was my left side. The bruises there had blossomed numerous eye-catching shades of yellow and purple.

My head felt fine. Well, not, fine but okay. I got up slowly, groaning, and made my way downstairs naked. I started my coffeemaker. I put down Lulu's breakfast. I threw open the sitting room curtains, the better to breathe in that fresh country air, only to find myself face-to-face with a pair of elderly ladies in pastel leisure ensembles. Stray tourists. One of them gaped at me, wide-eyed – the sight of me unclothed does have that effect on some women. The other one started fumbling for her camera.

A uniformed security guard came loping across the courtyard after them. "Area's off-limits, girls!" he called out. "Staff only. Follow me, please. Peacocks are this way."

Off they went, chattering excitedly. They're probably still talking about it. I know I am.

I showered. I dressed in the gray cheviot-wool suit while I sipped my coffee. Fern was being buried that morning. I hadn't known her for long, but I felt like going. I met up with Mavis, Mercy, and Charlotte in the courtyard. Mavis had on a severe navy-blue pin-striped pantsuit and was tense and quiet. Richard was backing the Mercedes out of the garage. He hopped out and opened the front passenger door for Mavis and closed it after her while Mercy and Charlotte got in back. There was room for me back there, too, but I didn't want to intrude. I was also anxious to get behind the wheel of the Jag again.

I was putting the top down when Charlotte got out and offered to take her own car so I could ride with the Glazes.

I thanked her but declined. "Why don't you ride with me?" I suggested. I did want to talk to her.

She turned me down. Mercy didn't.

"Do you mind?" she asked me shyly. She wore a jacket and skirt of matching black gabardine. She looked good in black. I have yet to meet a good-looking woman who doesn't. "I've always wanted to ride in an antique car."

"I prefer to think of it as a classic." I started it up. It kicked right over, began purring. "I don't mind a bit. Hop in."

"Okay with you, Father?" she asked Richard.

Richard wore shades against the bright morning. Sunshine can be somewhat rough on bloodshot eyes. "Fine, child," he replied unsteadily.

"Great." She climbed in next to me.

"Follow me, Hoagy," Richard said, with a lazy fly-boy salute that was straight out of *Dawn Patrol*.

"I shall."

He got in the Mercedes and was about to pull away when I heard the eruption. Mount St. Mavis. She immediately flung her door open and marched toward us, heels smacking sharply on the bricks.

"*What* do you think you are doing, Mercy?" she demanded.

"Riding to the funeral, Mother," Mercy replied mildly.

"Get in the family car at once!" Mavis ordered. "You will *not* ride to Fern's funeral in some flashy open sports car. This is the most preposterous, disrespectful thing I have ever – "

"Father said it was – "

"I said it was all right, Mave," Richard acknowledged from next to her, soothingly. "What's the harm?"

Mavis whirled on him, outraged. "How *dare* you interfere?"

"*Interfere?* Bloody hell, woman. She's my daughter."

"She's *my* daughter!"

Richard whipped off his sunglasses, twitching, red-faced. "She's *our* daughter!"

"She's *mine!*" cried Mavis, toe-to-toe with him, the cords in her neck standing out. "Shenandoah is mine. She is mine. *Mine.* And don't you forget it!"

"How can I forget it?" he snarled. "You never stop reminding me!"

Mavis faced Mercy again. "Get in the car, Mercy," she commanded, nostrils flaring.

"I'm riding with Hoagy," Mercy said defiantly.

"In the car, Mercy!" Mavis insisted.

"No!"

Mavis turned back to Richard, her chin raised, the better to look down her nose at him. "Are you happy now?" she demanded viciously. "You've turned her against me. Soured her. You've always wanted to. Are you happy now?"

"The only way I'd be happy, woman," he roared, "is if this were *your* funeral I was driving to!"

The slap caught him flat-footed. It was a hard, ringing blow and he took it full on the cheek. It knocked him back on his heels.

"That was a dreadful thing to say," Mavis whispered icily. She spun and marched back to the Mercedes.

Richard stood there for a second, stunned. Then he stormed after her. When she got in, he seized the car door and slammed it shut behind her with all of the strength his fury could muster.

Only Mavis wasn't all the way in. Her right foot was still sticking out when she saw Richard's hand on the door. She had only a split second to react. A split second to yank her foot inside the car. She just made it. Just missed having her ankle shattered by the heavy steel door. Just.

She stared at him through the window with her mouth open. She was genuinely frightened. I doubt she often was.

"Thought you were in, Mave," Richard growled in apology. "Sorry."

But he wasn't. She knew it and he knew she knew it. She glowered at him. He glowered back. Then he got in and they drove off.

"I don't understand them," Mercy said quietly after we'd tailed the Mercedes in silence for a few minutes.

"Don't even try," I said, enjoying the Jag's eagerness, the way it hugged the narrow country road. "You can never understand what goes on between two people. It doesn't matter whether you're related to them or not."

"But they hate each other."

"Seem to."

"So why don't they get divorced?"

"Could be they're happy this way," I offered.

"I don't believe that."

"Could be that facing the alternative – a life alone – is even worse than what they have now. Plenty of couples are like them. They complain. They fight. They make each other utterly miserable for forty or fifty years. I don't know why. All I know is if your parents wanted to get a divorce, they would. If people genuinely want out of a relationship, they get out."

"I don't understand you either," she said softly.

I glanced over at her. She was gazing at me. She looked more like an adult dressed this way. Or maybe I just wanted to think she did. Her eyes were a child's, utterly without guile. They caught and held mine a moment. Until I remembered the road. "What about me?" I asked.

"Why you never smile."

"That's a funny thing to ask someone who's on his way to a funeral."

"Why don't you?" she pressed.

"I smile all the time. It just doesn't show on the outside."

"Are you smiling right now?"

"Grinning my ass off."

"Hoagy?"

"Yes?"

"I like your car."

"So do I. Only it's my ex-wife's."

"You're divorced?"

"Somewhat."

"Because you wanted out?"

"Because one of us did."

There was no church service. Just a brief graveside ceremony. Frederick and Edward met up with us at the cemetery, each of them clutching a single long-stemmed red rose. Two dozen or so townspeople were there, too, most of them aged. It was a small cemetery set on a hill overlooking green pastures and a river that sparkled in the morning sunlight. It was a nice place to be buried, if you have to be buried.

Mavis wouldn't stand next to Richard during the ceremony. She stayed on the other side of the grave from him. Occasionally, they shot quick, poisonous glances across Fern's coffin at each other.

The brothers stood close together, their faces grim masks. After the coffin had been lowered into the ground they tossed their roses onto it. They left together.

I drove back to Shenandoah alone and changed into my work clothes. I always wear the same chamois shirt, jeans, and tattered pair of mukluks when I write. I do this because I wore them when I was writing the first novel. Ballplayers have their superstitions. So do writers. We're no more in control of our awe-inspiring gifts than they are.

I made a fresh pot of coffee and sat down before my Olympia with a cup. Alma's diary, my copy of *Oh, Shenandoah*, my sharpened pencils, and my blank sheets of paper were arrayed before me. I was all ready to go. Except for Lulu. She always dozes under my chair with her head on my foot when I work. This morning she wouldn't budge from her chair. She was acting shy and insecure now, as if she needed some kind of reassurance from me. Why hadn't we gotten a male? I asked myself. I went over to her and sat with her there in my lap for a while. I said a few things I won't bother to go into here. Then I went back to the typewriter. A few minutes later she ambled over and plopped down under me and rubbed my mukluk with her head. Then she went to sleep, still my girl.

He was a kind and decent man. Everyone spoke of his wisdom and his uncommon good sense. Truly, John Raymond was a man to admire. He was not, however, a man to love. And this was a sad thing, Evangeline reflected as she gazed across the dining table at him. For she had given this man her body and the past ten years of her life. And now she was miserable.

The work went quickly. Whenever I got stuck for a period detail such as an article of clothing or an eating utensil, I jotted it down on a list for Mercy. Occasionally, I found myself glancing up when I heard a noise outside, thinking it might be Sadie. Not that I wanted it to be Sadie. I just thought it might be, that's all.

I knocked off at lunchtime and went inside. Gordie was in the kitchen chewing on a peanut butter and jelly sandwich, his baseball and mitt next to him on the table. Charlotte, still dressed for the funeral, was pouring him a glass of milk.

"Hey, Hoagy," he said brightly. "Wanna play catch?"

"Maybe later, Gordie," I said.

"When?" he wondered.

"Gordie, why don't you go finish your lunch in your room," Charlotte broke in. "Hoagy is very busy."

The lower lip started to come out.

"Before dinner, Gordie," I promised hastily. "Okay?"

"Okay!" He snatched up his mitt and darted for the back door.

"Hey, Gordie," I called after him. "Take it slow."

He grinned, then slammed the door behind him.

Charlotte was puzzled.

"That's what McQueen said to people in *Bullitt* instead of good-bye," I explained.

She nodded, still puzzled. She obviously thought less of me now. It happens. I joined her at the counter and made myself a sandwich. The jelly was Fern's. Black plum.

"He sure does like you," she observed.

"Go ahead, rub it in."

"Hasn't said but five words to me," she confessed. "'I-want-a-Big-Mac.'"

Couldn't blame the little guy. I wanted one myself after I'd tasted her meat loaf. "So take him out for one."

"And if Mavis needs me while I'm gone?"

"Wouldn't she understand, under the circumstances?"

She stared at me.

"Of course not," I said. "How silly of me."

"I don't suppose I could talk *you* into taking him out."

"Sorry. Midget human life-forms are not my specialty."

"He's lonely. He needs a man."

"There's always Richard."

"He needs a *man*."

"You may be selling Richard short. I know you're selling me long." I poured myself some milk. "So, how are you at handwriting analysis?"

She frowned at me. "Handwriting analysis?"

I dropped Fern's bundle of love letters down on the counter. "I understand your father and Fern were romantically involved before he married your mother."

"It's true, they were." Curious, she picked up the letters and leafed through them, chewing on her lower lip. "If you're asking me would I recognize my father's handwriting . . . the answer is yes. And this isn't it." She handed them back to me.

"They're from a long time ago," I pointed out. "People's handwriting changes over the years. You might not recognize it at first glance."

"I *do* recognize it."

"You do?"

She nodded.

"Well, whose is it?"

She showed me her pointy little teeth. "You help me, I'll help you."

"All right, all right. I'll take the midget to McDonald's."

"Thanks, I knew I could count on you," she said, a triumphant glint in her eyes.

And then she told me who Fern's Sweet Prince was.

CHAPTER
TEN

A herd of tour buses was grazing outside the souvenir building. Hundreds of *Oh, Shenandoah* faithfuls sat at the picnic tables intently stuffing their faces on box lunches while they waited their turn to tour the old house. A number of them looked up hopefully at me as I eased the Jag past them down toward the front gate. I didn't cut a terrible figure. I had my navy blazer of soft flannel on over a turtleneck of yellow cashmere and pleated, gray houndstooth trousers. My plaid touring cap from Bates was on my head, Lulu's beret on hers. Still, it was Mavis Glaze they were hoping to catch a glimpse of, not the first major new literary voice of the eighties, and friend. Disappointed, they went back to cramming with both hands.

Edward Glaze had his law office in Barristers' Row, a choice little colony of 150-year-old carriage houses nestled across a courtyard from the domed Augusta County Courthouse in downtown Staunton. His reception area was small and neat, his secretary black, crisply dressed, efficient. He came right out to greet me when she buzzed him.

"Hoagy, I was so pleased you called," he said warmly, shaking my hand. "Lovely ceremony this morning, wasn't it?"

"It was."

"I've asked my cook to prepare us lunch at my house. We can walk. That be all right?"

"More than all right."

Edward strode briskly. He was in good shape for a man his age. Lulu trailed a few feet behind us, large black nose to the sidewalk. The town was hopping. Workers were stringing banners across Beverley Street. Shopkeepers were hanging colonial-style carriage lamps and hand-lettered wooden signs outside their stores. An ABC News crew was shooting background footage for the Barbara Walters special. The townspeople all seemed to know Edward and like him. They smiled and waved. He did the same.

"Hell, you ought to run for mayor," I teased.

He laughed softly. "Oh, no, that's much more Fred's style. I'm afraid I'm not particularly adept socially. It takes me a while to get comfortable around people."

"You're doing fine."

"Thank you," he said, coloring slightly. "I've been wanting to get to know you better, actually. Ask you about your work. Writers are such fascinating people, it's been my experience."

"I guess we've had different experiences." I tugged at my ear. "But feel free to ask."

The business district ended at Coalter Street. We turned there and started up a steep hill.

"They call this Gospel Hill," he informed me as we climbed, "due to the religious meetings held here in the late 1790s at Samson Eagon's blacksmith shop."

Soon we were among gracious Victorian and Greek Revival mansions set well back from the road behind blossoming magnolias and sourwoods.

"Not a terrible town," I observed. "Gorgeous, in fact."

"We try. We recently got the business district named to the National Historic Register. Quite an effort, but well worth it, I think."

Edward lived down the block from Woodrow Wilson's birthplace in a turn-of-the-century Georgian-style home of red brick. Fluted columns supported the ornate white frontispiece. An ornate fanlight topped the front door. It was a handsome place, though not unique. There was another next door exactly like it.

The entry hall was dark and cool and smelled of lemon oil. There was an ornate oak hatstand with a beveled mirror inside the door. I left my hat on it. Lulu held on to hers. Double doors led into a masculine front parlor lined with bookcases and furnished with matching leather wing-back chairs and a chesterfield sofa.

Edward went over to a butler's table next to the fireplace. "Sherry?"

"As long as it isn't the same brand Mavis serves."

He filled two glasses, smiling. "It isn't."

We carried them into the octagon-shaped dining room. It was sunny and airy. The French doors were opened to the garden, which was fragrant and ablaze with perennials. The dining table was a twin-pedestaled mahogany George the Third, set for two. A vase of tulips sat in its center.

"Lovely home," I observed.

"Thank you. It's somewhat large for one person, but I bought it a number of years ago for a good price and I've never regretted it. The garden, in fact, keeps me sane." He gazed out at it lovingly. "I spend most of my free time digging around back there."

"Where does your brother live?"

"Fred has a home of his own."

"The one next door?"

"Why, yes. How did you know?"

"Wild guess."

A uniformed black woman brought us our lunch. Veal marsala, boiled new potatoes, string beans. It was excellent. Sancerre wasn't terrible either.

I pulled Fern's love letters out of my pocket while we ate, placed them on the table before him.

Edward frowned, dabbed at his mouth with his napkin, and reached for them. It took him a moment to recognize them. He turned bright red when he did. "Lord, these are dreadful. I was all of eighteen at the time – the last of the great romantics." He laughed to himself sadly. Then his eyes began to fill with tears. "I can't believe Fernie saved them all these years. Dear, dear Fernie."

"Mind telling me about it?"

"Not at all – there really isn't that much to tell, Hoagy. We read poetry together in the tall grass and dreamt of running off to Greenwich Village and becoming great, starving writers. It was all so . . . *romantic*. And terribly tragic."

"Why so tragic?"

"Mother didn't approve of Fern," he replied. "Thought she was too common for her young college man. After all, Fern's father worked on our *car*. So Fernie and I overdramatized it, as we did everything. It was playacting. Kid stuff." He smiled faintly and sipped his wine. "Besides, Fern already had a serious beau, Frankie Neene. Frankie was a blustering, cocky kid then, a football player. Used to take her for rides in his car and make love to her. She told me all the lurid details. Told me he promised to marry her, too. He never intended to, though. He married a proper Mary Baldwin girl. Broke Fern's heart."

"I understand he committed suicide."

Edward's face darkened. "Yes. He was a broken man. Terrible business." He shook his head. "When I was your age, Hoagy, I wanted to lead three or four lives. Now that I've been around nearly seventy years, and seen what life does to people, I've come to realize that once is plenty."

"In her diary, your mother mentions that you got to be somewhat friendly with Sterling Sloan during the filming."

"As much as anyone could," he acknowledged. "Sterling was a strange, lost soul, a man who lived only for truth and beauty – the two things in shortest supply in this world. He was the saddest man I've ever known, and one of the most fascinating. Please stop me if I start to bore you. . . ."

"You won't."

"It rained the night before they were all due to arrive from Hollywood," he recalled. "The convoy of trucks, the specially chartered train, the hundreds and hundreds of production people – an invasion. In the middle of the night the doorbell woke me. Someone at the door. I heard our caretaker answering it. Heard voices. Then the doorbell started ringing again. I got up and went downstairs to see what was going on. No one else stirred – I was the light sleeper of the family. The caretaker said it was someone who claimed to be with the movie. He'd told the fellow to come back in the morning with everyone else, but he refused to go. I opened the door to find this thoroughly bedraggled-looking vagabond in a moth-eaten black cape seated out there in the rain on top of an ancient steamer trunk. He was soaking wet and unshaven and smelled more than a little of cow manure. He apologized for the late hour, explained as how he'd hitchhiked his way on a farmer's truck to be with the movie, and alas, had nowhere to stay and no money. He was unusually polite and well-spoken. 'What do you do?' I asked him. 'I drink,' he replied. 'I mean,' I said, 'who are you?' 'Oh, I am not any sort of person at all,' he replied. 'I am an actor.' A down-and-out one hoping for a bit role, I supposed. Still, he was shivering from the wet and had nowhere to go, so I let him in. It wasn't until he'd removed his hat and cape that I realized who he was. 'Why, you're Sterling Sloan!' I exclaimed. 'Someone has to be,' he replied in that cryptic, disembodied way he had. 'Unfortunately, I am that one.' I told him the cast would be staying at the Hotel Woodrow Wilson in town, and that I'd be happy to drive him there. But he was so pale and chilled I offered him a brandy first. His hand shook so badly half of it dribbled right down his chin. He hadn't eaten for days. I made him a sandwich, and he devoured it and drank several more brandies. He began to get some color in his cheeks. He told me I was a rare and kind young soul. Then he stretched out on the sofa in the parlor and fell instantly asleep. From then on, he attached himself to me. He seemed to like being around me. I have no idea why. Naturally, I was thrilled and pestered him for advice about acting. He told me to get proper classical training in Britain, learn to carry a spear, and play toothless old men and blushing young girls. He was quite generous – he even offered to write me letters of introduction to several theater companies over there. He was very offhanded about his fame. Had no use for the trappings of stardom, no star presence at all off camera, not like Miss Barrett or Flynn. You *knew* they were stars. Not Sterling. He came to life only when he was in front of the camera. The rest of the time, he almost wasn't there. He was so very quiet and remote. He spent long hours just stretched out on the daybed in his trailer, reading. And sometimes he really *wasn't* there. By that I mean he seemed disoriented, not totally sure where he was or what role he was playing. . . . He and his wife weren't at all close. He'd arrived from London, she from Hollywood. I felt he was a deeply lonely man. And then those headaches of his kept him in great pain for hours at a time."

Edward's cook came in and cleared the table. She left us a pot of coffee and a plate of cookies. Edward poured the coffee.

"Would you happen to know if he used morphine?"

"Not that I ever saw," Edward replied, nibbling on a cookie.

"Was there a doctor on the set?"

"There was. He arrived with the production team from Hollywood. Dr. Toriello. An older fellow with dirty fingernails and hair growing out of his ears. He spent a lot of time with Miss Darnell. I was told she suffered from severe menstrual cramps and refused to work when she had them."

"Sounds like a Dr. Feelgood," I suggested.

He frowned. "A what?"

"The studios always kept some borderline quack around to make the little green men go away. They still do. Did he spend time around Sloan?"

"Yes, he often looked in on him for his headaches." Edward's eyes widened. "Why, do you think he was . . . ?"

"I'm afraid so."

Edward shook his head sadly. "Morphine. It's for pain, isn't it?"

"It is."

"It was her, Laurel Barrett. She was so angelic, so delicately beautiful. Yet she was the dirtiest, rottenest tramp imaginable, Hoagy. God, how she tortured him. It was as if she took delight in punishing him for his love. She and Flynn – the two of them would go into his trailer in the middle of the day to have sex. Everyone knew. It was disgraceful." He lowered his voice. "She even made a play for me."

"Did you . . . ?"

"I was tempted. Lord, was I tempted. She was one of the most gorgeous women in the world. But Sterling was my friend." He sighed longingly. "I must confess I still wonder sometimes when I'm lying in my bed alone at night. I wonder what I missed out on." Abruptly, he reached for his coffee. "Drugs? Who could blame the poor man?"

"The night before she died, Fern told me she believed he was murdered."

"And you believe she was murdered, as well. Yes, I know all about your theory. Mavis phoned me first thing this morning. I was shocked, truly. It's been so many years since she'd phoned. I almost didn't recognize her voice."

"And my theory?"

"I'm skeptical, frankly."

"So is Polk Four," I admitted.

"Yes, I know. I spoke with him as soon as I got off the phone with Mave. I wanted to have the facts of the case. Lawyers, by nature, have an aversion to surprises." He sipped his coffee. "I've been curious about Mother's diary myself. Why those pages were torn out. Why Fern screamed."

"Did Fern ever say anything to you about it?"

"Not a word. The entire incident came as news to me."

"Do you have any idea who was there in Vangie's room with Sloan?"

"None."

"You said his wife was sleeping around on him."

"Gleefully."

"Was he doing the same?"

"There weren't any whispers," he replied. "As I mentioned, Sterling kept to himself most of the time. He certainly said nothing to me about anyone." Edward got up and went over to the French doors. "One thing you should bear in mind about Fern, Hoagy, is that she was always inclined to exaggerate. The fact is Sterling died of a ruptured aneurysm. The warning signs were all there. He had been complaining of blinding headaches. He acted strangely, he was frequently drowsy. The medical experts later agreed that these symptoms indicated the leakage in his brain had already begun. He looked particularly pale and drawn that last day of filming. He was so weak he was barely able to finish. That very night he was stricken in his suite at the Woodrow Wilson."

"Who else was there?"

"She was – Laurel. And Dr. Toriello arrived almost immediately. He was staying in the hotel. He sent for an ambulance at once, but Sterling died before it arrived."

"Did any other doctor besides Toriello see him?"

"I imagine so. Someone local had to sign the death certificate.

Toriello was licensed out of state."

"Were the police called?"

"Of course. The sheriff got there right away."

"Not the Staunton city police?"

Edward smiled. "Town was a lot smaller then. There was no city police force."

"I see. Who was the sheriff?"

"Polk Two," he replied. "Polk Four's granddad. Fine man. Only just gave up his senate seat in Richmond last year. Represented us there quite proudly for the past forty-five years. His legs are bothering him – he's eighty-seven, after all. But he's still sharp as a tack, old Polk Two."

"How would I get in touch with him?"

"If you wish to be gracious, you go through Polk Four and get his blessing. He's very protective of the old fellow."

"And if I don't?"

Edward stared at me for a moment, then turned and looked out the door at his garden. Stiffly he said, "He's in the book."

Polk Two lived on a small farm out off Route 11 on the way to Harrisonburg. The road to it wound back through lush, fragrant farmland and through time. A colony of Mennonites lived there. I passed a couple of their black, horse-drawn carriages clopping slowly along, and a farm where four women in bonnets, long dresses, and sneakers were planting vegetables in a garden. They waved as I passed. I waved back and fleetingly, wished I lived there with them.

A big silver Lincoln Town Car was parked out in front of the white, wood-framed farmhouse, which was badly in need of paint and a new roof. The broad wraparound front porch had a serious case of dry rot. There was a bank barn and grain silo out behind the house, a poultry house, hilly pasturage. All of it looked neglected.

I left the Jag behind the Lincoln and rang the doorbell and waited. And waited some more. Finally, I heard heavy footsteps inside and a cough.

"Sorry to keep you waiting, son," Polk Two said cheerfully as he opened the door. "It's my legs – they've pure gone to hell on me."

He was a tall, beefy man and he still had the lawman's air of authority even if he did have to walk with two canes. His coloring was fair. His full head of white hair was still streaked with blond.

His eyes were blue and twinkly behind the heavy, black-framed glasses, his loose, saggy skin so pale as to be almost translucent. I could see the blue veins on the backs of his hands as they clutched the canes, trembling slightly. He wore a white button-down shirt, black knit tie, a heavy gray wool sack suit, and hearing aids in both ears. He smelled like witch hazel and Ben-Gay.

"Come on in, son," he said. "Come on. Your dog, too, if she wants."

She didn't. She likes porches.

He moved slowly, waddling like a large, heavy penguin. Wheezing, he led me into a small parlor that hadn't been painted or aired out since V.J. Day. The air was heavy with cigarette smoke and dust and heat. Portable electric heaters were going strong in each corner. It must have been ninety in there.

"Too warm for you?" he asked.

"No, it's fine," I replied as I felt the perspiration beginning to run down my neck. "Cozy."

A radio was on, tuned to the police band. He waddled over to it and turned it off. "Can't get too warm when you get to be my age, you know," he observed. He chuckled. "I have to turn up the thermostat another degree every birthday. In three more years I'll be able to bake bread in here."

A captain's chair piled with cushions was set before a table. A large-type edition of *Reader's Digest* lay open on the table along with the phone and a carton of cigarettes.

Polk Two plopped *slooooowly* down in the chair. "Have a seat, son," he commanded, indicating an easy chair. "That one used to be mine. Most comfortable one in the house. I just can't get up out of it anymore."

I took off my cap and sat. "Nice place you have here, Mr. LaFoon."

He turned up his hearing aids. "Thanks. Been in the family a long time. And make it Polk Two, Mr. Hoag."

"If you'll make it Hoagy."

"As in Carmichael?" he asked, turning them up some more.

"As in the cheese steak."

He nodded. "Always like his songs. 'Stardust,' 'Georgia on My Mind' – you could hum 'em. Yessir." He lit a cigarette and looked around. "It'll all be Polk Four's when I pass on, if he wants it. Needs work, of course. Haven't done much to it since the wife died in '72. But the land's good. Twenty-five acres of it. My boy, Polk Three, he's retired down in Florida with his wife. I'm all alone here. But it suits me, except for this habit I got of not being able to shut up when I trap some poor fellow here like you." He chuckled. "Polk Four, he looks in on me regular as clockwork. He's a good boy. I just wish he'd take a drink of whiskey or a dip into a cute little blonde once in a while. A man needs to let off a little steam now and again, or he'll blow." He glanced at me sharply. "I phoned him after you called. He said he'd try to make it over."

"It sure is nice how everyone in the valley talks to everyone else."

"He said you were trouble." The old man looked me over with a practiced eye. "Don't know. You look to me like about as much trouble as a tub of warm grits. Take off your jacket, son. You'll sweat right through the material and stain it. Now what can I do for you? Something about this sequel to Alma's book, you said?"

I stripped off my jacket. "Yes. The publisher wants me to write an introduction recalling the sensation it caused when it first came out. The making of the movie, Sterling Sloan's death . . ."

He puffed on his cigarette. "Ah, that business."

"I understand you were there on the scene when he died."

"I was."

"I wondered if you could share some of your recollections with me."

"Newspapers covered the hell out of it." He moistened his thin lips. "You ought to go on over to the *News Leader* and go through their old issues. They give you any trouble, tell 'em I sent you. They'll treat you right."

"I'm not interested in what was reported," I said. "I'm interested in what *happened*."

He grinned at me. "Well, whatever you are you aren't dumb." He coughed, a deep, rumbling cough. "Okay. Sure. It's the recent things I can't remember, you know. Like what I had for dinner last night. But fifty years ago I can remember just fine. . . . Pork chops, mashed potatoes, and okra – that's what I was eating at my desk the evening I got the call. Sent over from Joe's Cafe across the street. They're out of business now. Joe got himself killed in Korea. No wait, that was Joe Junior. Joe had a coronary and dropped dead."

"The phone call . . . ?"

"Something about the movie folk over at the Woodrow Wilson," he continued. "Quite some hotel in those days, it was. Fanciest place within fifty miles. Fine dining room, ballroom, orchestra. I headed on over there, none too happy about it. Those movie fellas, they'd been making my life miserable ever since they got here. I had no complaint with the performers. Or with all them boys and girls from the fan magazines and newsreels neither. They behaved themselves. It was the damned film crew, dozens of healthy young roughnecks with money in their pockets. Whole bunch were like sailors on leave, drinking, chasing local gals, getting in brawls with the local fellows over 'em. I was sick of the whole lot, even if they did bring money into the town. But I'd had no trouble with the actors, like I said. Until that evening. . . . The manager and house detective, fella called Lou Holt, met me right at the front door, all agitated, and said there was an emergency up in the Sloan-Barrett suite. Quite some suite it was, too. Living room. Two bedrooms. Very first thing I noticed when I got there was the beds in both rooms were mussed. Odd for a man and wife, I thought. What I mean is, I don't believe the two of 'em slept together." He coughed. "I don't know if that's the sort of recollection you're interested in . . ."

"Go right ahead."

"Miss Barrett was standing there in some kind of flimsy dressing gown, without any makeup on. Or slippers. I remember she looked like a frail young girl standing there like that. She was a pretty thing, but no meat on her. Had the whitest little feet I've ever seen, like a baby girl's. Seems they'd been dressing for some big party being thrown that night down in the ballroom to celebrate finishing up the filming. Seems he, Mr. Sloan that is, got himself a blinding headache while he was dressing. She had sent a bellhop out for some aspirins, but by the time he got up there with 'em the fella had collapsed."

"Where was he?"

"On the sofa, unconscious. The doctor from the movie company, Dr. Toriello, was with him. Ambulance was on its way. But it was pretty obvious he wasn't going to make it. He was breathing with great difficulty, huge gasps. Died just a minute or two after I got there."

"Was anyone else in the room?"

Polk Two stubbed out his cigarette, thought it over. "The bellhop was still hanging around."

"What was his name?"

"Don't recall. Just some scrawny kid. I got rid of him."

"Anyone else?"

"One other fellow came in, some sort of take-charge right-hand man of Mr. Goldwyn's. Melnick. No, Melnitz. Seward Melnitz. One of those high-strung types, kept trying to boss me around. Telling me not to say a word to the press, not to let nobody in. Treated me like I was retarded or something."

"He was probably just used to dealing with producers. No

other witnesses?"

"If there were, they were gone by the time I got there."

"I see. What happened then?"

"Well, since Toriello was from California, I had to get a local man up to sign the certificate of death. It was Doc Landis I called. Discreet, professional man. He got right over, came to the same diagnosis as Toriello – that some kind of bubble had burst in Sloan's brain. After that the body was – "

"How?"

"Excuse me, son?"

"How did he arrive at his diagnosis?"

"Ah. Well, he asked Toriello a lot of questions. Don't recall what they were. I do remember they talked about Sloan's blood pressure. . . ."

"What about it?"

"It dropped dramatically after he collapsed, Toriello said. Apparently that told them something. And they discussed Sloan's symptoms of the previous few days. His headaches, way he'd been behaving . . ."

"Did you get the feeling Landis thought Toriello was negligent?"

"No, sir," replied Polk Two firmly. "Not at all."

"Did he examine the body?"

"His eyeballs. He looked at Sloan's eyeballs. Don't ask me why."

"To see if a pupil had dilated," I said. "A brain aneurysm would compress the optic nerve of one eye, possibly both. Was there an autopsy?"

"No, sir, there wasn't."

"Why not?"

"No reason to. The man died of natural causes. Medical men were satisfied."

"How long had you been sheriff at the time?"

"Three, four years."

"You'd been to a lot of death scenes, filed a lot of reports."

"My share of 'em," he acknowledged. "Yessir."

"Did you get any sense that something funny was going on in that hotel room?"

He frowned. "Funny? I'm not following you, son."

"That it wasn't what they said it was."

Polk Two reached for his cigarettes and lit one. "I'm still not following you, son," he said, a little chillier this time.

"Sloan's headaches, drowsiness, disorientation . . . And the collapse itself – loss of consciousness, severe drop in blood pressure, difficulty in breathing – all of it could point to an entirely different cause of death."

"And what's that?" he asked.

"Sloan was heavy into morphine. I think he died of an overdose."

Polk Two didn't react much. Just looked at the ash on his cigarette and tapped it carefully into an ashtray and took a puff and blew out the smoke. His blue eyes gave away nothing. "Doctors said it was an aneurysm," he said quietly.

"Of course they did. Sloan was a major star. Ugly things like drug overdoses had a way of being prettied up for people like him. Is that what happened, Polk?"

Polk Two shook his head. "No offense, son, but I genuinely don't know what the hell you're talking about."

"Was there a cover-up, Polk?"

"There was no such thing!" he fired back angrily. "I didn't run this county that way. Or my district when I sat in Richmond. And I don't like you coming here to my home and suggesting I did!"

"I'm trying to get at the truth."

"You *got* the truth, boy. The man died there on the sofa from an aneurysm. I don't know how I can make it any plainer."

"Okay," I said, backing off. "What happened then?"

"Body was removed to Hamrick's funeral parlor over on Frederick Street. He was cremated there next day."

"Quick, wasn't it?"

He shrugged. "There was a certain desire on everyone's part to get it over with. Town was so damned full of reporters, radio people, newsreel cameras – a real carnivallike atmosphere. Pretty ghoulish, you ask me. Miss Barrett, she took the ashes home to England for burial. Funeral service was held over there a few days later."

I took my linen handkerchief out of my pocket and mopped my forehead and neck with it. "I understand your father was Alma Glaze's lawyer."

He scratched his chin. "That's right."

"Shortly before her death she had him draw up a codicil to her will that sealed her notes for *Sweet Land of Liberty* for fifty years. Any idea why she did it?"

"Daddy said she was getting pressured by Goldwyn. He wanted her to hurry up and write it so he could get himself another movie. She didn't like the idea of being rushed, particularly by him. She detested the man."

"Isn't fifty years a little excessive?"

Polk Two chuckled. "Not if you knew Alma. That woman, she was *ornery*. Mavis is a pure pleasure compared to her mammy. It was about control, son. Alma was showing Goldwyn she was boss, not him, and she was rubbing his nose in it for good measure. That man simply was not going to make more millions off of her creation. Not as long as she was around, and not in the event of her death, either."

"In the event of her death – meaning she expected to die?"

"We all expect to die, son."

"But she was a relatively young woman. It seems like an extreme form of insurance to take, unless of course she had reason to believe she would die soon. Was she ill?"

"Not in the least. You had to know her. It was just Alma being Alma, sticking it to that Hollywood fella."

"She was run over soon after that on Beverley Street."

"That's right. Just after the movie came out. Biggest money-maker in history, you know, until all those damned spaceship movies come along." He coughed and shifted in his chair with no little effort. "It happened on a Saturday night, about eight o'clock."

"Any idea what she was doing in town?"

"Kids said she told 'em she had some business to do. The three of them were home alone when it happened."

"She was meeting someone on business at that hour?"

"I never did buy that myself," he confessed. "I figured maybe she had herself a fella in town. Didn't much matter. She was dead was all that mattered. Run down while she crossed the street. Some fool ran the traffic light."

"You never found out who?"

He got defensive. "I made some progress. Had the make and color of the car from a witness. A car matching it turned up ditched on the outskirts of town next morning, blood on the fender, seats and floorboard reeking of cheap whiskey. Had been reported stolen from an old lady's driveway an hour or so before Alma was hit. I figured it was a couple of local boys having themselves a toot before they headed off to the Pacific to get their poor dumb asses shot off. I followed up. Had my eye on a particular pair of young hotheads, but they'd gone overseas by the time I got on to 'em. And they never made it back. So I reckon justice was done, in its own way."

"There must have been a lot of pressure on you to catch them."

"There was indeed. Alma was an institution here."

"Any chance her death was something other than an accident?"

He peered at me intently from behind his heavy glasses. Then he chuckled and shook his head in amazement. "Son, you're not interested in the truth one bit. You're looking to spin wild yarns for the funny papers."

"I'm looking to figure out why Fern O'Baugh died the other day."

"Fell down a flight of stairs, I heard," he said mildly.

"Yeah. Lots of accidents seem to happen in this place."

"It's a place like any other," he said, grinning. "A little nicer, if you ask me."

A car pulled up outside, and someone got out. Lulu started barking from the porch. She has a mighty big bark for someone with no legs.

"That'll be Polk Four, I reckon." Polk Two lifted the window shade and glanced outside. "Making friends with your pup. Always has been good with animals. Yessir, that boy's just naturally likable."

"So I'm told." I got to my feet. "I won't keep you any longer, sir."

He started to struggle up out of his chair.

"Don't trouble yourself," I insisted. "Thank you for your time."

"My pleasure, son," he said, easing back down. "Helped fill the day. Retirement's a lousy deal. Better off if you die young."

"I'll do my best." I went outside, closed the front door, and stood there on the porch inhaling the fresh air and watching Lulu and Polk Four. I counted to ten before I hurried back inside.

The old man was on the phone. He panicked when he saw me, slammed it down, red-faced.

"Sorry," I said. "Forgot my hat." I plucked my cap off the arm of the easy chair and grinned at him. "Like I said, it sure is nice how everyone in the valley talks to everyone else."

Polk Four was scratching Lulu's tummy out on the thick grass by the mailbox. She was on her back, tongue lolling out of the side of her mouth. She'd fallen for him. What can I say – she happened to be vulnerable right now.

When Polk Four saw me, he stood to his full height and smoothed the wrinkles in his khaki trousers – not that there were any. "Pretty car," he said, gazing at the Jag.

"It is," I agreed.

"Yours?"

"My ex-wife's."

"So you're divorced?"

"We are but we aren't."

He frowned, puzzled. "What does that mean exactly?"

"It means we're both mad as hatters," I replied. "Why do you ask?"

He adjusted his trooper's hat. "I'm just trying to figure out why you're attempting to ruin my life."

"I wasn't aware that's what I was doing, Sheriff."

"Mercy called me first thing this morning," he revealed darkly.

"Oh?"

"Said she had something very important to tell me." He narrowed his alert blue eyes at me. "Any idea what it was?"

I tugged at my ear. "None."

"She's decided to go to Europe for a year when she graduates in June. She said she wants to experience life on her own.

"No kidding."

"No kidding." He clenched and unclenched his jaw. "She said it was your idea."

"I wouldn't go that far, Sheriff. I simply told her that's what I did when I was her age."

He crossed his arms. "I don't appreciate this at all, Mr. Hoag, you filling her head with crazy ideas."

"Not so crazy. She's kind of sheltered."

"She's kind of impressionable is what she is," he argued. "She's also kind of terrific, and I intend to marry her."

"I'm sure that's what she has in mind, too, Sheriff. She just wants to kick up her heels a little first. It'll be for the best," I assured him. "This way she won't wonder."

"Wonder what?"

"If she missed out on anything. She'd only end up taking it out on you."

"What makes you such an expert on the subject?" he demanded testily.

"You want advice on marriage, talk to a man whose own turned to shit."

"I wasn't asking for your advice," he said crossly.

"My mistake. Sorry."

He crouched back down and patted Lulu's soft, white underbelly. Out came her tongue again. "Sometimes Mercy . . . she gives me the feeling she thinks I'm a real clod."

I left that one alone.

"Has she said anything to you?" he pressed.

"She said she likes you."

He brightened. "She did?"

I suddenly felt as if I were back in junior high school. I hated junior high school. "Only she feels like you're being forced on her by her mother. It's got to be her own choice. Don't crowd her. Let her come around to it in her own time."

He mulled this over. "Think I should loosen up on the reins a little, huh?"

"If that's how you want to put it. But you'll do better if you start thinking of her as a woman and not an Appaloosa."

He shook his head at me, disgusted. "I really don't get you, Mr. Hoag. Bothering her. Bothering my granddad. Pestering everybody in town with your weird ideas about Fern O'Baugh being murdered – "

"She wasn't the only one, Sheriff. Alma Glaze was murdered, too." I glanced up at the house. Polk Two was watching us through the window. "Why she was, I'm still not sure. Something to do with Sterling Sloan's death – which was not caused by any brain aneurysm. That was just a cover-up."

"Uh-huh. Is there anything else?" Polk Four asked with exaggerated patience.

"Franklin Neene's suicide."

"What about it?"

"Maybe it wasn't. Suicide, I mean."

Polk Four stayed calm. Dangerously calm. "I have to tell you, Mr. Hoag," he said very quietly, "I've had just about as much of you as I can stand." He came up close to me now. I felt his breath on my face. It smelled of Tic-Tacs. "I'm not ordinarily one to get tough. You can ask anybody. But I sure do feel like taking off this badge and gun and punching you in the mouth."

"I'm real sorry to hear you say that, Sheriff. Because if you do, we'll have to fight, and one of us will end up in the hospital, and it won't be you."

"What I *am* going to do," he promised, "is advise Mavis you're a public nuisance and ought to be put on a plane back to New York."

"Mavis happens to need me," I reminded him. "As long as she does, I'm not going anywhere. Sorry."

"Not as sorry as I am."

"What is it going to take for you to realize that I'm not doing this for laughs, Sheriff?" I demanded. "You happen to be sitting on one of the biggest scandals in motion picture history. Bigger than Thomas Ince. Bigger than William Desmond Taylor. Bigger than Fatty Arbuckle. Well, maybe not bigger than Fatty Arbuckle, but *big*. People have been *murdered*. I realize these are your folks down here, your family, your friends. Their lives may be ruined. I can't help that. And neither can you. You have a choice to make. You can put your money where my mouth is or you can stand by and watch. Only, if you do, you'll be the one who is ruined. Because I will get to the bottom of this, and when I do, it will go very, very public, believe me."

He took a deep breath. Slowly, he let it out. "Why are you doing this?"

"Fern asked me to. It was her last request. You're supposed to honor those."

"Okay, fair enough. You've said your piece. Now I'll say mine: Number one, I think you're full of crap. I think you smell a buck and you don't care who gets hurt. Number two, I'll be watching you. You bother anybody in Augusta County, I'll be on you. You exceed the speed limit by one-half mile per hour, I'll be on you. You so much as smile at a girl under the age of eighteen or smoke in a no-smoking – "

"I don't smoke."

"Or step on a crack in the damned sidewalk, I'll be on you! Got it!"

"Got it, pardner."

"And *don't* call me pardner!"

Polk Four didn't wave good-bye when he went tearing off in his big sedan. He didn't smile or tip his big broad-brimmed trooper's hat either. I don't think he liked me anymore.

I drove slowly back through the Mennonite farms toward Route 11, wondering.

Say Sloan *had* died of an overdose – why had Alma been killed? Had she found out about the cover-up? Threatened to expose it? Was Goldwyn possibly behind her death? If not him, who? Why was Fern killed? Whom could she hurt now, all these years later? How much did Polk Two know that he wouldn't tell me? Did Polk Four know anything, or had he been shielded from all of it?

I was thinking about these things when I got to a stop sign. It was a rural intersection, nothing but farmland in all four directions. A four-wheel-drive Ford pickup came to a stop directly across from me, all styled up with racing stripes and fog lamps and chrome roll bar and tires so huge you'd need a pole vault to reach the seat. I'd seen a lot just like it since I'd arrived in the valley. They seemed to hold great appeal for cretins aged seven to seventy. I didn't pay too much attention to this one.

Not until I noticed the two men riding in it. The driver had a crew cut. The other man had a ponytail. And an over-under shotgun aimed out his window right at me. He pulled the trigger.

CHAPTER ELEVEN

I dove down onto Lulu just as the Jag's windshield exploded, showering me with broken glass. I stayed down, eyes squinched shut, breath sucked in, heart racing. He wasn't through – one more shot boomed in the country quiet. This one hit nothing. Then they took off for the hills with a screech.

I sat up at once, pellets of broken glass tumbling down the back of my neck. Lulu climbed down onto the floor under the glove box and cowered there, shaking. I assured her I could handle it.

Then I went after them.

I can't explain why. I had no idea what I'd do if I actually caught up with them. Die, maybe. All I knew was I had to do it. I tend not to be totally rational when I've been kicked in the head and shot at.

They were heading toward the Shenandoah Mountains and the West Virginia state line, moving fast but not that fast. Maybe they didn't know I was after them yet. The narrow farm road dipped and darted through the undulating pastures. No other cars were on it.

Merilee kept the Jag perfectly tuned. It responded at once as I tore my way through the gears, the wind biting at my face through the empty windshield. My eyes started to tear. I fumbled in the glove box for my aviator shades. Lulu glowered up at me, not liking this one bit. She had enough on her plate already.

The road started getting curvy right about when I got close enough for him to spot me in his rearview mirror. I could tell when he did – he speeded up. I did, too. His partner turned around. The cab's rear window slid open and the muzzle of his shotgun poked out. He took one wild shot at me, then another. Ignore those high-speed gunfights you see on TV – you can't get off any kind of a shot when you're bouncing down a country road at sixty miles an hour. Still, it crossed my mind that he might get lucky. So I floored it and cozied in right under the truck's upraised tail, the Jag's nose almost touching its *Keep on Truckin'* mud flaps. He was up so high on those stupid tires he couldn't get a clear shot down at me now even if he tried – the tailgate was shielding me. I was okay there. Unless they decided to hit the brakes.

Lulu let out a low moan. Again, I assured her I could handle it. There was no one to assure me I could handle it.

Faster. Seventy...eighty...veering past a Mennonite horse and buggy on a blind curve. Edging back over just before getting splattered by an oncoming car. Climbing hard into the mountains now, road twisting, narrowing. Signs shooting past . . . Head Waters – Elev. 2,925 Ft . . . Bullpasture Mountain – Elev. 3,240 Ft . . . Climbing up among pines now, swollen spring rivers roaring past. Climbing, curves blind, road a narrow ribbon hugging the side of the mountain. No shoulder. No rail. Only a sheer drop. And down, down, down . . . Jack Mountain – Elev. 4,378 Ft . . . The entire Shenandoah Valley laid out far below us now. I had no time to admire the view. I was too busy pushing him on. Faster . . .

We crested. Briefly, the road flattened out. Then we were descending. Flying down the twisting road, tires screaming, the Jag hugging the pavement like a panther. Twice he fishtailed, but held the big truck in check. We were playing a dangerous game of chicken now. I could stop at any time, turn around. I had his license number. But I didn't want to. I wanted to make him go faster.

He took his eyes off the road. Must have, because he didn't ever even try to hit the brakes. One moment he was flying down that twisting road. Next moment he was still flying, only there was no road under him. Only sky, his wheels spinning in the air.

I had just an instant to react. No time to weigh my options, to arrive at a sound, measured plan of action. There was only the Jag and the road that was no longer right in front of me. My brain shut down. My body took over. Feet rammed the brakes and clutch. Hands drove the wheel hard left. I spun out, wildly out of control. Skidded to a stop on the very edge of the road, facing uphill, stalled. I sat there like that for a moment, too dazed to move. Then the thought processes returned, and I jumped out to look.

The truck had touched down at the base of the mountain three thousand feet below, its wheels up, still spinning. A puff of gray smoke wafted lazily up from it, like from a campfire. It looked kind of peaceful. Until it blew. I saw it before I heard it. Saw the tongue of angry orange flame, the hunks of twisted steel flying off in every direction. I heard the explosion a second later. And for many seconds after that. It echoed across the entire valley, like a clap of thunder.

Lulu squirmed in between my feet and nuzzled my leg. I reached down and rubbed her ears. I got the battered silver flask of Macallan from the glove box and drank deeply from it. I stood there for a while taking in the panoramic view of the valley. I had time to admire it now.

And to wonder just whom Polk Two had been on the phone with when I'd gone back inside for my cap.

Pamela, housekeeper nonpareil, was waiting patiently outside the airline terminal in a sweater and skirt of matching bottle-green cashmere and knobby brown oxfords, her raincoat folded over her arm, two old leather suitcases beside her on the pavement. Pam's in her early sixties, plump and silver haired, and owns the loveliest complexion I've ever seen. Also the most unflappable disposition. I got to know her in Surrey a couple of years back when I was ghosting the life story of Tristam Scarr, the British rock star. Maybe you read it. Or about it. It got a little messy.

She smiled cheerily and waved when I pulled up at the curb and hopped out. "Yes, yes, it's so lovely to see you again, Hoagy."

I kissed her cheek. "Glad you could make it, Pam."

"Nonsense, dear. I'm thrilled you called – my life has gotten so appallingly dull of late. All of that new money buying up the country estates and trying so desperately hard to act the part. You simply would not believe how stuffy they are. Poor dears don't realize that the ruling class are, and always have been, utterly bats."

I grabbed her bags. "In that case you should find your new employer a refreshing throwback."

"Excellent."

"Though something of a challenge," I cautioned.

"Even better," she assured me. "Keeps one alert. You will tutor me, of course."

"Of course. What are friends for?"

One suitcase fit in the trunk, the other behind Pam's seat. Lulu wriggled around in her lap when she got in, happy to see her. Lulu is generally happy to see someone who has fed her kippers and eggs and will likely do so again.

"And hello to you as well, Miss Lulu," Pam cooed at her, getting her nose licked. "I see she hasn't changed her eating habits."

"No such luck."

"In the pink otherwise?"

"That," I replied, "is a long story – and not a particularly pleasant one." I found a spare pair of Merilee's sunglasses in the glove box and handed them to her. "You'll be wanting these."

Pam figured out why as soon as I eased away from the curb and picked up speed. "My Lord, you've lost your windscreen."

"Call me crazy, but I like the taste of bugs in my mouth."

She raised an eyebrow at me. "So it has turned into one of those, has it?"

I filled her in as we worked our way through the outskirts of Charlottesville to the highway. She listened intently, Lulu dozing in her lap.

When I was done, she said, "Sterling Sloan. My lord. Such a lovely, lovely man. I saw his *Hamlet* when I was a girl. He was so gifted and handsome. So tragic. I wept when he died. Every schoolgirl in Britain did. To think he was a drug addict. How sad. How very, very sad."

"I have an ulterior motive in bringing you in on this, Pam."

"I'm terribly flattered, dear boy. But how many times must I tell you? I'm much too old for you."

I grinned. I do know how. "Actually, I wondered if you could – "

"Quietly pick up what information I can from the staff and locals?" she inquired. "Of course. I'll get started first thing in the morning."

I glanced over at her. "How is it you always know what needs doing before anyone says so?"

"Because, dear boy, unlike so many others who make the claim, I am a professional. You've not said a word about Merilee. How is she?"

"Fine. We've entered into a state of peaceful non-coexistence."

"Meaning *you're* not ready to settle down again."

"No, we're equally qualmish about it."

"Why?" she demanded.

"It failed before. And there's no reason to think it won't again."

"Rubbish. When you fall off a horse you must get back on."

A bolt of electricity shot through me. *When you fall off a horse you must get back on . . .*

"Is something wrong, Hoagy?"

"Nothing . . . Meanwhile, I'm here and she's home and everyone's somewhat happy."

"More rubbish." Pam sniffed. "That's no home. One needs children to make a home."

"Pam . . ."

"I hate to see two such bright, lovely young people go without – "

"Pam, this car does have a reverse gear," I pointed out. "And they do have flights back to – "

"Very well. I'll shut up."

"Thank you. I knew you'd get the idea. Now I think we'd better start your tutoring . . ."

Mavis was a little tied up. There was her powwow with the ad hoc committee of Stauntonians coordinating the golden-anniversary festivities. Another with the media person handling the gala screening for the studio that was rereleasing the movie. There was her casual, reflective stroll through the grounds of Shenandoah with Barbara Walters and her camera crew. Still, Pamela swung into action just as soon as she got her chance.

We sat in the peacock parlor. Richard poured the bad sherry, he and Mavis circling each other warily. His cheek was still red from her slap. Her eyes made a point of avoiding his. She was giving him the same treatment she gave her brothers now. Serious punishment.

"We shall get along quite well, madam," Pam declared briskly, "provided you bear in mind a few vital facts about me."

Mavis gave her the regal glare. "Facts? What sort of facts?" she demanded stiffly.

"For starters, I have no use for mediocrity," Pam replied brusquely. "Never have."

"I assure you that is fine with me, Pamela," Mavis said, pleased. "As it happens, I myself am – "

"I speak my mind," Pam broke in. "You'll not find me the shy, retiring type. I believe a great estate needs a firm hand. Some employers cannot accept that, in which case I have little use for them. Not that you'll find me an impertinent woman. I abhor rudeness."

Mavis nodded eagerly. "Absolutely, Pamela. I myself – "

"Then we shall get along just grandly, madam. It's a lovely, lovely home. You're blessed to have it. The American Revolution is such a fascinating period, don't you think? Of course, being a Brit, I myself see it from a somewhat different vantage point. . . ."

"As do I, dear lady," Richard chimed in, helping himself to more sherry. Both of his cheeks had a rosy flush now.

"Yes, of course you do, Pamela," Mavis acknowledged readily. "And we must discuss that. I'll look forward to it. Would you care to see the old house now?" she asked her, a bit shyly.

"I would consider it a privilege, madam," Pam replied.

The kitchen door swung open just then and little Gordie wandered in, a cookie in one fist and a batch of comic books in the other.

Mavis whirled on him. "Yes, what is it, Gordon?" she demanded, pouncing on him as if he were a field hand who'd stumbled in, manure caked on his clumsy boots.

"Nothin', ma'am," Gordie cried, shrinking from her. He looked around at everyone, wide-eyed. He relaxed a little when he saw me there. "Hey, Hoagy," he said uncertainly.

"Hey, Gordie."

"Well, as long as you're here, you may as well say hello to Pamela," Mavis told him. "Our new housekeeper."

"Yes, yes, and what a sincere pleasure it is." Pam knelt with a refined grunt and placed her hands on Gorgie's narrow shoulders. "And how are you?"

Gordie withdrew from her, a turtle retreating inside his shell. He didn't respond.

"I said, 'How are you?'" Pam repeated, a bit louder. "Are you well?"

"Of course he is," said Mavis. "He's a very happy boy. Aren't you, Gordon?"

Gordie still didn't respond.

"Now run along outside," Mavis commanded.

He did, relieved to get out of there. The two women started out on their tour. Richard started to join them.

Mavis stopped him. "Richard, you're terribly underfoot. Go watch a ball game on television or something."

He made straight for the sherry decanter, twitching.

As they strolled out, I heard Pamela say, "The odd thing is, I can't help but feel I've been here before. You'll think it silly of me, but I happen to believe each of us leads a number of different lives through the ages . . ."

And then I was alone there with Richard. Defiantly, he downed his third sherry, clutching the delicate cordial glass tightly in his big, hairy hand. "One of these days, Hoagy . . . ," he growled between his teeth. He squeezed the glass tighter. It shattered in his hand. Blood began to stream down his fingers. He paid it no attention. "One of these days."

I started for my quarters. Before I could reach the back door, Charlotte appeared from her office to block my path. "Aren't you forgetting something, Hoagy?" she asked sweetly.

"Oh, God, I hate this."

"Boy, I never thaw nobody throw a ball like you can, Hoagy."

"It is a somewhat awesome sight."

We were seated in the McDonald's parking lot outside Staunton near Highway 64, where the newer, uglier sprawl was. Gordie wanted to eat in the Jag so we were eating in the Jag. Sadie was playing with a wad of paper at my feet. Lulu was curled on the floor at Gordie's feet, which he kept swinging up and down, up and down. He was a bundle of energy, squirming, waving his fingers, which were drenched with oily pink dressing from his Big Mac.

"You ever play in the majorth, Hoagy?" he asked.

"Yes, I did," I replied, trying to keep my eyes off his fingers. The sight of them was making me nauseous. Or maybe my own Big Mac was doing that. "Ever heard of Jim Palmer?"

"Uh-huh."

"I pitched for the Orioles at the same time he did. He threw harder than I did, but I looked better in my underwear."

"Did ya really pitch for them?"

"No."

"You shouldn't lie to people, Hoagy."

"You're right. Sorry." I stuffed the soggy remains of my hamburger back in the bag. Lulu sniffed at it disdainfully. "I did throw the javelin."

Gordie sucked on his Coke through a straw. "What'th a javelin?"

"A kind of spear. They throw it in the Olympics."

"Were you in the Olympicth? And don't lie."

"No, but I was once the third-best javelin thrower in the entire Ivy League."

"That the truth?"

"No one would lie about that."

"What'th the Ivy League?"

"It's a group of very expensive Northeastern colleges known for their academic reputations, their hard women, and their soft track stars – try not to drip Secret Sauce all over the upholstery, will you, big guy?"

"Thorry."

Sadie was chewing on my shoelaces now. I kicked at her. She thought I was playing and begain to swat at them. I grabbed her and put her down next to Lulu, who promptly scrambled over the gear-shift knob and into my lap with her head stuck through the steering wheel, which would be fine until I needed to turn it. I was starting to understand why they invented station wagons. Also baby-sitters.

"Tooth fairy came back, Hoagy," Gordie informed me happily. "Left me three more quarterth."

"Yeah, I had a feeling he would."

"Do I gotta go, Hoagy?"

"Go where?"

"The VADD cothtume ball. Mavith ith makin' me go, on account of I'm an object, um, object . . ."

"Object lesson?"

"Yeah. Do I gotta?"

"Whatever she says, Gordie. She's your mom, now."

"I hate her."

"Don't hate her. She's not a bad person. Just sort of difficult."

"You got parentsth?"

"Somewhat."

"What'th that mean?"

"It means we don't get along."

"Why?"

"They don't approve of me. And I don't approve of them."

"Why?"

I sighed. "How come you ask so many questions?"

"How long ya gonna be here, Hoagy?" he asked, waving his greasy fingers.

"A few more weeks."

"Then where will you go?"

"I don't know. My ex-wife lives on a farm in Connecticut."

"Where do you and Lulu live?"

"Manhattan. A fifth-floor walk-up on West Ninety-third Street."

"I'd rather live on the farm with her."

"Go ahead, rub it in. Are you done eating?"

"Uh-huh."

I seized him by his left wrist and wiped his hand clean with a napkin. Then I did his other one and stuffed the sopping napkin in the bag and wiped off my own hands. I got out and hurled the whole mess in the trash. I needed a shower now.

"Your wife got animalth?" Gordie asked when I got back in.

"Ex-wife. Couple of horses, some chickens, a pig."

"You be goin' there when you leave here?"

"Like I said, I don't know."

"Can me and Thaydie come, too? If you do, I mean. You don't have to thay yeth or no now. Think it over."

"Okay."

"Okay we can go or okay you'll think it over?"

"I'll think it over."

"Hoagy?"

"What?"

"I want another Big Mac."

"You'll get sick."

"Will not."

"*I'll* get sick. I'll buy you an ice cream cone on the way home instead."

He brightened. "Okay!"

I moved Sadie to his lap and Lulu to the floor under him. Then I started up the Jag and pulled away.

"My favorite'th chocolate," he confided.

"Mine's licorice."

"Ugh."

"You ever had it?" I demanded.

"No."

"Then don't say 'ugh.' You'll love it."

"Will not."

"You like Steve McQueen don't you?"

"Yeth . . ."

"It so happens licorice was his favorite flavor, too."

"How do you know?" he asked suspiciously.

"I just do."

"That another lie?"

"No, it's a supposition."

"What'th that?"

"You're too young to know."

Gordie asked if Sadie could spend the night with me. He was deathly afraid Pam would come into his room and find the kitten and send her off to the pound to be gassed. I assured him Pam was a very nice person and would do no such thing, but I couldn't convince him. So Sadie was parked on the love seat, asleep, when I came downstairs with Lulu at four A.M. for her nightly walk on the wild side.

She led me toward that same hole under the wall over by the souvenir shop. The shop loomed about fifty feet ahead of us in the beam of my flashlight when I heard the shotgun blast.

I pulled Lulu close to me on her leash and called out, "That you, Roy?" so he wouldn't blow our heads off.

It was. He stood near the hole, inspecting it by the light of his Coleman lantern, shotgun tucked under his arm.

"Evening, Roy," I said.

He peered at me, then back down at the hole.

"Have any luck?" I asked him.

He spat and reloaded. Then he sat back down in his chair behind the tree to wait for the return of the first great love of Lulu's life.

"Nice talking to you, Roy. Let's do lunch, okay?"

Lulu and I started back toward the house. Bowser intercepted us about halfway there, his stubby tail wagging furiously as he and Lulu greeted each other. I stood there wondering what the hell to do about him. Roy was sure to nail him when he made his way back out. His only chance was to hide out until daylight, then slip out after Roy had gone off watch. Only hide out where?

Lulu was gazing up at me imploringly now. She knew where. I sighed, and we three headed for home.

Bowser attacked the remains in Lulu's mackerel bowl when we got there – that'll give you an idea just how downscale he was. She watched him from her chair, tail thumping contentedly. When he'd had his fill, he stretched out on the floor next to her and licked his chops. He had no tags or collar, and more than a little gray in his muzzle. An older man. A breaker of young, innocent hearts. He probably had six or eight Lulus scattered around the neighborhood, waiting in vain for him to come home at night. But there was nothing I could do about it. Merilee was right. Lulu was a big girl now.

"I'll be turning in now, kids," I announced. "Don't play the stereo too loud. And stay out of my Macallan."

I went up the narrow spiral staircase and climbed back into bed. It wasn't easy getting comfortable. I was used to Lulu being on my head, not downstairs with a stranger old enough to be her father. I was just getting settled in when I felt something under the covers down near my feet. Something alive. Hurriedly, I flicked on the light and tore back the covers. Sadie peered up at me, all perky and bright-eyed.

"What are you doing down there?" I demanded.

I grabbed her and was going to hurl her downstairs until I remembered Bowser, who might enjoy her for dessert. I put her down on the floor and climbed back into bed. She promptly jumped up there with me and stretched out on my chest, dabbing at me gently with her paws, the small motorboat noise coming from her throat. Grudgingly, I scratched her under the chin. She moved up a little more and buried her nose in my neck, purring. She wasn't Lulu. She was more like a vibrating heating pad. But she did smell like mackerel, and that was some small comfort. I fell asleep with her there.

Lulu and I saw Bowser off at dawn. It was a damp, foggy morning. The two of them frolicked in the wet grass like a pair of frisky pups. Roy's chair was still there by Bowser's hole. But Roy and his shotgun weren't. Bowser squeezed under the wall without looking back and arfed once from the other side. Lulu answered with a strange moan that sounded like the air being let out of a balloon. It was a sound I'd never heard come from her before. It occurred to me for one awful moment that she might actually be considering joining him. Leaving me. But she just snuffled and turned her back on the hole. The two of us returned to our quarters.

Lulu ate an unusually large breakfast, then drowsed contentedly on my foot while I wrote. Sadie spent her morning chasing a fly around up in the bedroom, her claws skittering across the wood floor. Ah, to be so easily entertained.

He was the handsomest boy Evangeline had ever laid eyes upon, this stableboy. And he was a boy. His cheeks barely knew the edge of a razor. His complexion was fair and pure, his hair golden, his eyes the blue of the peacocks back home at Shenandoah. Her beloved Shenandoah.

"Shall I assist you up, m'lady?" he inquired.

"Please," she said, offering him her hand.

"Here we are, m'lady," he said as he boosted her up onto the chestnut mare.

She gazed down at him, trembling from his touch, from the earthy smell of him. He was gazing up at her, frankly, longingly, unashamed.

"What is your name, boy?" she whispered, her heart pounding.

"Andrew, m'lady."

"Mine is Evangeline, Andrew. I wish for you to address me by it. For

I am of Virginia, not England. And I am most certainly not a lady."

I took a lunch break a little before one. Pam was busy at the big round kitchen table reorganizing the household accounts, a plate of biscuits and a cup of tea at her elbow. Charlotte was on the phone in her office with a caterer.

"Getting settled in, Pam?" I asked.

"Quite nicely, dear boy," she replied cheerily. "It appears Fern had a filing system all her own. I have yet to fathom it, but once I have, I trust the operation will begin to make some form of sense. Fortunately, Charlotte is helping me prepare for the VADD Ball." Pam glanced over her shoulder at Charlotte's office, lowered her voice conspiratorially. "Are she and Richard . . . ?"

"He wants to, she's not so sure."

"Well, I shall help make the poor dear sure," Pam declared. "The man's a complete fraud."

"Oh?"

"Indeed. I discerned the faintest trace of commoner in his accent yesterday – not something one of you Yanks could detect. First thing this morning I rang up someone back home who knows of such matters. She assured me there is no title such as Richard described to you. No Kenneth Lonsdale, ill or otherwise. A fabrication, all of it. Oh, the man may be a second son. But certainly not one who is about to come into any family money in the near future."

"So that explains it," I mused aloud.

"Explains what, dear boy?"

"The snide little way the brothers have of calling him 'Lord' Lonsdale. It's all a pretension of his, and they know it. And like to rub it in."

Pamela sniffed. "I shall take it upon myself to inform Charlotte. I cannot allow her to get involved. She'll do herself no good. He's a miserable sort." She reached for a biscuit and nibbled on it. "Of course, what man wouldn't be – married to Mavis."

"What do you make of her?"

"She's a lonely woman," Pam replied. "I feel somewhat sorry for her, actually. But I can afford that luxury – I am not related to her. Speaking of which, her brother Frederick happens to owe everyone in town money."

"How do you know?"

"I've been ordering supplies for the ball. Each merchant has asked me who'd be signing the checks – because if it were Frederick, they said that they would have to have cash. They were quite apologetic about it, but also quite firm."

"Hmm. Interesting. Good work, Pam."

I heard footsteps on the stairs. Mercy came rushing in toting a knapsack full of books. She wore a plaid wool jumper over a pink cotton turtleneck, knee socks, and penny loafers. Her hair was in a ponytail. She looked good. Good and twelve.

She flushed slightly when she saw me there. "Oh, great, you're here," she exclaimed breathlessly. "I was going to have Pam give this to you." She handed me a manila envelope. "The historical details you wanted."

"Terrific. Thanks."

She flashed me a big smile. "Anything else you need just let me know – gotta run – I'm late for class – bye." She dashed out.

Pam raised an eyebrow at me.

"Something?" I asked.

"The girl gets positively saucer-eyed around you," she observed.

"I do have that effect on some people."

"You wouldn't be encouraging her just a bit, would you?"

"Now why would I want to do that?"

"Because she's young and lovely, and you're here and Merilee is in Connecticut."

"Makes perfect sense when you put it that way," I admitted. "Except that she's all but engaged to the redoubtable Polk LaFoon the Fourth, and I'm too nice a guy and he's in a lot better shape than I am. How are you getting on with Gordie?"

She frowned. "Not well. The child seems terrified of me, for some reason. Says next to nothing. All I've gotten out of him so far was something about the *tooth* fairy."

"And how generous he is?"

She peered up at me, amused. "You aren't becoming attached to him, are you?"

"Me? No chance. No use for him. None."

She shook her head sadly. "The poor little thing has been through so much. I can't help but feel this is not the ideal environment for him. He needs a home. He needs to feel he belongs. Here he seems to be somewhat in the way." Pam sipped her tea. "Mavis has been asking for you. She's read the pages you left her and wants to discuss them with you."

"Where is she?"

"On patrol somewhere in the northern portion of the estate. You, dear boy, are to find her."

I found her pink dirt bike before I found her.

It was lying in the brush alongside the dirt path that twisted through the woods out beyond the gazebo. The engine was running.

Mavis was lying another thirty feet or so up the path, facedown. Or I should say, what was left of her face was down. She'd been thrown – headfirst into the trunk of a tree. The tree won. Not much of a contest, really. She hadn't been wearing a helmet.

It wasn't a very civilized way to die. But I haven't come upon one yet that is.

CHAPTER
TWELVE

Polk Four pulled his car right out onto the lawn next to the trees. Two more sheriff's cars and an emergency medical services van were right behind him. So was a local news radio crew, until one of Polk's deputies chased them off.

Richard and Charlotte had been home with Pam. Frederick and Edward arrived from their offices within minutes. They brought Mercy with them from school. All of them stood there on the lawn in silence, gray faced.

Polk wouldn't let them anywhere near Mavis. He didn't want them to see her like that. He was polite, but firm. He handled it well, considering how upset he was himself.

"I told her a million times to wear a helmet," he said to me hoarsely, his blue eyes moist, as we stood over her body. "I told her it doesn't matter how slow you're going on these paths, you never know when you'll run into a stump or a rock or a – "

"Trip wire?"

He shot me an angry look and squared his jaw. "You already know I don't care for what you've got to say, Mr. Hoag. Right now is a particularly inappropriate time to – "

"Take a look, Sheriff."

His face reddened. He looked dangerous. "Get the heck away from me!" he snapped. "I mean it. Get away or I'll – "

"Take a look. That's all I ask. One look."

He hesitated. His shoulders relaxed a bit. Reluctantly he said, "Okay. One look."

I led him back up the path a ways to a slender, young redbud tree growing alongside it in the brush. A foot up from its base something had been wound tightly around its trunk, tight enough to cut through the bark, exposing the live green growth underneath.

Polk crouched next to me and examined the tree. "The bike probably did this when she lost control. So what?"

"The bike would have left a gash in one side of the tree, or broken it clean. It wouldn't have damaged the bark all the way around like that." I got to my feet. "Besides, there's another one just like it over here." I showed him the matching wound in a tree directly across the

322

path. "A wire did this, Sheriff. A wire stretched across her path. It stopped the bike cold. She went flying. She was murdered – same way Fern was. They were both murdered. You know it and I know it."

Polk stared down at his shoes. He swallowed uneasily. The emergency people were lifting Mavis's covered body onto a stretcher now. He glanced at them, motioned for me to follow him. We moved farther down the path to the rough old wooden gazebo where, fifty years ago, Alma Glaze had sat writing in her diary.

He sat down heavily at the weathered pine table, removed his trooper's hat, and smoothed his short blond hair, not that it needed smoothing. "I was going to come out and talk to you today," he said quietly. "Seems a couple of boys in a Ford pickup got themselves toasted on their way down Jack Mountain yesterday. Stevie Tucker and Tommy Ray Holton. I went to high school with both of them. Been in and out of trouble for as long as I can remember – breaking and entering, receiving stolen property, aggravated assault. They never did any serious time, but they were no great loss to the community either." Polk cleared his throat. "A passerby believes he saw them a few minutes before it happened . . . being pursued by an antique red car."

"I prefer to think of it as a classic."

"They the two who roughed you up?"

I nodded. "Someone hired them to try and get Alma's diary that day. It's worth a lot of money. Yesterday they were just trying to get me. They took out my windshield with an over-under shotgun"

"That checks. We found one near the truck. Who were they working for, Mr. Hoag? Who hired them?"

"I don't know, Sheriff. But I do know who can tell us."

"Who?"

I tugged at my ear. "You won't like it."

"I don't like any of this," he assured me quietly.

"Your grandfather can. Polk Two knows."

Polk Four slumped and let out a weary sigh. "No"

"Yes."

A look of genuine anguish crossed his earnest, unlined face. "What is going on here, Mr. Hoag? What the devil is going on?"

"I told you – a cover-up is what's going on."

"I know you did," he acknowledged. "And I didn't listen to you. Too unimaginative. That's what Mercy says I am – unimaginative. Christ, poor Mercy . . ." He looked at me sharply. "I'm thinking that all of this has happened since *you* got here."

"I know. And I'm the one who found the bodies. I could have done in both of them, hid the trip wire, then yelled for help. I look good for it. Only why, Sheriff? I've no reason to want either of them dead."

"I was thinking that, too." He scratched his jaw thoughtfully. "Publicity for your book?"

"It doesn't need it – not that badly. If you're looking for likely candidates to do in Mavis, there are plenty. There's Richard, who's been wanting to run off with another woman. There's the other woman, Charlotte, who also happened to blame Mavis for her father's death. There's Frederick and Edward, cut out of their mother's estate, bitter, jealous. . . . It could have been any of them. They were all familiar with her patrol route. Only, why kill Fern, too? What's the connection?"

"Maybe there isn't one," Polk suggested.

"I doubt that. Fern knew something. And so, it would appear, did Mavis. This whole business is about what got covered up fifty years ago, during the filming of the movie. I'm certain of it. I just can't figure out *how*."

He gazed out at the woods for a moment. Then he turned back to me, his face softening. "I'm sorry, H-Hoagy. About not listening to you before. Maybe Mavis would still be alive if I had. But I couldn't. I just couldn't. Nobody wants to believe that everyone they hold dear, everything they belong to, that all of it may have been built on something *wrong*."

"I know, Sheriff. And I know this is tough for you. You grew up believing that as long as you respected your elders and kept your nails clean and your shoes shined that good things would happen to you. And so far they have – you've been lucky. I'm sorry your luck has changed. Truly sorry."

"Whatever needs doing, I'll do it," he declared. "My personal considerations must be set aside."

"Glad to hear it."

"Any ideas?"

I had several things he could check out that I couldn't. He said he'd get right on them. He was utterly determined now. He had set a goal for himself and he would not be knocked off course. This was, after all, a guy who made it through law school.

"By the way, Sheriff, I'd also put Mercy under twenty-four-hour guard."

He frowned. "Mercy? Why?"

"She's twenty-one, isn't she?"

"Two months ago. I gave her a pearl necklace, belonged to my grandmother."

"Shenandoah is hers now. She's sole heir. If this whole thing is about money, and it probably is, she now owns everything. That means . . ."

He nodded. "You're right," he said grimly.

I didn't have to tell him what it meant. I didn't have to tell him that Mercy's life was now in danger.

CHAPTER
THIRTEEN

Mavis Glaze's death was front-page news across America. The television news crews stormed Staunton. So did *Entertainment Tonight*, *Time* and *Newsweek*, the major daily newspapers, *USA Today* and the tabloids. Within hours, reporters from all over were elbowing each other in the street for interviews with average townspersons. Barbara Walters landed an exclusive with Mavis's hairdresser, who wept on the air. Geraldo dug up a psychic who had foreseen that Mavis would die just as her mother had – in a vehicular accident, alone, wearing blue. Maury Povich, not to be outdone, found a Hollywood spiritualist who was convinced that Alma Glaze was haunting Shenandoah – how else to account for *two* accidental deaths at the estate in recent days?

Actually, that one made about as much sense as anything I had come up with so far.

Polk Four didn't breathe a word about the trip wire. Airing it in the press, the sheriff believed, would only turn Mavis's death into a bigger circus – and make her killer a lot warier. Better, she reasoned, if he or she figured they'd gotten away with it. He kept the truth from the family, too, since it would only frighten them. And since the killer was very likely one of them. I was the only one who knew Mavis had been murdered. Not even his deputies knew. Not the pair posted at the Shenandoah front gate to keep out the press and the gawkers – tourist visitation was suspended until further notice. Not the one in the house, who was partly there to screen phone calls and mostly there to keep his eye on Mercy.

Mercy didn't leave the house for several days. None of the family did. They just sat in the peacock parlor, dazed. Richard drank brandy after brandy and twitched a lot. Frederick chain-smoked. Edward kept coughing and opening the window, and Frederick kept closing it. Mercy sat on the sofa with a box of Kleenez, sniffling. No one talked. It was kind of pathetic, the silence. They had held such bitter feelings toward Mavis, yet they seemed lost without her. She had defined their lives. Her will, her demands, had dictated how each of them functioned and interacted. Without her there they were like strangers, sitting around waiting for a bus. And a new master. I had a pretty good idea who that master would be, too, only he was reluctant. He wasn't a family member. Not yet, anyway. But when it became obvious they needed him, Polk Four did step forward. It was he who made the funeral arrangements. Charlotte worked the phone. Pam kept the place running and meals on the table.

Little Gordie made for kind of a sad footnote to the story. The kid had already lost his natural parents. Now he'd lost his adoptive mother, too. Strangely, he didn't seem upset or hurt by it. I guess it was impossible to hurt him now. To him, this was just business as usual. And that was the saddest thing of all.

There was much debate in the *Staunton Daily News Leader* over whether or not to cancel next week's golden-anniversary festivities, the gala screening, the VADD costume ball. Naturally, the film studio was eager to capitalize on Mavis's death. They weren't alone. The Virginia tourism people had a lot riding on the anniversary, as did the town fathers of Staunton. Still, no one wanted to look too crass, so they left it up to the Glazes. Polk Four had to pull them together and make them decide. They decided the celebration would go on. Mavis, they felt, would have wanted it that way. Everyone was glad. I know I was. This meant Rex Ransom would still be coming to town. It also meant I'd actually have the opportunity to see Henry Kissinger in a powdered wig, red velvet knee breeches, and white silk stockings.

The Major League Editor who was publishing *Sweet Land* kept calling me from New York, and I kept ducking her. I returned her fourth call. It would have been unprofessional not to.

"Exactly how far along are you?" she wondered anxiously. "Not that I'm trying to pressure you."

"Exactly two chapters into it," I replied.

"That's *all?*"

"I've only been here a few days," I pointed out.

"I know, I know. I just . . . I mean, we're all over the front page right now. Do you need help, Hoagy?"

"Generally."

"I mean, is there something I can do to help speed things up? Anything?"

"Do you really want to help?"

"Absolutely. You're our top priority. Just name it."

"You could stop calling me."

"Stop calling you?"

"Yes. Every minute I spend on the phone with you is a minute I'm not spending at the typewriter."

"You mean like right now?"

"I mean like right now."

Click. She was gone. Smart lady. There's even talk she'll be getting her own imprint when she turns twenty-five.

My involvement with *Sweet Land* was actually out in the open now. Sort of. They put out a bogus press release saying Mavis had completed most of the manuscript herself before her fatal accident, and that I was being brought in to do a light polish. Hey, if you're looking for the truth, don't read the newspapers. And if you're looking for appreciation, become a licensed plumber – ghosting isn't for you.

I worked around the clock to the sounds of Garner and Gordie, who sat outside in the courtyard, tossing his ball against the wall for hours. I had no contact with the outside world, unless you count the telegram from Merilee: "I WANT YOU OUT OF THAT HORRIBLE PLACE RIGHT NOW, MISTER. STOP." To which I replied: "CAN'T. HAVING TOO MUCH GOOD, CLEAN FUN." Sadie was a frequent visitor, though unlike Lulu she kept climbing up on my desk and playing with the paper in my typewriter. I left my quarters only to eat and to take Lulu out for her midnight assignations with Bowser. Roy was keeping up his vigil by the wall. Mavis might be gone, but the precious Shenandoah peacocks were still in danger, or so he thought. If he thought. I had my doubts. Mostly, we caught him snoozing.

It was the morning of Mavis's funeral when Mercy knocked on my door, wearing a Mary Baldwin sweatshirt and jeans, face scrubbed, notepad in hand, composed, alert, all business. "I've looked into Vangie and John's marital vows, like you asked," she announced briskly.

"You really didn't have to do it now."

"I wanted to. It's keeping my mind off . . . other things, you know? I can come back later if you'd rather."

"No, no. Now is fine."

I gave her some coffee. She sat on the love seat with it, looked around at the room. It's entirely possible she'd never been in it before. She'd certainly never owned it before. Lulu sniffed at her, then turned her back on her and sat with a loud, disapproving grunt. Mercy watched this curiously.

"Don't mind her," I said. "She's just a little overprotective."

Mercy smiled. "She thinks I'm going to steal you from her?"

"From Merilee, actually."

Blushing, Mercy dove into her notes. "Okay, it seems the Anglican Church was the only officially recognized faith in the Virginia Colony," she reported. "And Anglican clergymen were the only ones empowered to perform marital vows. So I guess they would have had an Anglican wedding."

"Okay."

"What did people do who *weren't* Anglicans, I wonder?"

"Either pretend to get the faith or pretend to get married, I suppose."

She glanced through her notes, shaking her head. "Totally medieval. Do you know if you didn't attend an Anglican service at least once a month you could actually be fined? And if you . . . you . . ."

I heard a soft, plopping sound first. The sound of her tears falling onto the page. Then she hiccoughed once and her shoulders began to shake and then she was gone. I went to her. She hurled herself into my arms, heaved great sobs, held on tight. When she was done watering my shoulder, I gave her my linen handkerchief.

"Sorry," she said, sniffling, wiping her swollen eyes. "Didn't mean to . . ."

"It's okay. Nothing to be sorry about."

"I'm just not ready."

"For what?"

"Any of this. The estate, being in charge. I don't understand it. I don't understand anything." She buried her face in my chest. "I'm so *confused*."

"You're growing up all at once. Sorry to be the one to break it to you."

"I'm just not ready," she repeated.

"You'll be fine. You've got your father, your uncles, Polk . . ."

She shook her head. "I'm breaking it off with Polk."

"Since when?"

"It's something I decided I have to do."

"I wouldn't. At least not right now."

"Why not?"

"Because you're under a lot of strain. It's not a good time to make this kind of decision. Besides, he's not such a bad guy, in his own way."

Her eyes shone as they searched my face. "You surprise me. I thought . . . I mean, I thought you'd kind of approve." She lowered her eyes shyly. "You left someone out. You said I had Father and my uncles and Polk. There's also you."

"I'm not worth much on the open market."

"You are. You're so, I don't know, *sure* of things."

"The only thing I'm sure of is that I'm not sure of anything. I'm merely good at pretending. Comes with being old."

"Not so old," Mercy said softly. She raised her face to mine, her young lips parted slightly.

I shook my head. "That'll make things even more confusing."

My intentions were good. At least I think they were. Unfortunately, my timing stank. Richard stormed in just then without knocking. Finding us like that on the love seat didn't make him too happy.

"I've been looking everywhere for you, Mercy!" he roared. "I see I was looking in the wrong room! Go inside and get dressed at once! The *minister* is here!"

"Yes, Father." She gave me back my handkerchief. "Thank you, Hoagy. For everything." Then she went out.

Richard waited until she'd closed the door behind her before he lunged at me, grabbing me by the throat with his big hairy hands. "I don't believe there's a word in the language vile enough to describe you!" he spat out. "Taking advantage of a grieving girl, her mother not even in her grave yet!"

"Believe what you want, Richard," I gasped, sucking for air. "But you're wrong. She needed a shoulder to cry on. She happens to be the tiniest bit upset at the moment."

Richard stared deeply into my eyes. Abruptly, he released me, ran his hands through his hair. He slumped wearily into the easy chair. He seemed older to me. Mavis's death had aged him. "Sorry, lad," he said hoarsely. "Awfully damned sorry. Didn't mean to . . . Just not myself."

"I can't imagine why," I panted, fingering my throat.

Mercy had gotten coffee. Daddy got a single malt.

"It's a bitch, this," he confessed, sipping it gratefully. "An honest-to-Christ bitch. Mave was a hard, hard woman, lad. At times, I hated her more than I ever believed a man could hate a woman. But I did love her as well. I don't believe I realized just how much until now. I've no one now," he added mournfully. "No one in this world who gives a good goddamned about me."

"There's Mercy."

"She has her own life ahead of her. Marriage, children . . ."

"There's your brother, Kenneth," I suggested.

That one he left alone.

"Too bad he can't make it over for the funeral," I pressed. "Being so ill, I mean."

He glanced at me sharply. "You know the truth, don't you?"

I nodded.

"One of the brothers tell you?"

That one I left alone.

"Ah, well." He chuckled softly to himself. "We all play a role of some kind. I've played mine, and damned well, I like to think. Mave's idea from the start, you know. To impress the great unwashed. Meant a lot to her, bringing a fine English gent home to America with her, rather than a postman's son from Derby. I refused to play along at first. Wounded my pride. But I did it – for her. Sorry I had you on before. Been playing at it so long it almost seems real. It's certainly so to Mercy. She still doesn't know who I really am. That's how Mave always wanted it."

"She won't hear about it from me."

"Thank you, lad. Damned gentlemanly of you." He drained his whiskey. "I'm not coming into any money of my own, of course, other than whatever stipend Mercy gives me. I was having you on about that as well. Sorry."

"That's okay – I didn't entirely believe you. But I think Charlotte did."

He shifted uneasily in his chair. His face darkened. "Charlotte . . ."

"What are you going to do about her?"

"I honestly don't know, lad. What should I do?"

I sighed inwardly. I was getting tired of being the answer man. "Tell her the truth about yourself, for starters. If you don't, Pam will."

He grunted unhappily. "Dear, dear. And then?"

"Do I really look like Mary Worth to you?"

He stared at me, waiting.

I stared back at him. "Do you love Charlotte?"

"I don't know."

"Find out. See what happens now that you no longer have Mavis between you. See if a relationship grows."

He thought this over. "That's good advice, lad."

"It's true. I give excellent advice. I just don't take any of it myself."

There was a tapping at the door. Charlotte. She had on a black dress, drab, for the funeral.

"What are you doing out here, Richard?" she asked crossly. "You're needed inside."

"Sorry. Was on my way in."

She looked down at him. "You were not," she said gently. "You were sitting here jawing. Come along." She held her hand out to him, like she would to Gordie, if she cared for Gordie.

He reached up meekly and took it. "Yes, Charlotte."

Obediently, he followed her out. I watched him go. He needed this. He needed another woman to take charge of him. And Charlotte? I wondered about her. What was Charlotte capable of doing to get what she wanted? Did she figure in? How?

Mavis was buried that afternoon in the Glaze cemetery. It was a brief affair, and private. Immediate family only. And Charlotte and Polk Four and me. I don't know why I was invited, but I was, so I went.

She was buried next to her mother and father, beneath a big family stone. Frederick's and Edward's names and birth date were inscribed on it next to hers. A blank space remained – to be filled in when they died. Neither of them took their eyes off that space once during the entire ceremony.

CHAPTER
FOURTEEN

The *Oh, Shenandoah* golden-anniversary celebration was a truly major nonevent. Charter buses began pulling into Staunton shortly after dawn five days after the funeral, disgorging thousands of fans from all over America, most of them elderly ladies in pastel pantsuits who had seen the movie fifty times and knew every line, every detail, every morsel of gossip about the filming – or so they thought. The whole town gave itself over to the promotional frenzy. There were parades and banners and horse-drawn carriages and lots of people in Revolutionary War costumes. There were Vangie look-alike contests and movie memorabilia auctions and reenactments of battle scenes and panel discussions among self-proclaimed *Oh, Shenandoah* scholars. There were tours of historic homes and demonstrations of historic crafts and firearms. There were vendors selling peanuts and cotton candy. There were people, people everywhere, milling around the streets, stuffing their faces, taking pictures of each other, yelling, buying.

The Hollywood contingent began arriving later that afternoon. Most of them were billeted at The Shenandoan, a big new conference center built up on a hill on the outskirts of town. Such noted sons and daughters of the South as Chuck Heston, Ed McMahon, Shelley Winters, Gene Kelly, Roddy McDowall, Zsa Zsa Gabor, and Sonny Bono were on hand to pay tribute to Mavis Glaze's favorite charity and to get their faces on *Entertainment Tonight*. A number of them were granting interviews in the lobby when I got there. Sam Goldwyn, Jr., was on hand, attending to his father's interests. Cookie Jahr, the makeup girl who had been in the sitting room when Fern O'Baugh screamed fifty years before, was there. And so were Helene Bray and Rex Ransom, the two surviving *Oh, Shenandoah* cast members. Helene, the fast young actress who had played Vangie's friend Abigail was now the seventy-three-year-old proprietor of an art gallery in Carmel, California. She had short, severe white hair and a deep tan and wore a lot of heavy, jangly jewelry. She arrived in the company of a young, blond hunk of Eurotrash named Wulf. Rex Ransom arrived alone.

I found him lying down in his room with the shades drawn. "Stewart Hoag, Mr. Ransom," I said to the dim shape there on the bed. "We spoke on the phone."

"Oh, yeah, the writer. Sorry, musta dropped off – trip kind of wore me out." He reached over and turned on the bedside light.

It was some kind of mistake. This wasn't Rex Ransom. Not this bald, shriveled old man with no teeth who lay there on the bed before me with his shoes off. His color wasn't too good – unless you consider gray good – and he'd lost some weight. The skin on his face and neck fell in loose folds, and his polo shirt was a couple of sizes too big for him. So were his slacks. His belt was cinched practically twice around. He sat up slowly, put on his glasses, and lit the stub of a cigar that had gone out in the ashtray, his hands trembling. The cigar didn't smell too good, but it smelled better than his socks did.

He got to his feet with a groan and offered me his cold, limp hand. He was no more than five feet four in his stocking feet. "I know, I know," he said quickly. His voice was thin and slightly nasal. "You always thought I was a lot taller. That's 'cause I'm big through the shoulders and chest." He looked down at himself and frowned. "Used to be, anyways. And I wore lifts."

I was staring. It was so hard to imagine him as the Masked Avenger, that fearless doer of good who rode so tall and proud in the saddle. Now I knew why I hadn't seen him in anything for so long. And why Merilee had said, I hope he doesn't disappoint you.

"It's an honor to meet you, Mr. Ransom," I finally said. "I carried your lunch box."

"One of my kids, huh?" he said with a gummy smile. "Yeah, you look about the right age." He went into the bathroom. A moment later he returned wearing his teeth and his toupee. It was a bad rug. The hairs looked sticky and dead and didn't match the color of his sideburns. "Made two fifty a week to do that lousy show. Low point of my career. Christ, *television*. Wasn't until I had the job I found out they was gonna put me up on a goddamned horse. Damned horse hated my guts, too. Always tried to throw me. We used two different Neptunes, y'know. First one broke a leg doing some damned fool stunt, had to be put down. Nobody knows that. Go ahead and put it in your article. I don't give a shit anymore."

"Actually, I'm not writing an – "

"Hey, you got a pooch!" he exclaimed, noticing Lulu for the first time. "I love dogs. Landlady won't lemme keep one." He bent over and patted her. "Jeez, her breath . . ."

"Your landlady's?"

"No, the pooch."

"She has strange eating habits."

"It was the war, y'know," he declared, chewing on his cigar.

"The war?"

"Old man Goldwyn, he was gonna make me a leading man. I was on my way up when we wrapped this picture. Then I had to go into the service. None of that public relations flyboy crap, neither. I fought hand to hand in one lousy, stinking Pacific jungle after another. Killed three men. Woulda killed three more for a decent meal. When I came back, it was all different. They wanted dark and brooding – Greg Peck, Vic Mature, Bob Mitchum. I was an old face. Nothing worse in this business. Best I could get was two-line bits. Bartenders, cops, cabbies, maybe a few weeks here and there in a horror picture. . . . Hey, you want a drink or something? They said I can order room service. Food, booze, anything."

"I'm fine, thanks."

We sat in two club chairs by the window, which overlooked the tennis courts. No one was using them.

"That lousy series, it's all I got, y'know," Ransom went on. "On in reruns all over the place. I don't get a nickel off residuals, but I still do the sci-fi conventions, mall openings, junior high assemblies. I put on my costume and my mask, sign a few autographs, make a few bucks. My kids still love me. And I love them. They're my family. I got no one else." He shook his head. "And now they won't let me do it no more.

"Who won't?"

"These sons of bitches. Same studio that's doing this *Oh, Shenandoah* thing. Seems they're making this fifty-million-dollar *Masked Avenger* special-effects movie with some twenty-three-year-old weight lifter playing me. They want the public to think of him as the Avenger now, not me, so they're hassling me about making my appearances. Like I'm some kinda threat to 'em or something. All I make is a few bucks. I'm just an old man trying to get by. I got a one-bedroom apartment in Studio City, an eight-year-old car, no pension, hemorrhoids hanging from me like a handful of table grapes. And now they want to take it away from me. I tell ya, I'm so pissed off I didn't want to come to this thing. But what the hell, they're paying my way with a little something on top, so I can't afford not to. What kinda story you writing, kid? What can I tell ya?"

"I'm not a reporter, Mr. Ransom."

"Make it Mike. That's what my friends call me. My real name – Mike Radachowski."

"I'm working for the Glazes on the sequel to *Oh, Shenandoah*, Mike. Right now I'm collecting anecdotes for an introduction. I wondered if we could talk about Sterling Sloan's death."

"Sure," he said easily. "Some kind of stroke, wasn't it?"

"I don't think so. And I don't think you do, either."

He examined his cigar butt. It was cold. "What makes you think I know anything about it?"

"I have an idea you do."

He kept on examining his cigar. He looked worried now. "Sloan died a long, long time ago. What does it matter now?"

"It matters."

"I'd like to help you, kid," my boyhood hero said slowly. "But I really can't say nothing about it."

"About what?"

"The studio . . ."

"The studio is fucking you over."

"I still gotta make a living."

"They just said you can't."

"That's true," he admitted. He hesitated. "I don't know . . ."

"Why don't you do what I do when I'm in doubt?"

"What's that?"

"Ask myself what the Masked Avenger would do."

"That was comic book stuff," he scoffed.

"If we kept on believing what we learned in comic books, we'd all be a lot better off."

He looked at me curiously. "Y'know, you're kind of a strange young fella."

"Yeah, I'm what's known in the *New York Times* crossword puzzle as a oner."

"I don't know . . ."

"Trust me, Mike."

"Trust you? I don't even know you."

"Yeah, you do. I'm one of your kids."

"Look, I hate to let you down, seeing as how you are, but . . ." He thought it over. "What exactly do you want to know?"

"What you saw and heard."

"You mean gossip?"

"Okay."

He relaxed, relieved. "Well, hell, that's no problem. I can tell ya right off – it was a horny set. So what else is new. Errol, he was shtupping Laurel Barrett under Sloan's nose. Helene, Jesus, I had her, Dave Niven had her, we all had her – except for Sloan, who turned her down cold."

"Because of his wife?"

"Naw, on account of he had something else going. At least, that's what we all figured."

"Who with?"

"That got to be a major topic of conversation, you wanna know the truth. Sloan was very closemouthed. Not one of the gang. Didn't like to drink with us, play pinochle. You play pinochle?"

"Who was the smart money on, Mike? Who was Sloan's girlfriend?"

He crossed the room slowly and got a fresh cigar from the

nightstand. He lit it, puffed on it until he had it going to his satisfaction. Then he turned around. "Ethel," he replied, standing there in a cloud of blue smoke. "Ethel Barrymore."

"But she was – "

"Old enough to be his mother, I know. What can I tell ya – nobody's ever accused picture people of being normal."

"Any chance it was Alma Glaze?"

"The author? I doubt it. She wasn't exactly the cuddly type." He slumped on the edge of the bed and puffed on his cigar. "Still, you never know. Sloan was married to a great beauty. When a guy cheats, he always goes for something different. Coulda been. All I know is there was somebody, and I guess him and Laurel had some deal where it was okay for her to play around but not for him, on account of she let him have it but good."

"When?"

"That night. They had one hell of a fight in their hotel room the night he died."

"How do you know, Mike?"

"I had the room next door. Heard 'em hollering."

"What were they saying?"

"Couldn't hear no words."

"Then how do you know what they were fighting about?"

"What else do a husband and wife fight about besides money, and with their two paychecks money wasn't no problem."

"You're sure it was Laurel?"

"It was Laurel."

"And you were in your room when he was stricken?"

He nodded. "Getting dressed for the wrap party. Tux, studs, the works. I looked like a million bucks in those days. Rock hard, broads fallin' all over me. So I hear 'em goin' at it, a real doozy, and then . . ."

"And then?" I prompted.

"Then it got real quiet. I guess that's when the thing in his brain blew. Right away she comes running out in the hall screaming for Doc Toriello."

"As I understood it, he first complained of a terrible headache. She sent a bellhop out for some aspirin. Then Sloan got worse and *then* she called for the doctor."

He shrugged. "It coulda been that way. Sure. I don't remember so good."

"What really happened, Mike?"

He got up and went into the bathroom and filled a glass with water – an evasive maneuver. He returned with it and sat back down on the bed, mouth working furiously on his cigar. He said nothing.

I shook my head at him. "You've been holding the truth in a long time, Mike. You've kept your mouth shut, been a good soldier. And look what it's gotten you. Look how they've treated you."

He drank some of his water, smacking his lips as if it were good scotch. His eyes were on Lulu, who dozed at my feet. "I'd like to help you, kid. I would. But whatever a married couple does behind closed doors is their own goddamned business. And picture people – we don't tell stories on each other."

"Okay, Mike." I sighed heavily. "Only, you're really letting me down. . . ."

"Aw, don't pull that," he whined.

"I'm sorry, Mike, but it's true. You're letting one of your kids down. One of those eager, fresh-faced kids who grew up in front of the television set believing every single word you told him about truth and justice and tooth decay."

"That's low. That's awful fucking low."

Lulu stirred and looked up at me funny. I think she was having trouble imagining me as eager and fresh faced.

"People are getting murdered, Mike, and you're the only one who knows why. I can come back with the sheriff if you want, but if I do, everyone is going to find out you talked. Tell me now and no one will. You have my word."

"Jeez." He got up and started pacing the room, rubbing the lower half of his face with his hand. "The law. Jeez."

"What's it going to be, Mike?"

"You won't tell anyone where ya heard this?" His voice trembled.

"Not a soul."

"Okay, okay." He slumped back down onto the bed. "I was . . . I was dressing, like I told ya. And that's when I heard it."

"Heard what?"

"The gunshot," he said quietly.

"Gunshot?"

"Yeah."

"She shot him?"

"Blew half his head off. I pulled on my pants and went over there. Door was unlocked. He was on the floor. Blood all over the rug, the wall. Laurel was covered with it, screaming hysterically, the crazy fucking bitch. In and out of the bin after that, but they never prosecuted her. Whole thing got buttoned up nice and tight."

"Who was in on it?"

"They all were. The sheriff, Doc Toriello, the local doc, the hotel, funeral parlor . . . Money changed hands all the way down the line. Lots of it. Melnitz, Goldwyn's hatchet man, he took care of it. It was like it never happened. He came into my room later that night and told me just that – it never happened. I said okeydoke, you're the boss." He shook his head in amazement. "She was the star of a major motion picture. They could get away with murder in those days. She sure as hell did. And that's the story, kid. Kind of glad to be telling somebody about it, you wanna know the truth."

"What exactly was Laurel doing when you first went in there?"

"She was hysterical, like I told ya. I called the desk first thing. They got hold of Toriello."

"Was she holding the gun?"

"Uh . . . no."

"Did you actually see the gun?"

"No."

"Did anyone tell you for a fact that she did it?"

"Nobody said *nothin'.*"

"Then how do you know it was actually Laurel who shot him?"

"Nobody else was there," he replied. "Who the hell else could it have been?"

"A third party. Someone who arrived before the shooting, then hustled out before you got there."

He shook his head. "No chance of that. I could hear their door from my room. They didn't have no visitors."

"You said you were dressing for the party."

"Yeah?"

"Did you take a shower?"

"Sure I took a . . ." His eyes widened. "You're right, kid. I was in the shower two, three minutes washing my hair. Had a whole head of it then, thick and blond. Somebody coulda knocked and gone in then. I wouldn't a heard. Only, why are you so convinced it wasn't Laurel?"

"Because Laurel Barrett is long dead. No one here would bother to kill two people now, fifty years later, if she were Sloan's murderer. Someone local shot Sloan. Had to be. And someone local is still trying to keep it buttoned up." I got up out of the chair. "Thanks, Mike. You've been a big help. And it's been a genuine thrill to meet you."

"Sure thing, kid. Glad to have ya."

I started for the door, stopped. "Would you do it for me, Mike? Just once?"

He grinned at me. "Do what?"

"You know what I want."

He did indeed. Because something was already beginning to happen to him there on the bed. The blood was pumping harder in his veins. His chest was filling out, his shoulders broadening. He cleared his throat, and then he did it. He cried, "Neptune, *awaaaaay!*" His old cry. The one from long ago. He puffed on his cigar. "How was that?" he asked.

I tipped my cap. "It'll do, Mike. It'll do." I left before he started shrinking again.

Cookie Jahr would know. She had been there in the sitting room when Fern freaked. She knew who was in Vangie's room with Sterling Sloan. Whoever it was had shot him that night in his hotel room. That's why those pages had been torn from Alma's diary. Cookie knew. She was the one outsider who did.

Her room was down the hall from Mike's. Her door was open a few inches. I called out her name. There was no answer. I tugged at my ear, not liking this. People don't generally go out and leave their motel-room doors open. Not unless they've gone for some ice. I was standing ten feet from the ice machine. Cookie wasn't getting any ice.

Lulu was already heading straight for the car. She wanted no part of it. I called after her. I told her that after everything I'd done for her these past nights the least she could do was stay by my side when I needed her. Reluctantly, she returned to me. We went in.

Cookie was stretched out on the bed looking right at me. She had a cigarette going in the ashtray on the nightstand next to her. She was a frail, birdlike woman with bright yellow hair. She wore a floral-print blouse, white slacks, and a bright pink silk scarf. Whoever strangled her had used the scarf.

CHAPTER
FIFTEEN

Polk Four reached over and turned off his radio when it started squawking. We were sitting in his cruiser out in the parking lot of The Shenandoan, Lulu between us on the front seat sniffing gleefully at the tools of his trade on the dash. She likes sitting in police cars. Polk kept watching her. I don't think he liked her sniffing at his things. He certainly hadn't liked what I'd had to tell him – that his granddad had covered up a shooting. Cookie's body had been taken away. Polk had told the swarm of entertainment press she'd died of natural causes.

"No one saw anything?" I asked.

"Not a chance," he replied grimly. "Not with so many people coming and going. Plus the door at the end of the hall by her room opens directly onto the parking lot. She'd only been dead a few minutes when you got to her, too. So darned close. Now we may never know what happened."

"We'll know. We'll just have to work a little harder. You find out anything?"

"I might have." He glanced at me. "Except it goes no further than this car."

"Agreed."

"Your friend Pam was right. Frederick Glaze does have a rather serious . . ."

"Pain in the assets?"

He nodded. "In fact, the U.S. attorney's office has been quietly preparing to indict him."

"For?"

"Defrauding the Internal Revenue Service. Operating an illegal tax-shelter scheme involving some fifty-eight million dollars in bogus securities trades over the past three years. The way I had it explained to me, he claimed to be trading in government securities, only there were no actual transactions. Just fictitious pieces of paper. And hundreds of thousands of dollars in illegal tax benefits for his grateful, and unwitting, investors. It seems he's now scrambling to make good on what he owes the IRS and keep his name out of the papers and his butt out of jail. That accounts for where all of his money is going. Of course, the investors will have to pay back what they owe, too."

"Did he drag Shenandoah's holdings into this?"

"Some of them."

"Did Mavis find out?"

"She found out." The sheriff cleared his throat. "As a matter of fact, she was actively cooperating with the investigation."

"She was willing to testify against her own brother?"

"She was indeed."

"Hmm. Interesting, Sheriff. Who's Frederick's lawyer?"

Polk straightened the cuffs of his khaki shirt, not that they needed straightening. "His brother, Edward."

"Is Edward involved in the swindle, too?"

"No, he's clean. A conservative investor, Edward is. Just puts it in the bank. While we're on him . . ." Polk pulled a small notebook out of his shirt pocket and opened it. "He married one Danielle Giraud on August twenty-eighth, 1952 in Washington, D.C. She was attached to the French consulate. Marriage was annulled one month later. She married in '55, had two kids. Died in '84. Husband is still alive. A law professor, lives in Alexandria."

"Have a phone number for him?"

"Why?"

"I happen to be a very thorough ghost," I replied, writing it down. "Ask anyone I've ever worked for – if you can find one living."

Polk leafed through his notebook. "I also rechecked the medical examiner's report on Franklin Neene. It still turns up suicide. There was no sign of a struggle – he wasn't conked on the head or anything. No trace of drugs in his bloodstream – other than alcohol, but not so much that he might have been unconscious at the time of his death. The amount was consistent with what he'd consumed the night before. There's nothing to suggest it was anything other than what it appeared to be – suicide brought on by severe depression. Consequently . . ."

"Agreed. We focus elsewhere."

Polk bristled. "Who's *we*?"

"You're right, Sheriff. It's your investigation."

"Thank you," he said crisply.

We sat there in silence a moment.

"Have you spoken to Polk Two?" I asked him.

He stared straight ahead out the windshield. "I'm waiting until I have more facts."

I tugged at my ear. "Want me to do it?"

"I'll do it," he snapped in reply. "It's my job and he's my granddad. Just give me some time."

"Okay, fine. But you'd better hurry up, Sheriff. We're starting to run out of live bodies."

"Darn it, Hoagy, this isn't easy for me!" he raged. "I'm out here all alone on a shaky limb investigating people I've known and loved my entire life! One thing I don't need right now is your cheap sarcasm!"

"You're right again. Sorry, I don't mean to be hard on you. Seeing dead people just does strange things to me. Always has. I appreciate the effort you're making. I really do. And if Mercy survives this in one piece, I'm sure she'll thank you, too." I glanced over at him. He was staring grimly out at the parking lot. "Was that any better?" I asked gently.

"I'm trying, Hoagy," he said miserably. "I'm trying real hard to like you. For Mercy's sake. She thinks so highly of you. But it's no use. I just plain don't."

"It's okay, don't take it so hard." I patted him on the shoulder. "I'm used to it, pardner."

"And *don't* call me pardner!"

Polk Two had told me the Hotel Woodrow Wilson was once a fine place. It wasn't anymore. Now it was where Staunton stashed whatever it didn't want to look at. Its old geezers scraping by on social security. Its single mothers on welfare. Its discharged mental patients. Now it was one step up from the street, and a short one at that. The lobby had all the ambiance and charm of the Port Authority Bus Terminal. It certainly smelled just like it. Two musty old guys were dozing on a torn, green vinyl sofa. A gaunt, toothless black woman was screaming at her three dirty kids at the elevator. Signs were taped up all over the wall behind the reception desk. No credit. No overnight guests. No pets. No loitering.

The clerk was a thirtyish weasel with slicked-back black hair, sallow skin, and sneaky eyes. He looked down at Lulu, then up at me. "Can't you read?" he sneered. "No animals."

"They let you in here, didn't they?" I said pleasantly.

He curled his lip at me. "What are you – some kind of bad dude?"

"I like to think I am," I replied. "But no one else seems to."

"Well, what do you want?" he demanded coldly.

"Some information."

"This ain't the tourist information bureau."

"Tell me, does it wear you down being such an asshole or does it come easily to you?"

The weasel reached under the desk and came up with a nightstick. I reached in my pocket and came up with a twenty-dollar bill. I won.

"What do you want to know about?" he asked, the bill disappearing in his palm.

"The old days. Fifty years ago."

He yawned. "What about 'em?"

"Who worked here."

"How should I know?"

"Are there any employment records that go back that far?"

"All gone. Place has been under different ownership for years.

"I see. Any chance someone's still around who might remember those days?"

"Could be," he said vaguely. He was angling for another bill.

"I already gave you twenty," I pointed out. "And I can be back here in five minutes with Sheriff LaFoon."

"Okay, okay," he said quickly. "No sense being that way. I'm trying to think . . ."

"Yeah, I can see that. It's kind of like watching a Lego toy."

"Try old Gus," he growled. "He's always talking about how ritzy this shithole was back before the war. He worked here, I think."

"And where would I find Gus?"

"That's him over there," he said, indicating the two old guys nodding on the sofa.

One had a walker parked in front of him, the other a runny nose that was dripping freely onto his legs. "Which one?" I asked.

"The one without the walker."

"I was afraid you were going to say that."

I pulled a battered old armchair up in front of Gus and sat down. He stirred slightly but didn't waken. He was a burly old man in denim overalls, a faded flannel shirt torn at the elbows, and work boots. He needed a shave. Old men don't look hip when they're unshaven. They look like bums.

"How's it going, Gus?" I asked him.

He shifted on the sofa and grunted. Slowly, he opened one rheumy eye, swiped at his nose with the back of his hand. The other eye opened. I offered him my linen handkerchief. He took it and wiped his nose and his eyes with it, then carefully wadded it up and offered it back to me.

"You keep it," I insisted. "All yours."

His eyes focused on me for the first time. After a moment he said, "I know you. Sure I do."

"Sure you do," I agreed. "I used to play Smitty on the *Donna Reed Show*."

"No, you didn't."

"Okay, you got me. I didn't."

"You're Bob Dilfer's boy," he said, pointing a bent finger at me.

"I am not."

"Are too. Went down to Lauderdale to work construction."

"I did not."

"Got married."

"Well, that's another story, and an ugly one."

"How's your pappy?"

"We don't talk much anymore," I replied.

Gus nodded. "Know jus' what you mean. He can get ornery. Specially when he got liquor in him."

I glanced over at his dozing pal with the walker to see if we were disturbing him. We weren't. "There was a fellow who used to work here before the war, Gus."

His face lit up. "Billy."

I leaned forward. "Billy?"

"That's your name – Billy. Knew I'd get it."

"I never lost faith. A bellhop, Gus."

"Lots of bellhops here in those days, sure. Fine ladies and gents coming and going. They all stayed here. Roosevelt, Dewey. Harry S Truman. I once fetched Harry a fifth of bourbon. A fine gent. Tipped me ten bucks, he did."

"How about the movie folk?" I asked.

"Them had deep pockets all right," he sniffed, "but short arms."

"There was one guy who did real well by them though, wasn't there?"

"Weren't me."

"Who was it, Gus?"

His bleary eyes got a faraway look. "Hit the jackpot, he did. Got hisself a fancy new car. Fancy new job."

"Here at the hotel?"

"Naw, he got hisself into the easy pickings."

"Where did he go, Gus?"

Gus yawned, scratched his stubbly cheek and didn't answer me. I took out a twenty and laid it on his knee.

"I don't want your money, Billy," he said, staring at it.

"I know. It's a gift. Buy yourself something."

"Like what?"

"Like a handkerchief. Where did he go, Gus?"

Gus took the money and folded it carefully and stuffed it in the pocket of his overalls. Then he scratched his cheek again and told me where the lucky bellhop went.

I found him mowing the grass.

I brought Polk Four with me. I knew I'd get nowhere without him.

"Have a word with you, Roy?" I called to him.

He looked at me, then at Polk. Then he spat some tobacco juice and climbed down from the tractor mower and waited silently for one of us to say something.

"When did you come to work here, Roy?" I asked.

He stared at me blankly.

"About fifty years ago, wasn't it? You were working at the Hotel Woodrow Wilson when they offered it to you. Good pay, room and board. Glazes sure have taken fine care of you, haven't they?"

He kept on staring, jaw working on his tobacco.

"Fern wondered why they kept you around all these years," I went on. "Now we know why – to keep you from talking about Sterling Sloan's murder, right?"

He froze. Then his pale, deep-set eyes shot over to Polk Four. "Polk Two know 'bout you being here?" His voice was thin and reedy, almost a whisper.

"Let's leave my granddad out of this," Polk replied calmly.

"I'd call him, if I was you," Roy warned.

"I'd sit down and have a talk with Hoagy and myself, if I were you," Polk countered. "How would that be?"

Reluctantly, Roy said, "If you say so, Sheriff ."

"I say so, Roy. I do indeed."

Roy shut off the mower. We sat on the low stone wall that edged the vegetable garden. The peacocks strutted around us, watching us. Lulu growled at them from next to me and got honked at for her trouble. She burrowed into the ground at my feet and kept quiet after that.

Polk took off his broad-brimmed hat and placed it on his knee. "Want to tell us about that night, Roy? The night Sloan died?"

Roy watched the peacocks a moment, shifted his bony rump, spat some juice. "Manager, he sent me up there from the front desk," he began slowly. "Said to get 'em whatever they needed. Said something funny had gone on up there. He looked real nervous about it."

"Why did he send you?" Polk asked.

"Thought I know'd how to keep my mouth shut," Roy replied.

"Evidently a keen judge of character," I observed. "What did they need up there, Roy?"

"Towels. For the blood. Blood everywhere. Him on the floor with his brains spilling out. She were screeching her head off. Rex Ransom were there, only him went back to his room to be sick."

"That's my Rex," I said. "Did she have the gun?"

Roy shook his head.

"Did you see the gun?" I pressed.

He shook his head again. "Me and the house detective got him up on the sofa. Movie doc got there in a minute. Weren't much he could do though. Didn't have to be no doc to see that. Then this producer fella got there."

"Melnitz?"

"Never know'd his name. He pulled Polk Two aside and them two talked real quiet. Were the producer did most of the talking – one of them real persuasive types. Another doc come, signed some papers. I stuck around, in case they needed anything."

"And did they?" asked Polk.

"Later that night," Roy replied. "Two, three in the morning when the guests were all asleep. House detective got a van from somewheres. Him and me took up the rug, cleared the furniture out, all them bloody towels. Drove it all out to the dump and ditched it there. He told if I were smart and forgot what I seen, I'd do okay for m'self, and if I weren't, I'd be right sorry."

Polk stared down at his trooper's hat, his brow furrowed. "Who paid you off, Roy?" he asked, his voice quavering slightly. "Was it this Melnitz?"

Roy cleared his throat. "Were your great-granddad. Were Polk One. He called me to his big fancy law office next morning, give me five hunnert bucks. And a job out here. In case I got loose lips, I reckon. I took it. Sure I did. We all did. Times were bad. Them movie people could afford it. They wanted to pay money to cover the thing up, crazy not to take it."

"Laurel Barrett didn't shoot him, did she, Roy?" I said. "The Glaze family wouldn't have taken care of you all these years if she had. It was someone a little closer to home, wasn't it?"

Roy stared at me.

"Who else was there that night, Roy?" I asked. "Who else was in the hotel room?"

Roy glanced nervously at Polk.

"Tell us, Roy," commanded Polk.

Roy spat some juice into the dirt.

"Who was it, Roy?" demanded Polk. "Tell us, or so help me I'll haul you into – "

"Hidin' in one of the bedrooms," Roy muttered. "I saw 'em in there talking with the sheriff, real upset. Door was half closed, but I saw who it were. It were Miss Alma. Alma Glaze were in there."

CHAPTER
SIXTEEN

Pam brought me out my costume for the VADD Ball. My red velvet coat, waistcoat, and knee breeches were on a hanger. The rest was in a long white box – white silk stockings and black buckled shoes, white linen neckcloth and ruffled cuffs, black felt tricorne hat. There was one other box, squatly shaped.

"What's in that one?" I asked her as Lulu sniffed over all of it.

"Your wig, dear boy," Pam replied, smiling. "Freshly powdered."

It had a little pigtail at the back of the neck, held together with a black ribbon.

"Isn't all of this a bit silly, Pam?" I asked, trying it on in the mirror. I looked a little like Norman Bates's mother. I certainly looked more like her than I did Tom Jefferson.

"Of course it is. That is the point – it is a charity benefit."

"I could just wear my tux."

"You could not," she huffed.

"I don't look terrible in my tux."

"I'm well aware of that. However, this is a costume ball, not a Friars' Club roast," she reminded me airily. "Please, Hoagy. It's all been decided, and I've way too much to do to argue with you."

She did have a little to do. A thousand guests would be arriving by horse-drawn carriage that evening right after the movie. Trucks had been pulling up all week with party tents, tables, chairs, portable dance floors and toilets, floodlights, food, liquor, flowers. An army of carpenters and electricians were still putting it all together on the north lawn, while an assembly line of caterers was inside glazing the hams, baking the rolls. It was enough to send an average person bouncing off the ceiling. Pam was merely a bit flushed.

She started out the door. "A favor, Hoagy?"

"Sure, Pam."

"The family wishes for Gordie to appear at the ball, being the poster child and all, and the poor thing has the glums over it. Hasn't said a word or eaten a morsel all day."

"What makes you think I can bring him around?"

"He does happen to – "

"Like me," I acknowledged sourly. "I know."

"A lad of keen intelligence but questionable taste." She smiled. "Would you take him his dinner? Chat with him?"

"Soon as I get into my costume."

It took me a while. I had to climb into my breeches and stockings, put on my collarless muslin shirt, my neckcloth, my cuffs. It wasn't easy, and I wasn't happy with the way any of it looked until my coat was on and my hat was positioned rakishly atop my wig. I cut quite a figure in the mirror now. Erect. Commanding. Utterly Jeffersonian. I couldn't wait to see how Kissinger looked in his.

Lulu sat on her chair, watching me intently.

"Impressive, no?" I said.

She started coughing. She doesn't know how to laugh.

"Hey, I haven't made fun of your taste in men, have I?"

Stung, she got down from the chair and started her way mournfully up the staircase. I knew where she was headed – under the bed. Bowser hadn't shown last night. She'd been in a snit fit over it all day. Okay, it was a low blow from me. But hey, she started it.

I know Pam was impressed when I went into the kitchen to pick up Gordie's dinner. The place was mobbed with caterers. She didn't even seem to notice them.

"Truly magisterial, dear boy," she exclaimed, checking me out from head to toe. "And how are the shoes?"

"I've worn more comfortable bowling shoes," I replied, hobbling over to her. "Women's bowling shoes."

Charlotte came in from her office, frazzled and rushed. But not so rushed she couldn't stop and stare. And start snickering at me.

"Ignore her," Pam told me. "You're a stirring sight."

"I'm just glad Merilee isn't here to see this," I grumbled.

Pam opened a drawer and pulled out the Polaroid. "One must capture the memory," she declared, snapping my picture.

"I'll take that film."

"Nonsense. It goes in tomorrow morning's post."

"I'll get you for this, Pam. You owe me now."

"Yes, dear," she said patiently. She handed me Gordie's tray. "The carriages for the theater leave in thirty minutes. Don't be late."

I heard my phone ringing as I hobbled across the courtyard toward Gordie's rooms. It was Polk Four. He sounded very, very down.

"I tried, Hoagy," he said, his voice low and choked with emotion. "I really tried."

"Tried what, Sheriff?"

"Granddad. I-I went out to see him. Told him everything we know. Laid all my cards out on the table. Even told him we know he was involved. . . ."

"And?"

"He was very calm about it. Didn't get upset or anything. Just said that for the good of the valley and for my own future I should leave well enough alone. He said it's one thing for some outsider to try

digging up old bones, but another for me. He said he was disappointed in me. Like I'm some kind of little boy. I'm *sheriff* of this county!
Three women have been murdered! I asked him point-blank who it
was he phoned that set those two boys on you. He refused to tell me.
I don't know what to do now. I may have to nail him for obstruction
of justice if we're going to get anywhere. I don't know, Hoagy. I sure
don't . . ." He trailed off, was silent a moment. "It's all starting to
sink in, you know?"

"What is?"

"Who I am, what I stand for – it's all corrupt. Everything that the
LaFoons have built in this valley is corrupt."

"This from the man who was so sure that justice had the
upper hand here."

He breathed heavily in the phone. "I've never been so depressed
in my entire life."

"And you'll stay that way if you keep on thinking like you are."

"What do you mean?"

"I mean you can't deal in absolutes, Sheriff. Not when you're
talking about people. Your family wasn't as clean as you used to think
it was, and it's not as dirty as you think it is right now. The truth
is somewhere in between. It always is. I don't know what else
I can tell you, except that life sucks. But I think you're already
catching on to that."

I hung up and went next door. Gordie flicked off the TV when he
heard me knocking. He asked who it was. I told him. He said I could
come in. I did.

If the kid was gloomy, you could have fooled me. He started
giggling the second he saw me.

"What's so funny?" I demanded, setting his food down on
the coffee table.

"*You* are."

My close personal friend Sadie seemed to think Gordie's dinner
was for her. She started hungrily for it. I scooped her up.

"I am not funny," I said, putting her down on the sofa. "I'm a piece
of living history. You can learn an important lesson from all of this."

"Like what?"

"Like don't ever get talked into going to a costume ball."

Gordie's face darkened. He withdrew from me.

"Aren't you going to eat?" I asked him.

No reaction.

"Looks great," I observed. It did, too. Fried chicken, mashed
potatoes, greens. I wouldn't get to eat until after the movie, and
Oh, Shenandoah is one long movie. "If you don't eat it, I will."

Still no reaction.

"Suit yourself." I sat down, stuffed a napkin in my sleeve and calmly went to work on a wing.

"Do I gotta go, Hoagy?" he finally said.

"Don't want to, huh?" I said, munching.

"More than anything in the whole world."

"Then don't."

He brightened considerably. "Really!"

"Really. It's their thing, not yours. You didn't sign on as a performing seal. Anybody says different, you tell them to talk to me."

"Gee, thankth, Hoagy," he said gratefully.

He glanced down at the plate with interest. I nudged it over toward him. He went for the drumstick.

"What were you watching?" I asked as we ate.

"My favorite movie ever," he replied eagerly. "Theen it maybe a hundred timesth. Wanna watch?"

"You bet."

He reached for the remote control and flicked the tape on. James Garner and Donald Pleasence were emerging from a tunnel into the darkness. McQueen was helping them. The climax of *The Great Escape*, one of my three favorite McQueen films. The other two are *The Magnificent Seven* and *Bullitt*. I'd hate to have to pick one over the others. The Germans were on to them now. The searchlights came on inside the compound, machine guns fired, all hell broke loose. Off our heroes fled into the woods, each to pursue his own artfully conceived date with destiny.

If only real life were so neat. If only Sterling Sloan's murder made such sense. It didn't. The damned pieces still wouldn't fit together, no matter how hard I tried to make them. Say Alma Glaze was Sloan's mystery lover. Say he wanted to break it off when the picture wrapped and she didn't, so she showed up at his hotel room with a gun and blew his head off, the lover scorned. So far so good. Goldwyn's people and Alma's own people would be equally eager to cover it up. Only, who ran over Alma a few months later, and why? Why had Fern screamed? Whom had she seen in Vangie's room with Sloan? Not Alma – it was Alma herself who reported the outburst in her diary. Who had torn those final pages out? Why? And why had all of this reared its ugly head now, five decades later? Who was still being protected?

Lots more questions. And these answers weren't so easy to grab on to. Every time I reached for them they seemed to slip farther and farther away.

"Oh, boy, here'th my favorite part," exclaimed Gordie, breaking into my wondering.

McQueen was on his own now. Coburn had found a bicycle, Bronson a rowboat. Garner stole a plane. The others tried the train station. Not McQueen's style. He was looking for his own brand of transportation. It was while he was getting it that it suddenly happened – it all became clear to me. Horribly, finally, clear. So clear that I sat right up, stunned and dumbfounded. What can I tell you – sometimes it happens that way.

I wish I could say I was happy it had. I wasn't. The truth is, I felt lousier than I had in a long, long time.

"We have to talk, Frederick," I said into the phone after he said hello.

"Is that you, Hoagy?" he inquired in his husky, elegant voice.

"It is."

"I'm just climbing into this ridiculous costume . . . ," he groaned. "Go right ahead and talk. What's on your mind?"

"I know it was you who hired those two goons to get your mother's diary off of me." I waited for him to respond. There was only breathing from his end. I plowed ahead. "You were going to sneak it to the tabloids for a lot of money – money you desperately need. Taking it off me outside your office was your best shot. Once I had it with me at Shenandoah it would have been too obvious that an insider was behind it."

"I see," he finally said. He sounded weary and defeated. He sounded old. "And what else do you know?"

"I know it was you who Polk Two phoned after I visited him at his house. It had to be you – you were their contact. You sent them out there to kill me."

"Now that's not true, strictly speaking," Frederick protested. "I only meant to scare you. Get you to concentrate on your work and forget about this other business."

"And I know why. It's time for all of this to end, Frederick. I've no desire to hurt you or anyone in your family. Merely to see justice served. It's time for us to talk."

He breathed in my ear some more. "Yes. Okay," he said heavily. "I'd prefer to do it in person if you don't mind."

"I don't mind. Where and when?"

"Hell, let's do it right now – I've already seen the damned movie two hundred times. I'll come out there. We can go to the ball after we talk."

"That'll be fine. My quarters?"

He hesitated. "I'd rather we make it somewhere more private. Shall we meet at the gazebo? In half an hour?"

"See you then, Frederick."

Lulu didn't want to come with me. She was still sulking over the crack I'd made about Bowser. She only agreed to come when I begged her forgiveness. And mentioned the word *caviar* several times.

It was dark out now. The batteries in my flashlight were about dead from all of our late-night strolls. I found some fresh ones in the kitchen utility drawer, and put them in while the caterers rushed in and out with their fragrant trays.

"And what are you up to?" Pam wondered, watching me.

"Taking a small stroll."

"Where?"

"I don't know. Just felt like breaking in my new shoes."

"Must I remind you that the carriages leave in – "

"Please, Pam. You've stripped me of what's left of my dignity. Leave me my secrets." With that I straightened my tricorne hat and hobbled out the door.

The great north lawn was ablaze with the party-tent lights. Waitresses were setting the banquet tables. Musicians were testing their microphones. The peacocks were honking. A couple of old-fashioned movie-premiere kliegs stabbed way up into the black sky overhead, adding to the good old colonial effect. Lulu and I took the path that bordered the lawn, then plunged into the woods alongside the cemetery. It was dark and quiet in there. I could see only what was ahead of me in my flashlight beam, hear only the clopping of my shoes. Briefly, I thought I heard footsteps in the woods behind us, someone following us. But when I stopped, I heard nothing. And my flashlight beam found nothing. Lulu whimpered. I shushed her and moved on, sorry for the moment that Bowser wasn't with us. I could use someone like him, someone with no class or breeding. Someone who'd happily sink his teeth into a nice meaty leg if I asked him to.

I saw the weak flicker of a light up ahead. It was an oil lamp sitting on the pine table under the gazebo. Frederick was there already, seated at the table, smoking a cigarette. He stood when he heard me. He was dressed for the ball as I was, though he had a cape of peacock-blue silk over his outfit, and gold braid on his tricorne hat. I don't know why I didn't get gold braid on mine. I'll bet his shoes fit, too.

"Ah, here you are, Hoagy," he rasped pleasantly.

"Frederick," I said.

"Not exactly." He dropped the cigarette on the rough wooden floor and stepped on it. "Horrible things. My fingers will stink of nicotine for a week. . . . I'm afraid you've fallen for a trick we've played on people since we were boys, Hoagy. I do Frederick and Frederick does me. Drove our teachers crazy. I think I do him better. Just my opinion. You see, Frederick was in the shower when you phoned. I'd stopped over for my costume and answered it for him. Naturally, you assumed you'd reached Frederick. Your tough luck, I'm afraid. If you had gotten Fred, you might have lived." Edward reached under his cape and pulled out a revolver and pointed it at me. "But you got me."

CHAPTER
SEVENTEEN

"**K**ind of the wrong period, isn't it, Edward?" I said, my eyes on the gun. "A dueling pistol would be so much more appropriate."

"You'll forgive me the historical inaccuracy."

"I'll try. But I'm making no promises."

"You've gotten too close, young man. Much too close. And I have survived too long to be brought down now, particularly by some washed-up writer."

I glanced down at Lulu. "Are you going to take that from him?" In response she yawned and curled up under the table. Bowser. I needed Bowser, crashing through the woods, saliva dripping from his fangs. "Mind if I sit down, Edward? My feet are killing me."

"Please do."

He stayed where he was, the gun on me. "You know the truth, of course. That's why you wanted to speak with Frederick."

"Yes. I was off course for the longest time. Mavis and her damned collarbone kept throwing me. That business in your mother's diary about how little Mavis took a horse out one day, and fell, and was missing until Sterling Sloan found her in the pasture across the way. It seemed odd to me. Supposedly, Sloan rarely left his trailer. What was he doing out there with Mavis? And why was she still afraid to get back up on a horse so many years later? Because she broke her collarbone as a child? That didn't sound like Mavis to me. Some other form of childhood trauma seemed more like it. Like, say, the great Sterling Sloan trying to hand her his shlong. And maybe trying to do it again in Vangie's room on the last day of filming. I figured maybe *that's* what Fern saw, and what Alma walked in on. And I figured Alma shot Sloan because of it – the protective mother taking the law into her own hands. It all fit together, Edward. Except it didn't. Because if Alma killed Sloan, then who ran *her* down several months later on Beverley Street? Laurel Barrett? Possibly, except she was out of the country – I checked. And then there was now to factor in. Okay, Fern and Cookie were killed to keep things covered up. That part worked. But why kill Mavis? If all of this had been done to protect her, then why kill her? That made no sense. And it got me nowhere – except back to you.

"And how, may I ask, did you arrive at me?" he inquired calmly.

"You tipped me off yourself the day Fern died. We were all sitting there in the old house while Polk Four attended to her body. You were pretty upset about it."

"It's true, I was."

"So upset you messed up. You turned to Frederick and said, 'I keep thinking of the night mother died. I was at Fern's when I got the news, remember? She was the one who actually told me.' Frederick got somewhat curt with you and changed the subject. None of which meant much to me until later, when I interviewed Polk Two about that night Alma died. He told me all three of you kids were home when she was hit. A small discrepancy, but it stuck with me. And it didn't go away. Just got bigger and bigger. What had you been doing at Fern's? Why had Frederick gotten so snappish about your mentioning it? The answer was plain – Fern was your alibi for that evening in case Polk Two ever got around to checking up on you. Only he never did because Frederick covered for you, said you were home. And Polk Two accepted it. I guess he just didn't believe that you could murder your own mother, even though he was fully aware that you'd murdered once already. You murdered Sterling Sloan – the man you loved."

Edward lowered his eyes. The gun never left me. "It's true," he said softly. "I loved Sterling. I've never stopped loving him."

"It was *you*. You were Sloan's mystery lover. Fern saw you two together in Vangie's room. That's why she screamed. It must have come as quite a shock to a teenaged girl back in those days to discover that her Romeo, her Sweet Prince, was gay."

He was silent a moment. "It happened for me," he began slowly, "that very first night I saw him standing out there in the rain. I felt something I'd never felt before, not for any girl. Even Fern. She and I were so close. We gave each other our souls. But I'd never felt the *hunger* for her that one read about. The physical part, that was never real for me somehow. Until I met Sterling. He was . . . I suppose he was the very man whom I most wished to become. Brilliant, artistic, sophisticated. He was a soul in torment, a man locked in a loveless marriage. That simply made him all the more romantic. It was merely a business arrangement, their marriage. Good for both of their images. Laurel went her way, he went his. At least he was discreet about it. . . . I was so terribly flattered when he showed an interest in me. Of course, being a naive small-town boy, I had no idea *why* he was so interested. Not until the two of us were together in his trailer one afternoon. He got one of his terrible headaches and asked me if I'd massage his neck. As I did, I-I felt it happening to me – I felt myself coming alive. And then he looked at me and I knew he felt it, too. He took my hands in his and led me over to the daybed. We kissed. Gently, tenderly. And then he undressed me. I was powerless to stop him. I didn't want to stop him. It felt so right. For me it was. For me it was love." Edward's eyes moistened in the lamplight. "I loved him, don't you see? I've never loved anyone else in my entire life."

"You did try though," I suggested.

"I did," he acknowledged. "Years later, after I had finished law school, taken a job in the Justice Department in Washington." He chuckled softly. "I suppose I was the only murderer on the staff."

"Oh, I wouldn't be so sure," I said. "You took a wife."

"Yes, Danielle. A sweet, lovely woman. I hurt her badly."

"Indeed you did. Her husband told me all about it on the phone this afternoon. How she'd been married once before, briefly, to this man who'd wanted so desperately to conform. But he couldn't. It was clear from the first night he couldn't. Your marriage was annulled – on the grounds of nonconsummation."

"I wasn't being *me*," Edward explained. "Only with Sterling was I me."

"And he broke your heart, didn't he?"

"Such a tired old story," he murmured. "Such a cliché. But what did I know? I was eighteen years old. I thought he loved me as I loved him. I believed him when he said he would take me with him to Hollywood, to London, to wherever. That he would divorce her." Edward gazed out the gazebo at the woods. He seemed very far away now. The gun didn't. "How was I to know I was nothing to him? I was just some boy he'd diddled on location, one of the dozens he'd flicked and forgotten through the years, a bimbo. How was I to know? I didn't. Not until he told me. In Vangie's room, that last day of filming. That's when I found out. He said he wanted me to stay behind. He said he was no good for me, that I'd be better off forgetting about him. I couldn't believe what he was telling me. *Wouldn't* believe it. I threw myself into his arms, sobbing, begging, covering him with kisses. . . . That's when Fern saw us. That's what she saw. I heard her scream, saw her run away. A moment later Mother came into the room. Sterling and I were merely standing next to each other by then. But she *knew*. Somehow, she *knew*. Not that she said a word to either of us. She merely said, 'Excuse me,' in that stiff, proper way she had and walked out of the room."

"And put it in her diary – the pages you tore out."

"Her lawyer, Polk One, did it, actually. Before he sealed it and put it in the safe."

"And that evening you went to Sloan's hotel room and you shot him."

"I went up there to tell that evil bitch Laurel she had to let him go. I wouldn't believe him, you see. I wouldn't believe he didn't love me. I-I set Laurel straight, face-to-face. I told her Sterling was mine, not hers. I told her there was no love between them anymore and she should be sensible and divorce him. I thought I was being very adult, very mature. And she . . . she simply rolled her eyes at me and called to him in the bath: 'Oh, Sterling, dear, one of your little friends is here!' As if I were some irritating stray that had followed him home, some petty nuisance. And when he came out and saw me there, I realized from the way he looked at me that I *was*."

"So you shot him?"

"Never. I would never have. . . . I-I shot her. I shot Laurel."

"And you missed?"

Edward shook his head. "Sterling jumped in front of her at the last second. He took the shot. She screamed. I heard her screams in my ears as I ran out the door, down the hall, out of there."

"Your mother was summoned by Polk Two as soon as Laurel told him what had happened. Alma put the fix in for you. Both the townspeople and Goldwyn's people were only too happy to oblige her. No one wanted a scandal."

"Precisely," Edward agreed bitterly. "Mother protected her precious little boy. The studio protected their colossal investment. They weren't about to jeopardize it because of some faggot killing. Toriello dreamed up the aneurysm story, symptoms and all, and everyone went along with it. It was all covered up. Buried. And it would have stayed that way if it hadn't been for Sam Goldwyn. The greedy bastard had a hit on his hands and he knew it. Even before the movie came out he knew it. Right away, he began pressuring Mother to write a sequel. He even tried telling her how to write it – De Cheverier has to win the duel with John Raymond at the end, he said. After all, Errol Flynn was still alive. Sterling Sloan wasn't. Well, Mother didn't like being bullied by anyone, especially Goldwyn. She told him that if there ever was a sequel, she would write it in her own way and in her own time, thank you. He offered to buy up the rights to her characters and commission his own film sequel without any book. She declined. That should have been the end of it. Except he wasn't through, Goldwyn. Not so long as there was a gutter left to climb down into. He put it to Mother this way: Let me do my sequel or the whole world will find out that your son murdered Sterling Sloan and got away with it. Goldwyn figured that would break her. Break any mother. But he was wrong about Alma Glaze. Because she didn't care about me, not as much as she cared about her fool creation. She told him fine, go ahead and tell the world about Edward. She sold me out. Told me so to my face. She had a choice to make and she made it – she put her book ahead of her own son. I ask you, Hoagy, what kind of woman would do that? Only an evil one. Miserable, horrid, *evil* . . . I did the only thing I could do. I killed her. So Goldwyn could have his way. So that what had happened would stay private. Sterling and me . . . that was nobody's business. Nobody's." He chuckled softly. "Ironically, it was only after I'd killed her that I learned about the codicil she'd added to her will. I hadn't known. None of us had. Only her trusted legal advisor, Polk One. She did it to punish Goldwyn. Oh, the bastard thought about contesting it. Taking the estate to court. But the war was on by then. Wartime was no time for long, ugly court battles. Or big-budget Hollywood epics. So he quietly dropped the whole thing, moved on. . . . It was right, what I did. I've never been sorry that I killed her. Not sorry in the least."

"How nice for you. May I ask you how you did it?"

"You may. I overheard her on the phone with Polk One. A Saturday afternoon, it was. She wished for him to come out to Shenandoah at once. I suppose to talk about the codicil. He couldn't make it. She said she'd come into town that evening, meet him at his office at six. He agreed. After all, she was a rather important client. I moved swiftly, seizing the opportunity. I made a date for eight that evening with Fern. As soon as Mother left for town, I stole a bottle of bourbon from the liquor cupboard and did the same. I left my car near Fern's house, took the bourbon with me, and went hunting through the neighborhood for a car. I found one with its keys in it just a few blocks away. No one saw me take it. It was suppertime, the street was deserted. Polk One's office was on Beverley Street. I parked down the block and waited there for her to come out, my hat down over my face, my collar turned up. And when she did, she got what was coming to her. She flew fifty feet through the air when I hit her. God, it felt good. I kept right on going, until I was outside of town. I left the car there. Poured the bourbon all over the seats so Polk Two would think a drunk had done it. Then I ran to Fern's. I was only a few minutes late for our date. I was there when I got the news about Mother. Frederick phoned me. He knew I'd be there. And he knew why."

"Did Mavis?"

"Mavis was a child. She knew nothing about Sterling's death. And she never knew I killed our mother."

"And Polk Two never suspected you?"

Edward smiled. "If he did, he never said anything. You must understand that Polk Two was never anything more than a Glaze-family lapdog. His position as sheriff, his seat in Richmond, depended on staying in our good graces."

"I see. Why did Frederick let you get away with it? Why did he cover for you?"

"He's my twin, Hoagy. I don't suppose you can understand just how close that makes us, closer than any other two human beings can possibly be. Frederick loves me, and I love him. We've always watched out for each other, stood by each other. He is the only person I've ever completely trusted, just as he trusts me. Oh, we have our small differences. I happen to think he lacks personal discipline when it comes to money and women, for instance. But I'd still do anything for him. I'm helping him right now – trying to extricate him from his financial misfortune."

"That's certainly one word for fraud." I sat back and crossed my legs. At my feet Lulu paddled in her sleep, small whimpers coming from her throat. Dreaming of you-know-who no doubt. Edward stood there motionless, the gun still on me. "All of which brings us to the present, Edward. And to three more murders. You had to kill Cookie. Polk Four and I were starting to sniff around, and Cookie was the one living outsider who could name you as the person who'd been in Vangie's room with Sloan. Like you said, you've survived much too long to be brought down now. But Fern and Mavis were another matter entirely. How much did Fern actually know?"

"She knew of my relationship with Sterling, of course," Edward replied. "As to the circumstances of his death, Mother's death . . . Fern drew her own conclusions. Not that she ever said anything to me about it. Not then, not ever. We never talked about what Fern saw that day in Vangie's room. Or about anything else ever again. Oh, she was always cordial toward me, just as I was to her. But anytime I happened to look deeply into her eyes I saw . . . *pain*. Fern drew a line between us, and I was never, ever, to cross over it. It was an unspoken contract between us."

"Which she was prepared to break. My first night here she told me it was time for the truth to come out. Only, why kill her? I mean, I was prepared to ignore her. I just took her for a jolly, slightly paranoid old crank – *until* she was murdered. That made me think maybe she *did* know something. It was dumb for you to kill her and arouse my suspicion that way. Just as it was dumb for you to kill Mavis. What was the point? To get at her money? The estate goes to Mercy, not you and Frederick. There was no point, and that stumped me. Because if there's one thing you're not, it's dumb. You're a bright, sensitive, and extremely gracious psychopath. I couldn't figure Fern and Mavis out. Not until tonight, when I realized there was only one way it made any sense."

"And what way was that, Hoagy?"

"You didn't kill them. You had nothing to do with either murder."

Edward spread his feet slightly, took careful, steady aim at the center of my chest. "You're a gifted man, Hoagy. You should have stayed at what you know, writing. You're not as good at this sort of thing. Just good enough to die."

"Killing me won't solve anything, Edward. Polk Four knows too much. He'll follow the same trail right to you."

"And when he does, he'll do what he's told, just like Polks One, Two, and Three before him. The Glazes are the power in this valley. We *are* this valley. Young Polk, he has his sights set on the governor's mansion. He'll never make it there without our backing, and he knows it. I'm not worried about him. It's you I worry about. But my worries end here."

So here it was. The end. Staring at me from six feet away. I stared back at it. I wasn't afraid. There was no fear. Only regret. Because I was going to die here and now with nothing to show for my life, nothing except for two novels, a weird dog, and my independence. I was sorry I'd never see Merilee's green eyes again. Sorry we hadn't built a life together, only a truce. Sorry I hadn't said hello to my father in more than five years. He'd never hear me say it now. If only I lived I'd do something about that. But of course, I wasn't going to live.

Edward pulled the trigger. The gun made an odd sound when he did. As if it had fired twice at once. But I barely had time to register that thought. Almost instantly I felt a searing pain in my head, and the rough wooden floor of the gazebo was rushing up at me and I was hurtling down toward it, and then there was only blackness.

C H A P T E R
E I G H T E E N

It was Pam's face I saw first. She was standing over me looking very pale and grim. I was lying in a bed, the one in my slaves' quarters. I was dizzy. My head felt heavy and thick. I reached a hand up to it, fingered it. Something cottony was wrapped around it.

Pam wasn't alone. A crowd of people stood circled around me. Most of them wore costumes. Polk Two, Frederick – at least I hoped it was Frederick – Richard, Charlotte, Mercy. Charlotte and Mercy wore elaborate silk gowns over hooped petticoats, and wigs piled high under peacock-feathered hats. More damned peacock feathers. Polk Four stood there in his uniform. The weary old doctor who had signed Fern's death certificate was there, too. They were all staring at me, looking very serious. Everyone was there. Everyone except –

Two shots. Not one. Two.

I tried to speak, but my throat was too dry. Pam held out a glass of water with a straw in it. I drank some. "Lulu . . . ," I got out hoarsely. "Luluuuu . . ."

"Here she is, dear boy." Pam bent down to the floor next to my bed and hoisted her up onto the covers, where Lulu began to wriggle and whoop and lick my fingers. "Safe and sound," Pam assured me. "As are you."

Polk Four leaned forward. "You have Pam here to thank for that, Hoagy," he explained. "She tailed you out to the gazebo. Overheard the whole thing. She shot him just as he was about to fire at you. His shot went wild. Your wig took most of it."

"My wig?" I swallowed. "I admire your definition of a wild shot, Sheriff."

"Just got a shallow little groove over your left ear, son, the doctor informed me. "It bled quite a lot, but it's nothing serious."

"You wouldn't be saying that if it was your ear." I turned to Pam. "I thought I heard someone behind me on the path. That was you?"

She nodded. "When you left the kitchen, I took Fern's gun from my nightstand and followed you out there."

"But why?"

She reddened slightly. "You do have a tendency to get in over your head sometimes, dear boy."

"I sure do wish you'd filled me in, Hoagy," Polk Four said crossly. "Instead of making the hot-dog play."

"I honestly didn't know that's what I was making. You saved my life, Pam."

"Why, yes. I suppose I did."

"I owe you one.

"You could take me home with you when this is over."

"Please, Pam. Not in front of all of those people."

She smiled. No one else did. They didn't have much to smile about.

"Edward is . . . ?"

"Edward is dead," Frederick said quietly. He looked drawn and grief stricken. His eyes moistened. "We came into this world together. We've never been apart." He choked back a sob. "Not ever."

"I'm sorry it had to happen, Frederick," I said. "Only how could you do it? How could you cover for him all these years? He killed two people, one of them your own mother."

"He was my twin," Frederick replied simply. "Right or wrong, he was part of me."

"That works for you. Maybe." I turned to Polk Two. "But not for you, sir."

The big old man shifted slowly in his costume, hands gripping his canes tightly. His blue eyes were bright and clear and unapologetic. "I was an employee," he declared. "I was paid to do a job, and I did it. Nothing I was particularly proud to do, but I did it. People always make the mistake of thinking a politician leads. He doesn't lead. He follows."

"You agree with that?" I asked Polk Four.

"Not entirely," the young sheriff replied stiffly.

Polk Two let out a deep, hacking cough. "Now that Edward is gone, I believe it's best we put this whole sorry business behind us. Not make a big public spectacle out of it. Be bad for the valley. Bad for everyone. It's from long ago, and it's over now."

"Not entirely," I said.

"That's right," Polk Four agreed. "Pam swears she heard you say that Edward *didn't* kill Mavis or Fern."

"He didn't," I acknowledged. "Wasn't involved in their deaths at all. Merely an unfortunate chain of circumstances for him. Not to mention the two ladies."

Mercy frowned and shook her head, baffled. "But if Uncle Edward didn't kill them, who did?" she wondered.

They all seemed to stop breathing as they stood there staring at me, waiting for my reply.

"Steve McQueen," I said.

Polk Four frowned and glanced at the doctor, who leaned over me and stuck a light in my eyes. "I did sedate him," he murmured. "I'm afraid we may be losing him."

"You are not," I insisted, waving him away. "Remember *The Great Escape*, the McQueen movie?"

"I've seen it on television," replied Polk Four, baffled.

"What of it, lad?" inquired Richard, equally baffled.

"Remember how he got away?" I asked.

Polk Four scratched his chin. "He didn't get away. They caught him at the end. Brought him back, and his friend tossed him his baseball mitt as he was being led to the cooler."

"Right, right. But when he was on the run, before they caught him. Coburn took a bicycle, Bronson a rowboat, Garner a plane. And McQueen . . ."

"Wasn't there a car chase or something?" asked Mercy.

"No, that was *Bullitt*. He stole a motorcycle off a German – by stretching a wire across the road. The guy ran into it and went flying."

"A wire." Polk Four swallowed. "Okay . . ."

"McQueen happens to be Gordie's hero," I said. "And *The Great Escape* is his favorite movie. He told me he's seen it a hundred times."

"Wait one minute," declared Richard, incredulous. "Are you ctually suggesting it was that little orphan boy who murdered Mavis and Fern?"

"Ever since Fern fell down those stairs," I said, "I've been wondering what the hell she was doing upstairs in the old house when she was supposed to be serving up our lunch in the kitchen. She was chasing after Gordie. He was playing games with her, getting her mad at him. He got her to chase him into the old house, then up the stairs, and then he hid. When she went in one of the bedrooms to look for him, he tied a wire across the top of the stairs and ran down them, making sure she heard him. She chased after him and being blind as a bat, tripped over the wire and fell headfirst down the stairs to her death. Then he quickly gathered up the wire and hightailed it out to his room before I found her. Got to hand it to him – he's a clever little guy."

Polk Four gaped at me, aghast. "B-But why did he do it?"

"He hated her. He thought she was going to take Sadie away from him."

"Who is Sadie?" asked Pam.

"His cat."

"I didn't know he had a cat," said Richard.

"He used the same technique to kill Mavis," I went on. "He knew her patrol route. He tied a wire around two trees and hid. Then removed it after she'd gotten thrown. He killed her because she insisted he go to the VADD Ball. He didn't want to. The kid lost his whole family. Suffered a major emotional trauma. He needed someone to care about him. He needed help. What he got was a billboard and a room outside next to the garage. So he's withdrawn, drifted away.

Drifted so far he sometimes can't tell the difference between what he sees on TV and what's real. He worships McQueen in *The Great Escape*. He dresses like McQueen does in the movie. He sits and tosses a ball against a wall like McQueen does. He's even tunneling out in the middle of the night like him. And when Gordie gets real upset at someone, he solves the problem the way he thinks his hero would."

No one said anything.

"I'll be darned," Polk Four finally said under his breath. "Guess I . . . I ought to take the poor little guy into custody."

"Don't be too hard on him, Sheriff," I said. "He honestly doesn't know what he's done. And if it hadn't been for Gordie, we would never have found out who killed Sterling Sloan." To Pam I said, "How's the VADD Ball?"

"In full swing," she replied.

"I want to go," I declared.

"You're hardly up to it, dear boy."

"I have to go," I insisted.

Polk Four frowned. "And why is that, Hoagy? What else is left?"

"Kissinger. I have to see Kissinger."

The doctor leaned over me again. "I believe we are losing him."

And this time they were.

CHAPTER
NINETEEN

Edward Glaze's death made kind of a nice capper to the *Oh, Shenandoah* golden-anniversary festivities. At least all of the press who were around seemed to think so. They had loads of good, dirty fun with the story – the whole story. The deaths of Sterling Sloan and Alma Glaze fifty years ago. The deaths of the three women during the past few weeks. Polk Four insisted on a full and complete disclosure. Polk Two wasn't happy about that. After all, it didn't make him or the Glazes look too good. But Polk Four insisted on it. He showed me a lot of class by the way he handled the situation. He showed everybody a lot. Made quite a name for himself. Don't be too surprised if he does turn up in the governor's mansion one day soon.

I asked him to do me one small favor. I wanted him to impress on the media just how crucial the courageous testimony of actor Rex Ransom had been. The sheriff complied. Rex got a lot of attention as a result. Appeared on Letterman. Landed a lucrative series of denture-cream commercials. Even got carte blanche from the studio to keep on appearing around the country as the Masked Avenger. I never heard from Rex again, but I still watch the Masked Avenger in reruns. And he's still my hero.

The Major League Editor started calling me again. Not just to breathe down my neck either, although *Sweet Land* and how it was coming along did come up. She wanted me to write a book about the scandal after I finished up. Major advance. Major upside. Major excitement from her end. "True-life crime has become the fiction of the nineties," is how she put it, burbling. I turned her down. She immediately offered it to Frederick. He immediately accepted. He needs the money. He's still looking for a ghost. If you're interested, you can contact him care of Shenandoah, Staunton, Va. I forget the zip code. He's also looking for a new lawyer.

Gordie was placed in the children's ward of the state mental hospital in Charlottesville for observation. A team of child psychiatrists interviewed and tested him. It didn't take them long to diagnose that he needed permanent care. At the insistence of Mercy Glaze he was transferred to a private children's mental hospital nearby. The cost, seven hundred dollars a day, will be paid by the Glazes. His case will be reviewed every couple of years. He may get out someday. For now he has his own room and bath, and there's a baseball team.

Our last night at Shenandoah, Lulu woke me at the usual time for our usual date. She was particularly anxious. I'd been packing all evening – she knew we were leaving. I was anxious myself. I didn't know what she was going to do. Would she choose Bowser over me? Would she stay behind? Would I let her? Did I have a right to interfere? I didn't know.

Roy was still pulling wall duty. And still asleep on the job. He didn't hear us approach. Didn't see Bowser burrow under the wall and start toward us. Didn't see Bowser stop and turn and casually wait for his companion to burrow under it, too.

She was a collie. A real fox, too.

Lulu was so stunned she sounded as if she were going to choke.

Bowser wasn't particularly happy to see her. He sniffed at her coolly, as if she were a bad memory. The collie showed Lulu her teeth, the bitch. Then the two of them kept on going across the pasture. I guess they were just crossing Shenandoah on their way home. Or maybe he'd purposely gone out of his way – just to rub Lulu's nose in it. That's the sort of guy he was. Lulu sat there at my feet and watched them go, whimpering. Then she began to shake and tried to climb up my leg. I picked her up and carried her back to our quarters and gave her a bowl of milk with a slug of Macallan in it. She lapped it all up and fell instantly to sleep.

I didn't say it. I didn't say I told you so. It wouldn't have done any good, and she'd have bit me.

Polk Four stopped by in the morning to see us off. I was loading up the Jag when he pulled up in his cruiser, clean shaven and crisply pressed as ever. Still, he looked different to me. Not so certain of himself and his mission in life. That'll happen when the earth moves under your feet for the first time.

"Want to hear something funny, Hoagy?" he said, striding over to me.

"Desperately."

"I thought this whole business would drive Mercy and me apart. Send each of us running for cover. It hasn't. If anything, it's brought the two of us closer, in a way we never were before. It's as if we share something."

"You do. You've both joined the so-called real world. Welcome to it."

"Thanks." He stuck out his hand and smiled. "Thanks, pardner."

I shook it. "So long, pardner," I said, smiling back at him, liking him.

Pam came outside then with Mercy and Frederick. Richard and Charlotte followed. Those two seemed quite shy around each other now. She also seemed a little less drab to me now. There was a hint of color to her cheeks, a liveliness to her step. Maybe it was just my imagination. But I do know Richard's nervous tic had vanished. He was at ease. He was also sober. He carried Pam's suitcases. There was only room for one of them in the trunk. The other we'd have to ship north with the rest of my stuff.

"I'll be sending you more pages as soon as I have them," I informed Mercy. "Partly for your research assistance. Mostly for your approval. You're the boss now. The book won't get into print unless you like it."

"I know I'll love it," she assured me.

"Don't say that. I'm a writer like any other – I need someone to put their foot on my neck and keep it there." Polk Four frowned at this. "Figure of speech, Sheriff," I explained.

Mercy drew herself up. "Very well," she said sternly. "I'll expect several chapters by the end of the month, and they'd just better be up to Grandmother's standards."

"That's more like it, boss."

"Thank you." She giggled, made a quick, awkward step toward me, and kissed my cheek, blushing furiously. Then she lunged for the security of Polk, who put his arm around her, proud as can be. God, they were sturdy.

I shook hands with Richard and Charlotte and wished the two of them luck. Frederick as well.

"Absolutely sure I can't talk you into taking on this book of mine next?" Frederick asked me.

"Positive."

"That's too bad. Think they'd let me have a woman writer?" he wondered.

"I don't see why not," I replied.

"Yes, I think a woman's sensitivity would be a genuine asset," he mused aloud, nodding. "Any suggestions?"

"One. Keep your hands to yourself."

He turned to Pam, a mischievous glint in his eye. "Sure you have to leave, dear? Seems like we're just getting to know each other."

"Quite sure," Pam replied curtly.

We got into the Jag. Lulu and Sadie curled up on the floor together at Pam's feet, Sadie using Lulu as a pillow, and Lulu letting her. She was so depressed nothing bothered her. Actually, the two of them seemed to be growing on each other. Because of their shared diet, Sadie thought Lulu was a cat and Lulu thought Sadie was a dog. I wasn't about to break the truth to either of them.

Frederick's eyes hadn't left Pam. He waved good-bye somewhat wistfully.

"The man's an absolute beast," she murmured to me.

"We all are, Pam," I said, starting up the engine. "It's just that some of us are better at hiding it. I'd have thought you'd have no problem handling him."

"As would I," she admitted, sighing. "Except that when they're as terribly handsome as he is, I have a frightful time saying no. In fact, I can't."

"Why, Pam," I gasped, shocked. "You slut."

"It's high time you found out," she said. "After all, we are going to be living together."

Everyone waved good-bye. We waved back. Then I let out the Jag's parking brake and eased it down the twisting drive and out the front gate. We started for home.

I don't ever want to see another goddamned peacock again as long as I live.

I found Gordie sitting outside on the lawn, glumly tossing his ball against a retaining wall and catching it with his mitt. There were other boys out there playing ball, but he was ignoring them. The hospital had nice grounds, lots of grass, and trees and walking paths. You almost didn't notice the fence.

He lit up when he saw me. "Hey, Hoagy! How ya doing?"

"Just fine, Gordie. Heading up to Connecticut. I wanted to say good-bye."

"Can I come with you?" he begged. "Pleath?"

I shook my head.

"How come they're making me live here, Hoagy?"

"I guess they think it's for the best."

"How come?"

I took the ball from him. "Go deep. I'll throw you one."

He eagerly trotted off across the lawn. I wound up and sent one high through the air toward him. He picked up the flight of it right away, drifted back and to his left, and punched his mitt. He was there waiting for it when it came down.

I joined him, rubbing my shoulder. We walked.

"I'll be keeping Sadie for you," I told him.

"They won't let me have her here."

"I know. I'll take good care of her. She's still your cat. When you're ready for her, just let me know. I gave them my address at the desk in case you ever want to write her. Or me. Okay?"

"Okay." He glanced over his shoulder to see if we were alone, then looked up at me slyly. "Keep a theecret, Hoagy?"

"Sure."

A sneaky grin crossed his face. "C'mere. Wanna show ya thumthin'."

He led me into the trees over by the fence, behind some bushes. "You may sthee me thooner than ya think," he whispered, kicking at the undergrowth with his foot.

There was a big hole in the earth there under one of the bushes. He was digging. Tunneling out.

I must have gotten a whiff of pollen. My eyes were suddenly bothering me, and I had trouble swallowing. I grabbed him under his arms and hoisted him up, hugged him tightly to my chest.

He squirmed in my arms. "Hey, what'd you do that for?" he demanded, horrified.

"I don't know." I put him down.

"Well, don't do it again."

"Okay, I won't."

"I'm not a baby, y'know."

"I know. Sorry." I stuck out my hand. "See you, Gordie."

He shook it. "Sthee ya."

I started walking away.

"Hey, Hoagy!" he called after me.

I stopped. "Yeah, Gordie?"

"Take it thlow."

I smiled. "Slow's the only way to take it."

I went back to the car without looking back.

We cleared Washington by lunchtime and beat the rush hour out of New York onto the New England Thruway. It was nearing dusk when we crossed the Connecticut River into Old Lyme. Lulu jumped into Pam's lap and stuck her large black nose out the window as we made our way up Route 156 into the rolling hills of Lyme. Spring was happening all over again up here. The forsythia was ablaze, the apple trees and dogwoods blossoming. It would be nice to go through spring for a second time. This one might even make up for the first one.

Lulu started to whoop when I turned off onto the narrow country lane that dead-ended at those old stone walls flanking the dirt driveway. I stopped for a second to take it all in – the lush green fields, the fruit trees and duck pond, the snug old yellow house and chapel, big red carriage barn, Merilee's beloved old Land-Rover. Lulu, impatient, jumped out and sped up the drive without us.

She found her mommy out behind the house turning over her vegetable garden. She had on rubber boots and old jeans and a flannel shirt that once belonged to me. Her waist-length golden hair was in a braided ponytail, and she had mud all over her face. Lulu was whooping and moaning. Merilee knelt in the rich soil, stroking her. She looked up at me a bit warily when she heard me approach.

"Thought I'd finish the book here, if you don't mind," I said.

She turned back to Lulu. "I don't mind."

"I can stay in the chapel," I offered.

"If you wish," she said, her eyes still on Lulu.

"I don't."

"Then don't," she said. "Stay in the chapel, I mean."

"Okay, I won't."

"Good."

We both watched Lulu.

"It turned sour on her," I reported. "He dumped her."

"The brute."

"I did what I could, but she desperately needs a mother's touch right now."

"My poor baby," she said, rubbing Lulu's ears. "She's lost her innocence."

"It's true. She's already started reading Erica Jong."

Merilee looked up at me. "Hoagy?"

"Yes, Merilee?"

"Hello."

"Hello yourself," I said.

She got to her feet and started toward me. She stopped, peered at something over my shoulder. "Is that . . . Pam in the car?"

"She needs a place to stay. I figured you wouldn't mind."

"Mind? Gracious, I just hope I'm worthy of her."

"You'll more than do."

"But I look terrible," she said, brushing herself off.

"Just awful," I agreed, grinning.

She came up to me and kissed me and fingered the bandage on the side of my head, her brow creased with concern.

I took her in my arms and held her. "Just a minor brush with death," I said, getting lost in her green eyes. "How's Eliot?"

"Hmpht."

"What's that mean?"

"That's for me to know and you to never find out," she replied primly.

"What did he . . . ?"

"He got fresh."

"He got what?"

"You heard me. The big fat gherkin knocked me over and . . ."

"And what, Merilee?"

"Never mind."

"Did he put his snout where he shouldn't have?"

"*Mister* Hoagy!"

"You can't blame the fellow, Merilee. You put him back in the pink. It was just his way of saying thank you."

"That's not what Mr. Hewlett said.   He gave me a severe tongue-lashing."

"Elliot or Mr. Hewlett?"

"Stop it. He said I shouldn't have gotten so close to him, what with his age and the time of year and all."

"Don't sell yourself short. You're also a lot better looking than what he's used to. Smell a hell of a lot better, too. So what did you do?"

"Stick around for a somewhat tardy Easter supper and you'll find out," she replied wickedly.

"No . . ."

"Mr. Hewlett said it was the proper thing to do."

"Well, well. This is a whole new pioneer side of you, Merilee."

"It is. Producers had better watch themselves around me from now on, or risk the consequences. Ex-husbands, too."

"I'll remember that."

"Do so."

There was some business going on at our feet now. Sadie was rubbing up against my leg and yowling.

"And who might this be?" Merilee wondered, picking her up and cradling her in the crook of her arm. Sadie dabbed at her sleeve with her paws and began to make small motorboat noises.

"Don't ask me. Never saw her before."

"Hoagy . . ."

"Her name is Sadie. She's kind of on permanent loan. Not a terrible mouser. Every farm should have one, don't you think?"

She smiled at me. "I thought you hated cats."

"I do." I sighed. "It's a long story, and not a pretty one."

She gave me her up-from-under look, the one that makes my knees wobble. "I've got time."

"I haven't. Excuse me." I started for the house.

"Where are you going?" she called after me.

I went in the back door into the big old farm kitchen. I still had half a bottle of Glenmorangie in the cupboard. I poured two fingers in a glass and added some well water from the tap and drank it down. Out the window I could see Merilee and Pam cheerfully getting reacquainted out by the duck pond. I made myself another stiff one before I picked up the wall phone. I dialed the number from memory. My hands shook. My heart was pounding. It rang twice and then I heard the voice. And then I said it.

I said, "Hello, Dad."

David Handler

About the Author

David Handler was born and raised in Los Angeles and published two highly acclaimed novels about growing up there, *Kiddo* and *Boss*, before resorting to a life of crime fiction. He has written eight novels featuring the witty and dapper celebrity ghostwriter Stewart Hoag, including the Edgar-Award-winning *The Man Who Would Be F. Scott Fitzgerald*. He has also written five novels featuring the beloved duo off pudgy New York film critic Mitch Berger and alluring Connecticut State Trooper Des Mitry, including the Dilys Award-nominated *The Cold Blue Blood*. He has written extensively for television and films on both coasts and co-authored the international best-selling thriller *Gideon* under the pseudonym Russell Andrews. He is a graduate of the Columbia Graduate School of Journalism and began his career in New York City as a television and theater critic. He also served a stint as a ghostwriter. Mr. Handler currently lives in a 1790s carriage house in Old Lyme, Connecticut.

Visit David Handler online at www.davidhandlerbooks.com.

About the Illustrator

Colin Cotterill was born in London in 1952. He trained as a teacher and worked in Israel, Australia, the U.S., and Japan before training teachers in Thailand and on the Burmese border. He spent several years in Laos, initially with UNESCO and wrote and produced a forty-programme language teaching series; English By Accident, for Thai national television. Ten years ago, Colin became involved in child protection in the region.

All the while, Colin continued with his two other passions; cartooning and writing. His work with trafficked children stimulated him to put together his first novel, *The Night Bastard* (Suk's Editions, 2000). Since October 2001 he has written seven more books: *Evil in the Land Without* (Asia Books, 03), *The Role of Pool in Asian Communism* (Asia Books, 05), *The Coroner's Lunch* (Soho, 05), *Thirty Three Teeth* (Soho, 05) and *Disco for the Departed* (Soho, 06), set in Laos in the 1970s. The fourth book, *Anarchy and Old Dogs*, was published by Soho in summer 2007.

Since 1990, Colin has been a regular cartoonist for national publications and produced a Thai language translation of his cartoon scrapbook, *Ethel and Joan Go to Phuket* (Matichon, 04) and an anthology of his bilingual magazine column 'Cycle Logical' (Matichon, 06). Colin is married and lives in Chiang Mai in the north of Thailand where he lectures part time on the MA programme and rides his bicycle through the mountains.

Visit Colin Cotterill online at www.colincotterill.com.

About the Author of the Introduction

Dean James is an author of both mystery non-fiction—including *By a Woman's Hand* and *Killer Books* (both co-written with Jean Swanson)—and mystery fiction, including the Wanda Nell Culpepper novels (written as Jimmie Ruth Evans) and the "Bridge Club" mysteries (written as Honor Hartman). He has worked at Houston's Murder By The Book—one of the nation's oldest & largest mystery bookstores—since 1984.

The Man Who
Died Laughing
&
The Man Who
Lived By Night

OMNIBUS
①

by Edgar Award winner David Handler

Price $26, hardback
ISBN: 0-9767157-8-3

Price $18, trade paperback.
ISBN: 0-9767157-9-1

The first two mysteries starring celebrity ghostwriter Stewart Hoag & his neurotic basset hound, Lulu—in one volume! The hardback is the first hb appearance of these books! Featuring original cover art by award-winning crime novelist Colin Cotterill (*The Coroner's Lunch*)

The Man Who Died Laughing

With his cat food-eating dog, Lulu, and haunted by his ex-movie star wife, ghostwriter Hoagy finds himself ghosting the memoirs of the rich, the famous and the not-so-nice. Sometimes, the project dies on the vines. Sometimes, the client does.

The Man Who Lived by Night

Hoagy, a ghostwriter/reluctant amateur detective, and his catfood-eating hound, Lulu, return as Hoagy pens the memoirs of an infamous rock and roll star. He expected the assignment to be hot–but not quite as dangerous or deadly as it actually was.

"One of my all-time favorite series!"
—Harlan Coben

Sign up for
Busted Flush Press's free
e-mail newsletter at

www.bustedflushpress.com

RAVES FOR DAVID HANDLER
AND THE HOAGY & LULU MYSTERIES

"A wonderful series—fresh and fun and as good as mystery writing gets. Hoagy and Lulu are the best comic pairing since Fred and Ethel (and a darn sight better looking). If you're a fan of the genre, and even if you aren't, these are 'must reads' for any lazy afternoon."
—Mark Schweizer, author of *The Alto Wore Tweed*

"Hoagy and Lulu tickle your funnybone and touch your heart. Hooray for the return of this appealing and clever series."
—Carolyn Hart, *New York Times* best-selling author
of the "*Death on Demand*" mysteries

"Charming lead characters and good breezy writing."
—*Wall Street Journal*

"Sprinkled with clues and snappy one-liners in equal measure with some very nicely drawn characters."
—*The Denver Post*

"If I could get Stewart Hoag to ghostwrite my books they'd sell better, and I'd laugh myself silly. David Handler is a hoot, and his books are just the thing for what ails you. I find it hard to begrudge him his Edgar!"
—Parnell Hall, author of *You Have the Right to Remain Puzzled*

"Some books deserve to go quietly into that good night, but the works of David Handler are not among them. Busted Flush Press has brought back to print a master of the mystery genre. Stewart Hoag, amateur private eye, has smarts and intelligence. Handler brings his characters to life instantly—the voices are original and real. Best of all, though, Handler treats his audience with respect. He doesn't write down. And Lulu will steal your heart."
—Carolyn Haines, author of *Bones to Pick* and *Penumbra*

"When it comes to digging up dirt, there's nobody quite like natty ghostwriter Stewart 'Hoagy' Hoag and his neurotic basset hound Lulu."
—*People*

"One of my all-time favorite series."
—Harlan Coben, *New York Times* best-selling author
of *Promise Me*